SOMEBODY PLEASE LOVE ME

'Cat Willingham.' She heard her name called and looked at Sam, the head starter whom she had known almost from the day she began modelling. 'Where the hell have you been all this time?'

'I took some time off over the summer.' She smiled broadly. Recognition was always gratifying and being missed by Sam was tantamount to fame.

'You look gorgeous as ever.' He walked over to her. 'Even better than that,' he concluded looking at her more closely. 'Vacations obviously agree with you.'

The elevator arrived and she stepped in, smiling back at him. 'You're a love to say it.'

'Take Miss Willingham up,' Sam ordered the new young Puerto Rican elevator man. 'She's a star and stars wait for no one.'

AVIVA HELLMAN

SOMEBODY PLEASE LOVE ME

A Methuen Paperback

A Methuen Paperback

SOMEBODY PLEASE LOVE ME

First published in Great Britain 1985
by Severn House Publishers Ltd
This edition published and reprinted 1986
by Methuen London Ltd
11 New Fetter Lane, London EC4P 4EE

Copyright © 1984 by Aviva Hellman

Printed and bound in Great Britain by
Hazell Watson & Viney Limited,
Member of the BPCC Group,
Aylesbury, Bucks

British Library Cataloguing in Publication Data

Hellman, Aviva
    Somebody please love me.
    I. Title
    813'.54[F]   PS3558.E4764
    ISBN 0-413-60430-6

To the memory of my mother

CONTENTS

PART I
Prologue 1955 *1*

PART II
1973 *5*

PART III
Epilogue 1983 *295*

"We are molded and remolded by those who have loved us and, although the love may pass, we are nevertheless their work—for good or bad."

—*François Mauriac*

SOMEBODY PLEASE LOVE ME

PART ONE

PROLOGUE
1955

PROLOGUE

Cat watched Jeff slowly remove the photographs from the manila envelope and saw the look of bewilderment turn to recognition. She held her breath waiting for him to relate the glamorous creature in the pictures to her; for him to fully comprehend that she was no longer just his high school student, the daughter of Joe Wallenstein, the scrawny kid who sat on the stoop of her house hoping to catch a glimpse of him when he came home at night; for him to realize that she was eighteen, on her way to becoming a photographer's model and that she had been in love with him since she was fifteen.

Still holding the pictures, he looked up at her. A slow smile appeared on his face. The creases around his soft, sensuous lips deepened, but his dark eyes appeared troubled.

"A photograph appearing in a fashion magazine is exciting but that doesn't make you a famous model."

Cat knew she had to make him understand. Slowly she walked over to him and rested her head on his chest.

He pushed her away gently and looked down at her. His tall, lanky frame was slightly stooped and he looked tired and older than his thirty-four years. His thin shoulders were accentuated by the pull of his hands thrust deep into his cardigan pockets. He looked extremely vulnerable.

She threw herself into his arms and kissed him passionately on the mouth. His lips were soft and she could feel his desire. Then she was lifted off her feet.

Lying naked on the bed, his body barely touching hers, she felt his passion begin to grow, her head start to spin. Suddenly he stopped moving and for a brief moment she thought he was going to pull away.

She opened her eyes. He was staring down at her and the look was filled with wonder. She wanted to show him how much she loved him, how much she cared. She wanted to become part of him, of his being. Impulsively she pushed her lower body toward him, forcing his indecision, enveloping him completely. The slight piercing pain disappeared quickly as his movements grew more fervent and within minutes her body was in rhythm with his. The gasp of pleasure which escaped him sent an exquisite thrill through her. Then she felt his warm wetness.

She pressed him closer, reveling in the small tremors which continued to shake his body.

She wanted the moment to last forever. It had been a dream for so long and now it had come true.

Finally, he lifted his upper body away from hers and, brushing her long, dark hair from her face, he cupped her head in his hands.

"Do you love me?" she whispered.

"For always," he answered.

She closed her eyes and knew that she had created an image that could be loved.

PART TWO

1973

1

Looking at herself in the mirror, Cat Willingham lifted her head and studied her figure as her dresser finished zipping up the back of the white clinging satin gown. She had purposely darkened her makeup and, with her dark hair parted in the center and pulled back into a tight chignon, she was pleased with the overall effect. For a moment she wished she did not have to put on the poorly designed oversized chinchilla fur coat which she was about to model. Stepping into her white satin pumps, she started putting on the coat when Mario, the assistant designer, rushed over to her. He was followed by Bunny, the other model hired by Signor Varrucci, the Italian designer whose furs were being shown.

"Cat, Varrucci wants Bunny to model the chinchilla number and you can do the gray broadtail," Mario said quickly, and without waiting for her reaction, he turned to the dresser and spoke to her in Italian. Within seconds, Cat felt the white gown being unzipped.

"But why?" she asked, slipping out of the dress and handing it to Bunny. It did not really matter. Varrucci was one of the six unknown Italian designers on their way to South America. They had a layover in New York and had decided to show their designs to buyers in the United States who were beginning to gather in New York for the Spring and Summer collections. Still, she was curious at the sudden switch.

"A photographer from the *Daily News* and one from the New York *Post* just dropped by, and Signor Varrucci feels that Bunny would be better for them to photograph," Mario said, handing Cat a short black dress which was to be worn under the broadtail coat.

Cat looked over at Bunny, who was wearing only bikini panties and a bra and was waiting to be told what to do. Bunny was as tall as Cat and just as thin, but her narrow shoulders made her appear shorter. Her hair was blond and fell to her shoulders; her eyes were blue and had a vague, disinterested look about them.

Wordlessly, Cat put on the black dress and watched Bunny as she slipped into the white gown and then struggled into the enormous chinchilla coat. It engulfed her completely. The sight upset Cat. The coat had overwhelmed Cat; it looked ridiculous on Bunny. The luscious, puffy white-gray fur clashed with the long blond hair and the over-all line offended Cat's esthetic sense. She looked down at Bunny's feet and realized she was still wearing black pumps.

"The shoes are not quite appropriate," she said automatically.

"Well, give her your shoes," Mario ordered. His voice was tinged with hysteria.

"What size do you wear, honey?" Cat asked the younger woman as she stepped out of her shoes.

"Seven and a half."

"These are eight and a half."

"We'll stuff them with Kleenex," Mario said and proceeded to give instructions to the dresser. Then he turned back to Cat. "Will you be able to wear Bunny's pumps?" he asked.

"Hardly," Cat said icily. "But I have black pumps with me." Angrily she dug into her large leather bag and took out a pair of black shoes.

She got little satisfaction from the look of surprise which crossed Mario's face. "I also have a half slip, a full slip, a padded bra, two pairs of gloves, Tampax and several other items which every professional model carries with her when she goes out on an assignment." She tried to sound pleasant but did not quite succeed.

"Do you think you'll be able to work the broadtail?" Mario asked, ignoring her comments as he helped her on with the long, paper-thin fur coat.

"I think I can manage," she said, picking up a Kleenex and wiping off some of the dark makeup. It had been right for the white gown and the lush chinchilla, but it was not as effective with the gray fur.

At that moment the voice of the mistress of ceremonies came to them, announcing the Varrucci broadtail coat as the next item to be shown.

Cat fastened the last button of the double-breasted, tight-fitting coat which hugged her upper body and flaired out into a full-length skirt. Then, grabbing a long sash made of the same type of fur, she walked quickly toward the stairs which led down to the showroom, while tying the sash around her waist.

With measured steps she descended the stairs from the mezzanine floor of the St. Regis Hotel, which was being used as a dressing area.

By the time she reached the bottom stair and stepped into the glaring limelight of the small elegant Astor bar which had been cleared for the show, she had regained her composure and had succeeded in erasing the effects of the scene with Mario.

To the beat of the guitar player's rendition of "Arivederci Roma," Cat walked around, showing the coat to the half-filled room of buyers. Surreptitiously she scanned the faces of the audience and realized she knew none of them. This surprised her, since she knew most of the buyers from around the country. Turning her back to the spectators, she loosened the sash and undid the zipper which was hidden in the seam of the coat's waistline, separating the skirt from the bodice, and draped it on a nearby chair. When she faced the room again, the long evening coat was transformed into an Eisenhower jacket. The audience, who had been restive, grew silent and attentive. Cat was pleased in spite of herself. Then with equal ease, she unbuttoned the jacket and handed it to Mario, who was now standing in the shadow of the stairway. She then picked up the lower part of the coat and wrapped it around her waist. What had started as a long evening cloak was now a floor-length skirt.

Someone in the room began to applaud. Cat smiled and winked mischievously; then, unbuttoning the skirt, she threw it over her shoulders, molded the long sash into a collar and tied it loosely at the throat. The original coat was now a seven-eighth–length cape. Everyone began to laugh in appreciation and the sound followed her as she walked up the stairs.

"That was great," Bunny whispered with admiration when Cat reached the mezzanine. "I couldn't have pulled that off."

"Okay, Bunny," Mario whispered urgently, "go."

Cat watched the girl walk unsteadily down the stairs, looking like a little girl dressed in her mother's clothes. It was all so unprofessional, she thought with disdain as she handed her dresser the various parts of the broadtail ensemble and waited for her to put it together again for the grand finale, when all the models would go down and appear with their various designs for the last bow.

The elation she felt while showing the coat was quickly replaced by feelings of alienation. She lit a cigarette and looked over at the other models who were chatting amicably with each other. Like the buyers downstairs, she knew none of the girls she was modeling with. It upset her. In all the years that she had been working, this was the first time that none of her contemporaries were involved. It made no sense. She had only been away for six months, yet everything seemed to have changed.

She had felt so jubilant when Lucille, her booker at the Pamela Fitzpatrick Agency, called her late Sunday night from Fire Island to ask her if she could fill in for an incapacitated model the day after the Labor Day weekend. It had been less than a week since Cat told Lucille that her doctor was allowing her to go back to work. She had anticipated an endless round of go-sees before she could get back into the swing of things. Lucille's call, happening so quickly, seemed like a good omen.

When Cat arrived at the St. Regis, she was disappointed at not knowing any of the girls she was to work with; she was further depressed by the poor quality and gimmicky designs of Signor Varrucci. But she put her personal feelings aside and went through the brief rehearsal with professionalism and gusto. It was, after all, a job and that was all that really mattered.

Now, standing alone, the idea that Varrucci thought she could not be photographed by two press photographers began to rankle. It rekindled some long-suppressed emotions dating back to her childhood when she dreamed of becoming a model but dared not mention it to her mother. Cat shook her head angrily. She had overcome those complexes years ago. Yet suddenly she felt like that little insecure girl whom she thought she had buried forever.

The final bows taken, Cat rushed to get into her street clothes. She had to get out of the hotel, away from the models and designers who were causing her such anguish.

The bells of St. Patrick's Church announced the noon hour as Cat walked over to the corner of Fifty-fifth Street and Fifth Avenue. Her next appointment was at 1 P.M. and she wondered what she could do until then. She felt lonely and wished there was someone she could talk to. Gillis McGill would understand her feelings. They had modeled together for years and now Gillis had her own agency just two blocks away.

She started up the avenue briskly, but by the time she reached the building she had changed her mind. Gillis was busy and besides, what would she actually say to her? That she felt rejected? That would be ridiculous. The audience at the St. Regis certainly admired her. And she was being paid her full fee, which was quite substantial for one hour's work.

She turned the corner and walked toward Henri Bendel's. The minute she stepped into the posh store, her mood changed. There was something about the place which was special. The people had a quality, a chic, an aura which made her comfortable. She looked at the sales girls and the shoppers and it was almost impossible to differentiate between them. All were thin and elegant and attractive.

Cat ambled past the little boutiques displaying their wares as though they were part of a bazaar in some Middle Eastern country. She stopped and examined a colorful belt with beaded tassels, wondering if she needed it. She put it down quickly. She did not need anything. Instead she rode up to the designer's sportswear department.

"Well, I'll be damned, if it isn't Cat Willingham!" Fiona Lord, one of the store's buyers, was standing in front of her. "Where the hell have you been?"

"Oh, I took some time off." Cat smiled at the elegant woman whom she had known for almost twenty years.

"Well, you look great," Fiona said sincerely. "What are you doing here at this hour?"

"My daughter is going off to boarding school this evening and I thought I'd get her something pretty to wear on the trip up," she answered quickly.

"Well, I must say you're lucky. I could never get my kid to wear anything I brought home to her." Fiona laughed good-naturedly.

The phrase struck Cat and her smile wavered. "I'm not sure she'll wear it, but she saw one particular outfit the other day and loved it, so I thought I'd give it a shot."

"Let's get together soon," Fiona said. "Maybe lunch?"

"I'd love it," Cat said and watched Fiona smile and rush off.

Let's have lunch, Cat thought wryly. It was such an idiotic phrase. Who had time for lunch!

While waiting for her package to be wrapped, she wondered why she had bothered to buy the outfit for Alexandra. She would never wear it. When Cat was a teenager, she had hated it whenever her mother had bought her clothes. Instantly her mind rebelled against the comparison. This was totally different. Her mother did not understand fashion as she did and had no idea of what was right for the younger generation, whereas Cat was part of the fashion world, knew it intimately and understood the changing trends. A twinge of the turmoil she had felt while at the St. Regis returned, and she realized with surprise that it was the second time that day she had thought of her mother. Then she remembered that her mother was arriving that afternoon from Europe and decided that subconsciously the woman had been on her mind.

Looking down at her watch, Cat realized it was already 12:40 and suddenly she felt rushed. She had to get down to the garment district by 1 and getting there at this hour could be a problem.

With the package under her arm, Cat rushed out of the store just as a taxi came to a stop in front of her. She stepped in, ignoring a woman who had been standing at the curb before she arrived.

"550 Seventh Avenue," Cat said once she was settled. "And I'm awfully late, so could you try to get over to Seventh Avenue as soon as you can? There might be less traffic." Then, taking a cigarette out, she lit it, leaned her head against the window and closed her eyes.

2

The taxi driver edged his way through the dense midday traffic. The going was slow. At one point he glanced up at his rearview mirror and observed his passenger. She was chic and elegant, and although she was wearing large goggle-shaped sunglasses, in spite of the overcast skies, they did not hide her magnificent complexion, the high cheek bones, the strong chin or the marvelously sensuous mouth. He would have liked to talk to her, but she looked preoccupied. Instead he returned his eyes to the road and concentrated on his driving.

"You missed the intersection with Seventh Avenue," he heard her say and looked up, startled. She had removed her sunglasses and was staring at him with her incredible brown eyes which were blazing with fury.

"It's all the same," he said, feeling uneasy that he had ignored her requested route and was now stuck on Broadway at Forty-fourth Street without any possibility of crossing over to Seventh Avenue. "It's the day after Labor Day and everyone is back in town. And when there's a forecast for rain, everyone comes in with their cars."

"If you would have done what I asked . . ."

"Lady, look over there," he interrupted, pointing to Seventh Avenue. "It's just as bad."

He was getting angry, too. He'd picked her up in front of Bendel's instead of taking the matronly lady standing next to her because she was elegant and striking and he loved looking at the chic models. "Believe me, I'd love to get you to where you're going. I work for a living and the more fares I get the happier I am."

"Well, I work for a living, too," she snapped back, "and I'm terribly late."

With that, she dug her hand into her enormous leather bag, took out her wallet and handed him a five-dollar bill.

"I'm sorry to do this to you," she said, trying to be pleasant. "But it'll be easier for me to walk from here. That Forty-second Street crosstown traffic looks like it won't clear for quite a while." She smiled for the first time. "I know it's unfair, but I am late."

He watched her rush down the avenue. She was extremely tall but graceful and was wearing boots. He wondered what her legs were like. He looked at the two-dollar tip and shrugged. These models made a fortune and they could afford it, he thought, as he revved up his motor. She was right to walk. He'd be stuck there for at least ten more minutes.

The humid warm air made breathing impossible as Cat headed toward her destination. She should have taken a subway, she thought, but the idea of going down into a crowded subway was unbearable. The leather bag she was carrying was heavy and the Bendel box was cumbersome. A slight pain began to throb in her lower abdomen but she ignored it. Bo Shephard was expecting her at 1 P.M. and she wanted to be on time. In spite of their close friendship, doing his show was as important to her as it was to him.

Arriving at 550 Seventh Avenue, the Mecca which housed many of the top fashion designers and manufacturers of New York, Cat paused to catch her breath. Briefly she glanced at the coffee shop across the street and wished she could go in for a Danish and coffee. It was out of the question. Instead she headed toward the elevators, glancing briefly at the clock. It was just 1 P.M.

"Cat Willingham." She heard her name called and looked over at Sam, the head starter whom she had known almost from the day she began modeling. "Where the hell have you been all this time?"

"I took some time off over the summer." She smiled broadly. Recognition was always gratifying and being missed by Sam was tantamount to fame.

"You look as gorgeous as ever." He walked over to her. "Even better than that," he concluded, looking at her more closely. "Vacations obviously agree with you."

The elevator arrived and she stepped in, smiling back at him. "You're a love to say it."

"Take Miss Willingham up," Sam ordered the new young Puerto Rican elevator man. "She's a star and stars wait for no one."

Once the doors shut, Cat leaned against the elevator wall, hoping to relieve the pain, which was growing worse. Within seconds she felt better and her mind turned to Sam's enthusiastic greeting. He had an eye for noticing the slightest change that took place in the models who had been around his building for as long as she had. He also had a way of finding out their most intimate secrets, and yet he had obviously not heard of her recent operation. Normally, she would not have been that discreet about her state of health, but a hysterectomy was somehow different and the fewer people knew about it, the better.

"Where is everybody?" Cat asked when she walked into Bo Shephard's reception room. The place was unusually quiet.

"They're out to lunch," the girl said. "And Mr. Shephard asked me to send you right in. He's very hyper today and gave strict instructions that you and he were not to be disturbed, no matter what."

Cat smiled with satisfaction. She had been the fitting model for Bo's forthcoming collection, had worked intimately with him on many of the concepts and today they were going to pull the whole thing together.

Just before going in to see Bo, she glanced at herself in the wall-lined mirrors. She had seen two designers that morning before the fur show with the hopes of pinning down some shows for the Spring and Summer collections, plus going to Bendel's and she was exhausted. She was also terribly uncomfortable in what she was wearing, having overdressed because the radio forecast early that morning predicted rain and cool temperatures. But neither the fatigue nor the discomfort was evident as she pushed open the doors to the showroom.

Bo was standing in the middle of a pale pink room looking out of place in his tight-fitting dungarees and faded T-shirt on which the word LUV was gaudily imprinted. He did not hear her come in and she took a minute to observe him. They had known each other since high school and it was he who was mainly responsible for her being a model. From the time they were in sophomore year, he had been determined to become a designer and was always sketching outlandish outfits. When he asked her to pose for him, she was shocked but flattered. Contrary to everyone else, he loved her height and loose-jointed slouch and kept referring to her as his Brooklyn Audrey Hepburn. Posing for him while he sketched sparked something in her, and a deep-rooted subconscious dream came alive. By the time they reached their senior year, he was hounding her to get some photographs and try for a modeling career. It was from him that she learned design, fabrics, makeup and what fashion photography was all about. But most important he taught her to understand her body, her face, to use her inner sources and be selective in whatever she did.

In spite of his scholastic mediocrity in high school, Bo got a scholarship to the Pratt Institute of Design, which kept him near at hand. Their friendship grew. She continued to pose for him and their dreams took shape. He was going to be a world-renowned designer. She would be a famous model who would marry a rich man and wear Bo's designs to all the elegant parties around the world.

Her marriage to Jeff was the first dose of reality for them both. Jeff Phillips was hardly the globe-trotting, dashing millionaire who was to be part of that glamorous future. But she had not counted on falling in love and getting married at eighteen, even though being married did not interfere with her modeling career. If anything, Jeff appreciated her work and encouraged her. It was Bo's career which did not take off as they had dreamed. His talents were not appreciated in this country, and he left for Paris where he worked as a sketcher and stylist for the designers in small couture houses. Still their friendship continued. He was there when she came to Paris for the first time to be photographed in the European collections for *Vogue*. She was young and frightened and Bo took care of her. He was especially helpful after the birth of Alexandra when she had to reestablish herself. It had been a difficult pregnancy and she was away from work for nearly the whole nine months. Doing the French shows was crucial. She took the infant with her and Bo took over, leaving her free to do the work. Jeff would never have allowed her to take the baby if Bo had not been in Paris to take care of her. Somehow Bo was always around when she needed him. She, in turn, tried to help him when he first came back to New York in the mid-sixties. At that time she was at the pinnacle of her career as a photographer's model, earning a great deal of money, still she did his fittings as well as his fashion shows and posed for photographs in his clothes, without charge. The Regency Agency, with whom she was signed, was furious. Aside from the fact that runway modeling was a comedown for someone of her stature, it also meant a loss of money. She did not care. Bo was struggling and she had faith in him. After two seasons, though, he felt completely defeated and he left for London, hurt and humiliated, swearing never to come back.

For the next five years, Cat tried to persuade him to return. More and more designers were beginning to design under their own labels and she was convinced his unique talent would finally be recognized. His return coincided with her emergency operation and since she was in the process of moving into a new but not yet furnished apartment, she went to Bo's house in Connecticut to recuperate.

She noticed the change in him the day she got to his house. Ambitious as ever, his priorities seemed to have changed. Hard as he worked on his designs, he was working even harder at creating a unique, almost eccentric personality. Getting his name mentioned by the press, being seen at all the right parties, going to the "in" places, took up almost all of his time. They fought over it constantly and it was only her presence which forced him to put in the time needed to complete his Spring and Summer collections. He was grateful and, as the weeks went by, their relationship returned to what it had been when they were in school in Brooklyn. Then one day Bo announced that a photographer named Greg Butler was arriving from London. The day Cat met Greg, she felt she would lose Bo.

Now, standing in his syrupy pink showroom, Cat shuddered. The whole ambiance was so unlike him.

"I think the white ivory bracelets would be best for that lavender and aqua shirt," Cat said quietly as she watched him place a jade bracelet on the cuff of the shirt.

He looked up startled, then he smiled. "Ya, I know, but where the hell are they?"

"Under the chair," she said, pointing.

"But of course." He rushed over, picked them up and placed them on the colorful shirt's cuffs. Then standing back he squinted his eyes, examining the effect. "That's perfect and the red belt should make it a smashing outfit."

"White belt," Cat said.

"I'm trying to make a statement," Bo said emphatically.

"Well, it's a loud one. That's for sure."

Walking over to her, he put his hand under her chin and their eyes met. "Are you all right?" he asked seriously.

"Raring to go," she answered, touched by his concern. "As a matter of fact, let's get to it."

He handed her a pair of slacks, a shirt, sandals and some jewelry and Cat walked into the dressing room. Undressed she stared at her naked body for a minute. She was as thin as she had been when she was eighteen, she thought with relief. Her small breasts were still firm and her shoulders were broad and emphasized her tiny waist and narrow hips. Her diaphragm was smooth, her rib cage barely covered with flesh and her stomach was flat, except for the scar from the operation, which the surgeon had thoughtfully placed below the bikini line. It was almost completely healed and although it still protruded slightly, she succeeded in camouflaging it by wearing tight elasticized pantyhose. For a moment she longed for the days in the 1960s when models wore girdles, waist cinchers and other supports to achieve the lines required for designer's clothes. But then again, that was her true talent; the ability to move with the times, change with the styles, to please the buyer's insatiable passion for something new and different. Her eyes wandered down to her long, slender legs. They were as shapely as any young woman's. She smiled wryly. Maybe not quite any young woman and her brow furrowed. The preoccupation with youth was growing worse. There were times when she wanted to cry at how young some of the girls were these days. She raised her hand to her forehead and smoothed away the wrinkles. She must remember not to frown, she thought with annoyance.

"Hey, Cat, we don't have all day," she heard Bo calling.

Quickly she slipped into the clothes and, erasing all thoughts from her mind, she walked back into the showroom and struck a pose. Bo handed her a scarf which she donned expertly and she walked around the room while he scrutinized the overall effect. They worked in silence as she modeled one outfit after another. Occasionally Cat made a comment about a sleeve being badly set and which felt uncomfortable, or a hem which she thought was incorrectly proportioned. She refrained from saying too much about the accessories he chose, which she found outrageous. They were friends and he respected her opinions, but he was the designer and she did not want to overstep her position. It was the sloppiness of the finishings around the buttonholes and seams which finally made her explode. She was struggling into a flimsy gold lamé skirt and wrapping an intricate white and gold scarf around her midriff when she could no longer contain herself.

"Bo, for crying out loud, the workmanship on this scarf is revolting."

He raised his brows and his eyes flashed with fury. "The workmanship is fine," he said through clenched teeth.

"I don't understand what's gotten into you." She held her ground. "You're the one who broke your back on each buttonhole, screamed and ranted when a buckle was not just so or a seam was a fraction off and now you'll let this crap go into the most important fashion show of your life?"

"It's a look I'm after." His voice rose. "I've eaten shit for years worrying about perfection and where did it get me? Well, this time 'round I'm going to make everybody sit up and take notice of Bo Shephard, not my seams. Balenciaga, Dior, Fath are dead. Nineteen seventy-three people don't look for that finesse anymore. If I could come up with a disposable dress, wear it once and throw it away like a Tampax, believe me I'd do it. People looking at my clothes will buy them because of my name. MY NAME! That's what I'm selling now."

Lowering her eyes, Cat turned away and continued working, the outburst seemingly forgotten.

"I think this outfit should have a couple of snake bracelets around the upper arm," Bo said at one point as he walked over and started wrapping them around her upper forearm. She felt them pinch her flesh and she cried out.

"Flabby, flabby, flabby," Bo jeered.

Cat looked down at her arm. It was almost skeletal yet the bracelets caused her flesh to protrude.

"Bitchy, bitchy, bitchy," she answered sweetly. "Those bracelets wouldn't fit a chicken bone, my love."

"I don't really like them, anyway." Bo smiled and the anger was gone. They had been friends too long and cared for each other too much.

"You rushed or something?" Bo asked, aware that she kept glancing at the wall clock.

"Don't worry about it." She forced herself to sound calm. "It's just that Alexandra is leaving for boarding school tonight and I'd hoped she would let Bernie drive her up. But she insists on taking the seven o'clock train."

"Train!" Bo spat the word out. "How gauche," he said, handing her a pair of earrings and several bangles. "I don't know how you could have given birth to a child who would prefer going up by train rather than a chauffeured limo." The words were couched with affection. "That child is too much."

"That's just it. She's not a child any more. She's almost sixteen and as stubborn as hell." She became agitated. "As a matter of fact, we had a terrible fight last night." The words slipped out in spite of herself.

"About going up to school in a limousine?" Bo asked suspiciously.

"Oh, come on. That's where it started but not where it ended." She heaved a sigh. "Let's face it. Life has been a nightmare since Jeff started teaching at Boston U. Last year wasn't too bad. He came down on weekends or we went up there. But this year, forget it. And now that I've moved to this new apartment plus my operation . . ." She shrugged her shoulders helplessly. "I just don't know what's going on. I rant and rave and Alexandra barely reacts. It's eerie."

"What's happening between you and Jeff?" Bo asked tentatively.

"I don't know the answer to that, either. He hasn't said anything, but I think he's angry that I moved."

"Want to talk about it?"

"No. I better not." Cat regained her composure. "Let's get on with what we're doing."

"What time is it, anyway?" Bo asked, respecting her wishes.

"Quarter of five."

"Why don't we finish it all tomorrow?" he suggested.

Cat was grateful. Bo, more than anyone, knew the trauma which Alexandra's departure was causing.

"What time can you be here tomorrow?" Bo asked, becoming professional again. "I've got to get all this stuff together by the twentieth of September, latest. The printers are screaming so they can make up the brochures, I've got to get the press releases out and I want some promotion pictures done before the show. And now that I've got to straighten out some seams and buttonholes . . ." He paused and grinned.

Scanning her schedule for the next day, Cat's thoughts lingered on the word "pictures." Was it possible that Bo was not going to have her pose for the publicity shots? She dared not ask.

"How about nine o'clock in the morning?" she asked instead.

"It's a date."

Together they walked into Bo's office and Cat slid into a deep down-filled rust-colored chair. The exhaustion which she had ignored was now overwhelming.

"Have you got time for a drink before you go?" Bo asked.

"I'll just have a cigarette. Bernie will be downstairs in fifteen minutes." She tried to relax and looked around while Bo poured himself a glass of wine. The office was a further testament to Bo's determination to create an "impression." Although far more in keeping with the tasteful kid she had grown up with, the decor was still ostentatiously extravagant. Bo was spending money as though it were going out of fashion. Money, she knew, he did not have.

"If that stupid brat insists on taking the train, can I have Bernie for the evening?" Bo asked, interrupting her thoughts. "I called his answering service and they said he was busy. But if you're not going to be using him, I'd like to have him drive Greg and me over to the Metropolitan Museum. They're having a big gala and everybody will be there. Then we're going to Elaine's and after that Capote is having a small midnight soiree." He emphasized the last name, obviously trying to impress her. "Have you ever met him?" he continued, sipping his wine.

Cat laughed. "You know I haven't." Then, growing serious, she continued quietly, "And I am impressed, if that's what you're trying to do. But I really don't think you need a limo for the evening. It'll cost a fortune and everyone will know it's rented." She tried to keep the sarcasm out of her voice.

"You're using it and God knows you're probably in worse financial straits than I am," he said childishly.

Cat winced. He knew exactly how broke she was. Still his reference to it made her uncomfortable.

"I needed the car anyway, since my mother sailed into New York at noon. So I figured I'd hold onto it in case Alexandra changed her mind."

"Doesn't your mother usually stay in Vienna until the end of September?"

"Usually, but long ago I learned not to ask too many questions."

"She sure lives a good life," Bo sneered. "When will you finally tell her you can't afford her extravagances?"

"Oh, Bo—get off it. She's so lonely and those six months with her cousins mean the world to her."

"Sorry I mentioned it."

"Have you hired the models yet?" she asked after a minute. "Lucille tells me she hasn't heard from you."

"Lucille Taub is a great booker, but Pamela Fitzpatrick isn't the only modeling agency in the world, you know."

"I know you don't care for Pamela personally but she does have the best runway girls in town." She squashed out her cigarette, stood up and started collecting her things. "Have you or haven't you hired the girls?" she repeated her question.

"Sort of," he answered cautiously.

"Aren't you pushing it timewise? Most houses are all set and the best models are not waiting around, you know." She cleared her throat nervously. "I know. I'm going on more go-sees in the next couple of weeks and let me tell you, even designers who know me and love me are all booked up." It was a painful admission, but she felt she had to jar Bo into action. Suddenly she realized what he said. "What does 'sort of' mean?"

"I'm going to be using mainly print models," Bo said quietly.

"You have got to be kidding!" Cat was stunned. "Are you out of your mind? Your first important show in New York where the press is going to be out in full force and you're going to trust it to girls who do photography?"

"I've got you and I'll get a couple of other experienced runway models, but the look I'm after is—young." The last word was spoken quickly, as though he hoped it would be ignored.

Cat turned away pretending to be looking for something and trying to hide her irritation and embarrassment. The phone rang at that moment.

"Hi, luv," Bo said and Cat bristled. It was one of Bo's latest affectations, acquired as far as she was concerned since his involvement with Greg Butler. She wanted to leave but knew she had to wait for the conversation to end. To her relief she heard Bo ask whoever he was talking to if he could call back later. She understood the conversation was not for her to hear. It saddened her. They had never had any secrets from each other.

"Okay, I'm leaving now," she said, walking toward the door, where she nearly collided with Greg Butler, who rushed in at that moment.

"I've got it," he shouted childishly to Bo, ignoring the fact that he had nearly knocked Cat down. "The editors flipped over me and loved, simply loved, my work."

Cat turned around and looked at Greg. He was young and looked like a member of the British Royal Family. His blond hair was cut in a Prince Charles style, falling attractively over his forehead, his eyes were light blue, the nose short and thin, his teeth small and very white. She shifted her gaze over to Bo. Her tough Irish friend was completely transformed. This diamond-in-the-rough, the serious designer, the bright, introspective, tasteful and hard-working man was suddenly effeminate, almost cute.

"That's swell, baby." Bo seemed to have forgotten Cat was still in the room.

"They're thrilled with my slides and that picture I took of you flipped them out," Greg said, walking over to the bar and pouring himself a glass of wine. "It's all set for January and I can pick the models." He almost giggled. "I want to find the most gorgeous girl in the world for this job."

At that moment Cat caught Bo's eye and he became flustered. Whether it was the content of the conversation or his embarrassment over his total infatuation with Greg, Cat could not say. It was obvious, however, that Greg was talking about something that dealt with Bo's career and it did not include her.

"I'll run along and see you at nine o'clock tomorrow," she said stiffly, picking up the Bendel box which had fallen to the floor.

"What's in the box?" Bo asked, looking and sounding normal again.

"An outfit for Alexandra."

"Whose?"

"Burrows," Cat said almost maliciously.

"His clothes are all wrong for her."

"She thinks he's divine." Cat emphasized her words.

"She'll never wear it."

"Where there's life, there's hope." Cat smiled, nodded her head to Greg, who was too wrapped up in himself to notice, and walked out of the room.

Her friendship with Bo was being jeopardized by that little faggot and there seemed nothing she could do about it, she thought as she pressed the elevator button.

3

"Hi, Mom. I'm on the phone with Dad," Alexandra called out when Cat entered the apartment. She sounded friendly, as though the fight the night before had not happened.

"I'll be right in," Cat answered, looking through the mail which she found outside the front door. She could not decide what upset her more—the handful of unpaid bills which she was holding or the idea that Alexandra had probably not been out of the apartment since she woke up.

Entering her daughter's room, she noticed two small suitcases standing in the middle of the chaos, with a guitar and a large drawing portfolio propped up against them. Alexandra was sitting on her unmade bed, the phone held between her shoulder and chin. The ashtray on the floor was overflowing with cigarette butts. The sight infuriated Cat but she held her temper.

"He wants to talk to you," Alexandra said, handing her the phone.

Cat reached for it haltingly. Somehow, Jeff's going off to Boston two years ago had not really changed their relationship. Her moving did. It was not meant to have any significance. They had spoken about moving many times in the past. It was his attitude after the fact which gave rise to the idea that their relationship was undergoing a change. It confused her. She was not sure of what it was she wanted or expected from her marriage at this point in her life.

"Hi, Jeff," she said brightly.

"How are you, Cat?" Jeff sounded formal.

"Exhausted for a change." She regretted the phrase immediately.

"Cat, I'm coming into town toward the end of the month and I'd like to come by and see you."

"That's great," Cat said, simulating an excitement she did not feel. "When?"

"Last Wednesday in the month."

"Fine," she said, trying to remember her schedule for that day, but not wanting to make him wait while she checked her calendar. It would be a replay of their life together—his needs being usurped by her work schedule. "I'll be home by eight. Is that too late?" she asked, vaguely aware that she had a six o'clock show at Gimbels East.

"No problem. I'll see you then."

"Should I put the water on for coffee?" Alexandra asked when Cat hung up.

"We don't have much time," Cat answered, throwing the Bendel box on the bed. "Are you all packed?"

"Sure am," Alexandra said, looking at the package. "What's that?"

"It's the outfit we saw the other day at Bendel's which you loved and I thought it might be something you would wear up to school."

"The one with the studs?" Alexandra sounded incredulous. "Oh, Mom. I thought it was nifty, but really nothing I could wear."

"Why not?" Cat asked with pretended nonchalance. "What are you planning on wearing anyway?"

"I'm dressed," Alexandra answered, and the apathetic tone surfaced as she started moving around the room nervously.

Cat bit her lip as she scrutinized her daughter. The child was no more than five feet two inches tall and very overweight. Her complexion was sickly and her dark eyes were slightly bloodshot. The pale lashes gave them a vacant look.

"You want to tell me you're going to wear those baggy jeans, an oversized sweatshirt and dirty sneakers?" Cat found her voice.

"I feel comfortable in them and I don't think they'll care how I'm dressed if we can afford the tuition."

"Alexandra, just try on the outfit. For my sake," Cat pleaded.

Alexandra snatched up the box and stalked into her bathroom. As soon as she was out of the room, Cat opened the closet door. It was packed with clothes. She proceeded to open the built-in drawers and discovered that they too were filled to the brim.

"What are you taking with you anyway?" she called out.

"Everything I need."

"What happens if you go out to something a little more formal?"

"Mom, leave me alone," Alexandra said, coming back into the room still dressed in jeans and sweatshirt. "As for this lovely outfit," she said, throwing the skirt and bolero on the bed, "they're a size eight. I happen to be a size twelve, closer to fourteen."

"Oh damn. I asked for their largest size." She became agitated. "The sizing is so different these days."

"Suppose I leave it here and you can return it," Alexandra said patiently.

"No. I won't return it. Besides, you're planning on losing weight, aren't you? So why don't you take it with you and work your way into it?"

"Will that make you happy, Mom?" Alexandra asked and her voice was suddenly soft.

"Oh, babe, never mind if it makes me happy. I think it would make you happy."

The downstairs buzzer sounded.

"That's Bernie."

"No way." Alexandra's face reddened. "I'm taking the train!"

"May I take you to the station?"

"No!" Alexandra said emphatically.

"Will you call me the minute you arrive?" Cat asked anxiously.

"I promise."

"Now, are you sure you have enough money?"

"You gave me a hundred dollars in cash and I have the credit card you got me."

Cat lowered her eyes. She should not have given the child a credit card, but the deep-seated guilt about Alexandra had triumphed again.

Alexandra picked up the two suitcases and Cat took the guitar and drawing portfolio. Standing in front of the elevator, Cat reached out and smoothed Alexandra's mass of brown kinky hair, worn long and coming down the side of her face in an unflattering manner. She held back a comment about the style, which was all wrong. It would make the last minutes unpleasant.

When the elevator arrived, Cat reiterated the need for a phone call when she arrived at school. Suddenly Alexandra threw her arms around Cat's shoulders and Cat froze. The fleshy softness of her daughter's body discombobulated her. She forced herself to hug the child. As though sensing her mother's discomfort, Alexandra looked up at Cat briefly, then ran into the waiting car. Just as the door shut, Cat glimpsed an unbearable sadness in the child's eyes. She was tempted to ring for the elevator to come back but decided she was probably projecting her own feelings. Slowly she walked back into the apartment and went directly to Alexandra's room. Seating herself on the unmade bed, she stared vacantly around her.

What had gone wrong?

When very small, Alexandra was a warm, sweet, cuddly child who seemed to accept the endless stream of nurses, housekeepers, mother's helpers and maids, with ease. A petite, almost Dresden-like creature, her skin was alabaster white, framed by flaxen-colored hair. Her features were small and doll-like and she peered at the world through large brown, twinkling eyes. She smiled easily and strangers would stop on the street to admire her.

In spite of it, Cat knew Alexandra would not grow up to be a beauty. Her skin was sensitive and fragile. Her tiny features were deceptive and her lashes were colorless, giving the eyes a strange, naked look. By the time Alexandra started first grade, she did not look like her daughter. What was even more distressing was the disparity in their personalities. Alexandra grew into an introverted child, dependent, clinging and incapable of making friends. She spent her time alone, sketching and playing her guitar, or going to the movies with whatever housekeeper happened to be working for them at the time. Cat understood her daughter's loneliness, knew that she should be helping her make social contacts, inviting friends over, teaching her child to communicate with her peers, but there was no way she could stop working at that point in her life. Still, as long as Jeff was in New York, Alexandra had her father, who, even though preoccupied with his writing, was there physically, and Cat was not too concerned. It was when Jeff was asked to teach a post-graduate seminar at Boston University that the strain on Cat became overwhelming. She suspected it would happen and was tempted to ask Jeff to forgo the offer, but it meant a great deal to him and she did not have the heart to stop him. Left alone with Alexandra, material things were all she could offer in compensation. They had little effect on their relationship and Cat's frustration mounted. But, remembering her own childhood with a disapproving mother, she covered her unhappiness by being tactful, helpful and constructive. It was a losing battle. Alexandra could in no way compete with her mother's glamour and she simply gave up. A hostility developed which was there at all times; sometimes overt, sometimes thinly disguised, but it existed, and Cat's disappointment was clear. Both mother and daughter were aware of it.

The decision to send Alexandra to boarding school was difficult, was an admission of defeat, but Cat knew the time had come for emotionally uninvolved people to take over if Alexandra was to survive. As with the purchase of the apartment, Cat did not consult Jeff, convinced he would insist that the child come to live with him, which she felt would be equally damaging. She informed him of her decision as a *fait accompli*, and to her relief and amazement he did not object. She assumed he had seen the wisdom of her act.

Now Alexandra was gone, pretending an assurance which Cat knew she did not feel. Unhappy as she was for herself, it did not compare with the pain she felt for her child. That was a pain she could not cope with.

Heaving a deep sigh, Cat took in the room once more. It contained a box spring and mattress, a desk and a chair. The white walls were pockmarked by tiny pieces of tape which had held up Alexandra's charcoal drawings. Cat was relieved they were gone. She hated them. They reminded her of the people in the Crown Heights sec-

tion of Brooklyn where she had grown up, especially the ones who
arrived in the neighborhood after the Second World War. Cat had
avoided going there for a long time after she married Jeff. But at one
point, she started taking Alexandra to visit her mother. She could
never figure out what prompted the decision, except that she felt it
might be nice for Alexandra to know her grandmother. The rapport
between the two delighted Cat. On occasion she would even allow
Alexandra to spend the night there and although she wondered what
the two had to say to each other, she did not delve into it too deeply.
Then the strange sketches began to appear on Alexandra's drawing
pad and they seemed to affect her to the point of morbidity. When
the child became preoccupied with the Holocaust and began to ask
endless questions about the past, Cat put a stop to the visits. Somehow Cat decided that Clara and her surroundings were not what an
impressionable child needed. But it was already too late. The sadness
and loneliness which were an intrinsic part of Alexandra's existence
grew deeper. With Jeff's departure the apathy appeared and grew
worse with the passage of time.

Cat closed her eyes in anguish. The fight which they had had the
night before came back to her vividly. It had started over Alexandra's
weight and sloppiness when suddenly Cat found herself attacking
the drawings which Alexandra was fondling with great care as she
took them off the wall. Somehow Cat had always avoided the subject
of Alexandra's art. It obviously meant a great deal to the child. But
last night Cat wanted to provoke some sort of reaction in her daughter. In frustration she lashed out at the sketches and their subject
matter. It had been the wrong thing to do. She had touched a nerve
and Alexandra had indeed reacted. Even now Cat shuddered at the
angry "I hate you" which had rung out in a tone of despair. But the
lively reaction was short-lived and within seconds Alexandra with-
drew, leaving Cat more bewildered than ever.

Cat tore her mind away from the sadness which lived within her
daughter and her eyes fell on the Bendel box lying on the bed, the
outfit carelessly thrown over it. It was the only patch of color in the
drab room.

Something had gone wrong in her relationship with her daughter and Cat could not understand what it was. She had tried so hard to
be a good mother. She worked for Alexandra, worried about her,
tried to give her everything which she herself had missed while
growing up. But somehow it was not enough.

Cat stood up. The pain in her lower abdomen, which she had
ignored for too many hours, was now quite severe. She rushed to her
bathroom, found her pills and swallowed one. Although she had fully
recovered from the operation, the doctors had warned her about

exerting herself and on her first day of going back to work, she had overdone it.

Returning to her bedroom, Cat felt the evening stretch out into a long and dreary time. Bo came to mind. She knew he was busy, but in the past they had always been a comfort to each other. If the situation were reversed, he would have called and she would have responded without hesitation. She decided to phone him.

Greg answered. He did not acknowledge her. He simply placed the receiver down and she heard him call out, "Cat wants you, but don't take too long, we're late."

She was tempted to hang up.

"Can I have the car?" Bo asked the minute he came on the wire.

"That's not why I called." She swallowed hard.

"Anything wrong?" The old concern was there, but there was also impatience.

"I'll be in a little later than nine tomorrow," she said hurriedly.

"Oh shit, Cat, is that why you called?"

"Sorry," she said and hung up quickly.

They were friends, they were responsible for each other, they needed each other, but that was in the past. Now she still needed him, but he no longer needed her. Therein lay the difference.

Unconsciously she flicked on her answering machine.

Lucille had left an urgent message and Cat realized she had not called the office all day. A couple of models had called just to chat. David Thomas had called and said he was home for the evening.

She debated whether to call him. In all her years of modeling, David was the first male model she had ever befriended.

The phone rang and Cat picked it up quickly.

"Are you okay?" David asked.

"I was just thinking of you," she said impulsively.

"Did Alexandra get off all right?" he asked with concern.

"Just fine." She hesitated. David, more than anyone, knew how difficult a time she'd been having with Alexandra. He had spent a great deal of time with them since she moved into the apartment and Alexandra had come back from summer camp. "Well, you know how she is." Cat laughed briefly and wondered if she should invite him over.

"Anything I can do?"

"Actually not." She decided against the invitation. She needed time alone. "I'm exhausted and I've got a big day tomorrow."

"So do I. I've got several go-sees tomorrow and I'm up for a Macy's catalogue, but I'll call you in the evening and maybe we can get together."

"That sounds great."

She hung up, feeling better. David was a friend, a good friend, and in a way he had begun to take Bo's place in her life.

Lighting a cigarette, she lay down on her bed, her mind still married to thoughts of David.

She had noticed him when Pamela first signed him up. He was difficult to overlook, being extremely tall and well built, with copper-colored hair and incredible amber eyes. Still, it was not until she started going into the office during the summer while recuperating from her operation that she got to know him. She discovered he was an orphan, had spent time in the Army and was now trying for a modeling career, for which he was ill-suited. In spite of his extraordinary good looks, he photographed poorly and was awkward on a runway. He was, however, very bright, kind, gentle and extremely knowledgeable and tasteful. He helped her with the moving and furnishing of the new apartment, was a delight to spend time with and most important he made her feel good about herself at that point in her life. Whenever he was around, she felt attractive, glamorous and worldly. Also, in contrast to a lot of men she had known, whose passes and vulgar innuendos she had had to fend off through the years, David's manner toward her was always correct and beyond reproach.

Suddenly she found herself wondering if she wanted to have an affair with David. It was a strange thought. Throughout her marriage she had occasionally considered going to bed with someone other than Jeff, but she never did. She was too much in love with him to jeopardize their relationship. She was also not a woman who could have a casual affair, for she was bound to become emotionally involved. It would have disrupted her life with Jeff and would have interfered with her career, which was extremely demanding. Things of course had changed in recent times, but she dismissed the thought of going to bed with David. An affair with him or anyone else at this point could still prove disastrous. She was much too vulnerable. Alexandra was gone, her marriage was going through a crisis and her career was at a precarious stage. She and David were friends and there was no reason to change that relationship.

Cat looked at the clock. It was nine-fifteen and she realized that she had not yet spoken with her mother. She picked up the phone and remembered that she had not reactivated the number with the phone company. What an obvious Freudian slip, she thought and smiled. Talking to her mother was always nerve-wracking. The woman's unspoken demands, her total self-absorption, her disapproval were there at all times. She would demand that Cat come to Brooklyn and she did not have the time or the inclination to do so.

There was, after all, nothing she could do to relieve her mother's loneliness.

Cat was almost asleep when Alexandra finally called. It was a short conversation, but she was too tired to notice its brevity. Alexandra was safe and that was all that mattered.

4

For the next three weeks Cat tried to fill every waking moment with appointments, scheduling her days and evenings so that by the time she got home at night she was too tired to think about her loneliness. She succeeded except for the early morning hours when, out of habit, she woke even before the alarm clock went off.

It was no different this morning as she reached over and shut off the shrill blare of the alarm clock. It was six forty-five and she had been awake since six. In the past she had loved that morning quiet. It was like no other. It soothed her, gave her time to organize her thoughts and prepare for the events of the day.

But since Alexandra's departure, the silence of the predawn hour had a different quality; it was accompanied by a sadness rather than affording her the tranquillity she had loved. It made little sense, since neither Jeff nor Alexandra ever woke early. Still, in the past she knew they were there and that had made the difference.

"At the sound of the tone the time will be 7 A.M.," Cat heard the radio announcer state. He then gave the weather forecast.

The prediction was for rain and she readjusted her thoughts about what she would wear. Then leaning over, she turned on the delicate porcelain-figured lamp and was about to light a cigarette when the phone rang.

"Cat, I'm sorry to call so early," Lucille Taub said. She sounded troubled.

"What the hell are you doing at the office at this ungodly hour?" Cat took a cigarette and lit it.

"Fashion week is always hectic." Lucille seemed harassed.

"What's the problem?" Cat decided to ignore the tone.

"I've got several more go-sees for you," Lucille said slowly, "and Pauline Trigére wants to see you before booking you."

Cat stiffened. She hated the go-see routine and now, even someone who knew her as well as Pauline was not willing to take a chance.

"If that's the way it has to be, that's the way it will be," Cat tried to sound cheerful.

"Got your book?" Lucille did not brighten up in spite of Cat's obliging manner.

Cat opened up her appointment book. Staring at her in bold letters was the reminder that Jeff was coming by that evening. It had slipped her mind completely and it took her a minute to regain her composure.

"Incidentally, I'm going up to the Grayson Agency about a new cosmetic campaign," Cat said when she had finished writing down the appointments. "I'll let you know the exact date when it's set." She tried to sound nonchalant, unwilling to give away the importance she was placing on the forthcoming interview.

"For the Chameleon ads?" Lucille sounded surprised.

"I think that's it. I bumped into Dan Grayson and he specifically asked me to come by," Cat said defensively. She had, in fact, called Dan, who was an old friend, to tell him she was back at work. He was genuinely pleased to hear from her and did ask her to come and see him. "I'm very pleased." She continued, "Something like this would certainly help the bank account, not to mention the career."

Lucille did not react.

"You are aware that they're about to launch a whole new line of ads, aren't you?" Cat asked. Lucille's silence was disconcerting.

"Oh, sure," Lucille said quickly. "I just didn't think you'd be interested."

Cat bit her lip. There was something wrong with the statement, but she did not want to delve into it too deeply.

"Anything else?" she asked instead.

"Well, Cindy Jones can't make the Scavullo appointment."

"Why not?"

"She has a hangover or something." Lucille sighed.

"What does Pamela say?"

"Pamela is in Mississippi judging a beauty contest, don't you remember?"

"Of course," Cat said absently and was about to suggest that she and Cindy were the same type and that she might go instead. She caught herself before the words were uttered. Cindy was nineteen years old! "What about Jill Howard?" she asked.

"Jill can't get a sitter for her baby," Lucille answered.

"Oh come on, Lucille." Cat exploded. "Try to get a sitter from the nursing service and if they can send one over, check with Scavullo and find out if he agrees to the switch. If I remember correctly, Jill was his first choice anyway. And I know the editors at *Cosmo* prefer Jill." She spoke with great authority and could not decide if she was pleased or not. She sounded like someone running an agency rather than a working model.

"Okay," Cat heard Lucille say quietly. "By the way, will you have time to drop by the office today?"

"Why, is anything wrong, anything you can't handle?" Cat tried to cover her discomfort. It was unlike Lucille, head booker for the agency, to be so unsure of herself.

"The new head sheet has to be approved before going to the printer and I would like you to see it."

"I wasn't planning on it," Cat said stiffly. "But if you really need me, I'll try to stop over at the end of the day."

"I could have David bring them to you if you'll tell me where you'll be during the day."

"David? David Thomas?" Cat cried out in spite of herself. "I thought he was doing the Macy's catalogue this afternoon."

"They canceled him, obviously." Lucille sounded malicious.

"Why obviously?" Cat tried not to show her concern.

"Cat, my love, he's a lousy model and I'm damned if I can figure out what Pamela sees in him. For a savvy lady who can pick winners every time, she sure has a lemon in him."

"He works and earns his keep," Cat snapped. "He may be inexperienced and a little stiff, but he certainly has the looks and you know it." She caught her breath. "As a matter of fact, why don't you and David decide on the head sheet without me? I'm sure Pamela would agree."

"That's something I won't do." Lucille's manner changed and Cat knew she would not move from her decision.

"As you wish. I'll come by late this afternoon," Cat said and hung up.

The conversation left her limp. What was Pamela up to? Cat wondered. Throughout the summer Cat had been vaguely aware that Pamela was spending a great deal of time away from the office, was getting more and more involved with her daily column, and demanding social life. But Pamela was still tops in the modeling agency field and she could afford to take the time off. Cat was recovering from her operation and she did not mind helping out. Pamela's trust and confidence were gratifying, and secretly she hoped that one day Pamela would ask her to join the agency on the management side. It was a reasonable thought, almost a logical progression. But now Cat wanted to go back to work in the field where she belonged.

She looked down at the pad on which she had scribbled her appointments. It was a far cry from what her schedule looked like a year ago at this time. Was it possible that if Pamela were around more . . . Cat did not finish the thought. Pamela had been good to her and she had no right to question her actions.

"Damn that operation," she whispered, slamming the book shut furiously. But even as she did, she was aware that her true frustration was not with Pamela or her own lagging career. It was the prospect of seeing Jeff that evening which was troubling her.

She looked around the room. It was decorated in a mélange of yellow and white patterns, with the walls lined in a soft shirred floral fabric, except for the wall opposite her bed, which was mirrored from floor to ceiling. A bolder, yet complementary print hung at the windows and was repeated in the fabric of her canopied bed. A round lace-skirted table stood in front of the window, flanked by two deep yellow velvet boudoir chairs. The thick-piled wall-to-wall sculptured carpet incorporated the overall soft, muted colors, giving the room an aura of rich, warm elegance. The utter femininity of the decor was somehow a statement. It certainly was not in keeping with the personality of the girl Jeff Phillips married nearly eighteen years ago. He had not seen the new apartment and he was bound to notice that she had not given thought to his needs while putting it together.

Slowly Cat got out of bed and walked over to shut the window. She shuddered slightly as she pulled on her soft white terry cloth robe, tied it tightly around her waist and started toward the door which led to the rest of the apartment. Passing the mirrored wall, she glanced briefly at her slim silhouette, which was vaguely outlined in the dim early morning light. The lithe, shadowy image was somewhat reassuring.

Walking past the living room, Cat stopped and looked into it. In contrast to the frivolity of her bedroom, this room with its bare bleached floors and lacquered walls, was stark and streamlined. It was more in keeping with who she was, but it too was different from anything she would have chosen in the past.

But that was the point, she thought helplessly. After years of bowing to the needs and comforts of others, she was now determined to indulge herself. It had taken her almost eighteen years to move out of the dingy apartment on the West Side of New York and into the high-rise East Side building. And although the apartment was nowhere as large as the one on West Eighty-seventh Street, with its high ceilings, narrow hallways and ornate moldings, it was sufficiently big for her and for Alexandra. It had two bedrooms and L-shaped living room and above all it had terraces. They were the most important feature. The one outside the living room was not large, but accommodated a table and chairs, a lounge and planters. It wrapped around the apartment narrowing down to a ledge outside the kitchen and dining area. "Cat's Walk" is what she had named it when she first inspected the apartment. The sizes did not bother her. The idea of having outside space represented freedom.

Impulsively she walked into the living room and fluffed up the pillows strewn on the low white modular couches. The couches and low glass coffee table, set on a heavy stainless steel stand, were the only pieces of furniture in the room. That was all she wanted. Once she decided to move and found the apartment, she asked Jeff to come down from Boston and take what he wanted from the old apartment. She had the rest picked up by the Salvation Army. She had no use for the secondhand, cumbersome furniture they had collected through the years. She hated everything there and except for an antique desk she had picked up in Florence when she did a fashion show there, a small Botticelli painting her father had given her for her sixteenth birthday and the huge enlargement of her first *Vogue* cover photograph, she wanted no part of her former life in her new dwelling.

Well, it was done, and somehow she would resolve things with Jeff. He was an intelligent and reasonable man and she had been a good, supportive and loyal wife. They were two grown-up, sophisticated people who cared about each other and understood each other's needs. Surely he would appreciate her wish to improve their living conditions. He could not fault her for that.

With renewed confidence she walked toward the kitchen, throwing a brief glance at Alexandra's room. The door was open and the emptiness still jarred her.

Entering the kitchen, Cat plugged in the coffee maker, popped a thin slice of white bread into the toaster and waited for the coffee to brew. Within minutes her breakfast was ready and she walked over to the kitchen window and pulled up the shade. In spite of the weather forecast, a dim sun was rising over the East River and she stared at the incredible spectrum of colors which were visible at that hour. The beauty of the sight struck her and for a moment she wished she had someone to share it with. She turned away quickly, trying to ignore the fleeting glimpse of the emptiness which accompanied being alone.

Pouring herself a second cup of coffee, Cat turned back to the window. The beauty which had captivated her was still visible and she immersed herself in its loveliness. She refused to think of herself as a lonely lady. She was one of the top fashion models in the city and had been for many years. She was elegant, successful and highly respected. She knew many people and was extremely well liked. If she rarely went out, it was because she had long since made the decision that her personal life had to bow to her work schedule. She saw no reason to tire herself on late nights where everyone overate and overdrank and the men treated models as though they were playthings rather than serious working women. She was a working woman, whose work meant everything to her. Work meant independence. Work meant money. Work meant meeting obligations. It meant paying the rent when Jeff was not earning enough, getting the best care for their child, paying medical bills and all other unexpected expenses. It was work which made it possible to send Alexandra to boarding school, pay for the extras which could make her daughter's life exciting and interesting, support her mother with a monthly allowance and even allow herself small luxuries. It was work which made it possible to buy the apartment she was in and even though she knew her modeling career would not last forever, it was still a while away before she had to retire. She was thirty-six, but she was one of the lucky ones who succeeded in appearing ageless.

Thirty-six. She smiled to herself. In truth she was well on her way to being thirty-seven and she forced herself to linger on that fact. Years back she had decided she would quit when she was thirty. She was twenty-five then and it seemed that thirty was eons away. It did not work out. At thirty she made the deadline thirty-two. That too had to be put off. Thirty-four became the goal and she had actually begun to map out some ideas for a new career when Jeff left for Boston. It was the first time she was truly conscious of her age and felt fear. But fortunately she was in great demand as a runway model that season and she was able to put off thoughts of retirement. She also stopped setting deadlines. She was going to be in charge of her destiny and it would be *she* who would decide when to quit. Her sudden operation reversed everything.

"Damn that operation," she whispered again. Quitting because of an unexpected illness represented a defeat. And it could not have happened at a worse time. Being away from the fashion world for six months at this point in her life made even people who knew her well, people who had booked her for years, hesitate about hiring her when she announced she was ready to go back to work. Still, she thought with determination, she would climb back to the top again. Experience, she was convinced, counted for something, even in the world of high fashion.

Downing the remains of her coffee, Cat hurried back to her bedroom. She could not afford maudlin thoughts crowding her mind. She had to focus in on her lagging career. Although most of the top designers had already booked their models through October and November, there were still quite a few who could use her. The important thing was to be seen.

5

The bathroom was steaming and the mirrors were clouded over when Cat stepped out of the tub and patted herself dry. Then, wrapped in a huge, soft bath towel, she sat in front of her dressing table and switched on the bright makeup lights. Slowly she wiped away a small patch of steam and stared at herself.

"A beauty you ain't," she said out loud and made a face at the image but even as the words were spoken, she could not help but smile. Staring back at her from the small clearing in the mirror was, as far as she was concerned, a preliminary outline of a face, a pencil sketch which needed defining before emerging as a complete portrait. She raised her hand and touched the taut olive-toned skin. It was drab and lifeless. The thin brows needed to be darkened, the long lashes made to look thicker to emphasize the huge, deep-set, brooding brown eyes and give them the proper frame. The nose was imperfect and almost too prominent, the mouth wide and sullen with the lower lip nearly bursting over the strong chin and exaggerated width of the jaw bones. Every feature had to be modified or amplified, just as the unruly dark hair had to be handled so as not to detract from the overall chiseled bone structure. But all the imperfections would be corrected. She had learned through years of tireless work and total dedication that by the time she was through she would succeed in looking completely exquisite.

The mirrors were now clear and with meticulous care, Cat proceeded with her task. Her hair had grown frizzy from the dampness and she pulled it back expertly into a tight, small chignon and started applying her makeup. She chose each shade of lipstick, mascara, eye shadow, eye liner, rouge and powder with forethought. To her, makeup was an intrinsic part of fashion. Finally done, she put on a silk shirt, stepped into an ultrasuede skirt, slipped on a matching fitted vest and pulled on her high-heeled boots. Scrutinizing herself again before leaving the room, she added a small polka-dotted scarf which she tied around her neck. She was the pinnacle of elegance and although times had changed and most of the younger models did not bother to dress before a call—she could not relax her standards. She was from the old school that believed that the public image had to be preserved at all times.

Throwing a trench coat over her shoulders, Cat picked up her large leather bag and was almost at the front door when the phone rang again.

"Shit," she whispered under her breath. It was nearly nine o'clock and first appointment was at ten.

"It's Mel Black," the harsh, garrulous voice announced, "and, baby, I need a favor."

"Oh, Mel," Cat wailed. "I'm late."

"It'll only take a minute." He rushed on, "I've got a big thing to ask of you."

"Okay." Cat settled herself against the wall and listened. Mel was a press agent who had done her favors in the past and she owed him a few.

"I've got this babe who's got to be the best-looking kid that I've ever laid my eyes on and I need help."

"What kind of help?"

"Well, she's gorgeous, see, and she wants to be a singer and an actress. You know the scene, but I think that by handling her right, I could get her a movie deal."

"So?"

"She needs classy exposure and I wondered if you could get Pamela to sign her up."

"If she's that gorgeous, what's the problem?"

"I gotta maneuver it right. She's shy and scared."

"How old is she?"

"Nineteen but she's only been in the city a short time and she's immature."

"Does she have pictures?"

"She has some, but if they're not right I'll get the best to have them redone. Scavullo, Stern, Penn, you name it."

"That's expensive."

"Money is no object," Mel said slowly.

"Who's footing the bill? You?" Cat laughed knowing Mel was usually broke.

"No. There is somebody . . . Oh, for crying out loud, Cat, do it without asking so many questions."

"Are you sleeping with her?"

"Good God, no!" Mel exclaimed in horror. "As a matter of fact if I didn't know better, I'd swear she's still a virgin."

"Okay. When do you want me to see her?"

"This evening?"

"Not a chance. But I'll be at the Plaza Hotel on Monday next and I could see her around three in the afternoon."

"That would be perfect. She goes to five o'clock Mass." He emphasized the last words.

"Mass?" Cat exclaimed.

"Oh, yes, she's very religious and I find it refreshing." He sounded serious.

"You're putting me on, aren't you?" Cat laughed good-naturedly.

"Well, you've got to admit it's different."

"That it is," Cat agreed. "What's her name, anyway?"

"Megan Baynes and she's got an apartment at the Osborne on Fifty-seventh Street."

"Megan Baynes?" Cat repeated the name. It struck a chord. "Hey, isn't she the Southern girl who recently came to New York? I think I've read about her. Is that possible? She's religious all right and she sings and plays the guitar, if I remember correctly."

"I should hope you've read about her." He laughed briefly. "I'm working my ass off trying to get her that coverage."

"Well, I'll see what I can do to help," Cat said with amusement and hung up.

Waiting for the elevator, she dug into her bag and took out her appointment book. She had a show at ten o'clock and a fitting at eleven-thirty. A go-see at two o'clock and a show at three. She could probably see Lucille at five. She also marked in the appointment with Megan Baynes.

"You're a sight for sore eyes, Miss Willingham." The doorman smiled, opening the front door for her.

His appreciation always gave her a lift. Living on the East Side was certainly different from living on the West Side and the cost and effort were worth it, she decided.

As she was stepping into the cab, a fine drizzle had started coming down.

6

"Just one more shot, Cat," a young man with a press card stuck in his hat called out.

Cat struck an alluring pose and smiled broadly. Several flash bulbs went off, as a couple of other photographers took advantage of the extra minutes she allowed them.

Turning away from the photographers, she stepped into the small dressing room and collapsed into a chair. She had just finished a difficult showing of evening clothes where everything had gone wrong. None of the accessories arrived on time. A couple of the girls had been late and clothes were shown by models who were not meant to wear them. The designer was beside himself and the strain had taken its toll on Cat.

"You've got a face made of rubber and the patience of a fucking angel," Zoe Smith said, and Cat realized she was not alone.

"Are you trying to flatter or insult me?" Cat asked, looking over at Zoe, who was busily reapplying her lipstick. The ebony-colored face with its small flat nose and sensuous lips was immobile and the dark eyes, half hidden by gold-shaded lids, were expressionless. She reminded Cat of an Egyptian goddess.

"Don't knock it," Cat said, lighting a cigarette. "A picture in *Women's Wear Daily* or any newspaper can't harm me at this point. I need to remind people I exist."

"It's the way you turn on the charm and turn it off which gets me." Zoe stood up, smoothing out the skintight cashmere sweater-dress which showed off the total perfection of her body. "I personally think you're much too democratic."

"With the way my career is going I can't afford to be any other way," Cat laughed good-naturedly. She could say it to Zoe. Zoe would understand.

"I know and that's going to be your downfall." Zoe smiled for the first time and the imperious statue-like creature disappeared and was replaced by a warm lady.

Zoe, who had been modeling almost as long as Cat, was one of the top black models in the world, one of a group who were responsible for the revolutionary change in the fashion world. Those black models, with their free abandoned movements and their incredible lack of inhibitions, made designers create clothes for the contemporary woman, clothes which were comfortable, flowing and adaptable for everyday living. Yet in spite of her success, Zoe was still setting standards of behavior for her race in the fashion world. Every black model who entered the field imitated her impeccable behavior and professionalism.

Cat had known her from her Paris days when Zoe was working for the House of Dior as a mannequin. Their friendship started then and continued without interruption.

"How's the marketplace?" Cat decided to change the subject. She did not want to talk about herself.

"I'm off to Greece for a couple of weeks to do a collection for a designer whose name I can't pronounce, on some island I never heard of and then back to Atlanta." Her eyes sparkled with excitement.

"Sounds divine," Cat drooled. "When will you be back in New York?"

"Not coming back," Zoe said, and Cat sat up in shock.

"What do you mean, not coming back?" Zoe was one of Pamela's most important models. She had put her on the head sheet long before it became fashionable to have black girls on the list and had personally fought for her both with designers and advertisers. Cat also knew that it was Zoe's reputation that gave Pamela's agency an edge on all up-and-coming black models and she was still a drawing card for Pamela. Her departure would be a terrible blow. "But why?" Cat asked more urgently.

"Well, my little boy is starting first grade. My mother is getting too old to take care of him and my husband and I feel I should be around more. Also, I don't want to be pushed out of modeling. I'd rather leave while I'm ahead. But the real reason I'm going is that I've decided to open my own modeling agency in Atlanta, exclusively for black girls."

"A segregated modeling agency?" Cat tried to smile but knew Zoe was serious. "Meaning if I come to Atlanta and want to join your agency you won't take me on?"

"You, I'll take. You're one of the few white girls who can shimmy down a runway like we do."

"I had you as a teacher and that's as good as they come."

"That's bull. I've tried to show other girls how to swing with the music, but they somehow still succeed in looking like they've got a broom up their ass."

"Pamela will be upset," Cat said after a minute.

"Too bad." Zoe threw a matching cashmere knee-length cardigan over her shoulders. "I think I've paid my dues and now that Pamela doesn't seem to give a damn anymore, I feel I'm free to do what I want."

"What do you mean, doesn't give a damn?" Cat asked cautiously.

"You haven't been paying attention, but she's never around. I adore Lucille, but I can get my own bookings at this point in my career. I want an agent when there's a contract to be negotiated or a problem to be thrashed out. But she's never there."

"Wouldn't it make sense to talk to Pamela before making this drastic move?" Cat asked slowly. "Maybe you can open a branch in Atlanta that would tie in with the agency here," Cat pressed on.

"Don't be a fool, Cat. If Pamela so much as got wind of what I'm doing she'd cut me to ribbons. She's a mean son-of-a-bitch, always was. And she's becoming worse."

"Do you have the money to do it?"

"Well, my earnings will go on for a couple of years and if I play it right, I think I can make it."

"I'll miss you." Cat put her cigarette out, feeling that a chapter in her life was coming to an end. She felt sad.

"I'll miss you, too," Zoe answered. Then throwing her shoulders back, she assumed her grandiose manner, as if fortifying herself before facing the world, and ambled gracefully away.

Cat slumped down in her seat and closed her eyes, trying to block out the relevance of Zoe's situation to her own. Vaguely she wondered if she could ever open her own agency. The thought confused her. She could never do that to Pamela. But more important, she could never do it on her own. As soon as Pamela came back to town she would talk to her about the future.

She started dressing quickly. She had promised Lucille she would stop by, and she did not want to disappoint her.

7

The Pamela Fitzpatrick Agency was housed in a new location on East Sixty-second Street, off Madison Avenue. Pamela had recently bought the narrow three-floor structure as an investment and a symbol of her success. It was a far cry from the little offices she had on West Fifty-fifth Street, which had consisted of a barnlike space where everyone from bookers to receptionist sat together handling the phones and doing all other chores involved in the running of an agency. The place was a beehive of activity, with girls coming in for unscheduled interviews, delivery boys running in with packages and food, and models stopping by to freshen up or rest. Pamela had her own little space, separated by a plasterboard wall and, although set apart, she was involved in everything that was going on.

The new offices were totally different. They were thoroughly thought out and extremely luxurious. The outside was painted pale blue, Pamela's favorite color. Going up the front stoop, one entered the parlor floor which was enormous and served as a reception area. The wall-to-wall carpeting was plush and a decorator had placed several large plants in various spots around the room. The track lighting was dim but was specifically directed at enormous blowups of the top models, past and present, who were connected with the agency. Small divans hugged the walls with elegant tables in front of each. Important magazines from every corner of the world, copies of *Women's Wear Daily* and other literature connected with the fashion world, were neatly piled on an antique iron rack. Pamela Fitzpatrick models were featured or mentioned in every one of them, and the implication was clear: being a model with Pamela's agency meant you could reach the top. The receptionist's desk was strategically placed between a stairway which led down to Pamela's office and another stairway which led up to the third level. There, rooms were set up for important or potentially important models who were in town but had not yet settled in their own apartments. Miss Mack, the receptionist, an elderly woman with blue-white hair, impeccably groomed, with steel blue eyes behind blue-rimmed glasses, sat guard. She had been a Lilly Dache model in the thirties and although past the age of retirement, she still carried herself as a woman who had been beautiful and refused to accept the passage of time.

One could see Pamela's office from the top of the stairway, but it was not until you reached the bottom step that she came into view, since her desk stood at the far corner of the room. She, however, could watch the girls descend and, as everyone who knew her understood, Pamela would usually decide even before meeting the girl whether she would be interested in representing her. Her office walls were paneled in a light wood on which she had hung pictures of models in various poses, taken in many parts of the world dating back to the 1940s and '50s when Pamela reigned as a legend. A huge armoire, lined with Clarence House fabric, stood slightly ajar and contained albums and magazines, along with endless bric-a-brac which she collected from her travels. Most were scheduled to be packed as Christmas gifts and sent to important clients. Her desk was large and piled high with papers and photographs and two telephones. Her swivel chair was thronelike and she could turn it with ease toward the little typing table which stood to one side. Opposite her desk were two large armchairs which were deep and comfortable. They too had a specific purpose. Pamela would observe her potential models while they struggled to get up from them. Doing it gracefully was a feat.

Standing in front of the building, Cat observed it for several minutes and felt a longing for the old place which had been her home away from home for many years. These new offices, she decided, were more like a racetrack with hurdles than an office meant to encourage and help girls who were after a modeling career. Before her operation, Cat rarely went there. She simply called in for her appointments and picked up any messages which might have been left for her. She mailed in her work vouchers every few days and Lucille would send the money to her. It was as though Lucille understood her reticence. Suddenly Cat wondered if she could talk to Lucille about her future, if she could ask Lucille openly if her modeling career was over. She was sure Lucille would be honest about it.

Quickly Cat ran up the front stoop and tried to push open the front door only to find it locked. It was only a few minutes past five and this made no sense. She rang the doorbell and within seconds it was opened by Mack. The woman looked pale and frightened.

"Oh, it's you, Cat," she whispered. "Come in quickly."

"What's going on here?" Cat asked, walking in, when she caught sight of Cindy Jones sitting on one of the small settees. It took Cat a minute to recognize her. The girl was skeletal. Her shaved head resembled that of a cadaver; her eyes staring into space appeared like empty holes. Her posture was rigid and her legs jutted out like spindles in front of her.

"My God!" Cat gasped and rushed toward her. "What happened?"

Cindy looked at her and grimaced. "I'm tired."

"Mack!" Cat hissed. "Why isn't someone doing something?"

"Lucille is taking care of everything," Mack answered, throwing a disdainful look at Cindy.

Cat ran into Lucille's office and found her talking on the phone. She waved Cat to a seat without interrupting her conversation.

Cat was too nervous to sit down. Instead she lit a cigarette and listened absently to what Lucille was saying.

"Yes, *bubee*," the woman cooed sweetly, "I know that, but I haven't seen her in days, weeks to be exact—maybe it was even months—and you know these girls; they do, on occasion, exaggerate the need to be thin." She made a face and raised her eyes up to the ceiling, controlling her exasperation. "Listen, my love, I'll have six girls down at the studio before nine tonight. You're shooting at midnight on the *Queen Elizabeth* and I promise you one of the girls will be as great as Cindy." She started shuffling through pictures and gesturing to one of the other bookers to come over to her desk. "Yes, my darling, you will have your girl, I swear it."

Lucille hung up and the syrupy sweetness was gone. "I want these girls called," she ordered, handing a list of names and telephone numbers to the three bookers who had been sitting around looking numb. "I don't care where they are, or how you find them. And when you do, I want them hand-delivered to Newton's studio. Understand?"

"Lucille, what's going on?" Cat started the minute Lucille stopped talking. "What about that poor child out there?"

"That poor child out there has obviously been on a starvation diet. She's living with some oriental guru and his diet is herbs and pot and coke, and probably everything else that's healthy according to his theories. She had this job locked up months ago and as far as I knew it was all set. I called her yesterday and the guru assured me that she would be there." She smiled wryly, "Of course he was speaking in some strange dialect and I might have misunderstood."

"Stop the wisecracks. What are you doing about her? You can't just leave her there."

"Don't be an ass, Cat. I've called her doctor and he's sending an ambulance and getting her into Bellevue as soon as possible."

"Where is the boyfriend?"

"He went to the studio with her this morning and when Newton saw her he hit the roof. So the gentleman brought her here. Practically carried her in and then he ran."

"Where's her family?"

"I called her mother in Spokane, Washington. She went berserk and said she would sue us."

"Is she coming to New York?"

"On her broomstick. Yes, she and her husband are taking the first plane in." The strain was beginning to show as she picked up a ringing phone.

"Hello, my love." Her smile was back. "Thank you for returning my call, but Joyce Sterling can't make the sitting tomorrow. Her plane was grounded over Shannon Airport and it's, as we say, an act of God. But Suzanne Brady is available." She began to sift through her books. "They could almost be twins. Oh, you know her? Of course you do. Yes, of course, and you loved her." She listened for a minute. "Five A.M. shooting? That's double fee, right?"

She hung up, picked the receiver up and dialed a number.

"Okay, Joyce, you can relax. I've found a replacement and you can go ahead and do the television commercial, but for Christ's sake, don't sign any releases before Pamela checks them."

"When do you think the ambulance will get here?" Cat asked when Lucille hung up.

"I hope to God it gets here before Pamela does. She'll have a fit."

"Is she back in town?"

"She breezed in here earlier in the day. I forgot she had a date in court and since she'll probably have to talk to the lawyers for a while after it's all over, hopefully she won't be back here before seven."

"What's she doing in court?"

"Fanny Nelson signed up to do an ad for a pharmaceutical company, which was great. It was her first big job and she was thrilled so she misread the release. It wasn't for a pill which prevented menstrual pains, it was for a birth control pill. Get it? Prevent was the misleading word. Now, not only are they using the ad, but they want the picture for packaging. The fact is, Fanny couldn't care less, but her family is Catholic and they'll have a fit."

"But if she signed the release what the hell can Pamela do? She's over eighteen and that's binding."

"Yeah, but just so it won't be a total loss, she's going to try for more money. A one-time ad is one thing. Using the picture as they plan on doing should be worth a hell of a lot more."

"Will she win?"

"You bet your bottom dollar she will." Lucille stood up and started arranging some flowers in a vase.

Cat watched her carefully. Whereas Miss Mack looked like someone who belonged in a glamorous modeling agency, Lucille would have been more at home behind a counter in a small dress shop on the Grand Concourse in the Bronx. She was dressed in a large mu-

mu, which camouflaged her fleshy body; her makeup was put on with a heavy hand, the Evelyn Marshall false eyelashes were too long and the wig was too obvious. Still, the warmth and enthusiasm she exuded could not be overlooked and when she smiled the room seemed to light up. Her reputation as tops in her field was well deserved. For a brief moment, Cat remembered the uncertainty in Lucille's voice when she called her earlier in the day and she wondered if Lucille was possibly neglecting her. Obviously there was plenty of work around but it was not coming her way. Was this the moment to ask about her waning career? Cat wondered. She could not bring herself to do it.

"Who's the admirer?" she said instead, pointing to the flowers.

"Jeannie Lester sent them over with love." Lucille made a face.

"Who's she?" Cat asked.

"One of Pamela's new discoveries from England. And she's got to be quite something since she's getting the royal treatment. She's staying upstairs at Pamela's insistence, even though she can well afford a hotel."

"You haven't met her?"

"No. She arrived from London this morning and she's been booked to the hilt from the minute she landed."

"She's not very original with the flowers," Cat said disdainfully.

"Listen, it's better than the chocolate boxes some of the girls send, which are fattening, or the perfume, which I never use, not to mention the junky jewelry some of them try to palm off on me."

"Would you really send a girl out on a job because of flowers or whatever?" Cat asked curiously.

"Not unless they were right for the job, anyway."

"But does it make a difference?"

"Yes and no," Lucille said slowly, then paused with embarrassment. "You see, now that the agency has grown and we have almost two hundred models, sometimes it's a reminder that they exist."

"I've never sent you anything," Cat said seriously.

"You're different." Lucille looked directly at Cat. "You've got to remember that we started with fifteen girls. And although every one of you was a pain in the ass in one way or the other, you were family." She looked up at an aging framed head sheet which hung over her desk. Cat did, too. There were head shots of fifteen young women, some smiling, some serious, some showing off a semi-profile, but all were exquisitely glamorous. "From that we've got seven of you left." Lucille continued, "So I didn't need a reminder that any of you exist. Besides, you've always been special to me." She said it with great emotion.

Cat looked briefly over at Lucille and smiled gratefully. Then returned to look at the old head sheet.

"Are we really only seven?" Cat mused.

"Yup, and I have a feeling that the seven is going to be reduced further."

"Oh?"

"Bibi Thompson is retiring to get married. She always said she'd quit when she was thirty-two and bingo, she's doing it. Gloria Lang is going to the Coast to try for an acting career and I have a feeling she's going to stay there. Zoe, I think, is restless, and something is brewing in that black sphinx-like head of hers. Although she'd be a fool to leave. She's got a good two years more as a model." She shook her head disapprovingly. "When you consider what Pamela did for her, you'd think she'd be a little more loyal and grateful."

"Hold it," Cat interjected. "She's more than contributed her share into making this agency what it is. I personally think she should do what she wants if she can afford it." Her vehemence was misplaced and Lucille raised her brows.

"Franie Lynn is still going strong, so I guess she'll stay." Lucille decided to ignore Cat's reaction. "Beth Grower is sewed up for two years with Revlon, so she's not really around and then there's Terry Crouse, who's over the hill and I wish Pamela would call her in and tell her so."

"Well, that sure covers the seven, when you include me." Cat smiled reflectively. Again she wondered if she could ask Lucille about her standing in the marketplace, but the words stuck in her throat.

"The little men in white uniforms are here from the looney bin." Miss Mack was standing in the doorway.

Lucille and Cat ran out to the reception room. Two male nurses were strapping Cindy onto a stretcher. A doctor was directing their actions.

Cat walked over and placed her hand over Cindy's naked head. The girl was cold and her eyes were dull, but she recognized Cat. "Thanks," she whispered, as she was carried toward the front door.

"Must she be taken to Bellevue?" Lucille asked the doctor and the flippancy with which she discussed Cindy earlier was gone. Instead, a concerned, almost motherly, tone had replaced it.

"Miss Taub, someday modeling agencies are going to be put out of business with their emphasis on being thin. Anorexia is serious business everywhere, but in your field it's reaching epidemic proportions."

"Every model with this office is an adult and we don't force anyone to do things against her will," Lucille said angrily.

A strained silence followed the doctor's departure.

"Incidentally, where's David?" Cat asked, breaking the somber mood.

"Not here, thank goodness," Lucille snapped.

"What's this thing you've got about him?" Cat kept her voice at a level of indifference.

"Well, for starters he's a lousy model. I don't think he's had a job in the last three months."

"People have their dry periods and you know it better than anyone."

"Bullshit," Lucille sneered. "As a matter of fact, I think I finally figured out what he's all about." Her tone became confidential. "He's being groomed to become the new assistant." She winked as she said the last word.

Cat was speechless. Pamela always had beautiful young men around as escorts, errand boys, attendants and bodyguards. They were usually homosexuals signed up as models, but everyone knew the truth. They were, in fact, Pamela's playmates. Cat dismissed the idea. David did not fit the bill. He was too bright, too well informed, too sophisticated and he certainly was not a homosexual. Her conviction concerning David's sexuality surprised her. Bo was a homosexual and it did not bother her.

"I doubt it," she said finally. "You just don't like him."

"I happen to hate him," Lucille said firmly. "And frankly, I think Pamela has bitten off more than she bargained for. He's conniving, which the others were not. He's ambitious, which the others were not. And he's awfully hungry."

"Oh well." Cat did not want to hear anymore. "I think you're wrong but time will tell." She looked at her watch. It was nearly five-thirty. "I've got to be at Gimbels East at six," she said "and I only hope I find a cab at this hour."

At that moment Pamela appeared in the doorway. Her face lit up with pleasure at the sight of Cat. "What a pleasant surprise!" she said, throwing her white briefcase on the desk. "I hope you're not rushing off and can stay and talk for a while."

"I wish I could," Cat answered with genuine regret. "But it's the rush hour and I've got to be on Eighty-sixth Street in half an hour."

"You can use my car," Pamela said as she picked up several messages from Lucille's desk and scanned them quickly. Cat had a moment to observe her. She was indeed a phenomenon. She had arrived from out of town that day, had spent hours in a courthouse and still she looked as if she had just come from a day of rest in the country. She was a tall woman who carried the fashionable oversized man-tailored Ralph Lauren raincoat to perfection. The brown Gucci shoulder strap bag matched the brown medium high-heeled boots and were in keeping with the tweed skirt and brown turtleneck sweater. Her blond-tinted hair was softly permanented and was cut just below the ear lobe. Her makeup was subtle. The overall demeanor was of a high-powered executive and she exuded confidence and authority. Just being in her presence made Cat feel more secure.

"Is the driver outside?" Cat asked tentatively. She could not afford to be late for the Gimbels showing.

"Come, I'll walk you out and tell him to drive you." Pamela said, putting her arm around Cat's shoulder.

Sitting in Pamela's car, Cat felt better. She could talk to Pamela openly about what was going on at the agency as well as about her personal problems. They had known each other for twenty years and although they had never been intimate friends, there was a strong bond between them.

8

It was nearly 8:30 when Cat arrived home and found Jeff waiting in the lobby of her building. She was contrite and apologetic all the way up to the apartment while Jeff tried to reassure her.

Watching her nervously trying to unlock her front door, Jeff was tempted to take the key and help her but restrained himself. That was the role he had played for too long and it was time to stop. It gave him time, however, to observe her. She was thinner than ever and the heavy makeup did not hide the fatigue which was etched around her eyes and mouth. She was obviously driving herself as she had always done and he wondered when she would stop and realize she needed to redirect her energies.

Entering the apartment, Jeff stood by as Cat flicked on a light. It took him a minute to adjust to the brightness and then he found himself blinking at the stark white sterility of the decor.

"Is this what you wanted?" He found his voice.

"Well, I don't know that it was thought out, but I just love it," Cat said with confidence as she moved toward the living room. "Do you like it?" The assurance was gone and he heard the childish plea behind the bravado.

"It's certainly interesting and different." He tried to sound convincing.

"Let me have your coat and then I'll get out of these work clothes and make us some coffee." She walked toward him. "I'm sorry I was late coming home. I did so want to get some cheese and crackers but it's been a terrible day. Everything went wrong with the show at Gimbels. You know how it is when several designers get together." She was talking compulsively as she started to help him off with his coat.

He caught her arm and she stopped in confusion.

"Relax, Cat," he said quietly. "You look all in and you seem to have forgotten to whom you're talking." He paused and smiled. "It's

Jeff, remember? And if there's one thing I know better than anyone, it is that you make the lousiest coffee in the world."

An uncertain smile began to hover over her lips.

"So why don't you go and make yourself comfortable? Take that slop off your face, get into a robe and lie down. I'll make the coffee and bring it in when it's ready. Just point me in the direction of the kitchen."

"Touché." Cat tried to laugh, then taking his hand she guided him toward the kitchen.

"Have you had anything to eat?" he called out but she had disappeared into her bedroom.

The bareness of the kitchen struck him much as the living room did. It looked unused. Opening the refrigerator door, he saw a container of milk, a yogurt, diet white thin-sliced bread and a can of coffee. He slammed the door shut and his eyes fell on the stove. The oven was still taped up. The cupboards contained a set of white china and except for the cups and saucers, the dishes were still covered with packing straw.

The feeling of wanting to take care of her returned more forcefully. Grown up and successful, he knew that behind the brittle self-assurance was the little girl he met when she was fifteen and a student in his English class.

She made little impression on him then, except that she was extremely shy and self-conscious about her height. Curiously though, she always carried herself with grace and dignity. A good student, she became tongue-tied whenever he called on her and it took him a while to understand that she had a crush on him. It was touching and he felt sorry for her since she had no way of hiding her feelings.

He got to know her better as Joe Wallenstein's daughter.

It was in the mid-fifties and Jeff had taken a sabbatical from his teaching job at Ann Arbor, Michigan, with the hopes of embarking on a writing career and finding a publisher in New York. It proved to be quite difficult and within a short time he was broke and was forced to accept a teaching position in the Crown Heights section of Brooklyn. He moved into the upper floor of a small house opposite the Wallensteins.

He was not particularly interested in meeting the people of the area, but he became acquainted with Joe Wallenstein while taking his nightly strolls around the neighborhood. The silent sad man, who walked around at night deep in thought, touched him. Joe's story, which came out over a period of months, was no different from that of many Austrian Jews who had come to the United States on a visit in the late thirties only to discover that because war was imminent, they could not return to Europe. He met Clara, also a refugee from his hometown in Austria, shortly after he arrived, and they started their life together as war raged in Europe, torn with feelings of guilt about their families, who were left behind. Neither was young when they married and the idea that they would one day return home and rejoin their families never left them. It was the revelation when the war ended that most of their relatives had perished in the Holocaust which finally put an end to that dream. Joe accepted his fate, aware that their daughter was an American and should be brought up in the United States. Clara never gave up the hope that one day she would go back home.

An art dealer by trade, Joe Wallenstein was a truly artistic, tasteful and cultured man and he clung to the Old World habits in spite of himself. The neighborhood they lived in had begun to change with the influx of thousands of Orthodox Jewish survivors from Europe and although he and his wife had little in common with the new arrivals, their religious fervor seemed to feed Joe and gave him a sense of security. Clara wanted to move but Joe prevailed. It was a difficult decision, since it forced the Wallensteins into observing strict Jewish Orthodox rules, and although Joe knew such observances were a burden on their daughter, he could not let go.

At one point Jeff began to be invited to the Wallensteins' Friday night dinners and it was then he met Clara and observed Cat more closely. The older woman was extremely elegant, very extravagant and quite frivolous. She spent a great deal of money on her home and herself, seemingly oblivious to Joe's modest income. Appearances seemed to mean everything to her and it was quite clear that she was totally displeased with her daughter. Jeff could see and feel the antagonism even though the child appeared to want to please her mother and gain her approval. He often wondered why Joe did nothing to relieve the tension, aware that the man adored his daughter. He just sat by in brooding silence, obviously torn between the love he felt for his wife and for his child.

Like her husband, Clara spoke with a heavy Austrian accent, but unlike him, she would often lapse into German, seemingly unaware of her rudeness. The fact that Jeff did not understand what she was saying was of little consequence. The idea that Cat was being excluded broke Jeff's heart. He was tempted to stop coming to the house, but Cat's obvious pleasure at seeing him, her pathetic relief at having him there, caused him to continue the weekly visits.

Jeff was not home the night Joe Wallenstein died. It was late on a Friday night and he was about to enter his house when he noticed the lights were on in the Wallensteins' living room. It surprised him and he was wondering whether to walk over when he saw Cat sitting on the front stoop of the house. He had grown used to seeing her there when he came home, no matter how late, and he usually ignored her. But that night something about her uncharacteristic, sagging posture raised his concern. As he approached her, he noticed she was deathly pale and her eyes were swollen from crying.

"Cat?" he started slowly, fearful of frightening her.

She looked up, dazed. "He's dead," she said and her voice lacked inflection. "He's dead and he's lying on the floor in the living room wrapped up like a mummy."

Jeff sat down beside her and put his arms around her, trying to hide his frustration and anger. Although Jewish by birth, he had long since given up observance of the rituals.

"He died after sundown and the rabbi wouldn't let the ambulance take him away." Cat's eyes widened with terror. "And he's going to stay there until sundown tomorrow."

Jeff stiffened. He was sure that in spite of Joe's adherence to tradition, he would have forbidden this ghoulish aspect of Sabbath observance from being followed. But he was dead and no one was aware of how his daughter was reacting to a sight which was bound to haunt her for many years to come.

"Where's your mother?" he asked, cuddling the frightened girl.

"She's been given some medicine so she would sleep." Her voice cracked and she began to sob.

"Let me take you inside. It's late and you should get some sleep."

"I don't want to see him," she cried out hysterically.

He lifted her gently and carried her into the house, using his body as a shield against the sight in the living room, and placed her on her bed. She fell asleep holding his hand.

He was only vaguely aware of Cat over the next few months except that Clara became extremely possessive of her. They were always together and on the rare occasions when he did see Cat alone, he would stop to talk to her. She seemed grateful for his attention.

It all changed the night he woke up to the gentle knocking on his door and found Cat standing in the door, her overly made-up face streaked with tears, her hair disheveled and her dress smeared with vomit.

"Good God!" He pulled her in, fearful that his landlady would wake up. "Where the hell have you been?"

"I went to a party with a friend. She's a model and she was going to help me get a job in a showroom."

"And what happened?"

"I drank too much and Mr. Kimmel, the one who was going to hire me, realized I was under age and he threw me out."

"Where's your friend?"

"She went to another party and I was going to meet her at her home." Tears began to stream down her cheeks. "It's the first time my mother let me sleep at a friend's house and I was so thrilled.

Instead I got mixed up with this Mr. Kimmel and now I feel like a whore."

He wanted to laugh but controlled himself. "But why?"

"Mr. Kimmel gave me a hundred dollars for cab fare."

"Poor baby," Jeff said seriously but he could not help but wonder if Cat had been to bed with Mr. Kimmel. The thought made him look at her more closely. She was still scrawny, all arms and legs, but for the first time he realized she was no longer a child.

"Well, if you're that unhappy about it, why don't you send the money back?" he suggested, trying to be helpful.

She looked up and suddenly her expression changed and her eyes narrowed with determination. "Oh no," she whispered. "Mr. Kimmel may not give me the job as a model, but this hundred dollars might help me with my modeling career."

"You really want to be a model?" Jeff was amused. She was the most unlikely candidate for a modeling career.

"More than anything in the world." She paused and a faraway look came over her face. "And I will be one."

He could not persuade her to go home at that hour. Instead, he had her undress, take a shower and as she lay down on his bed, he held her hand, much as he did after Joe's death. There was a difference, however. Suddenly she was very desirable. When she opened her eyes and reached out to touch his face, he leaned over and kissed her full lips. She responded passionately and he got up quickly and walked to the far corner of the room. Cat was no longer his student, having just graduated from high school, but she was still very young. Finally in control of himself, he came back to where she was lying and tried again to persuade her to go home. She shook her head defiantly and kept staring at him with wide, bewildered eyes.

Mrs. Wallenstein would not be pacified when she found out that Cat had spent the night at Jeff's. Somehow, word got around the street and, within days, Clara had him dismissed from his teaching job for molesting a minor.

Cat would not let go. In defiance of her mother she started visiting him in his room whenever she was through with her daily chores. He could hear the arguments in the Wallenstein home late into the night and he wondered what it was he could do for Cat.

Finally Clara recruited the neighbors and he was forced to move. He also found it impossible to get employment as a teacher in another school. The stigma of being a child molester followed him.

Thoughts of returning to the Midwest were with him constantly, but he had started writing articles for the *Village Voice*, and his career was coming along so he stayed. But it was Cat, rather than his work, who kept him in New York. He felt responsible for her. She was alone, lost and frightened.

Living in a small room in Greenwich Village, Jeff concentrated on his writing and socialized with his contemporaries. A confirmed bachelor, he had several girlfriends whom he enjoyed and who enjoyed him. He became involved in the liberal political movements of the city and, although broke most of the time, he was happy with his lot. As for Cat, she was taking a secretarial course at a nearby business school and would stop by after classes on days when her mother was out shopping or playing cards with her neighbors. She still treated him as though he was her teacher and was still infatuated with him, but he was sure it would pass. His concern for her diminished, but he was always pleased whenever she appeared.

It was a year before he discovered she was not attending school. It was in late May when she arrived in the early afternoon, which was unusual, and handed him a manila envelope. Thinking it was her diploma, he kissed her in a fatherly fashion.

"Open it up," she ordered, and there was a timbre in her voice he had never heard before. He also took note that she was dressed up and had put on makeup. She looked different, although he could not pinpoint the reason.

"Made the honor roll?" he laughed approvingly.

"Better." She smiled broadly and threw herself on the bed, never taking her eyes off him.

He looked at the envelope suspiciously. The name Cat Willingham was boldly printed on it.

"Who's Cat Willingham?" he asked.

"That's me," she answered aggressively. "I couldn't hope to be a model with a name like Catherine Wallenstein."

He raised his brows in surprise. Slowly he opened the envelope and removed several photographs from it. Staring at them, Jeff was stunned. They were all of Cat dressed in glamorous clothes. There was barely any resemblance between the excruciatingly thin, self-conscious girl he knew and the glorious creature he was seeing. But it was Cat and she was ravishingly beautiful.

"When did all this happen?" he started.

"That represents almost a year of hounding photographers, their assistants, their grip carriers, anyone with a camera who would take pictures of me." The assurance with which she spoke struck him again. "Until now they were all lousy and I never bothered to show them to you. But these were taken by Penn and he's already had me meet the editors of *Vogue*. I'm being photographed with Pamela Fitzpatrick tomorrow in a Balenciaga gown." She pronounced the name with reverence.

"I don't understand what you're talking about." He tried to be patient. "A photograph appearing in a fashion magazine is exciting but that doesn't make you a famous model."

"I've been booked by *Vogue* to do six editorial pages for their September issue and a cover for January." She got up and walked over to him. "And the Helena Rubinstein people are talking about using me as their model for their forthcoming ad campaign, which is being launched sometime next year." She paused to catch her breath. "And that means money." The last words were said triumphantly.

He did not react. He had been expecting Cat to grow up at some point and he knew he did not want her to go. For the first time he realized he was deeply in love with this woman-child and it distressed him. He had so little to offer her.

"Now you can afford to write that great book and not have to worry about anything." She was standing close to him and she rested her head on his chest.

He disengaged himself angrily. "That's hardly your problem."

"It's not a problem. I want to help you. Sure I want to be a model, more than anything in the world, but I don't want it just for me. I want it for us." The childish fear of being abandoned had replaced the exuberance of pending success.

"Does your mother know about this?" He pointed to the photographs.

"No. And she won't until I can show her a tear sheet." Her eyes began to sparkle again. "Jeff, I've done it, oh, I've done it." Suddenly she threw her arms around his neck and kissed him passionately. Then, moving away, she looked at him seductively.

He smiled inwardly, not wanting to offend her. But the look betrayed her youth and vulnerability and all his feelings, which had been kept under wraps for so long, surfaced.

Lifting her up gently, he placed her on the bed. With trembling fingers he started to undo the buttons of her shirt. Her eyes were closed but her arms were pulling him toward her and then he felt her body rise toward him. Her warmth surrounded him eagerly and he pressed himself deep into her. Vaguely he thought of withdrawing before consummating the act, but his need for her, coupled with hers for him were too overwhelming.

When he came to himself, he lifted his upper torso and, cradling her head in his hands, he looked down at her. She was staring at him with wide bewildered eyes.

"Do you love me?" she asked.

"For always." And he meant it as he had never meant anything before in his life.

They were married under threats of police action by Mrs. Wallenstein, even though Cat was over eighteen. It was humiliating and for a long time they did not see Clara. Then she began to appear in their lives periodically and, though he made an effort to accommodate her demands, both emotional and material, it was impossible to do.

Cat's need for her mother, however, was always there. She tried to hide it, but Jeff knew it existed. Unspoken most of the time, it would surface when she was under stress, such as the time when Alexandra was born. Clara was in Europe and when she did not rush back to the States, the estrangement between mother and daughter deepened. But Cat's need never really disappeared. At one point, Cat started taking Alexandra to visit Clara in Brooklyn, hoping her child would gain her the approval she never had. The visits lasted for several years, but stopped abruptly when Cat decided Clara was having a morbid effect on their daughter.

Jeff did not interfere, hoping Cat would grow more secure as a person and the strange dependence would lessen. It leveled off when Cat began giving her mother an allowance. That seemed to pacify the guilt.

Somehow the stormy relationship between Cat and Clara did not affect their marriage. Their relationship withstood all hardships. Each was deeply involved with work and although he was concerned when Cat got pregnant that a child would disrupt their idyllic life, his fears were groundless. Theirs was a love affair which seemed unshakable.

The gap in their ages narrowed, and he continued being father, teacher, husband and lover, while Cat assumed the role of wife, mother and breadwinner. Their dependence on her income lessened, but there was no way of persuading her of that fact and he did not press the issue. His ego could take it and since Cat's happiness meant everything to him, life moved along with little change.

It was Cat's second pregnancy, twelve years after they were married, which finally changed everything. Although he, too, did not want any more children, he would never have allowed her to go through an illegal abortion. But she went ahead without telling him and the operation had a devastating effect on her. She had always been zealous about her work. Now it became an obsession. The idea of giving it up, even for a short period, terrified her.

After that, the spontaneity of their life together was gone. She became totally self-absorbed. She was past thirty and hidden fears surfaced. Her career as a photographer's model began to wane and she went into runway work. Although she quickly became one of the top models in the field and her earnings hardly suffered, she felt her life was coming to an end. The paranoia about youth dominated most of her thoughts and actions. It affected their physical relationship and his love, adulation and admiration were not enough. Both he and Alexandra circled around her, trying not to upset her, but her needs were insatiable. The tranquillity which had been part of what made

theirs a unique marriage began to come apart. When the offer to
teach at Boston University came up, Jeff accepted it as the perfect
opportunity to relieve some of the pressures which were beginning
to affect him. Cat's protests were feeble and he knew she, too, was
relieved.

Now, after nearly eighteen years of marriage, he was tired of the
game-playing. He was past fifty and needs which he had tried to
ignore, both his own and Alexandra's, came into play.

Jeff sighed deeply and looked over at the rain-drenched terrace.
It looked forlorn and the sight deepened his feelings of sadness. Cat
living alone after all these years worried him but he could no longer
protect her. Would she make it? he wondered.

9

As Cat undressed and removed her makeup she felt happier than she had been in quite a while. From the minute she saw Jeff waiting for her in the lobby downstairs, the comforting feeling of belonging came back to her, and she realized how much she had missed it. Having him in the apartment, hearing his footsteps approaching the bedroom, gave her a sense of security. She wondered if she could ask him to come back to the city and resume their life together. With Alexandra away at school, it was possible that they could recapture the dreamlike quality which existed between them when they were first married. She had loved him so.

The gentle knock on her door puzzled her. Jeff was behaving like a guest.

She watched him place a tray with cups and saucers, creamer and sugar and neatly folded cocktail napkins on the table. As always, he had a way of making things look appetizing, and she wished his formal demeanor would go away.

"That looks delicious." She smiled warmly at him.

"And you look exhausted," he said with concern. "Why don't you lie down and relax."

Obediently she got into bed and watched him look around.

"This is some room!" he said finally, and she caught the hurt in his voice. "Talk about a change of personality." He regained his composure within seconds. "No wonder you didn't want anything from the other apartment."

"It's no reflection on you or us," Cat said quickly. "It's just that everything there represented so many unfulfilled dreams."

Jeff came over and sat on the edge of the bed, brushing her hair away from her face. "They were your dreams, Cat, not mine," he said seriously.

Cat caught his hand and held it. "I kept hoping you'd succeed with your writing."

She saw him wince. "I did succeed," he said quietly. "I never intended to write that great American novel. You wanted that, I didn't. What I write now gets published and that's almost enough for me."

"Almost?"

"At the risk of sounding banal, writing is a lonely job and I've always hoped that someday I could go back to teaching. You see, Cat, I suddenly realized I need people around me."

"Were you lonely?"

"Not for a long time." He sounded hesitant. "But sometimes I wished you'd been around more."

"We needed the money."

"I could never compete with your earnings, but we could have managed on what I was making."

"You never asked me to quit," she said slowly.

Jeff raised his brows. "Nobody ever forced you to work."

"I know. But you never asked me to quit," she repeated childishly.

"And would you have quit?" he asked, and before she could answer he continued. "Cat, I don't know when it happened, but at one point you no longer worked to earn money. You became obsessed with being a model. Like the social drinker who one day takes that one extra drink and becomes an alcoholic, somewhere along the line your modeling took on another dimension. A deeper meaning."

Cat felt helpless. Her work had always been equated with high earnings. That was the reason she was a model, worked as hard as she did. But that was not what Jeff was saying.

"I wanted you to ask me to quit." She found her voice.

He looked at her for a long moment. "You'd better have your coffee before it gets cold." He turned away and picked up a cup and handed it to her. "And since we're on the subject, how are your finances?"

"Well, the operation was unexpected and cost a blooming fortune." She was relieved to be off the subject of her work.

"It's true, your timing wasn't the best."

"An emergency hysterectomy with complications was not exactly what I had in mind at this time," she concurred. "As a matter of fact, I might not have bought this apartment had I known it would happen."

"Can I be of any help?" he asked.

"In what way?"

"Do you need any money?"

She lowered her eyes. In spite of what Jeff had said, he could never have taken over the financial responsibilities for their lives. He was the dreamer, the artist, and she was convinced he had no idea about what their expenses really were. Besides, that had been the bargain she had made with herself. She was to be the breadwinner.

"I'll manage," she said stiffly.

"Cat, give yourself a break." Jeff's voice softened. "You're pushing yourself and you should take time off and rest."

She took a deep breath and her eyes moistened. She covered her face quickly.

"Are you all right?" he asked with concern.

"I feel old and unfeminine since the operation," she whispered, and was stunned by the confession.

"That's a crock. You don't look any different than you did when we first got married. As for your femininity, think on the bright side. You can relax and maybe even enjoy yourself now that you can't get pregnant." The last words, although said lightly, barely hid the suppressed anger.

The tears which were on the verge of flowing dried and her head shot up. "That was unnecessary and unkind," she said through clenched teeth. But she could not deny the validity of his statement.

After the abortion she was terrified of getting pregnant, but she hid her fears whenever they did make love and until this minute she was convinced she had done it well. Even after he left for Boston, she made a serious effort to spend weekends with him and behave as a wife should. The idea that Jeff had not been fooled was shocking. That he should have chosen to bring it up in reply to her impulsive confession was devastating. She could not understand what had made her mention her feelings about her femininity. Having said it, however, she had assumed he would be understanding, even reassuring.

"How about dinner?" Cat asked after a long, uncomfortable silence. "I can call a Chinese restaurant and have them deliver." She tried to smile.

"Cat, when did you speak to Alexandra last?" He ignored her offer.

"I tried reaching her several times, but she's been busy, which as far as I'm concerned is a good sign." She was taken aback by the sudden change of subject. "We've got to face it, she's not a scholar and at this school they have a good art department and great riding stables."

"How long are you going to go on with it?"

"With what?"

"Riding stables, horses, riding camps. You keep pushing that child into a mold which she simply does not fit. You're grooming her for a life she does not want and frankly, you're not doing her a service." His voice hardened.

Cat lit a cigarette and did not answer.

"Have you any idea who Alexandra is?" he asked after a minute. Still she did not answer.

"Cat, she's a funny little girl who's overweight and unhappy about it. She's warm and cuddly and sensitive. And she wants your approval more than anything."

"Sensitive to what?" Cat exploded. "To herself and her needs. Is she sensitive to mine, to yours?"

"She'd like to be but doesn't know how. She also wants to please, I assure you, but she can't help it if her needs are different from yours."

"What are her needs that are so different? Drawing morbid little men and women in black and white?" Cat shot the words out furiously.

"They're quite beautiful and extremely well done." Jeff got angry, too. "If you'd only bother to look beyond your own complexes."

Cat wanted to protest but his words upset her into silence.

"Do you really believe Alexandra enjoys riding?" he asked after a minute.

"I know she does," Cat said defiantly. "Ask her if you don't believe me."

"I wouldn't dream of putting her in that position."

"Please, Jeff, let's not fight," she said wearily. They had been through this conversation in the past and she was too tired to pursue it.

"Cat," Jeff said, and something in his voice made her look directly at him. "I've been asked to give a series of lectures at UCLA in Los Angeles. I'm leaving next week and I'll be gone until June."

"Oh, Jeff, I couldn't possibly take the time off."

"I'm not asking you to." He walked over to the far end of the room and sat down in a chair. "On the contrary, I think this will give us a chance to see if, after all these years of pretense, we should possibly call it quits."

Cat was too stunned to speak.

"But what I do want is for you to let Alexandra come with me," he continued after a moment.

"Take Alexandra away?"

"What about it?" Jeff asked, and Cat realized he was serious. He really wanted to take Alexandra away from her.

"It's a ridiculous idea." Cat tried to sound calm. "What about school?"

"School?" Jeff laughed mirthlessly. "Cat, that child can't concentrate on anything and hasn't been able to for quite a long time. I saw it when she spent time with me while you were in the hospital and I've spoken to the headmistress at her present school. She's cutting every class. She's in a bad emotional state." He stopped and shut his eyes as though in pain. "Cat, she needs help."

"What are you talking about?" Her voice rose, although instinct told her he was right.

"Let's not belabor it."

"Are you suggesting I've neglected her?"

"Good God, no. You've done everything in the world for her. Everything you possibly could. If anything, you've done too much."

"And what's that supposed to mean?"

"Have you by any chance gotten your American Express bill this month?"

"I don't think so," she said cautiously.

"Well, the school finally took it away from her. Seems she's been using it to buy things for other girls and getting the cash." He controlled himself with difficulty. "Cat, she's into drugs in a very serious way and she needs help. And an open bank account will not do it."

"You've always been jealous of the money I've given her." Her voice rose. "As for the drug bit, I don't believe you." She was aware that her hysteria was mounting because she did believe him, but somehow she could not face it.

"Would you like to speak to the school psychologist?" he asked quietly.

"I certainly would," she said, and picked up the phone.

She was aware of Jeff watching her as she started to dial the school number. She stopped midway and hung up.

"But who will take care of her?" she whispered.

Jeff looked uncomfortable for a minute. "Cat," he started slowly. "I won't be going to the Coast alone. Neva Green is already there and she's rented a house . . ."

"Neva Green!" Cat gasped. "You and Neva?" The idea was preposterous. "Jeff, Neva is one of my best friends."

"You don't have a best friend, Cat," Jeff said dryly. "Neva was the lady who helped you out whenever the maid was off and Alexandra needed to be cared for. Neva was the good neighbor who was there when work was more important than anything and anyone; the lady who shopped and ran errands for you, who listened to you moan about gaining an ounce, or finding an eyelash out of place. She did it willingly. She loved you. She thought, and still thinks, you're the most beautiful creature in the world. She was your friend. You weren't hers." His voice rose in anger. "When did you see her last?" he demanded. "Have you thought of her once since you moved from the West Side?"

Cat could not answer. Neva Green. Her frumpy, heavy-set neighbor who lived on the fourth floor on West Eighty-seventh Street. Big-bosomed, motherly, warm and kind, they had met shortly after she and Jeff moved into the building, and she and her husband George became Cat's surrogate parents. Cat remembered how surprised she was to learn that Neva was only five years older than she was.

"How long has it been going on?" Cat found her voice.

"What the hell difference does it make?"

"Were you having an affair with her while George was still alive?"

"Is that the only thing you can come up with at this time?" he said bitterly. "Good God! When will you ladies begin to understand that sleeping with other women, having affairs, is not where it's at. I won't bother to answer your first question for one simple reason. Whether I slept with Neva or not is irrelevant, because nothing I did took anything away from our relationship. And you know it. And in answer to your second question, no, I did not sleep with Neva while George was alive. But over the past couple of years, Neva and I grew close to each other."

"Is that why you moved to Boston?"

"Partly. We wanted to put an end to it for your sake, and Alexandra's, but we weren't sure what we should do. We're still not sure, but this California thing came up . . ."

"And you discovered you couldn't live without each other." Cat was suddenly angry. Neva was a fat, old housewife and in a way it was humiliating to be replaced by her.

"Don't be bitchy," Jeff said threateningly.

"But with Neva?" Cat could not cope with the thought. "How could you?"

"Easily," Jeff snapped. "You simply never grew up and I suddenly wanted a woman. But more important, I wanted a friend, someone who wanted me, reached out to me, helped me, thought about me. Someone who talked to me." He caught his breath. "Frankly, you finally grew to bore me." For the first time he wanted to hurt her. He regretted the words the minute they were spoken.

"I bore you?" She stood up shakily. "I bore you!" She repeated the phrase and wanted to laugh, but no sound came.

Jeff had turned away and was staring out the window. Cat looked at him and tried to see him objectively. He was fifty-three years old and she was almost thirty-seven, yet at that moment she felt as though he belonged to a different generation. Characteristically, he was wearing his ill-fitting corduroy jacket, which did not match the pants, and the orthopedic space shoes, which she hated. Still, he exuded a warmth and dependability which had sustained her for so long. She was tempted to walk over to him and ask him not to leave her. She rejected the thought. Jeff was an old man and she was still young.

"Are you in love with Neva?" she asked in spite of herself.

"Stop being childish," he said impatiently. "What about Alexandra? That's really what's important." His manner softened. "The doctors feel that six months with me might help her and she's always liked Neva."

"What happens after six months?" Cat felt drained.

"I really don't know. I've been asked to give a series of lectures at Brooklyn College in September and I'm anxious to do it."

"Going back to Crown Heights?" she said with disdain.

"Brooklyn Heights, as a matter of fact. I'm thinking of buying a house there."

"You mean, you'd really go back to Brooklyn and teach?"

"Brooklyn, Buffalo, Barcelona. What difference does it make if you're happy with what you're doing and have come to terms with who and what you are."

"But they humiliated you so back then," she persisted.

"Well, who better than you would understand that I find justice is finally being done." He stood up. "But all that's beside the point. What I do know is that right now Alexandra needs a home. I believe that's part of the problem. With all that we've given her, we haven't given her a solid base. It's been flakey, unformed. The values, both yours and mine, have been lost in the shuffle of trying to exist. The emphasis on what's important was sorely missing."

"I don't know what you're talking about," Cat said angrily.

"I know you don't."

"Jeff, what the hell do you want from me?" she screamed out of control.

He looked at her for a long moment and suddenly his expression changed.

"Oh, Cat, what I want is for you to be happy. That's what I've always wanted."

"But I am happy," she said uncertainly.

"You've been so busy that you really haven't any idea what I'm talking about."

"Jeff, do you want a divorce?" she asked coldly.

"Not really, but I think you have to decide if you do."

"I won't consider living with you again if you go through with that crazy plan of going to Brooklyn. That would really be the end of this marriage."

"That's part of what this six months is all about. It'll give us both time to think of what we really want from each other."

"How does Neva fit into all this?"

"Cat, I never thought I'd marry. Had no intention of getting married until you came into my life. You are my wife. If our marriage should end, I have no intention of marrying again. Neva knows that. She's my friend and I'm hers but that's where it sits." He was in full control of himself again. "My main concern at this moment is Alexandra. What we need to consider at this time is her welfare. And the question is will you let her come with me to the Coast?"

Cat was tempted to refuse but knew Jeff was right.

"I'll call the school in the morning," she whispered.

"Thank you," Jeff said after another strained silence. "I appreciate it." For a minute he looked as though he wanted to say something, but changed his mind. "It's late and I've got a train to catch."

Standing in the doorway, his wrinkled raincoat draped over his shoulder, she could see his concern for her.

"Will you be all right?" he asked.

"Of course I will," she said with exaggerated confidence.

"With it all, I'll still always be only a phone call away."

"I know." She forced a smile. "But I think you're right. I should take time to think things out."

After Jeff left, Cat walked into the living room and threw herself on the sofa. It was for the best, she thought wearily. The next six months would give her a chance to get herself in shape physically, emotionally and financially. It would also be the first time in her life that she would be responsible to no one but herself.

The phone rang beside her and Cat picked it up quickly.

"How about leaving your husband and flying off with me to Outer Mongolia?" It was Kevin Dawson, a photographer whom she'd worked with through the years.

"When?" Rather than be annoyed at the intrusion, Cat could not help but be amused by his question.

"The plane leaves in forty-five minutes."

"I'm ready," she answered and, holding the phone between chin and shoulder, she got up and started pacing. "And now that I've accepted, what do you do for an encore?"

"I hang up and try again with the hopes that you turn me down as you always do."

"When did you get into town?" She laughed appreciatively.

"A couple of hours ago. How about dinner sometime this week? I've got an assignment which I need help with."

"Serious?"

"Not really. *Elle* magazine wants me to do a story about Soho, of all places, and I'd like to talk to you about it."

"Sounds fascinating. When would you like to meet?"

They made a date and Cat hung up. Was it possible that Kevin wanted her for the assignment? She did not know much about Soho but that was unimportant.

She continued to pace, nervously, and then walked out to the terrace. It was a moonless night and a feeling of foreboding rose in her. Her conversation with Jeff returned all too vividly, although she felt calmer about it, perhaps because the phone call with Kevin gave her some perspective on her life. There were so many things she could do if she were alone. She could have her eyes done and no one would know about it. She could start entertaining, living like the glamorous singles about town which everyone expected of a high-fashion model.

She could begin to enjoy herself as an unattached woman. She could even have an affair. She could have as many affairs as she wanted. Many men had courted her through the years, desired her, wanted to spend time with her. Now she was free to accept the attention.

She closed her eyes, trying desperately to hold on to the feelings of elation which her mind was formulating.

The tears welled up in spite of her and started streaming down her cheeks. Within seconds her body began to shake and she gave in to the uncontrollable sobbing.

10

The chaos which greeted Cat when she walked into Bo Shephard's showroom was complete. Bo was dressed, as usual, in his tight-fitting, faded dungarees, but now he had on a magnificent pure white silk shirt with full sleeves, gathered tightly around his wrists with huge gleaming cuff links, sneakers, red socks and a necktie instead of a belt tied around his waist. He was running around frantically, and although the piped-in rock music was deafening, it did not drown out his panic. He kept calling everyone "Luv," and Cat wanted to hit him. It was so affected, so unlike him.

"Cat! Thank God, you're here," he screamed when he saw her, and rushed over to kiss her on the cheek. "I need help desperately. Some of those girls in there are a total mess. You've never seen a dirtier collection of garbage in your life." He caught his head between his hands. "I swear, they look as if they haven't taken a bath in a week."

Cat was about to point out that she had warned him against using print models rather than experienced runway girls, but knew it would be pointless. Instead, she preceded him into the dressing room where hair stylists, manicurists and dressers were trying to help the girls who were to do Bo's all-important show. In the far corner of the dressing room she saw three runway models sitting around relaxed and chatting amicably. She wanted to walk over to them. They were her family, her friends. They had worked together for years, knew each other's habits, helped each other in a pinch while on a runway, covered up little mishaps which occurred while doing a complex new line. But today she knew she had to concentrate on Bo's show. It was going to make him or break him.

"It's a blessing we had a rehearsal last night," Bo said, following her. "Or I'd swear these guttersnipes aren't the same ones I hired to begin with."

"Take it easy, Bo," she said quietly, suppressing her own nervousness. It was, after all, her first big show, too, since starting to work again.

With exaggerated confidence, she smiled graciously at the younger women and her sense of professionalism took over. She walked around, making suggestions to one of the dressers, helped a girl find her accessories, showed another how to paste down her nipples with tape. Suddenly she spotted a young model who looked completely dazed and Cat realized the girl was squashing out the tail end of a marijuana butt. For a minute she almost lost her poise. Who the hell were these kids? she wondered. What right did they have to be doing fashion shows, earning more money than most models in the world, and abusing their privileged position just because they happened to have been born with good looks.

"How do you get your hair to stay that way?" one of the girls asked.

Cat walked over to her and quickly arranged the chignon into place. The girl was young, thin and tall, but her figure was not as good as hers, Cat noted with satisfaction. She felt better. Bo had chosen girls who somehow resembled her, since she had been the fitting model for the entire line, and she knew that once out in the showroom she would overshadow them all.

"Have some champagne," Bo said, pouring some into a paper cup. It was an inexpensive brand and he was using it as a cheap ploy to perk up the models, give them a look of excitement and verve which none of these inexperienced girls was capable of assuming at that hour in the morning. Cat did not fault him for doing it. She did resent the idea that he seemed to have forgotten who she was. She did not need a drink to affect the proper look when doing a job, no matter what hour. Shaking her head pleasantly, she walked over to her rack of clothes.

"When did you start being mother hen?"

Cat swung around in amazement. Standing beside her was Nancy Stuart.

"What the hell are you doing here?" She was genuinely pleased to see her, and the impulse to rush over and hug her was overwhelming but she held back. The gesture would have been phony. Nancy had been ill, in a sanitorium, rumored to be a result of drinking, and Cat had not even called to ask about her.

"I was in town for the day and I heard Bo was having a show, so I thought I'd drop by." Nancy smiled and lit a cigarette. Cat noticed her hand shake ever so slightly and she turned away quickly and started rummaging through the clothes. She and Nancy had started their modeling careers together but Nancy had quit when she married a young policeman and moved to the country when her first of four children was born. The marriage surprised everyone. Nancy had always sworn she would marry money. At the time Cat envied her for being able to make the transition from the glamorous life she led to being a housewife. They saw each other on and off for a while, but their lives were so different that the friendship petered out. At one point Cat heard the marriage had broken up. She meant to call but never got around to it. Recently she heard that Nancy had married a very rich man. Cat remembered being pleased for her. It was something Nancy had always wanted.

"Why do you bother?" Nancy was saying, as she leaned against the wall, inhaling deeply on her cigarette. "These girls aren't worth it. They're a mess and they don't really give a damn."

"I know," Cat said sadly. "It was different when we first started."

"We were hungrier." Nancy smiled wanly.

"You sound as though you miss being hungry," Cat said and looked closely at Nancy.

"You know something? Sometimes I actually do miss it." Nancy's voice was barely audible and then she started coughing. Cat watched helplessly as Nancy tried to quell the spasm. It was over in a minute and Nancy groped for a chair.

"You know you don't mean it." Cat lit a cigarette and tried to figure out what it was that bothered her about Nancy's appearance. She was dressed in the latest Galanos tweed suit, which fit to perfection. Her hair, as always, was very blond, cut short and perfectly coiffed. The bone structure with the high brows, the deep-set green eyes, the perfectly shaped nose and wonderfully full lips were all there, yet there was a distinct change. What was missing was the youth, Cat realized, and the thought upset her. Nancy's face seemed to have settled into maturity. Gone was the fun-loving, uninhibited, almost wild young woman Cat had known. Parties, drinking, being promiscuous, were Nancy's way of life. She loved her liquor and held it well and although she overindulged, it had little effect on her ability to do her job. She was ready to take on the world even though she was usually broke. Now, obviously wealthy, having achieved her dream she looked defeated.

"Cat, they're all here." Bo rushed over, his face flushed with excitement.

Cat was grateful for the interruption. "Of course they are," she said encouragingly.

"Everyone, everyone who's anyone," he continued. "*WWD*, Saks, Carrie Donovan from *Harper's Bazaar,* Bernadine Morris from the *Times,* Gerry Stutz from Bendel's, Nancy Benson from *Cosmo* and the lady from *Vogue* . . ." He snapped his fingers trying to recall the name.

"Grace Mirabella," Cat interjected automatically.

"Sure." He smiled sheepishly. "I'm so nervous I could forget my own name this morning." Then realizing Cat was still in her street clothes, he started pleading with her to hurry.

"I'll be ready," she said reassuringly. "Don't worry."

She watched him rush off.

"Nothing changes, does it?" Nancy stood up. "Can we get together after the show?" she asked.

"I'll be dashing out as soon as this is over, but let's make a point of having dinner or something soon."

"Sure, I'll be in touch," Nancy answered, and started to walk away.

"Where can I reach you?" Cat called after her.

"I'll call you," Nancy said quietly, disappearing behind a rack of clothes.

Slowly Cat removed her shirt and pulled the first garment she was to show over her hips. Only then did she remove the leather pants. She did it quickly so that none of the younger models noticed, but she knew she was self-conscious about appearing naked in front of the others in the room. She had done it instinctively and she was shocked. She had never before been inhibited while working.

The applause started the minute Cat stepped out into the small clearing in the showroom. The appreciation filled her with exquisite joy and she rose to the occasion. Mustering up all her years of experience, she succeeded in giving Bo's bizarre wedding dress an elegance which, as far as she was concerned, outweighed the importance of the design. Wearing a suitable air of high seriousness that verged on aloofness while still maintaining a slightly humorous manner, she waltzed around carelessly, allowing the bird-feathered cape to open partially before swinging around to show off the fullness of the back. Then, with a swift spontaneous gesture, she undid the hook at the neck and whipped the cape off, exposing the transparent mini-skirted dress which was tightly fitted over the upper body, then flared out in numerous layers of chiffon, the longest coming down to mid-thigh. The body suit underneath was flesh-colored and it appeared as though she were naked. The textured white stockings and white baby jane shoes completed the outfit. Bo had created the dress on her and although she felt the design was too campy and secretly believed she was the wrong model to show it off, the appreciation from the audience proved Bo knew exactly what he was doing.

Seemingly relaxed, Cat turned around several more times, although she knew she had to get to the Plaza Hotel by one o'clock. Bo was having her model this outrageous outfit at a charity show where several designers were showing their favorite designs for the occasion. The applause grew louder as the models and Bo came out to take the final bow.

"I better get out of here," Cat whispered to Bo while maintaining her pleasant smile.

"Walk to the back and I'll do the rest." He bowed low and walked over to the audience, who stood up and rushed toward him, giving her time to escape.

"I'll never make it." Cat ran toward the dressing room.

"You certainly don't have time to change," one of the dressers said frantically.

"Okay, let's get a sheet of canvas and wrap it around me," Cat ordered. "There *is* a limo downstairs, right?" She directed her question to Sue, Bo's newest assistant.

"Oh my God, I forgot," the young woman wailed.

"Well, get your coat and come with me. You'll have to find me a cab, although at this hour it should be impossible."

Wrapped in the white canvas sheet, her trench coat flung over her shoulders, Cat tapped her foot nervously as the elevator started down. "Oh, shit, I forgot my bag." She turned to Sue. "You run back up and get it and bring my clothes while you're at it and if I find a cab before you're down, get another one and meet me in the grand ballroom of the Plaza.

"Sam," Cat called out to the head starter when the elevator door opened. "Any chance of getting me a cab? I'm frantically late."

"It ain't going to be easy at this hour." He rushed toward the front door.

Cat followed him out, aware that the feathered cape was almost touching the wet pavement, when she saw an empty cab come to a halt in front of the building. She ran to it and nearly collided with a man who was heading for the same taxi.

"If you're going my way, I'll drop you," Cat said, starting to get into the cab.

"I happened to have hailed this taxi," the man said angrily.

"Oh, come on, I'm in a terrible hurry. You can drop me and take it on from there."

She seated herself and the man came to sit beside her after slamming the door shut.

"The Plaza," Cat called out and leaned back, heaving a sigh of relief.

"I happen to be going to Wall Street," the man said pointedly.

"Well, it's only a few blocks out of your way." She threw her head back and closed her eyes, trying to relax.

"Are you going to your own funeral?" she heard the man ask and she opened her eyes and looked over at him.

"Funeral?"

"Well, that shroud you're wearing would lead me to believe it."

"Oh." Cat smiled and pulled aside the muslin sheet, exposing the wedding cape and gown beneath it. "No, it's a wedding dress."

"What?"

"It's the latest wedding dress designed by Bo Shephard and I'm showing it as the finale of the benefit show which is being presented at a charity luncheon at the Plaza."

"You mean it's a costume show," he said with relief.

"You don't like it?" Cat asked coolly.

"I'd hate to think of what the groom would wear."

"I think Bo could come up with something appropriate."

"Well, it sure as hell wouldn't be for any man I know."

Cat sat up and with a low, disdainful look, ran her eyes over her companion and found herself staring at an extremely attractive man. His salt and pepper hair was cut short and shaped in a monk's style, which although severe, was extremely becoming. He was clean-shaven and the cleft in his chin was clearly visible. Behind rimless glasses his eyes staring pleasantly at her were electric blue, so light they appeared almost transparent. The white collar of his shirt was perfectly starched, the tie, in red and navy stripes, was in keeping with the conservative dark gray flannel suit and vest. His raincoat and leather briefcase were lying on the seat between them. Her eyes came back to his face. He looked to be in his early fifties, and there was an animal sensuality about him which made her uncomfortable. "No, I'm sure it wouldn't be proper for any man *you* would know."

"I'm sorry," the man said, realizing he had offended her. "I'm Clay Whitfield and I'm rather removed from the world of fashion." He fished out a wallet and took out his card. "I'm in banking and I didn't mean to hurt your feelings."

Cat stared at the Cartier card, which had a Wall Street address. It was beautifully engraved and very much in keeping with the whole demeanor of the man. She looked back at him. He was staring at her and she grew uncomfortable.

"No, it's okay," she said, and turned her head away, determined to ignore him. She was tired and hungry and wondered if Sue would get to the Plaza on time so that she could have a bite to eat before going to the various appointments she had that afternoon.

"Excuse me," Clay interrupted her thoughts. "I've never thought of it before, but do you ladies dress this way in real life, too?"

Cat looked over at him. "What's real life?"

"That'll be two dollars and seventy-five cents," the driver called out before Clay could answer and Cat realized they were in front of the famed Plaza Hotel.

"I don't have any money on me," Cat cried out in embarrassment. "I forgot my bag."

"That's quite all right," Clay smiled, "considering I thought I was going to a funeral and then realized I was actually escorting a bride, I'll be happy to take care of it."

Cat stepped out of the taxi and smiled at him. "You're really okay, even if you are a little too conservative for this day and age."

11

David Thomas did not join the audience in the tumultuous applause which reverberated through the large ballroom, as Cat did her final swing on the runway and started toward the curtain where the models had their dressing room. Instead, he leaned back, lit a cigarette and tried to understand her charisma. She was certainly no beauty. Almost too tall, she was much too thin, yet she succeeded in appearing positively regal. She had a way of parting her lips as though she were about to smile, and her dark eyes seemed to focus on everyone in the room, giving the audience the feeling she was showing the gown to each person individually. Yet he knew she always made eye contact with just one person to achieve that effect. He also knew that on this day she had chosen him. He had been furious when Lucille ordered him to deliver an envelope to Cat. Now he was pleased he had come.

People began to leave but David remained in his seat watching them amble out. It was a society-studded audience. He had met most of them at one time or another since joining the Pamela Fitzpatrick Agency, but now, sitting alone, he watched their eyes sweep past him with no sign of recognition. He knew that if Pamela were at his side, these same people would have stopped to chat and would have even been gracious to him. He tried to emulate her manner of aloof indifference, but the knot in his stomach began to form into a silent rage. Since becoming a model he seemed to have diminished in stature. Even his extraordinary good looks, which always made people take note of him, did not receive the superficial acknowledgment he had grown used to while growing up. Being a male model made him less than a nobody. He slumped in his seat and covered his face with his hands. Things had not worked out for him.

When he first arrived in New York, he had one thought in mind. He was going to find someone in a position of power who would help him become somebody. Ultimately he was sure he would have the power, but first he needed recognition. It was all vague, but he was young and was convinced that time was on his side. He had just been released from the Army and was no different from others of his generation who were confused, searching and frightened. Except that he was completely alone in the world.

Within weeks of his arrival he was almost broke and feeling frantic. Although he was street-smart from years of being on his own, that did not prepare him for the loneliness he discovered in New York. He started working as a waiter in small East Broadway bars, which proved disastrous. Everyone around seemed as desperate as he was.

He was in the city for nearly six months when someone who ran a modeling agency approached him and suggested he sign up as a model. His first reaction was shock and revulsion, but the promise of decent money for part-time work appealed to him. He signed up and although the jobs he got were for sex-oriented magazines and horror paperback book covers, he did succeed in getting some decent photographs to make up a composite. Out of habit, he began to acquaint himself with the world he was involved in, discovering that Pamela Fitzpatrick ran the most successful agency in New York. He also discovered she wrote a weekly syndicated column. The latter pleased him. It meant she was well connected, which was far more important to him.

Becoming a Pamela Fitzpatrick client became the focal point of his existence. The problem was meeting her. He knew he could go up to her office on a cattle-call day and stand around with all the other models who wanted to be seen by her. But that was not the way he wanted to present himself.

His break came the night he was having a drink in a small, dilapidated bar in the East Village. He was sitting on a barstool when she walked in. She was magnificently dressed in a pale blue gown, decorated with matching feathers and beads reminiscent of the style of the 1920s. Her jewelry was elaborate, almost to the point of poor taste, which was incongruous with her chic demeanor. She was also more attractive than he imagined. But what impressed him most was the vibrant power she exuded, and he could not understand what she was doing in these shabby surroundings, being fawned over by her escort who was an effete-looking young man.

David did not take his eyes off her as she and her escort were seated in a dark corner of the room. He watched her scan the room carefully and when her eyes met his, he stood up and walked over to her.

"Excuse me, Miss Fitzpatrick," he said respectfully. "I have a question to ask you." Before she could interrupt, he went on. "I've often wondered why you don't devote more time to being a serious writer, instead of running a modeling agency."

"You've often wondered, eh?" Her laughter was mocking. "And who the hell are you to wonder?"

"I'm David Thomas."

"Should I know you?"

"*I* think you should."

"Oh, God, you're not one of those new semi-nude male actors who goes around fornicating on the screen, are you?"

"No." David grinned. "I'm a brilliant young journalist who admires you for your writing."

"Do you admire me enough to get me a double extra-dry martini?"

He could feel her watching him as he walked toward her with her drink.

It was working just as he had imagined. He had mentally rehearsed this first meeting numerous times and it was being played out successfully. She finished her drink, and without saying good-bye to her escort, walked out of the bar with David.

Stepping into her chauffeured Mercedes, David felt confident. He was sure he was on the threshold of great things.

"Drive through the park," Pamela ordered the driver. Then turning to David she said simply, "I suppose you want to be a model."

"Just until I earn enough money."

"And then?"

David lit a cigarette and it took all of his will power not to shake as he did it. He wanted to impress her as being more than just a beautiful face.

"I want to help kids, kids who grew up in poverty as I did in the orphanage, who got pushed around and never got the breaks. I want to help the less fortunate. Too many people get themselves into positions of power and then abuse it. I saw it in the orphanage and in the Army. Now I want to earn enough money to become independent and begin to write. I want to expose those people." David concluded his little speech and he felt small beads of perspiration forming on his upper lip. He had rehearsed that speech, too. He wondered if she believed him.

"My dear young man, others have felt as you do. Feel as you do," Pamela said quietly, but he noted that she was not jeering.

He grinned a boyish grin, which he knew was appealing. "Not quite, Miss Fitzpatrick. There's an advantage in coming from nowhere, being nobody, belonging to no one and having no one belong to me. I don't have any obligations. I can say what I want because I am a true orphan. I, David Thomas from the orphanage, have the ultimate weapon. I am alone in the world and I can say truths that I know the grass roots of America will understand because I am one of them."

She started to laugh. "You don't believe that. You believe you're much more than most people." Then she grew serious. "And you probably are in a small sort of way."

David did not flinch at the last remark.

"Be at my office at noon tomorrow and bring your pictures," she said suddenly and, turning to the driver, ordered him to take them to her house.

When they pulled up in front of the town house in the East Eighties, Pamela restrained David from jumping out. He was taken aback. That was not the way the script ended in his preconceived rehearsals. He looked inquiringly at her.

"I'll consider representing you." Her smile was insulting. "Isn't that what you wanted?"

Effortlessly she got out of the car, walked up the steps to her house and within seconds she was inside the door.

Condescendingly the driver dropped him off at the subway station.

That meeting had taken place nearly two years ago and nothing had changed. A bitter anguish shot through him. He was a bad model in spite of his looks and they both knew it. He never understood why she kept him on and even titillated him with promises of a future at her side. He was also painfully aware that he had taken the place of the young man who was her escort the night he first met her, but there was nothing he could do about it. He had nowhere to go. He was totally dependent on Pamela and his only satisfaction was that in a strange way she was becoming dependent on him. With the endless vermouthless martinis and tranquilizers she consumed plus a schedule that began early in the day and rarely ended before the small hours of the morning, she was close to the breaking point and needed someone like him around. And it was because of her state that thoughts of taking over her agency began to crop up in his mind. He was sure he could run it as well as she did. He also had no doubt that he could open up an agency of his own. It was simply a matter of finding the models who would be ready to sign up with him at the beginning of his venture.

"Sir, we've got to get the place cleaned up," someone said and David looked up. The huge ballroom was empty except for the people moving around clearing away the tables and chairs.

He got up quickly and headed toward the improvised dressing room where he knew he would find Cat. Thoughts of seeing her made him feel better. She was one of the few models he liked, and felt comfortable with. She was also the one model he hoped to persuade to join him if he were to leave Pamela and start his own agency.

He found her sitting in a director's chair, her hand covering her face. She looked tired and dejected.

"Cat?" he said gently.

She sat up and composed herself. "David, how wonderful! I saw you out front and wondered if you would come by."

He walked over to her and taking her hand he pressed it and kissed her lightly on the cheek. "You look upset, when the fact is you were the hit of that idiotic exhibition of poor taste to which we were all exposed back there."

"It's nothing, really," she said, holding onto his hand. "I was so rushed coming from Bo's show that I forgot my clothes and I'm waiting for Sue to bring them over. She's still not here and I'm running late." Her smile broadened. "But you're here and I can't say that I mind it."

"Well, I'm of use to someone," he said, pleased. "Would you like me to get us some coffee while we wait?"

"No, stay and talk to me." She still did not let go of his hand and there was an intimacy in the physical contact which caught him off guard.

"What's your schedule for the afternoon?" he asked, disengaging himself, trying to regain his composure.

"I've got to see someone at the Osborne as a favor to Mel Black and then I'm going over to the Grayson Agency about a cosmetic ad."

"Who's at the Osborne?"

"A potential model, whom Mel is pushing."

"Are you seeing her with Pamela in mind?"

"Maybe."

"I wouldn't bother. She barely has time for the ones she has."

"What are you talking about?"

"I can't really pinpoint it, but there's something screwy going on at the office." He paused for a long minute. "Every agency in town is opening up their lists, getting involved in careers other than print and fashion shows. There's a future in television commercials, television in general, even motion pictures. Pamela's agency could and should become sort of a career guidance place and God knows she's involved with every big ad agency in the country, knows everyone who's anyone, intimately, yet she doesn't seem to want to get into it for her models."

"That's not the type of agency she wants, I guess," Cat said slowly.

"She's just being old-fashioned and frankly, unless there's more versatility in her shop, everyone is going to look elsewhere." He stopped, aware that Cat was looking at him intently. "An awful lot of models are unhappy and thinking of leaving her, you know," he concluded in an offhand manner.

"That's very interesting." Cat tried to hide her anxiety. Zoe had said much the same thing a few days ago and in a way it confirmed some of her own thoughts.

"I don't know what to say," she said after a minute. "Maybe I should talk to her when she comes back to town." She cleared her throat. "When is she coming back, anyway?"

"She rushed back to Mississippi after the court case and I don't really know when she's due back." Getting off the stool he started pacing. He had pushed hard, he thought, maybe too hard.

"How did Bo's show go?" He turned back to Cat.

"I think it went well, except that a friend named Nancy Stuart stopped by and it threw me." She seemed relieved at the change of subject. "She looked great but there was something depressing about her."

"Nancy Stuart?" David repeated the name. "Isn't she the woman who married Jack Hastings recently?"

"Yes, I believe so."

"I wonder why he married her?" David asked curiously.

"What's that supposed to mean?" Cat said indignantly. "She's a sensational lady."

"She's over the hill, for Christ's sake."

"How old would you say she is?" Cat asked cautiously.

"I don't know. Forty?"

"Not quite." Her tone changed and David wondered what he said that had offended her.

"Are you doing the Scassi show?" He didn't want to upset her.

"Scassi is still booking?" Cat gulped. "I've done his shows for years and years."

"Why yes, he called yesterday," David said innocently. "I know for a fact he wanted two models."

"Are you sure?"

"I'm almost positive." He became flustered. "You want me to check it out?"

"Yes," Cat said quickly, then reconsidered. "No, let me ask about it myself."

An awkward silence followed and David again felt that he was upsetting her. That was not what he meant to do.

"How's Alexandra?" he asked, hoping to recapture the friendly feeling which usually existed between them.

"She's fine," Cat said too quickly.

"She'll be home for Thanksgiving, won't she?"

Cat's face clouded over. "She's gone to Los Angeles with her father."

"When did all this happen?" David was flabbergasted.

"Last Wednesday."

"Is that why I didn't see you this past weekend?"

"I was too broken up to talk to anyone."

"That's pretty dumb. I'm your friend, remember?"

"I know, but I had to be alone." Her voice was suddenly filled with pain. "David, what's the matter with Alexandra?"

"The matter with her?" he asked in surprise. "I think she's a great kid who's got some problems."

"But she's so unhappy."

"It's the age."

"David, you've seen her often in the last few months and you've talked to her. Has she said anything about what's troubling her?" She hesitated for a minute. "Anything about me?"

"Look, she's fifteen years old, she's all wrapped up in baby fat and it's not easy being your daughter, under the best of circumstances." He paused briefly. "But she worships you. That's for sure."

"What do you think of her drawings?" Cat ignored his last remark.

"They're sad, but that's an expression of the times and her age." He smiled warmly at her. "Don't be so worried. She'll be fine. You may be a hard mother for a kid to take, but you're a smashing lady and she's very lucky to be your daughter, even if she doesn't know it now."

"I wish I could believe you." Cat's voice was edged with tears. "I'm so hurt and confused. I feel as though I've been kicked in the gut and I don't understand why. I get up in the morning and the pain is there, as though I've lost something and then I remember that she's gone and I want to die." She looked over at him helplessly. "I must have done something awfully wrong all these years, but I'm damned if I know what it is."

"Cat, relax. Sooner or later Alexandra will find out how lucky she is," he said sincerely.

"I wonder."

"Listen. I think you've got to start getting out more. You've been cooped up for a long time, and there's a world out there that's waiting for you."

"I suppose you're right," she sighed. "I haven't socialized on my own since I got married."

"That's what I mean. Between husband, home and child, you're a positive recluse. You should start meeting people, going to parties, any party, be seen and see what's going on. The place is really jumping."

Sue walked in at that moment carrying Cat's clothes. "Traffic," she started to explain.

"It's okay," Cat interrupted. "Don't worry about it."

"I've got to get back to the showroom." Sue handed Cat her clothes.

"Thanks." Cat could not wait for the girl to leave.

"David, I've got a sensational idea," she said, the minute Sue was gone. "Why don't I give a party. We can give it together. A Christmas party, or a housewarming, something great, extravagant and stupendous." Her excitement grew. "We'll invite everybody who's anybody and we'll have a ball."

"That's the spirit. And it would also do you good and bring you to the attention of people who might not be aware that you're back in circulation." David smiled at her encouragingly.

Picking up her clothes, Cat walked behind a screen.

"How about dinner tonight?" David asked.

"Can't tonight," she called out. "I'm doing an evening show at the Pierre Hotel which should go to ten." She reappeared, fully dressed, and was scanning her appointment book. Then she looked at her watch.

"God, it's three o'clock already," she said with annoyance. "Damn that Mel." Then looking up she continued. "The rest of the week is a bitch. I've got a couple of evening shows and on Thursday I'm going with Bo to a soiree at the Goodmans' at Bergdorf's. There's a bash being given for some Italian princess who's decided to become a designer and Bo asked me to go with him. But how's this weekend?"

"We'll talk before then," he said stiffly.

"But we'll definitely spend this Saturday together?" Cat was ready to leave.

"Sure. Incidentally, Lucille sent these over for you to look at." David handed her a large manila envelope.

She took it quickly, feeling embarrassed for him. It was wrong for Lucille to use David as a messenger boy, and unnecessary. Taking out the photographs she scanned the faces of the two young women.

"What do you think of them?" she asked, trying to give him the feeling that he was part of the decision-making.

"They should both lose weight, for starters," he said, replacing the pictures in the envelope.

Cat laughed. "You sound just like Pamela. That's exactly what she would say."

"It's safe, anyway." He laughed, too.

"Why don't you decide and tell Lucille whatever you want," she said nonchalantly.

Walking out of the Plaza, Cat took David's arm and squeezed it. "I think we make the handsomest couple on Fifth Avenue," she said, looking up at him.

"You could make anyone look good," he answered sincerely.

Suddenly she leaned over and kissed him on the lips. Then turning around she ran down the steps and turned into Fifty-eighth Street heading west.

David watched her until she disappeared from sight.

Could she be the one? The familiar thought which had given him hope since he was very young, returned. He had never succeeded in establishing a relationship with anyone, but Cat was different. Throughout the years, his efforts toward people turned sour and he would find himself on the losing end. Everyone took and no one was willing to give. Pamela was his latest aborted effort. She had turned out to be mean and vindictive. Yet now all his childhood hopes were rekindled because of Cat Willingham. She was warm and kind, bright and successful. But most important, she was alone and needy, just as he was.

Walking toward Pamela's office, David felt better. Things could be different for him if he had someone like Cat beside him.

12

The hallways at the Osborne were ornate and gloomy and Cat wished she had not agreed to meet Megan Baynes. She rang for the elevator and in a minute she heard the ancient creaking sound of the chains announcing its arrival like an aged servant who should have long since been retired.

The elevator man matched his vehicle but he brightened when she mentioned Megan's name.

"That's my little beauty," he said with pride, and Cat was touched. "You a friend of hers?" he asked after a minute.

"Well, sort of."

"Be good to her," he said, and scanned her face anxiously. "Someone should take care of her," he concluded as though talking to himself.

The corridor of Megan's floor was dimly lit, the carpet, old and tattered. Still the majesty of the structure remained. The walls were paneled in dark oak, the banisters thick, hand-carved with figures and classic designs reminiscent of days when carpentry was an art. Care and devotion had gone into their making. Cat felt chilled. It brought back memories of old houses she visited with her father when she was very young and he would take her along when he examined their contents for auctions. The faded memory shook her. It was all so long ago . . .

She hastened her step. She refused to be drawn into the past which she had succeeded in erasing from her life. It was too painful.

Reaching the end of the long corridor, she found herself standing in front of a heavy oak door. The name card was written in a childlike script. She rang the bell, which seemed to make no sound. Suddenly a burst of light illuminated the dark hallway and Cat found herself blinking at the brightness. It obscured the features of the young woman who was standing in the doorway.

"Won't you come in?" the girl said, moving away and allowing Cat to enter.

It took a second before her eyes adjusted to the light. Then, looking around, she was struck by the enormity of the room. The ceilings were unusually high and the Gothic windows looked as though they had been moved from some medieval cathedral. At the end of the room, a fireplace, huge, black and cavernous seemed like the gaping jaws of some monster. It contrasted sharply with the stark white brick walls.

"You look scared," the young woman said, and Cat turned her attention to Megan Baynes and she felt herself gasp. She was the most beautiful creature Cat had ever seen. She was almost as tall as Cat and very thin. The glossy black hair hanging in soft waves to her shoulders made the simple white dress she was wearing look like a religious habit, and the effect made her seem unapproachable and ageless in her innocence. She wore no makeup, yet the startling bushy eyebrows appeared painted on the flawless skin and her bright blue eyes rimmed with thick bristly dark lashes, staring childishly at Cat, reaffirmed the quality of purity which emanated from her.

Cat's first impulse was to turn around and walk out. She could not understand why, but there was something about the young woman which caused an unfamiliar reaction to rise within her. It was not jealousy. Cat had been in the business too long and always had to contend with younger models entering the field. Sometimes she did envy some of them for their youth and beauty, but envy was not what she was feeling at that moment. She regained her composure with difficulty.

"I don't know what I expected," Cat managed to laugh politely, and walked to the center of the room. "I've never been in any of the apartments in this building." Her voice trailed off.

"Why don't you sit down?" Megan said, waving Cat into an armchair which stood across from an old overstuffed couch. A small glass-topped table on a wrought-iron stand stood between them.

Cat did as she was told and an awkward silence followed.

"Would you like something to drink?" Megan asked finally. It was not asked graciously and the Southern accent, along with the gruff quality in the voice, further irritated Cat.

"A coffee would be lovely," Cat said, taking out a cigarette as she watched Megan walk out of the room.

Left alone, Cat took in the surroundings more closely. The floors were in need of staining but the magnificent parquet was still very much in evidence. A picture of the Madonna and Child hung over the fireplace, next to a large wooden cross. A devotional candle stood on the mantle. Cat remembered Mel Black mentioning Megan and her piety and she could not help but wonder if religion was the theme which Mel was going to use to bring Megan to the attention of the public. Using religion as a gimmick was a cheap shot, Cat thought and made a face. Still, people were known to use any means to make a name for themselves. Vaguely she wondered if Megan was in on the scheme.

"It is a super room, though, isn't it?" Megan said as she returned, interrupting Cat's speculations. Her accent was more pronounced and the question sounded like a demand.

"It reminds me . . ." Cat stopped. She was not sure what it reminded her of, but the feelings that enveloped her in the corridor returned.

"I decorated it myself and modeled it after Mother Alba's room." Megan said with pride. "She was the Mother Superior at my convent and she was the greatest."

"How long were you in the convent?" Cat asked, putting out her cigarette.

"I was there for a while and I was very happy there."

"You were?" Cat asked absently, "How can anyone be happy in an institution?"

"Mother Alba was very good to me." Megan's voice softened. The edge of harshness that had jarred Cat, was gone.

"Kind or not, a convent's still an institution," Cat said and regretted the words when she saw a hurt look come into the young woman's face.

"But this certainly is a very spacious room," Cat rushed on quickly, trying to make amends and hide her feelings. "I mean, it's wonderful to have so much space when you think of the way they build houses today."

The hurt look disappeared and Megan smiled for the first time. The extraordinary beauty was enhanced.

"Would you like to see the rest of it?" Megan asked and without waiting for a reply she walked toward a little stairway. Cat followed her and found herself standing in a compact but fully equipped kitchen. A vast assortment of pots and pans lined the entire wall. The stove and refrigerator were the latest models.

"Do you like to cook?" Cat asked politely, examining the girl closely.

Her beauty was truly unusual and she probably photographed well, since her bone structure was perfect. She was extremely graceful and moved with ease. The question was how agile she would be in front of the camera? If she were as poised there as here, she could make it to the very top as a photographer's model. She could probably also do commercials, although both the accent and the quality of the voice would have to be worked on. Voice-over could be used in the interim. Cat found herself wondering if she would take time out to work with Megan.

"No, I don't, but my mom does. She's the greatest cook in the world."

It took Cat a minute to remember what the girl was talking about.

"Oh, is your mother here?" The softness which had appeared when she spoke of the Mother Superior was even more pronounced.

"Not yet, but she will be soon. Very soon. I'm bringing her to live with me. She's the most wonderful person, and you can't imagine how hard she's worked all her life to bring me up." Megan's face flushed with excitement. "Now, if you'll come this way, I'll show you my bedroom."

Cat followed Megan across the living room where Megan opened a door which Cat had not noticed earlier since it blended in with the walls.

"This is my bedroom," Megan said with pride.

Cat peered over her head and she was stunned. The room looked like a nun's cell. It contained a white iron bed and a tiny night table with a simple lamp standing beside it. A black rosary with a little white cross was draped over the shade. On the opposite wall from the bed stood a dressing table with a mirror encircled by lights similar to those found in theatrical dressing rooms.

"Oh dear," Cat said teasingly. "Such vanity. What would Mother Alba say?"

"I need it for putting on makeup when I model and certainly when Mel gets me the acting jobs and . . ." She stopped and looked at Cat with an expression of rage mingled with guilt.

Cat regretted her cruelty. It was unlike her and she was embarrassed. She lowered her eyes and found herself staring at a photograph sitting on the dressing table. It was a picture of a lady with a thin, wan face whose eyes stared vacantly out into the room.

"Is that your mother?"

Megan walked over to the picture, picked it up and looked at it tenderly. "Isn't she beautiful?" The child-like quality returned.

Cat could not answer. The picture bothered her. There was no emotion in that face, no love, no compassion. She let Megan's question pass.

"What about your pictures?" Cat wanted to be away from the cell-like room, away from the unpleasant face staring out of the photograph.

"Sure thing." Megan came back to herself. "You go have your coffee and I'll bring them out."

Cat wandered about the living room, trying to understand its mood and the personality of the young woman who lived in it. She picked up a book which lay on the mantel of the fireplace. It was a worn Bible. The pages had obviously been fondled countless times. Nearby she saw several other religious books. Suddenly she caught sight of a guitar resting in a corner and it made her think of Alexandra. For the first time Cat wondered how old Megan was. Mel had said she was nineteen, but she was obviously older. She certainly looked older. But then again there was that childish quality about her when she spoke about her mother. Cat's thoughts became muddled. She was being irrational. To her relief, Megan walked in at the moment and handed her a large leather-bound album.

Looking through the photographs, Cat realized that Megan had done more modeling than Mel had led her to believe, but it was clear that most of it had been done outside New York. The unprofessional quality of the pictures did not hide Megan's beauty, although most of them verged on the vulgar. Cat understood Mel's concern. Whoever had handled Megan's career, had exploited her.

Cat was glad she had come. Her first piece of advice to Mel would be to send Megan home to Mama. But if he insisted, she would suggest that Megan take a whole new batch of pictures and then she would show them to Pamela. Cat doubted that Pamela would be interested. Megan's vague, elusive manner would put her off. But at least Mel would then have a proper portfolio and could take it elsewhere.

She looked up at Megan, who was lighting a candle, and the strange feelings which had struck her when she first saw her was reinforced. Was it possible that she was jealous of Megan after all? It made no sense. Yet from the minute she walked into the apartment, she was struggling with emotions which were totally foreign to her, and she forced herself to understand them.

The answer came slowly. She wished Megan were her daughter, rather than Alexandra. She felt an affinity with Megan that she suspected she would never have with her own child.

"What do you think of the pictures?" Megan asked, turning toward Cat.

"Some of them are quite good," she said carefully. "Where did you work before you came to New York?"

"In the South," Megan answered. She was obviously not going to be more specific.

"How did you get to Mel?"

"Doc Kimbrough told me to listen to Mel."

"Who's Kimbrough?"

"He's a friend of my mom's."

"What kind of a doctor is he?"

"He's not a doctor. He's just a very important man in my home town and everybody calls him Doc." She smiled. "He's always been very kind to me."

"And now you want to be a model in New York?"

"I want to be a movie star, and make a lot of money," she answered seriously.

The phrase made Cat smile.

"I sing and play the guitar," Megan continued, unaware of Cat's reaction. "And I'm taking dancing lessons and acting classes."

"Have you ever performed in front of an audience?" Cat asked curiously.

"I did in church back home and at the convent. Mother Alba loved to hear me sing." She sucked her breath in with pleasure. "And Father Francis at my church here is going to have me sing to the children at St. Dominiques."

"You're very involved with your religion, aren't you?" Cat asked haltingly, again wondering if Megan was aware of Mel's intentions.

Megan's eyes widened in surprise. "But of course. It's the most important thing in my life." A look akin to fear crept into her face. "Why do you ask?"

"It's just a bit surprising to find someone as dedicated and devout in this day and age, especially in our field," Cat said defensively.

"Is it wrong?" Megan whispered. "Is it wrong to have faith in a Being who is going to make everything better? I believe that you belong to God and He takes care of everything." Her cheeks grew pink and her eyes glistened as she spoke. "I'd be lost without Him."

The sincerity with which the words were uttered was inescapable. Megan believed every word she said and whatever Mel had in mind, Cat was convinced that Megan had not been consulted.

The phone rang at that moment. It was a quiet muffled sound and for a minute Cat was not sure it was a telephone at all. Megan did not seem to hear it.

"Megan, I think your phone is ringing."

"Yes, I know." Still she did not move toward it.

"Well, aren't you going to answer it?"

"No. Mel takes care of everything like that."

"But suppose it's a friend who wants to talk to you?"

"I don't have any friends in New York other than Father Francis and I see him at early Mass and at evening services," she said simply. Then her expression changed. The child-like quality disappeared and was replaced by the harsh, gruff young woman who had greeted Cat when she first came in. "Let's not talk about me anymore," Megan said and settled herself on the sofa opposite Cat. "Tell me about you, instead."

"I should have thought Mel would have done that. But if you're interested, I'm a model, a fashion model, have been for a long time," Cat started out and felt foolish.

"Do you make a lot of money?" Megan asked.

The question was asked so guilelessly as to compensate for its rudeness.

"Well, yes, but being with Pamela Fitzpatrick helps. And that's where Mel wants you to be."

"Who's she?"

"You haven't heard of Pamela Fitzpatrick?" Cat was amused.

"No, I haven't," Megan answered, and her brow furrowed. "Should I have?"

"Well, she's a very famous and powerful lady in the modeling world, in the theater, in society, you name it. Everybody's heard of her."

"What does that mean, powerful?"

"It means she can . . ." Cat could not form the answer. In all the years she had known Pamela she had never once had to explain who she was or what her source of power consisted of. "Let me put it another way." She started again. "Pamela has the best and most prestigious modeling agency in the United States. People pay attention to what she says and take note of what she thinks. She's a trendsetter, knows everybody worth knowing, and frankly, in the modeling world, she can actually make or break a person."

"Is that possible?" Megan asked suspiciously. Then after a moment she said, "She sounds like a bad lady."

"One doesn't judge the Pamela Fitzpatricks of the world as good or bad. She is. She's like an institution," Cat said emphatically.

"You don't like her, do you?"

"Of course I do."

"A few minutes ago you said you didn't like institutions." It was a strangely perceptive remark spoken harshly and Cat was taken aback. Megan was more of an enigma than ever.

"Megan, what do you really want out of your life?" she asked, deciding she would try just once more to help Mel in his quest for Megan's career.

"I told you. I want to be a movie star. I want to become famous so I can earn enough money to support my mom."

"And how will you achieve that?"

"By working. Mel thinks I can make a lot of money in the movies but he thinks I should start as a model." She smiled indulgently.

"Well, there you are. For that you need people like Pamela to help you."

"Oh, I wouldn't want her to help me," Megan said seriously, "but could you?"

Cat stood up, confused. "Let me take these pictures with me and I'll see what I can do," she said stiffly. The girl was upsetting her and she had to get away. "I'll speak to Mel in a few days and we'll figure something out."

The relief on Megan's face was touching. Suddenly she threw her arms around Cat's shoulders and hugged her. "Thank you so much. You're the first person I've met since coming to New York, other than Mel, who's been kind to me. Truly kind to me."

Cat nearly ran out of the apartment. Instinct told her she should not help Megan get into modeling. She was too fragile and could be badly hurt. Mel knew that, too, and she realized that he had called her because he felt she would understand.

As she settled herself into a cab and gave the driver Grayson's address, Cat found herself wondering what photographers she could ask to take pictures of Megan. Kevin would be good, but Greg would be the likeliest candidate. Bo's clothes would look superb on Megan and Greg had said he wanted the most beautiful model for his pages in *Harper's Bazaar*. She also knew that someone would have to take Megan under her wing and hold her hand until she could fend for herself.

13

Waiting for the elevator to take her up to the Grayson offices, Cat took out her compact and scanned her face to make sure she still looked fresh. It had been an emotion packed day. Bo's show had taken a great deal out of her. The talk with David about Pamela needed further consideration. All that, topped by the meeting with Megan, caused her to feel drained. There was some strange connection between the disjointed events which made up her day, but she could not figure out what it was. All she knew was that she felt unusually conscious of the passage of time. Megan made her miss Alexandra more than ever. There was no physical similarity between Megan and Alexandra but somehow she kept coupling them in her mind. She tried to conjure up her daughter's image the day she left. Alexandra had thrown her arms around her shoulders and hugged her. She saw it vividly when suddenly the picture changed and it was not Alexandra who was hugging her, it was Megan.

"Going up to Grayson's?" Tammy Dickenson, a model from Pamela's office was standing beside her, and the confusing memory evaporated.

"Yes, and you?"

"Sure thing." Tammy took out a huge magnifying mirror and ran her fingers through her long, sleek blond hair. "I was out with Grayson's account executive and he thinks I'd be ideal for their new ads." Tammy put the mirror away. "He's a dreamboat and a fair-haired boy at the agency and I hear he pulls a lot of weight with Grayson." She giggled. "He feels it's in the bag."

David was right, Cat thought, as the elevator shot up to the penthouse floor. She had to get out more, meet people, be seen and remind people of her existence. It may not have been important when she was on top, but now it was. She caught her breath. It was the first time she actually admitted to herself that she was no longer at the top. "Be nice to everyone on the way up because you're bound to meet them on the way down." The phrase ran through her mind. She had been nice, she thought wearily. Very nice. She looked over at

Tammy. But probably not as nice as Tammy was. It was a rotten thought and most unlike her. Tammy was a beautiful girl, a good model and to the best of her knowledge, a decent, hard-working kid. Kid. That was the word. Tammy was a kid and they could not possibly be going up for the same job.

Reaching their floor, Cat headed for the large double doors, her feelings of discomfort growing. Tammy was right beside her. She pushed the doors open with assurance and held it open for Cat. The gesture was respectful and it infuriated her.

The sight of the overcrowded reception room confirmed Cat's suspicions. Standing around were about a dozen models. Cat recognized them all, some she'd worked with for over a decade, and they were all considered past their prime. The call was obviously for an older woman, probably someone who could appear as Tammy's mother.

Cat's first impulse was to leave. She was not ready to face that reality. The others were probably right for the part. She was not. It also explained Lucille's not mentioning it.

"Miss Dickenson, please go to the conference room at the end of the hall," the receptionist said as they entered, "and Miss Willingham, Mr. Grayson asked me to send you into his office the minute you arrived. I'll let him know you're here."

In spite of feeling uncomfortable about the roomful of waiting models, Cat's unhappiness was eased by the preferential treatment. She called out hello to several of the women and felt their eyes following her as she escaped into the long hallway leading to Dan Grayson's office.

They need the job as much as I do, Cat thought, but she dismissed it immediately. Needs, like pain, could not be weighed. Her need was real. No matter what Jeff said, the fact remained that she needed the money. But more important, if she got the job it would be a fitting conclusion to her career. She had started as the Helena Rubinstein girl and she would conclude it with a cosmetics campaign. She realized she was again thinking of the end of her career. Was it really the end? Was she ready for it? Somewhere in the back of her mind she knew she was not.

Dan came toward her and put his arm around her shoulder. "You're as gorgeous as ever."

"I wouldn't have missed the reunion for the world." She kept her voice light, but he knew what she meant.

"You're my first choice, but I have to put up a show."

"But why did you have to make it a general call?" she asked. "You know damn well that some of those gals won't stand a chance. There's something cruel about what you're doing."

"Oh, I don't know," Dan answered, leading her toward the conference room. "Most of those broads out there don't really have feelings."

"Bullshit. Everybody has feelings."

"So maybe they don't have brains. If they did, they would have given up a long time ago," Dan said with finality.

"Well, for Christ's sake, when you come to feel that way about me, try to be honest," Cat said slowly.

She preceded him into the large conference room. Several young account executives were standing around talking to Tammy. One of them had his arm around her shoulder and was looking at her with affection. Cat knew none of them. After the introductions there was a brief, uncomfortable pause.

"May I see your portfolio?" someone asked.

Cat handed it to him and smiled pleasantly. He opened it and everyone crowded around as he flipped through the pages. Nonchalantly, she walked to the far corner of the room and watched them. Their expressions were noncommittal and then they started whispering. She wanted to die.

"Want a drink?" Dan said when they were back in his office and Cat was settled on the small sofa facing the magnificent view of New York from the oversized windows.

She shook her head trying to compose herself. Finally feeling she could control her voice she looked over at Dan. "The only thing they didn't say was 'Don't call us, we'll call you.' "

"Cat, you were wonderful." Dan gulped down a straight Bourbon and wiped his mouth. "I wanted them to see you as I do, so I didn't tell you what it was all about, but now I can."

Cat narrowed her eyes. "Go on," she said, although instinct told her she did not really want to hear what he had to say.

"Well, this is going to be the biggest cosmetic campaign we've ever launched. It's a fragrance as well as bath oil, deodorant, a complete line, and we'll be spending several millions on it. Television, billboards, packaging, magazines, the works. We still don't know who the model will be, but we want someone to represent it, build it up, promote it for months before we're actually ready to go with it."

"We don't know who the model will be." The words stood out clearly. And you're not it, Cat thought bitterly.

"Dan, get to the point," she said out loud.

"I would like you to be our sales rep. I want to sign you up to travel around the country, talking it up on television talk shows, at stores, at women's groups, with editors . . ."

"Forget it, Dan." She stood up. "You're sweet to think of me, but had you told me over the phone what you had in mind, I could have saved you the trouble and the time. Saved myself the time as well."

"It's a smashing opportunity," Dan persisted. "And you're ideal from every point of view. We can't use a young model. She wouldn't know how to handle herself. The ones in their late twenties or early thirties either have a husband and small kids and can't travel or if they aren't married and don't have kids, they don't want to move around the country. You're made to order. I understand your husband lives in Boston and your daughter is at the age where it wouldn't be too much of a problem. The money is great so you can afford to hire the help you need."

She started to protest.

"Thirty thousand dollars a year is no chicken feed," he threw the figure out deliberately.

Cat burst out laughing. "You've got to be kidding. I make twice that amount, at least." She said it with assurance and hoped the doubt was not too evident. "And I stay put, sleep in my own bed and although my daughter is probably old enough to be on her own with a housekeeper, it's something I just won't do."

"I'll go to thirty-five thousand for you," Dan said seriously. "You've got to remember this is firm, not speculative."

He knows, Cat thought in dismay. He knows I'm past my heyday and the fifty thousand, sixty thousand, seventy thousand which I had earned for years was very speculative, indeed.

"Thanks anyway." She put her hand out. "Don't think I don't appreciate the offer. But it's really not for me."

Just before reaching the door, she turned around. "Dan, is Tammy up for the job as the model?"

"You've got to be kidding." He waved his hand in a deprecating manner.

14

Cat was completely dressed and ready for the Goodmans' reception for the Italian princess as she looked longingly at her bed. It was out of the question. If she lay down, she would never get up. Instead, she turned on the overhead lights in the bedroom and inspected herself carefully. Again she was wearing one of Bo's creations and she wondered if she could tell him that she disliked his latest fads. She would have in the past, but their relationship had changed and she knew it would be pointless.

Moving around the room nervously, Cat tried to fall into the character which the outfit required. A mannish tuxedo made of black shiny heavy silk, the trousers had black velvet stripes running down the sides, and were tight-fitted to mid-calf and then flaired out outrageously to the ankles. The lapels were also in black velvet and the jacket hugged her waist when buttoned. In contrast to the masculine look of the suit, Bo had created an extraordinarily frilly blouse, Victorian in style, with white Belgian lace visible at the wrists and repeated as a handkerchief in the breast pocket of the jacket. The cummerbund around her waist was in flaming Chinese red satin as were the ballet slippers.

She wore no jewelry except for a heavy gold chain accented by a magnificent, colorful enameled pendant in the shape of a cross. When she first saw it, she was surprised. Bo had designed it, something he had started doing recently, but he was hardly a religious man, and the religious symbol was out of character for him. When he saw her reaction, he assured her it was simply an ornament which inadvertently ended up in that particular shape. Cat felt strangely ambivalent as she clasped the chain around her neck. The effect of the colorful ornament was dazzling and her feelings of discomfort disappeared.

Bo also chose her makeup for this occasion. The nearly white base was contrasted by heavy dark eye shadow and liner with silver highlights. The rouge and lipstick were a Chinese red. Her nails were painted the same color. Bo had wanted her to cut her hair, but she refused. Instead, she affected a Rudolf Valentino style, parting her dark tresses severely in the center, plastering them down with cream and pulling the rest into her famous chignon. It created the effect of a short bob. She felt like a fop, a dandy from an Oscar Wilde novel, but that was what Bo wanted. He was not going to let up until he forced his way into the marketplace, even though he was breaking all the rules in order to achieve his goal. Tonight he would be dressed in an identical outfit. As much as she hated the whole idea, she had to admit it would attract attention.

She lit a cigarette and sat down in one of the small chairs trying to calm herself. She knew she was not really angry at the design or at Bo but was struggling with something she refused to confront and which had to be faced. Her modeling career was coming to an end and she was not ready to accept it. The conversation with Dan was the most telling of all.

Although everyone she had seen since she started making the rounds had been extremely kind, gracious and seemed happy to see her, few had come up with jobs. Most of them promised to call her for the Fall and Winter collections, whereas Dan had offered her something concrete. But more important, all her interviews were taking too much out of her emotionally. The effort to appear at ease, make jokes, come up with the knowing, clever remarks, trying to prove she was still "good old Cat" were draining her. Go-sees had always been difficult, but now the fear of rejection had taken on a new dimension and she wondered if she could take it for much longer. Still, she was being booked and the money was trickling in, she thought defiantly. Suddenly her conversation with Jeff came back to her. Was it really the money which was at stake? He had indicated that it was something deeper, more insidious.

She stood up angrily and caught sight of herself in the mirror. She looked great, there was no doubt of it, but even Bo was deserting her. He was taking her to the Goodmans, which was a coup, but he was not going to have her photographed for the feature story which *Harper's Bazaar* was doing about him. Greg had implied it that day in Bo's office. Bo had obviously prevailed with the editors to use Greg, who was a totally unknown photographer in the States, but he was not going to fight for her.

Lighting another cigarette, she continued to stare at herself. She was being absurd. She could not possibly expect Bo to use her in his photographic layout. But that was no longer the issue. Now the question was whether she could still do fashion shows. Could she ask Bo? Would he tell her the truth? And, most important, could she take it? The answer eluded her.

She squashed out her cigarette and picked up the heavy double-breasted velvet coat, which was interlined with stiff muslin and lined with red silk, put her cigarettes and lipstick into a small black clutch bag and unwrapped a long cigarette holder which Bo insisted she carry. She felt ridiculous and for the first time since she started modeling she was tempted not to go, in spite of knowing the evening could be construed as a job. It was an extremely unprofessional thought and she rushed out of her room.

The downstairs buzzer was ringing as she emerged into the front hall. A delivery boy with flowers was on his way up, the doorman announced. Cat was relieved. They were probably from Bo. That was the sort of thing he would do. She opened the front door and waited, wondering if she had misjudged Greg's influence on him after all.

The box was long and the flowers were sent from MacDonald Forbes, the florist of the Carlyle Hotel. *That* was overdoing it, Cat thought, as she signed for them. Opening the box, she removed the green tissue paper and found herself staring at the most exquisite long-stemmed roses she had ever seen. It looked as though there were at least two dozen of them. With trembling fingers, Cat tore open the enclosed card.

"Imitation, as perfectly done as possible, lacks the texture and aroma of real life and I know you agree with me." It was signed "Clay Whitfield." It took her a moment to remember who he was, and then she wondered how he got her address. Reaching out, she touched the flowers. They were made of delicate silk and were quite perfect, except for the one rose in the center of the bouquet which was somehow less perfect, and she realized that it was real. She felt cheated. She pulled it out and pricked her finger. It had thorns. The silk ones did, too, but they were blunt. She was almost late for her appointment with Bo, but she rushed back into her bedroom, found Clay's card and called his office. It was nearly 7 P.M., but she knew instinctively that he would be there. He looked like a man who lived for his work.

She proved to be right when the secretary answered and within minutes he was on the wire.

"Real life pricked my finger," she said when she heard his voice.

"Real life has a way of doing that," he answered and laughed self-consciously.

"How did you get my name and address?"

"Well, you said you were doing a fashion show at the Plaza and once I knew that, it wasn't very difficult to identify the lady who was wearing the outrageous interpretation of a wedding dress. Everybody seems to know you and my secretary remembered that you had some dealings with our office when you bought your apartment. We handled the transaction."

"Were you the one who gave me such a hard time when I was trying to get the mortgage?"

"Not exactly, although actresses and models and people in the arts are not really the most reliable ones, you know."

"Thank you, Mr. Whitfield." Cat resented the last remark and wanted to end the conversation. "I'll enjoy the silk roses and they will compensate me with their beauty as I watch real life die within days. Although I must admit you did make your point."

"How about having dinner with me on Friday . . ."

"Tomorrow?" Cat wanted to laugh. The prim Mr. Whitfield had all the old-fashioned ideas about models and their lifestyle.

"No, the stock market will be dead this Friday because it's the eve of the holiday, so I'm off for a long weekend."

"What holiday?" Cat asked.

"It's an important Jewish holiday, Yom Kippur."

Cat was about to say she was Jewish and knew all about Yom Kippur and its importance, although until this minute she had, in fact, forgotten about it, but she held her tongue and could not understand why.

"Oh, of course," she said, and wondered if Clay Whitfield was Jewish. He did not look it. The thought amused her. Everyone was always saying that to her.

"I meant next Friday," Clay persisted.

"Okay," she said, and regretted it immediately. Somehow she felt threatened by him.

"I'll send the car around for you at seven."

Sitting in the taxi on the way to Bergdorf Goodman's, she reconstructed her conversation with Clay. Her omission about her being Jewish was a strange throwback to the days when she first started modeling. At that time, in addition to changing her name, she had worked hard to separate herself from her background, family and home. Certainly Orthodox Jewish tradition was out of place in her existence. Somehow she was convinced that being Jewish would be a hindrance, unnecessary baggage in her struggle to become a top photographic model. Her marriage to Jeff helped. He was Jewish, but not observant, and she was relieved of any contact with formal religion. Years later, when she grew more secure, she never actually denied her origins, but she never flaunted them either. Being Jewish receded in importance until it was almost completely ignored. Yet now, her conversation with Clay bothered her and she decided she would cancel her date with him.

Bo was waiting for her at the side entrance to the store. Standing next to her, wearing an identical tux, she felt they looked ridiculous. He took her arm firmly, as if guessing her discomfort, as they entered the waiting elevator.

The evening at the Goodmans' was the epitome of fashionable elegance. The apartment, high up over the plaza bordering on Central Park, was exquisitely elegant, yet succeeded in being cozy and intimate. Most of the people who had attended Bo's press show were present, along with some of the known jet-setters, theatrical and motion picture personalities, and several of the best-dressed women in the country. Cat felt out of place, as she walked around chatting with the various guests. It was when she lit her cigarette and felt the pain from the thorn prick that it dawned on her that she was there because she was a model showing off a designer's creation, not because she really belonged. It was a revelation and she wondered why it had never occurred to her in the past. But then she had had Jeff . . .

"What are you doing here?" Pamela Fitzpatrick asked and Cat looked around, surprised. Before she could answer, Pamela continued, "Oh, you're showing off a Shephard monstrosity."

The question and answer were a reaffirmation of her own thoughts, and she was both hurt and embarrassed.

She scanned the room quickly, wondering if Bo were within earshot. He was off in a corner engrossed in conversation with Sally Kirkland, the editor who ran the fashion section when *Life* magazine was still on the stands, and he was oblivious to his surroundings. She turned back to Pamela and wanted to say something clever, but could think of nothing appropriate. She also knew it would be pointless. Whenever Pamela started needling people it was because something was bothering her and that was her way of getting it out of her system.

"Let's say it's different," Cat said, trying to smile. "When did you get back into town?"

"I came right from the airport. My darling husband Peter met me there and drove me in."

Cat was surprised. Peter rarely socialized with Pamela's business world. Except for seeing him at Pamela's famous Christmas parties, where he was a gracious and charming host, Cat did not really know him.

"Is he here?" Cat asked.

"Over there." Pamela nodded. "He's talking to Fairchild." She did not offer to take Cat over.

"Pamela, I'd like to come in and talk to you," Cat started haltingly. "Will you be in tomorrow?"

"Only in the morning. The city closes down early tomorrow because of Yom Kippur, especially in our field." She paused. "You should know that better than most, or have you decided to take a stand and convert?" With that she reached over and touched the cross Cat was wearing.

"Don't be silly." Cat felt herself blush. "It's a piece of jewelry, like any other."

"Looks like a bona fide cross to me," Pamela said sarcastically.

Cat looked down. The back of the pendant was facing outward and, since the underside was made of gold, it did indeed appear to be a simple, if rather large, religious symbol.

"Of course I haven't converted." Cat tried to smile, but Pamela's statement offended her and she felt more out of place than ever. Still, she wanted to continue talking to her. "Pamela, who's Clay Whitfield?" she asked for lack of another subject.

"Clay Whitfield has got to be one of the powerhouses on Wall Street." Pamela was visibly impressed. "Why do you ask?"

"I met him the other day and he asked me out."

"You have got to be kidding." Pamela squinted her eyes suspiciously. "Oh, of course, Margaret died last year."

"Who's Margaret?"

"Mrs. Clay Whitfield." Pamela made a face. "What a pill she was. They'd been married for years and years. One of those money-marries-money scenes. She was an unbearable snob. A classic beauty, the perfect hostess, superb mother of two nasty kids and a pain in the ass. Rockefeller was not really 'in' as far as she was concerned. So you can imagine how she felt about us, the poor working class."

"Sounds rather revolting," Cat said slowly. In spite of Pamela's description of Margaret Whitfield, there was a dose of resentment in the statement.

"Are you going to go out with him?" Pamela asked, and before Cat could answer, "You'd be a fool not to."

"Pamela, I'm a married woman."

"Don't give me that crap about being married," Pamela snapped. "You've carried that spineless parasite long enough. Why don't you give yourself a break. Most women would give their eyeteeth to be seen with Clay, believe me."

The tirade against Jeff had been going on for years and Cat was tempted to lash out but refrained. She wanted to hear more about Clay. She also felt she was impressing Pamela and after all these years, she still wanted and needed Pamela's approval.

"Have you ever met him?" Cat asked.

"Once, years ago at his Oyster Bay home." Pamela became flustered. Cat was unaccountably pleased. She had gotten a rise out of Pamela.

"I could use a drink." Pamela looked around for a waiter. Spotting one, she moved quickly toward him.

Cat watched her take the drink, gulp it down and walk toward Peter. She was dressed in a long, sapphire-blue matte jersey dress covered with sequins and although beautiful it was meant for a younger and thinner woman. Pamela was past fifty and brilliant in many areas, but she had not come to terms with the fact that she was no longer the high-fashion model of the 1940s and '50s and was now quite matronly. Cat had met her when she was first starting her career and Pamela was ending hers. Pamela took a liking to Cat and was her champion from the start. She was instrumental in building Cat's reputation. It was Pamela who persuaded her to go to Paris after the birth of Alexandra and was responsible for her ultimate success. No one understood Pamela's motives, least of all Cat. They were totally different in every way. Cat never stopped being awed by her, taking guff from her which she never would from anyone else.

The invitation to join her agency came as a surprise to Cat. She was the most popular model with the Regency Agency and saw no reason to change.

"Mine will be the biggest agency ever," Pamela said with assurance. "I'll start going into runway modeling in a more serious way and it will be *the* agency to be with." The tone was cold, almost menacing. "You'd better believe it."

"I don't think I can leave Regency," Cat said, hiding her fear and annoyance. Pamela had done so much for her.

"You can't afford not to," Pamela answered. "Besides, I'm going to have the voucher system and I'll give you a break on the commissions."

It was tempting. No matter how much she earned, it was difficult to meet her monthly financial obligations. The idea of getting her money every week or two, no matter when the client paid up, could not be ignored.

"Let me think about it," Cat said cautiously.

"Don't take too long. I'm counting on you," Pamela said pleasantly, but there was a threat in the voice. It was the first time Cat saw a different Pamela from the one she thought she knew.

For the next four weeks Pamela got an enormous amount of publicity and it became clear that hers was going to be *the* agency to be with. Cat's decision to sign up with Pamela was finally made because she was concerned that everyone in the industry might suspect she had not been asked. She joined Pamela's agency with great trepidation, which diminished only when she realized Lucille Taub was going to be the head booker, she, too, having been lured away from Regency. It was months later that Cat discovered that Pamela had used her name as bait to get Lucille and several other models to go with her. It upset her, but Pamela did keep her promise and Cat's income nearly doubled.

Now, watching Peter and Pamela, Cat wondered about them. Their relationship had always intrigued everyone. It was a well-known fact that Peter was a homosexual and people often asked Cat what the marriage was all about. She never answered, pretending loyalty to Pamela. The truth was she did not know. There was an air of mystery attached to the marriage. Pamela had married Peter in Paris shortly after the Second World War, where Peter was connected to the American State Department and wrote controversial articles for various European magazines and newspapers. Cat knew that Pamela had given birth to a little girl who stayed with Peter when Pamela was working and that the child died. It was never clear when she died since the subject was never discussed. It was expected that Pamela would move to France permanently when she retired, since Peter did not want to return to the States. And she did for a while but one day they were back in New York and within a short time the Pamela Fitzpatrick Agency was created. Cat always suspected that the death of their child had something to do with the move but it was sheer speculation on her part.

Cat turned her attention to Peter. He had his arm around Pamela's shoulder and Cat had the feeling Pamela was leaning against him, as though for protection. The sight disturbed her. Cat had never thought Pamela needed protection from anyone. She was so independent, so sure of herself, so strong. Pamela's voice drifted toward Cat. She was speaking with great authority, her hand flailing to make a point. Cat tried to catch the words but the room was too noisy. Pamela with her biting tongue, probably making a joke at someone's expense, or talking about anything and everything, never allowing facts to hamper her opinions. It obviously did not matter, since she usually succeeded in being completely captivating. She was not only accepted by the crowd, she was a focal point for it. Pamela belonged and Cat felt like the hired help.

The thought was upsetting. Pamela had started out as a model, just as Cat had. They were equally successful, yet Pamela had made the transition from working girl to jet set entrepreneur. It had never been something Cat wanted. Being a successful model, earning a good living, being independent was all that mattered. Now, for the first time in her life she wondered if she would want to change places with Pamela. And if she did, could she? Jeff would certainly not be interested in this world of fashion and glamour. Clay Whitfield came to mind. With someone like Clay she could probably bridge the gap between her world and the one Pamela was involved with.

"Will you be going to visit your mother this weekend?" Cat was relieved to hear Bo's voice breaking into her thoughts and she turned to him quickly.

"I should, shouldn't I?" she said sheepishly. "I haven't seen her since she came back but the idea of going to Brooklyn is so depressing."

"Well, it just seems right that you should," Bo said, sipping his champagne. "This is the holiday when you atone for all your sins, isn't it?"

"What's going on with everyone today?" Cat said impatiently. "I've suddenly become the house Jew, the expert on the Jewish religion."

"Don't be so touchy, luv," he said bitchily.

Walking toward the french doors which led to the terrace, Cat moved with as much dignity as she could muster and stared at her image in the darkened panes. For the first time in years she wondered if she looked Jewish. Clay obviously did not think so. She had always been considered exotic, the South American type. She put her hand to her face. It was icy.

When Cat arrived at her apartment, she decided she would visit her mother after the holiday. The idea of spending Yom Kippur with Clara in the predominantly Jewish neighborhood was unbearable. They would not even be able to go out to lunch, which usually diffused some of the tension which existed between them.

She also changed her mind about going out with Clay. It would be her first date as a single woman and she realized she had never actually dated a man. She'd been out with numerous men, all over the world, but that all came under the heading of work, since most of them were involved in the fashion world in one way or another. Clay was different and she was suddenly looking forward to it.

Just before she fell asleep she wondered how tall he was and if she should wear high heels and risk towering over him.

15

In the most uncharacteristic fashion, Cat overslept and woke up to the voice of the radio announcer relating the news. She sat up startled as the words coming from the radio reached her slowly. It was Saturday, October 6—Yom Kippur—and the Middle East was in the throes of a war again. She caught the words, which were obviously the repeat of the first bulletin, and realized it was 8:05. She had never been to Israel, had no interest in going there, but whenever the country was mentioned, she thought of her father. He would not move out of Crown Heights, except if he could move to Israel. That was the main point of disagreement between her parents. Although Clara hated Brooklyn, she refused to consider moving to Israel.

Turning on the television, Cat went through her morning routine while waiting for David, and kept glancing at the small screen. Pictures of war planes and comments by various commentators filled the room. War in living color was invading her home and she was mesmerized. Israel had been attacked by bordering Arab nations and was being badly beaten. Thoughts of her father returned. She remembered his total involvement when the Israeli state came into being. His joy and sadness for the country. Unaccountably she suddenly identified with him and a feeling of panic took hold of her. She wanted to turn off the TV, but felt paralyzed. Israel, Egypt, Syria, Jordan were countries far away. They had no bearing on her, yet she felt lost and frightened. She picked up the phone and called David.

"Have you heard the news?" she asked haltingly.

"Yeah, it's quite something, isn't it?"

"Is Israel going to lose the war?"

"God only knows. I must say it was pretty clever of the Arabs to attack them when they did."

The comment angered Cat and that confused her even further. "It seems unfair," she said quietly, hiding her feelings.

"Oh, I don't know. The Israelis have made surprise attacks in the past so why not try to do the same to them?" David sounded objective and completely logical.

"I guess so." Cat was sorry she had called him. "Are you coming over?"

"Be there around noon," he answered, and hung up.

The conversation left Cat more bewildered than ever. She picked up the phone again and called a couple of her model friends. None had heard the news and when she mentioned it in passing, they were almost indifferent, although one felt it was wrong to attack a tiny country on its holiest of days.

Cat continued to look at the television set and as the news grew more tense and muddled, so did her feelings. She wished it were a working day surrounded by people she knew. She would have felt more comfortable listening to the comments of some of the dress manufacturers and buyers who were Jewish. She felt terribly lonely and tried to think of someone who could help sort out her feelings. She could think of no one. She glanced briefly at the clock. It was 11 A.M.

David's arrival relieved the unhappiness temporarily. They measured the living room windows for vertical blinds, made a list of kitchen equipment she wanted to buy at Bloomingdale's and went out to lunch at Maxwell's Plum, their usual Saturday routine. Cat hid the turmoil which was rising in her, but was conscious that the city was unusually quiet, the shops quite empty and, although she had never fasted on the Jewish Day of Atonement, she was unbearably self-conscious while eating her hamburger. It was while they were at the movies that she could take it no longer. Her childhood with her parents in Brooklyn, her father's strict adherence to tradition, the numerous religious rules she had grown up with, were suddenly alive. She could not understand why her lack of religious observance was now causing her feelings of guilt. Suddenly she knew she could not sit through the movie, and on the pretext of not feeling well, pleaded with David to forgive her for wanting to leave. They left the theater midway through the film.

Sitting opposite David in a small coffee house on Third Avenue, Cat could not bring herself to drink her tea.

"You're as tense as a bitch in heat," David said, eyeing her critically.

"I think I'll call my mother."

"I didn't know your mother was alive," David said in a strange voice.

Cat blushed. She never discussed her family with anyone and her statement did seem ridiculous. "Oh yes, she lives in Brooklyn. We don't really get on too well, but she's been away and I haven't seen her since she came back, which is really awful." Her voice trailed off in embarrassment.

"Do you have any other relatives?" David asked quietly. "Is your father alive?"

"He died when I was sixteen."

"And your mother never remarried?"

"No. She's still devoted to his memory. Theirs was a true love."

"What does your mother do?" David asked.

"My mother?" The question was almost funny although why it struck her as such she could not tell. "Well, she travels quite a bit and spends six months of the year in Vienna with a cousin. She's always wanted to go back there to live." The last phrase seemed superfluous. "But now she's back," she concluded.

Thinking about her mother's life was something Cat avoided at all times. It gave her feelings of helplessness.

She got up nervously. "I think I'll call her," she said quickly. "It won't take but a minute." She ran to the back of the shop, shut the door of the booth and dialed her mother's number.

The phone rang several times and Cat remembered that her mother would never answer the phone on Yom Kippur. She slammed the phone down and walked slowly toward David. Somehow the unanswered call made the need to get away from the city more urgent. She did not want to talk to David about furniture, careers or office gossip. She wanted to be close to something which she could not pinpoint and which she was frightened to delve into too deeply.

"David, my mother isn't feeling well and I think I'd better go out to see her. Would you mind?"

He looked crestfallen. "Would you like me to go with you?" he asked.

"Oh, I wouldn't do that to my worst enemy." The idea of introducing David to her mother was ridiculous. "No, I'll just grab a cab and we'll get together tomorrow."

Seated in the cab, she gave the driver a destination which was two blocks away from her mother's house. There was no way she could drive up to Clara's house on the holiday. Then, settling back, she realized she was dressed in dungarees, a sloppy heavy sweater, loafers and an old trench coat. She had barely any makeup on and her hair was braided unceremoniously down her back. Hardly appropriate attire for a Jewish neighborhood on Yom Kippur. She was tempted to ask the driver to change his course and take her home to dress but stopped herself. They hadn't even crossed the bridge to Brooklyn and she was already being sucked into a mold she had broken years ago. She sat back, lit a cigarette almost defiantly and said nothing.

As soon as the taxi left the Brooklyn Bridge and was nearing

Crown Heights, the silence of the holiday took over. Fewer people were seen walking about, all the shops were closed and the atmosphere was somber. Cat's temptation to ask the driver to turn back and head for Manhattan was overwhelming. She had left all this behind when she was married and moved away from Brooklyn.

After paying the driver, Cat walked quickly toward the neighborhood where she was born and grew up. Her discomfort about her dress was dispelled almost immediately since the streets were empty. It was early evening but not yet sundown and Cat realized that people were either in the synagogue or at home. She passed the familiar landmarks of childhood—the schoolyard, the candy store, the delicatessen which had become even more dilapidated with time. The latter was nestled between the hardware store and the green grocer. The shoemaker and the five-and-dime were next. She stopped to look through the window of a small dress shop which used to be run by a friend of her mother's. It was empty and a small sign on the door indicated it was for rent. Cat made a mental note to ask Clara what had happened to the woman who ran it. Was she dead? The thought jarred her. Were any of the people who owned the stores she had just passed still around, or had others taken their place? She had been away for eighteen years and they had all been old, even then. Or had they? Suddenly Cat found herself running. As she turned the corner into the tree-lined street, she stopped and an overwhelming sense of doom shot through her. Memories were forcing their way into her consciousness and she refused to allow them to surface.

She stopped in front of the simple two-story semi-detached house, her heart pounding, and was relieved to see it was almost in total darkness except for a dim light coming from the living room. That night, years ago, it was all lit up and her mother's crying could be heard through the silent street.

Slowly she turned to look at the building across the street. Jeff had lived there and the memory of him sitting in his room reading calmed her. He had always been there when she needed him.

Turning back, she looked at the house where she was born. Since her father's death, her mother had rented out the second floor and Cat wondered who the tenants were.

Entering the small vestibule, she tried to push the door open only to discover it was locked. That was strange. In the past it was always open. She rang the bell and waited.

"Who is it?" Clara sounded frightened.

"It's me. Catherine."

Then she heard three locks being unlatched and her mother opened the door.

Cat was taken aback. It had been a little over six months since she had seen Clara, but the woman had aged greatly. Her hair was completely white and her blue eyes seemed shaded over. Always a petite woman, she seemed even smaller now. Her skin, however, was smooth and the inborn elegance of the past was still very much in evidence.

Cat leaned over and kissed her mother on the cheek, trying to hide her shock.

"Come in, Catherine, come in," Clara said, moving away and letting Cat walk by her into the small living room, "and let me look at you."

"Let me look at you" was her mother's standard comment whenever they met. Cat gritted her teeth. She had anticipated the request.

"You're so thin," Clara continued, looking at her more closely. "And so pale." Clucking her tongue in disapproval, she walked toward her oversized wing chair and sank into it. "Are you sure you're eating enough?"

"Mother, I'm fine. Really fine." Cat hid her annoyance and observed her mother surreptitiously. Her face looked younger in the subdued lamp light, giving the skin a richer color. Her blue eyes were clear and observant and the hair, pulled back into a loose bun, suited her. The robe, a light shade of blue velvet, complemented the deeper blue of the chair, as everything in the room was done to set off her mother's appearance to its best advantage. Cat's eyes came to rest on her mother's hands, which were neatly folded in her lap. They were gnarled with arthritis and wrinkled with age and the large diamond ring glimmered conspicuously. Furtively, Cat looked around the room. It still contained most of the antiques her father had bought years back, as well as the precious bric-a-brac which he had given Clara during their years of marriage. Even the huge, ancient sewing box, which always stood at the foot of her mother's chair, was in place. Cat sighed with relief. Joe did not leave a great deal of money, and Clara had started selling off the precious furniture and other items to support herself. When Cat realized what was happening, she began giving her mother an allowance to prevent any further sales. Somehow it seemed sacrilegious to give up the things which meant so much to her father.

"How are you, Mother?" she asked finally.

"I'm all right. A little tired today since I've been fasting, but it's nearly time to break the fast and then I'll have some tea." She took a small lace handkerchief from her pocket and wiped her brow on which tiny beads of perspiration had begun to form.

"I'm sorry I haven't been in touch more but it's the Spring and Summer collection showings and I've been awfully busy."

"Don't apologize," Clara interrupted the guilty barrage. "Are you all right?"

"Of course I am," Cat said indignantly. "Why shouldn't I be?"

"Well, after an operation . . ."

"How did you know about it?" She had purposely not told her mother about it.

"Dr. Goodwin saw your name on the nurses' chart at New York Hospital when you were there."

"Who is he?" Cat tried not to sound too angry.

"He's Norma Goodwin's son. They lived up the street from us when you were little. He was much older than you so you probably don't remember him."

"Mother, did you hear about the war in Israel?" Cat changed the subject.

"Yes, I did," Clara sighed deeply.

"What'll happen?" She sounded like a small child but could not help it.

"I don't know. Everyone is in *shul* today and the people who could explain it to me are not going to answer the phone if they were home. Dr. Goodwin told me about it this morning when he came by."

"Why did he come over? Are you sick?"

"No, he just dropped in."

"Are you sure?" Cat persisted.

"I'd rather not talk about it," Clara said with finality.

The silence which followed was awkward and the room was suddenly stifling. Cat wanted to get away, even though she had just arrived. Impulsively she started toward the far end of the room, which overlooked the little garden in the back, eager to breathe the cool air. As she drew aside the curtains and pushed up the window, a gentle breeze swept past her. She could hear the rustling of the dried leaves and the sight of the desolation of the small patch of earth, which had been her father's pride, deepened her misery. It was growing dark rapidly and the sky took on a shade of menacing gray smoke. For one timeless minute she wanted to be a child again. She closed her eyes and allowed herself to pretend she was a little girl, her father's little Chatsie. The daughter he adored, who was always at his side, who infused him with a desire to live and enjoy the beauty of life. She could feel his love even now, and the feeling was delicious. She tried to cling to the memory of that time, that bittersweet moment when excitement came easily, when the magic of discovery created new and exciting worlds, when there was still unwavering faith in the hope of all good things.

"How is Alexandra?" Clara's voice reached her and Cat walked back into the living room and sat on the sofa facing her mother.

"She's in boarding school. It's up in Connecticut and it's a very good school." Cat decided not to mention the separation from Jeff or Alexandra's new living arrangement.

"Didn't she come home for the holidays?" Clara asked in amazement.

"Mother, school just started and it would be ridiculous for them to start celebrating every holiday."

"It's been a long time since I've seen her," the older woman said sadly.

"That's not true. We saw you off when you went to Europe," Cat said defensively.

"But you never bring her here, anymore."

"It's a long trip and she has such a full schedule."

"We used to have such a good time together," Clara said wistfully.

"May I turn on the radio and hear what's going on?" Cat wanted to get off the subject of Alexandra.

"In a few minutes." Clara leaned back in her seat looking quite pale.

"Of course," Cat said in resignation. Since her father's death some of the rigid Orthodox rules had been relaxed but there were certain traditions which her mother still insisted on and one of them was the sanctity of this day, the holiest of Jewish holidays.

They sat in silence, and Cat again wondered when she could leave. It had been foolish to come and expect her mother to relieve her of the unknown fears which had taken hold of her earlier in the day.

The ringing of the doorbell made them both sit up. Clara's face took on a look of terror and Cat remembered the locks on the door.

"Who do you suppose that is?" Clara whispered.

"Mother, what are you scared of?"

"There have been several robberies around here recently. The neighborhood is not what it used to be."

Cat walked toward the small front hall.

"Ask who it is before opening it," Clara called out in panic.

"It's Mark Goodwin," the voice answered when Cat inquired.

Opening the door, Cat found herself staring at a distinguished bearded man. He was dressed in a long black coat and had on a black hat, which he removed when he saw her. She did not know what she had expected but the man staring pleasantly at her had a gleam of humor in his eyes which was captivating. She liked him immediately.

"You must be Catherine." He smiled warmly at her.

"Why, yes," she said haltingly, trying to remember him from the past.

"You don't remember me, but I remember you." He walked into the hallway. "And I must say you've grown into a beautiful young woman." He looked at her more closely. "I prefer you in person to the pictures your mother showed me."

Cat was surprised. She never knew her mother kept any of her pictures, much less showed them to anyone.

"How are you, Mrs. Wallenstein?" Mark walked quickly over to Clara. "You're as pale as a ghost."

"I forgot you were coming by." Clara tried to smile.

He took her thin wrist in his hand. "Did you fast in spite of what I told you?" he asked, and Cat could see he was upset.

"Dr. Goodwin, I'm all right." Clara removed her hand from his. "Catherine, would you put some water on to boil and make your mother a cup of tea?"

While Cat was waiting for the water to boil, Mark walked into the kitchen. "I've made her lie down." He sounded preoccupied.

"What's wrong with her?"

"She's a very sick lady, Catherine. Always was. As a matter of fact, I forbade her to get out of bed today, but with you here I could hardly expect her to follow my instructions. I'm afraid the strain on her is great."

"Is she that sick?"

"I'm afraid so. These trips she keeps taking to Vienna are exhausting her. I've been wanting to call you but she wouldn't hear of it. This last one was really too much."

Cat took the tea and toast to her mother, who thanked her wanly, then she walked back into the living room.

"I'm glad you're here," Mark said when Cat settled herself into the couch. "I would have called you in a few days in spite of her protests." He paused, weighing his next phrase. "She can't go on living alone."

"What about those relatives of hers in Austria?" Cat felt as though a trapdoor was closing in on her. "Wouldn't it make sense for her to live with them?"

"There are two cousins and they're sicker than she is, so I think that's no help at this point," the doctor said quietly.

"Oh, shit," Cat said through clenched teeth.

"That's one reaction. But I'm afraid you'll have to do better than that."

"What are my choices?"

"Well, Emma comes in several times a week so that worked out until now, but it's not a satisfactory arrangement. The fact is you either find her a home or . . ."

"A home?" Cat gasped. "An old-age home?"

"Do *you* have room for her?"

Cat turned her head away. Her lovely new home was about to be invaded and she was not going to permit it. "Can't Emma come and

live here?" she asked. The old housekeeper had been with them
when she was a child and for many years came in to help out even
after her father died.

"It would cost a fortune for starters," Mark answered soberly,
"and even if you could afford it, I doubt your mother would agree.
Although I must say that woman is a gem. She drops in every few
hours anyway."

"I'll have to try to figure something out," Cat said slowly. Alexandra's room was empty and it was the obvious solution. She wanted to
cry in frustration. "We'll have to start with the Emma idea," she said
after a minute. "If that doesn't work out, I guess I could make some
other arrangement."

"Thank you." He smiled for the first time since they started
talking. "I was sure you'd help."

"You mean you discussed it with my mother and she did not
think I would?" Cat asked sarcastically.

"She forbade me to tell you about anything at all. She has this
unbearable need to protect you."

"Not me," Cat said emphatically.

"You'd be surprised." Then getting up he asked if he could turn
on the television. "The war has upset me so," he said as the picture
cleared and the evening news came on with the horrors of what was
going on in the Middle East.

"What does it all mean?" Cat asked.

"It looks really bad," Mark said thoughtfully. "I wish I could go
and help." He slammed his fist into his hand. "Those bastards. They
just won't give us a chance."

"Us?" Cat said, bewildered. "Who's us?"

"Us Jews."

"But we're Americans," Cat stated indignantly.

"I pray that we never have to make that choice," he answered
quietly.

Cat had heard that phrase throughout the years at her father's
table but as with most of the sayings picked up in childhood, she
never delved too deeply into their meaning.

"I think I'll sleep here tonight." She changed the subject. What
Mark was saying upset her and she did not want to continue the
conversation. "And maybe I'll get a limousine tomorrow and drive
her into the city for a little while."

"That would be nice." He seemed to come back to himself.
"She's been cooped up in this house too long. A change of scenery
would do her good." He walked over to Cat. "Take it easy, Catherine.
You've been out of this neighborhood for a long time, but if you give

it a chance, think back to when you were a little girl, you'll realize it wasn't all bad."

Cat stared at him. She had just met him, yet he seemed to perceive so much about her. He felt like family.

16

With Mark gone and her mother fast asleep, Cat called Bernie and asked him to pick them up from Brooklyn at ten the next morning. Then she dialed David's number. He was not in and she left a message with his recording machine asking him to come by her house at 2 P.M. instead of 12 noon. There was no reason to impose her mother on David. She would bring Clara to New York, spend an hour with her at the apartment, then take her back to Brooklyn. She would be back in the city by two at the latest.

That done, Cat turned off the lights in the apartment and walked into her childhood bedroom. The sight which greeted her stunned her. It appeared as though time had stood still for the past twenty years.

The familiar cot was made up with the same simple white cotton sheet and old-fashioned European downfilled comforter folded at the foot of the bed. The faded chintz-covered armchair was still standing next to a chest of drawers with the small reading lamp atop it. Haltingly, Cat opened the narrow cupboard and the odor of camphor flooded the room. She peered into it and realized it was filled with clothes, both hers and her father's. It made her shudder. Her mother was clinging to a past which would never again be realized. Tenderly she ran her hand over the folded sweaters when she caught sight of a rust-colored skirt and ribbed black sweater. It was the outfit she wore the day she went for her interview with John Robert Powers. Pulling both garments out, she put them up against her face and tears which had been held in check started streaming down her cheeks, as the memory of that day, twenty years ago, came back.

It was dark out, but Cat knew that dawn was about to break. She lay on her bed listening to the clanking of the garbage cans being tossed around by the garbage collectors and heard them curse under their breath as they lifted a particularly heavy load. The grinding of the machinery eating up the refuse was even louder. Finally the truck moved down the street and the silence of early morning returned. She waited. Within seconds she heard her father's footsteps, overhead, but instead of walking into the bathroom, she heard him come downstairs, open the front door and close it gently behind him. Cat sat up bewildered. She could not remember when he went out without first showering and shaving.

Nervously, Cat turned on the overhead light and started out of bed. Her father's unusual behavior was disturbing and threw her plans into confusion. She had worked it all out just before she fell asleep the night before. If her father had followed his usual morning routine, she would have had time to go into her parents' room and take some of her mother's costume jewelry before he came into the kitchen to start breakfast. Now everything was changed. She had no idea when he would be back, and the thought of being discovered stealing was devastating. Still, she had no choice. She needed the jewelry and she would simply have to risk it. Quickly she walked up the stairs and slipped into her parents' room. She did not look at Clara's sleeping form as she treaded her way, through the boxes and shopping bags strewn around, to the dressing table. She opened the jewelry box. While feeling around for some gold hoop earrings and a heavy chain, her eyes caught sight of a picture of her father with his mother standing next to him. Her grandmother's beauty always captivated her. How she wished she could be as beautiful. Then her father would love her, too. Angrily she grabbed a handful of trinkets and started toward the door, but now she stopped to look at Clara. She was lying on her back, the sheet barely covering her nakedness. Her face was deathly pale and she seemed not to be breathing. For a minute it occurred to Cat that her mother was dead. She felt dizzy and there was a choking pain in her throat as if she were stifling a scream. Terrified, her eyes wandered down and took in Clara's body. The imperceptible movement of her rising breasts proved she was alive. She ran from the room feeling sick with guilt mingled with relief.

She barely made it to her room when she heard her father walking up the stoop to the front door.

"Catherine, it's time to get up," Joe called, going into the kitchen.

"I'll be there in a minute," she called back, looking down at the jewelry she had taken. Fortunately, the earrings and necklace were there. Slipping everything into her bag, she grabbed her clothes and went into the bathroom.

"You okay?" Joe asked when Cat walked into the kitchen. It was the largest room in the apartment and looked out onto a small backyard, which in contrast to the front of the building, was beautifully planted and cared for. That was Joe's greatest pleasure—tending to his little patch of land.

"I'm fine, Papa," Cat said, and turned to look at him. He was unshaven, his eyes were bleary, his shirt was wrinkled and his hair was disheveled. His appearance shocked her. She seated herself at the kitchen table, and focused her eyes on the glass of orange juice standing next to her plate. It looked appetizing, except she knew it contained the vitamins Joe insisted on her having every morning. She held her breath as she picked it up and tried to gulp it down, but the vile taste of the vitamins could not be ignored and she gagged.

"Don't you dare throw up," Joe said threateningly as he came over and placed the eggs and toast in front of her.

She grabbed for the toast and crammed it into her mouth, hoping to quell the aftertaste of the juice. It did no good. She put her hand to her mouth and started heaving.

"Don't you dare." Joe's voice became ominous. "You're as thin as a rail and you'll get sick, get tuberculosis or something unless you get some flesh on you."

She knew he was quoting her mother and she felt the hot tears almost spill over. She swallowed hard and picked up her fork and stared at her plate. Then, unable to control herself, she jumped up and ran from the kitchen, holding back the vomit until she reached the bathroom.

"You can throw up all you like," Joe said when she returned, "but damn it, you'll finish your food if it's the last thing you do."

"May I have some tea?" she asked feebly.

As Joe started to prepare it, Cat tried to shovel the food into her mouth. In spite of her abhorrence of the food, it was the loveliest time of day for her and she hated to spoil it. Usually sitting across from her father in the early morning while her mother slept was her earliest memory. The kitchen would be flooded with the pleasant aroma of his aftershave lotion, he would be wearing a crisp shirt, with sleeves rolled up exposing his muscular arms, his fair hair wet from the shower, brushed back, exposing his wonderfully kind face. They would talk and laugh as though they did not have a care in the world. Clara did not exist, the unhappiness which shrouded their daily existence was forgotten. Joe would tell her lovely tales of his boyhood in Vienna and Cat would drift into a fantasy world of green pastures, clean fresh air, blue skies where rain never fell, where misery was unknown, where everyone was beautiful and fair and laughing with happiness.

"You'd better hurry or you'll be late for school," Joe said gruffly. Then placing the tea before her, he started clearing away the dishes. He sounded tense and his accent, which embarrassed her, but which she only heard when strangers were around, was suddenly grating.

"I've got a little time yet," she whispered, not looking up. His unkempt appearance disturbed her.

"That's fine, but don't wake your mother. She didn't sleep well last night," he said, walking toward the door.

Cat lowered her head on the table. Didn't sleep well, she thought bitterly. How could she? She had ranted and raved through the night, oblivious to the hour. Her parents' fights were usually about moving to Israel and were spoken in German. Cat had learned to sleep through them. Last night, however, she was dozing when her father came home. The argument started in German, but at one point Cat realized her mother was speaking English and that Cat was the subject of the tirade.

"I can't take it," Clara cried. "She doesn't eat. She looks sickly and I don't know what will happen to her. She also doesn't seem to stop growing and she's only sixteen."

Joe said something which Cat did not understand, but Clara would not be stopped.

"It's all your fault. You spoil her. She can get anything from you. And when you think of the things I need . . ." Her voice grew soft and within minutes it was very quiet and Cat knew her parents were making love. She could never understand how her father could make love after all the abuse showered on him.

She could not fall asleep again. Staring at the ceiling, she was unable to quell the pain. She knew how her mother felt about her appearance. Still, the words stung. But what hurt most was that her father had not defended her.

"I'm leaving now, Chatsie." Joe was standing in the doorway and Cat looked up in surprise. Chatsie was her grandmother's nickname and her father had not called her that in a long time. She wanted to run over to him, have him hold her close as he used to when she was small, but the look in his eyes stopped her. His expression was filled with pity.

Joe reached into his pocket and took out a five-dollar bill and placed it on the table.

Cat stared at it. She knew he was trying to tell her he understood her hurt and she wished there was some way she could show him that she loved him and that she was grateful.

"Go on, take it, my little Chatsie." He pushed the money toward her. He continued looking at her for a long time. Then he turned away abruptly and in a minute she heard the front door slam shut. She had to check the impulse to run after him. She wanted to tell him that one day she would make him proud of her. That she might not be able to replace her grandmother, the beautiful Chatsie of his youth, but that she would make something of herself and give him cause to love her as he once did.

Picking up the money, she started walking out of the kitchen when she heard Bo calling her. She turned and saw him standing at the window. Small and freckled face, he had his books strapped together, flung over his shoulder. He was freshly shaven, except for the light fuzz which was beginning to grow over his upper lip. He was eighteen and had only recently begun to shave and Cat knew how much it meant to him. In spite of her unhappiness, she smiled.

"You'd better shake a leg or we'll be late," he said.

Cat walked over to the window. "I'm not going to school today."

"Oh, come on, they're cracking down on truants and if your parents find out they'll kill you."

"They couldn't care less," she said defiantly. "I'm going to New York." She paused, tempted to confide in him, but decided against it. "I'm meeting a friend and we're going to the Paramount."

"What friend?" Bo asked suspiciously. He knew better than anyone that she had no friends. Having won the fight with her parents over attending the Wingate Public High School rather than the religious school of the neighborhood, she was never accepted by her classmates. They looked at her as the oddity who came from "that neighborhood," where people dressed strangely and adhered to weird religious customs. Much as she wanted to belong, she dared not invite anyone over. She was too uncomfortable about her father's habits and foreign accent and did not trust her mother to be cordial. Bo was the exception. They had something other than school in common and although her parents disapproved of him, they were friends.

"Come on, Cat. What friend?"

"A girl I met at Friday night services a few weeks ago," she lied.

At that moment she saw Jeff Phillips walk out of the house across the street and she became flustered. Bo looked around.

"I'm damned if I know what you see in him," he said childishly.

"I think he's the handsomest man in the world," Cat whispered.

"He's too tall and too thin and I hate the clothes he wears," Bo said critically. "Also his hair is too long and his glasses too big and I think you should try and be a little less obvious in class when he calls on you. You're making an ass of yourself."

"He looks just like Arthur Miller and that's divine as far as I'm concerned." Cat sighed childishly.

"Well, there's no accounting for taste."

The grandfather clock in the living room struck the half-hour and Cat panicked. "I've got to run," she said hurriedly.

"You'll get caught."

"I don't care," she repeated. "I'll meet you at three so we can go to graduation rehearsal together." She turned away from him.

"Cat, don't go to New York," Bo pleaded.

"I've got to go," she said forcefully.

"Well, it's your funeral."

"I know what I'm doing," Cat said, and walked out of the kitchen.

Once in her room she reached under her bed and pulled out a large manila envelope. Opening it, she took out four blow-ups of her graduation pictures. She scanned them carefully and the sight of her own image, staring at her, gave her untold pleasure. Even the photographer who took them had commented on how well she photographed and although he charged her a great deal of money to enlarge them, she was convinced it was worth it.

She turned and looked at herself in the mirror. Automatically she put her finger to the bridge of her nose and tried to change its shape. It was her worst feature. If only she had the money for an operation! Her mother's statement of the night before came back to her and doubts beset her. Was it possible her mother was right?

"She's wrong!" Cat whispered, hoping the words spoken out loud would dispell her doubts.

She dressed quickly. The rust-colored skirt was just the right length and showed off her shapely legs. The black ribbed sweater tucked in by a large tight belt gave her tall thin frame the limpid look of the models in *Vogue* and *Harper's Bazaar*. Forcing her body to relax, she pushed her hips forward and moved around, causing the full skirt to swirl seductively. Putting on makeup took a while. Her skin was flawless and needed little base, but she outlined her eyes as well as her brows with heavy dark eye liner. Using a lip brush she gave her full lips a distinct shape. It was all exaggerated but she was aiming to be extraordinary. Clasping on the hoop earrings, she stood back. The outfit was perfect, the makeup superb. She felt as though she had been born for this moment in time and her confidence soared. In spite of what her mother had said, in spite of her father's sad eyes when he looked at her, she would make it. Bo saw it and she was sure that everyone in the fashion world would see it, too.

17

Cat was surprised when she entered the reception room of the John Powers modeling agency. It was filled to capacity with what appeared to be hopeful young girls. When she called the office she was told to be there at ten-thirty on Friday, and she had assumed that meant she had a special appointment. The idea that she was to be one of hundreds had never occurred to her. The temptation to leave was great but she felt compelled to stay. It had taken a great deal of courage to come this far. To retreat because of the competition was foolish.

"Your name, please," the receptionist said.

"Cat Willingham," she answered promptly. It was a name she had settled on from the day she started thinking of becoming a model. Catherine Wallenstein seemed inappropriate.

"Please write it down and I'll call you when your turn comes."

She moved to the corner of the room and felt sweaty. It would take forever, she thought, panicking again. She had to meet Bo at three and had to be home by five. It was Friday and her father insisted she be home before sundown.

"Do you have a cigarette?" a girl standing next to her asked, and Cat found herself staring at a stunning, tall blond girl with enormous green eyes and perfect features.

Fumbling in her bag, Cat took out a crushed pack of Chesterfield cigarettes, grateful that she had them to offer.

"This your first interview?" the young woman asked.

"Yes." Cat took a cigarette and lit it, too.

"My name is Nancy Stuart," the young woman smiled. Her teeth were white and even. She was the most beautiful creature Cat had ever seen and the thought of leaving returned.

"I'm Cat Willingham," she said quietly, trying to hide her admiration and trepidation. "Have you done this before?"

"I've tried a couple of other agencies, but haven't heard from them. So I figured since I have the morning off I'd come over for the cattle call."

"Cattle call?" Cat mulled the words over. They sounded distasteful. "Is that what these things are called?"

"Sure is and don't we look it," Nancy laughed good-naturedly.

"Will it take long?"

"You playing hooky or something?" Nancy asked suddenly.

Cat felt her cheeks go red.

"Don't worry. I won't tell a soul, I promise," Nancy said quietly. "When do you have to be out of here?"

"Latest, two."

"You can go ahead of me," Nancy said generously. "I don't have to be at work until quite late this afternoon."

"You work as a model?"

"Yes, showroom," Nancy said, and inhaled deeply. "I hate it more than anything, but it brings in the weekly paycheck and you meet some pretty nice people, if you know what I mean."

Cat had no idea what she meant. But that was the least of it. Her confidence was evaporating quickly. If someone as gorgeous as Nancy wasn't accepted as a photographer's model, what chance did she have?

"Thanks for letting me go ahead." She remembered the kind offer. "What does happen in there?" Cat asked as a girl was called to go through a massive door which opened discreetly and shut almost immediately.

"Well, you go in and if the spirit is with him, Mr. Powers will be there in person and will look at your pictures, give you advice and tell you you'll be hearing from him. He will also give you a small lecture about what's involved in becoming a model and probably try to discourage you." She smiled. "And most of the time he's right."

Cat stared at the door. She watched girls walk in and tried to figure out which ones came out more quickly than others. She also tried to read their facial expressions, wondering how they felt after the interview.

Time moved slowly and Cat began to make mental notes as to which type stayed in longer with Mr. Powers. She could get no clue from her mental machinations. As far as she could tell most of the girls were unusually beautiful, graceful, poised and could be models. Her feelings of discouragement grew. Was she fooling herself in thinking she could compete with all these fantastic-looking creatures? Was her mother right after all?

"Cat Willingham," the receptionist called out, and for a minute Cat forgot it was she who was being paged.

"Having waited for nearly three hours, you'd better get to it," Nancy said.

The room was very large and beautifully decorated, Cat noted when she entered. Huge windows faced her and she could not make out the features of the man sitting behind the large desk. She felt dazed and wilted. She had meant to look in her compact mirror before walking in but forgot.

"Why don't you sit down?" a woman said, and Cat looked around. She had not noticed that anyone else was present.

She walked slowly toward a chair which faced the desk, trying to achieve the walk she had practiced during the weeks before she came to this moment. Instead she felt clumsy and awkward.

"May I see your pictures?" Mr. Powers said.

She handed them over and tried to decipher what was going through his mind. The woman came to stand next to him, peering over his shoulder. She came into focus. She was a large, matronly-looking woman who smiled warmly at Cat.

"How old are you?" Mr. Powers asked.

"Nineteen," Cat said with practiced assurance.

"A very young-looking nineteen," he said tersely. Then clearing his throat he continued. "The pictures are very nice and you have good bone structure but you would need a nose job and I honestly don't think a modeling career is what you should be after." He looked at her for a moment. "You're tall enough, but there is a certain look which high-fashion models have, a sophistication, a mysterious quality which you may develop, but at nineteen," he paused, making it eminently clear that he did not believe her, "you still have not acquired it."

Cat swallowed, trying not to cry out in protest.

"Let me show you what I mean," he said, taking a large photo album off the table and opening it up. "Here, look at this lady." Cat found herself staring at a photograph of a blond woman, dressed in a black tight-fitting dress. Her waist was minuscule, her hands were held over her thin hips, her legs were poised, one slightly in front of the other, giving the skirt a tight-fitting look around the shins. Draped around her shoulders was a black fox scarf framing the perfectly shaped face, which was expressionless. She was looking straight into the camera and the eye contact with the viewer was hypnotizing.

"Who is she?" Cat whispered.

"Pamela Fitzpatrick," John Powers said with pride. "She's one of the top fashion models in the business and the reason is that she's got that something that every woman wants to emulate."

Cat felt sick and wanted to leave as quickly as possible. The defeat was crushing and she was not sure she could hold back the tears.

"Thank you." She stood up shakily and turning around quickly she rushed out of the room. She wanted to be back in Brooklyn where she belonged. She was grateful that she had not mentioned the interview to Bo. It was all too humiliating. Having someone know about it would have made it worse.

"How did it go?" Nancy Stuart stopped her.

"It was a mistake for me to come, that's for sure," she whispered wanly.

"Don't take it so hard. He's not God, you know."

Waiting for the elevator, Cat felt her life was over. Her mother was right. Her father's pitying looks were justified. The dream of making him proud of her had come to a shabby end.

"You forgot your photographs." The woman who had been in the room with Mr. Powers was standing next to her.

"Thank you." Cat no longer wanted them, but she took them politely.

"You need new pictures," the woman said quietly. "You've got the makings of a model. Top, top, top." She smiled knowingly. "But not with those." She fished in her jacket pocket, took out a card and handed it to Cat. "There's my number. Call me." Her smile broadened. "But graduate first."

Cat looked down in embarrassment. "Is it that obvious?"

"Oh, honey, so many girls get their graduation pictures blown up. We can spot them a mile away and frankly, those damned photographers should be shot for making all that money for the lousy pictures they take."

The elevator arrived and the woman winked at her. "And for Christ's sake, don't touch that nose," she said as the door closed.

Cat looked down at the card. "Lucille Taub" and an address on West End Avenue with a phone number were neatly printed beneath the name. The tears of joy came as the elevator let her off on the main floor. She had the makings of a model. Mr. Powers was not God. She did not know if Lucille Taub was, but she had spoken with authority.

As the subway wound its way back to Brooklyn, passing the bridge and going underground, Cat felt euphoric. She was going to be a model. She knew it more conclusively than ever before. She needed pictures and they cost money. Somehow she would get it. "But graduate first," Lucille had said. Well, it was not that far off. Then she would get a job, any job, save her money and get the pictures. She would ask Bo who should take them. Now she could confide in him and he would help her. Convincing her father that she would not be going to college would be a problem, but she would do that, too.

Thoughts of her father and the way he looked at her that morning returned. She would erase it, wipe it away. She would rekindle a relationship which had existed between them in the past. She would be Chatsie again. It would be just as it was when she was a child. He had loved her and cuddled her then, praised and encouraged her.

She was his pride and joy and they were always together. He loved and missed his mother and wanted his daughter to be like her. She had never met her grandmother but from what she knew of her she had been a highly cultured, brilliant art dealer and filled her son with the values which she felt were important. Her father adulated beauty and he, in turn, tried to instill in her a love of beauty. Going to museums with him was like reliving the enchanted life of every painter and every painting. Visiting antique shops re-created the past to the point where she could touch it. Examining the furnishings of old houses made the oldest and shabbiest place seem like a palace. He infused her with love for beauty, charm and grace.

Then one day it changed. The war had ended in Europe and he had gone to Vienna. She was about seven or eight. When he came back, she was no longer his little girl. He'd been gone for only three or four months, but somehow she must have changed, since he looked at her differently. It was a look filled with dreadful sadness which eventually turned to pity.

It would all be different now, Cat thought with growing excitement. Although it was still a while away, she would again be the daughter he obviously longed for, the daughter he loved when she was small.

The rehearsal lasted until five and Cat was frantic to get home.

"Can you pose for me for just half an hour?" Bo asked, trying to keep up with her. "I have this idea that I want to enter into a contest and I need a model."

"Sorry, but you know how furious my parents get when I'm late coming home on Fridays. It's all shit and I hate it, but I'd rather not have a scene tonight." She sighed contentedly. "I'll meet you tomorrow if you like. I'm sure I can get away when my father goes off to synagogue."

"Ten-thirty?"

"I'll be at your place," she replied, but her voice was drowned out by the sound of a siren.

They were just rounding the corner into her street when an ambulance shot past them.

"What did you say?" Bo asked.

Cat could not speak. She looked at Bo for a minute and suddenly she started running. She knew before she reached her house, with a certainty which astounded her, that the ambulance had just left there. She also knew her father was dead, and knew that nothing would ever be the same in her life again.

18

It was just past twelve noon when David unlocked the door to Cat's apartment. She had left a message on his recording machine to say she would be late, but he decided to ignore it. He loved Cat's apartment and looked forward to the time alone there.

He was about to enter when he heard voices and froze. He caught sight of Cat standing with her back to him talking to someone whose voice he could not identify. His first reaction was to close the door and ring the doorbell, but Cat turned at that moment and although she still did not catch sight of him, her appearance upset him to the point of immobility. She looked haggard, unsure of herself, almost humble. Nowhere could he detect the poise and striking presence which she normally exuded. Caught off guard, she appeared frightened and vulnerable. Briefly, he wondered if she were talking to Pamela. Pamela was the only person who could reduce Cat to such a state. But he knew that was impossible. He had dropped Pamela off at four in the morning and she was now on her way to the country.

He was trying to figure out what he should do when a small, impeccably groomed woman, wearing a long black coat, came into view. David knew immediately the woman was Cat's mother. Different as they were, there was still a noticeable resemblance.

"It's a lovely room, Catherine," the woman was saying. "It just doesn't look lived in."

"I know it's different from what you have, but I like it." There was a tremor of anger in Cat's voice. "Frankly, I think it's a reaction to what I grew up with."

"Didn't you like our home?" the older woman asked, sounding hurt.

"That's not what I meant," Cat answered, looking down at the frail, winsome woman.

David was fascinated. He watched Cat's anger subside only to be replaced by what appeared to be a look of guilt. Suddenly he felt like a Peeping Tom. He was also aware that he was witnessing a private family feud, laden with emotion, and wondered how he could get away. He started to close the door but it squeaked in the process and the sound seemed to thunder through the apartment. Both women looked around and he was trapped.

"I'm sorry I frightened you." He said walking quickly toward Cat.

"Oh, David, you gave me a start." She looked even more strained than before and there were dark shadows under her eyes. "Didn't you get my message?"

"Message?" he asked innocently.

"I called—" she began. Then abandoning the thought, she smiled wanly, and turning to her mother she continued, "My mother, Mrs. Wallenstein, David Thomas."

David took the woman's extended hand and his confusion mounted. She was smaller than she appeared from the distance and looked almost fragile, yet her hand gripped his like a vise.

"My pleasure, ma'am." He found it difficult to talk.

"How do you do?" The accent, which eluded him until now, was quite heavy and it surprised him. It was, however, the look in her eyes which threw him off balance. Although smiling, they were cold, appraising, aloof and condescending. All his pretended self-assurance, the façade cultivated through the years, disappeared and within seconds he was again the little boy in the orphanage being inspected by prospective parents. He wanted to run from her. Like a fleeting, yet clear-cut, memory, he knew that she too would never adopt him, as no one had during all the years he was growing up.

"I would like to go home now, Catherine," Clara said, turning to Cat.

It gave David a moment to regain his composure.

"Let me change into some fresh clothes," Cat said in a subdued voice. Before leaving the room she threw David an imploring look and he wondered what it was she wanted.

Left alone with Clara, David tried to think of something to say.

"Do you work with Catherine?" Clara broke the silence.

"Yes and no." David tried to speak naturally. "We both work out of the same agency."

"Agency?"

"It's a modeling agency. Pamela Fitzpatrick's agency."

"What does this agency do?" she asked. "I'm afraid I'm not familiar with the procedures of my daughter's work."

"The agency helps us get various modeling jobs."

"Oh, it's like an employment agency."

David grew more uncomfortable and could not think of an answer when, to his relief, Cat returned.

"Are we ready?" Clara asked, obviously not interested in hearing what David had to say.

"Yes, of course," Cat said quickly.

Standing in front of Cat's house, David watched Cat and Bernie help Mrs. Wallenstein into the limousine. He turned away and lit a cigarette. Nothing ever worked out as he planned, he thought forlornly. There was so much he had to say to Cat, plans to discuss, ideas to explore.

"David?" He heard Cat's voice beside him. "I'm sorry for my mother's behavior. She has a way of being brusque, but she doesn't really mean to be unkind." She tried to smile, shrugging her shoulders with an air of futility. "Why don't you go back up and wait for me," she continued hurriedly. "I'll just take her home and come back to the city in a couple of hours."

"Okay, Cat." He was genuinely grateful that she had come back. "As a matter of fact, why don't you make a reservation at some smashing restaurant for this evening and we'll go out to dinner."

She sounded as though she were bribing him and he smiled. "Don't be silly. Just get back as soon as you can and we'll plan the evening then."

"Miss Willingham." The driver came over. "Your mother said she isn't feeling well."

"I'm coming, Bernie," Cat said impatiently. "You will be here when I come back, won't you?" She looked imploringly at David.

"Of course," he answered, and watched her hurry off.

As soon as the car was out of sight, David reentered the building and rode up to Cat's apartment. Unlocking the front door, he walked directly into the kitchen and put water on to boil.

He had helped Cat furnish the place, was responsible for many of the items in it and in a way he felt a sense of ownership. Knowing he would be alone for the next couple of hours gave him a sense of untold pleasure.

Pouring himself a cup of coffee, he was about to leave the kitchen when the phone rang. He picked it up without thinking. A man asked for Cat but his voice was interrupted by Cat's message recorder. Unable to hang up, David listened to the recording end and heard the signal of the beep.

"It's Clay Whitfield, Catherine. I came back earlier than expected and frankly, you're the reason. If you come in early enough please call me at seven-five-eight-four-three-four-eight. I want to speak to you and see you long before next Friday." The phone went dead and David hung up.

Carrying his cup to the terrace, he wondered about the call. The idea that Cat was involved with some man had never entered his mind. She was one of the few models who did not play around. She

was married, had a child and was noted for her fidelity. At first David
assumed she was simply more discreet than other models, but since
getting to know her, the legend was confirmed. She was simply
uninterested in extramarital entanglements. Her work, her home
and her child preoccupied her at all times. When she spoke about her
husband, it was with deep affection and respect. The call from a Clay
Whitfield and the affectionate message was a surprise. To have to
contend with someone other than an absentee husband was something David did not count on. Clay Whitfield. The name sounded
familiar and he made a mental note to check it out.

Although it was October, the weather was unusually mild and
David settled himself on a chaise at the far end of the terrace. The
exhaustion from his night on the town with Pamela surfaced and
thoughts of the evening with her came to mind. Normally, he would
not have been home on a Saturday night, but since Cat had left him
to see her mother, Pamela reached him and insisted he join her. The
pattern rarely changed. It started pleasantly enough. He drove her to
a cocktail party at someone's house and although he knew no one
there and, as usual, was not introduced, he enjoyed the surroundings.
The artwork was excellent, the ambiance pleasant, the canapés expensive. Dinner at Elaine's was fair, but watching the celebrities was
always exciting. Pamela's light, friendly manner, combined with the
proper aloofness, fascinated him. He envied her charm and precise
correctness of behavior, which she succeeded in exhibiting on command. It was the strange party, in a filthy loft in the East Village with
strange people involved in the drug scene, that she took him to after
dinner which angered him, even now. He had escorted her to numerous parties of that sort in recent months and he had accepted
being a voyeur while she indulged herself. What bothered him,
though, was her drinking, which was reaching unmanageable proportions. Almost in self-defense, he had consumed more liquor than
he normally did and now the slight hangover plus the lack of sleep
were catching up with him.

A cool breeze rose and swept across the terrace. David sank
further into the seat, erasing Pamela from his thoughts. It was pleasant being high up above the city, safe from a world he was not able to
adjust to or be accepted by. Except for Cat. She accepted him and
more important she liked him. She treated him like an equal,
respected and appreciated him. They complemented each other and
could do things for each other. It was reaffirmed during their conversation at the Plaza. Since then he had given a great deal of thought to
how they could open up their own agency. Theirs would be a small,
exclusive agency and since Alexandra was away they could use her
room as an office. It would throw him into closer contact with Cat,
which made him uncomfortable. Women, as such, did not interest

him. His sexual experiences to date had been limited to young girls he picked up at parties or bars. They rarely excited him. Neither did Cat, but that was one of the nicest things about their relationship. She made no physical demands on him.

Thoughts of sex and relationships with women always upset him. His hand shook as he lit a cigarette and looked up at the sky. The clouds, like amorphous puffs, were moving slowly by and seemed to be trying to form into some definitive images. Watching them, David felt soothed and an almost forgotten memory of long ago sifted into his conscious mind.

He was eight years old and it was his birthday. It was hot and all the kids from the orphanage were allowed to go swimming. He and his brother Frankie swam across the lake, leaving the others on the opposite shore. He was alone with his brother, who was seven years older, and he felt supremely happy. Frankie was a leader at the home. Everybody looked up to him. Frankie was all David had and he loved him very much.

They reached the shore and David lay on the bank looking up at the sky, trying to define an animal formation from the changing patterns of the clouds.

"I see an elephant, Frankie," he called out in triumph and looked over at his brother. Frankie did not seem to hear him. He was sitting on a log and was absorbed in fondling himself. David had seen other boys doing the same thing and they were usually punished for it. He watched his brother intently. Frankie looked angry.

"Don't do that," David yelled in frustration.

Frankie lifted his eyes and they were glazed over. David felt frightened.

"I hate you," David screamed angrily. "I hate you and I wish you were dead."

When Frankie still did not react, David ran toward the lake and jumped into the water. Within seconds his lungs began to ache as the water filled his mouth and nose. He heard Frankie's voice calling his name. He could not react. Then he felt Frankie's hand around his neck and he lost consciousness.

A siren woke him from a deep slumber. He put his hands over his ears trying to shut out the harsh noise. His chest was hurting and he could barely breathe. Then he smelled smoke. He saw blinding lights flashing outside his window. Rough hands jerked him out of bed, loud angry voices were yelling in the darkness. He was herded down a black iron fire escape which led to the grounds below. Someone was there waiting for him to take him away. He looked back and saw billows of thick dark gray smoke coming out of the windows. He knew instinctively that Frankie was still somewhere inside the burning building. He called out but his voice was lost in the noise. He hovered with the other kids, shaking and crying. The fire engines arrived. He knew Frankie was burning to death. What happened at the lake came back vividly. He had yelled out that he wished Frankie dead. That was the last thing he said to his brother. It was a painful thought and he tried to dismiss it. Frankie was all he had. Frankie was his brother.

The sirens continued late into the night. Then an ominous silence followed. The fire was put out and everyone started walking toward the charred building.

"Your brother Frankie is dead." David heard the words but his mind rejected the idea. Frankie could not be dead.

The wail of a siren in the distance made David open his eyes and look around. It took him a minute to realize that he was not at the orphanage. He was on Cat's terrace. He was safe.

Picking up his coffee, David sipped it slowly, trying to understand why the memory of his brother had suddenly come back to him. It made no sense.

He shut his eyes and within seconds fell asleep, unable to cope with the scene which had happened so many years back.

19

Cat was disappointed to find the apartment in darkness when she arrived back from Brooklyn. The trip had taken longer than expected and she assumed David had gotten bored and left. Then she noticed the living room door was open.

The sun had gone down and dusk had settled. It took Cat a minute before she caught sight of David lying on the chaise at the far end of the terrace. She approached him quietly and stared down at the sleeping boy. His face, in repose, appeared extremely young, sad, and frightened. While awake and animated it was not as visible, but now it was deeply etched. Slowly her eyes wandered down his body and she felt uncontrollably attracted to him.

"David," she whispered, reaching out to touch him. "David, it's me, Cat."

He opened his eyes and for a moment it seemed as though he did not recognize her. Then as full consciousness returned, he smiled apologetically. "I must have dozed off."

"I'm sorry it took so long for me to get back," she said quickly, trying to shake her reaction to him of minutes before.

"Nonsense." David stood up briskly. "I was exhausted and it's so pleasant here that I didn't mind one bit."

"It is lovely up here, isn't it?" Cat said, feeling more in control as she placed a large manila envelope on the wrought-iron table next to the chaise and threw herself into a chair.

"What have you got there?" David asked, pointing to the envelope.

"Mel delivered the pictures of his latest protégée," she answered.

"What's she like?"

"I can't quite tell," Cat said, and her voice became strained. Since meeting Megan her ambivalence about her was greater than ever. "She's got to be the most beautiful girl I've ever seen, but I don't think she's someone Pamela would want to sign up."

"Is she photogenic?"

"Unbelievably."

"So why wouldn't Pamela want her?"

"I don't know," she said thoughtfully. "And you know what? I don't know if I would take her on if I were running an agency."

"May I see the pictures?" David reached over and picked up the envelope.

He opened it slowly and took the photographs out. The face staring up at him caused a sensation in him which he could not understand. Whatever the feeling, it was excruciatingly painful. He was aware that Cat was watching him and he tried to compose himself but an insidious fear seized him. It seemed to grow until it dominated and almost conquered him. A blurred memory, which he could not bring into focus, was hovering at the edge of his consciousness. He wanted to look at Cat, as if her presence would help him, but dared not. Instead, a feeling of futility gripped him and he felt as though he were drowning in a whirlpool of emotions from which no one could save him.

Cat watched him closely. The expression on David's face was similar to the one she had seen just before she woke him.

"I think I'll go make some fresh coffee," she said, wanting to get away.

David came back to himself. "Nonsense," he said, and threw the pictures carelessly on the chaise. "You've had a hectic day and I've just been sitting around." He started to walk away, then stopped. "Hey, why don't we have a drink for a change? It'll do us both good."

"Why not!" She smiled for the first time.

Things had not been going right from the minute she'd decided to visit her mother, Cat thought when David left the terrace. Clara emphasized the unsettled state of her life recently. Just a few hours with Clara and she was back to being the bad girl who displeased her mother. She felt ugly, unwanted and unloved, just as she used to feel when she was growing up. All the adulation, all the acceptance showered on her by thousands of people through the years, were wiped away as though they never were. Even her reaction to David seemed misplaced.

"With it all, you look gorgeous," David said, coming back and placing a tray on the table.

"That's sweet of you to say," Cat said gratefully. "My mother isn't pleased, that's for sure." She sighed deeply. "I never seem to please her."

"How is she feeling?" David asked with pretended concern.

"Not too well. As a matter of fact, I think I'll have no choice but to have her come and live here for a while. She can't be alone and her doctor feels it's the right thing to do."

David's heart sank. Cat's mother living in the apartment would spoil all his plans.

"You'd have to give her Alexandra's room," he said cautiously.

"Obviously." Cat tried to cover her discomfort. Although Clara had not mentioned David's name after they left the apartment, it was clear to Cat that she did not like him. "But let's forget it for now," she said, trying to cheer up. "Why not talk about happy things?" She took a cigarette and allowed David to light it. Then pulling her knees up under her chin she looked at him with affection, as he handed her a drink.

They toasted each other silently. The strained mood disappeared and a feeling of intimacy replaced it.

"David," Cat said finally, "is a modeling career what you want from life?"

"Of course not," he cried out in exasperation. "What I'm doing now is just a way to make some money. Let's face it, I've got to eat. But I do have plans."

"What are they?" Cat asked encouragingly.

David got up and started pacing. Pamela had asked him that question when they first met and he had answered her quite honestly. It got him nowhere. Now, he had to be careful. Cat was important to his future. "Eventually I want to write. I want to give people a full picture of what is really happening around. I believe that poverty, despair and hopelessness are not necessarily the ingredients that make up life." As he spoke a sense of urgency and excitement crept into his voice and his eyes grew unusually bright.

Cat gulped her drink down and reached out for a refill, observing him closely. His fervor was exciting. She had been right about him. He had substance. Together they could build a productive future.

"So why are you working as a model?" she asked haltingly. "You should be working for a newspaper or a magazine."

"I wanted to when I first got to New York, but no one was waiting for me." He poured himself another drink and sat down opposite her. "And as I look back, I wasn't really ready." He cleared his throat. "As a matter of fact, I don't know that this is the time either. You see, Cat, I have quite a few talents, but my looks are what brought me to Pamela's attention. I know I'm not a good model, but I've been watching and learning." He emptied his glass. "Let me give you an example." He seemed to be groping for words. "Take Pamela. Who is she?" he asked carefully, but did not wait for an answer as he rushed on. "She runs a modeling agency. But it could be much more. There's a potential there which can be developed into something much more important." He searched Cat's face as if daring her to disagree. "That agency could be turned into an empire, and Pamela is just pissing it away."

"Pamela has been in this business for over thirty years," Cat said slowly. "I don't know what she wants to do with the rest of her life, but she has one of the best modeling agencies in the country and I think she actually loves what she's doing and cares about her stable of girls."

"Stable is right," David said with disgust. "And she treats it as such." He got up and poured Cat and himself another drink. "If you must know, I believe you have more interest in what goes on there than she does."

Cat's eyes narrowed. She understood what David was driving at and in a way he was giving voice to something which had been churning in the back of her mind since she started working again.

"She's exploiting that agency for all it's worth." David seemed oblivious to Cat's reactions. "She's exploiting everything and everybody, including you." He paused as though waiting for his words to sink in. "Have you any idea how much she earns compared to what you make?"

"I do all right," Cat said defensively.

"Why should you be content with just doing all right?" he snapped back. "You're one of her best models, for crying out loud. If I were in your shoes I'd go out on my own like a shot." He stopped and waited.

Cat sipped her drink and said nothing.

"You don't need an agency to get you bookings," he started again. "Every designer, editor and photographer knows you and as soon as you're back on your feet you'll be in demand as never before. So why should you pay her a commission?"

"David, you're being unreasonable. There are services which an agency gives a model which are invaluable."

"If you had your own agency, you could have the same services. What's more, you could choose the jobs you wanted to do whenever you wanted them for as long as you wanted to and at the same time, you could be giving other models the benefit of your experience. And it would be you who would be collecting the commissions." He caught his breath with excitement. "God damn it all, Cat. How many times have you sat in for Pamela when some new model needed to learn about makeup or practice her walk, or figure out what to wear and how to appear?"

She'd been doing it for years but never gave it a thought. "But, David, I can't work and run an agency," she said finally.

"Stop being an ass. I'll help you. As I just told you, I don't want to model. I'm more interested in running this business and I'd love to do it with someone like you, whom I like and respect."

Cat felt unaccountably nervous. "David, I couldn't possibly take models away from Pamela. You don't understand my relationship to her. She seems rough and gruff but I owe her a great deal." There was little conviction in her statement.

"Who's talking about taking anyone away from her?" He stopped and looked around for Megan's pictures. "Take this girl. I bet you could make her one of the biggest models around. Between you and her and a few more models who are frantically looking for decent representation, you'd be in business like a shot." He looked at her for a long moment. "Cat, an agency makes 90 per cent of its money on 10 per cent of its models. With your experience and personality, all you'd need is the 10 per cent."

Cat's laughter rang through the air. "David, if people knew what horse was going to win the race, they wouldn't have so many horses running."

"That's very funny, but if you're smart, real smart, you could choose the winners, certainly for starters, especially if you didn't race them against each other."

Cat stood up and her head was spinning. She rarely drank and the liquor she'd consumed made clear thinking difficult.

"You need money to start an agency," she said, aware the conversation had taken a strange twist. What had started out as a talk about David's future had turned into a conversation about her own.

With measured steps she walked to the far end of the terrace. David's thinking was fallacious, twisted, almost dishonest, but she could not ignore it completely. He was right about Pamela's agency. And although Pamela was good, and Lucille was great, they were involved with so many new faces that they were overlooking hers. The idea of operating an agency had crossed her mind but she always assumed she would do it when her modeling career was over. David was saying that it did not have to be so.

She leaned over the terrace rail and stared down at the street below. It was dark except for the lights of the city, which were twinkling up at her. For the first time in months, she felt as though she could reach out and gather them up. They were again within her grasp. The feeling was delicious. She straightened up and turned around to find David standing next to her. She leaned against him for support, then impulsively she raised her face to his and kissed him on the mouth. His lips were pressed together and she forced them open with her tongue. Finally his jaw slackened and he responded to her passion. She held him close and there was an abandon in her action which surprised and thrilled her. Her excitement grew and she wanted to reach down and touch him.

"Let's go inside," she whispered.

She undressed quickly, holding on to the passion she had not experienced since the first years with Jeff.

The bedroom was in total darkness and Cat held her breath as David came to lie beside her. He, too, was naked. She ran her fingers down his body. It was young and firm and amazingly smooth. She leaned over and kissed his eyes, his cheeks, his mouth. His lips were soft and warm. Suddenly she could control herself no longer and she swung her leg over his body and straddled him with her thighs, forcing him into her. She threw her head back and stared blindly at the darkened ceiling aware only of David's organ inside her as she made frantic love to him. Finally exhausted she rested her upper body on his chest, nestling her head on his shoulder. Her heart was pounding furiously in rhythm with his. Only the sound of their breathing could be heard in the silence of the room.

Reality came back slowly. Cat raised her head and touched David's face with her fingertips. His cheeks were wet with tears. A wave of embarrassment washed over her. She had behaved outrageously and had been insensitive to him and his needs.

Without a word she moved away and turned on her side. She fell asleep almost instantly.

The ringing of the phone jolted her out of the deep slumber. It was still dark out and she looked over to where David had been and realized he was gone. The events of the night flashed through her mind. The ringing of the phone would not stop. She did not want to answer it. She never wanted to talk to anyone ever again.

"It's obviously not for me," David said, standing in the doorway of the bathroom. He was fully dressed and his hair was still damp from the shower he had taken. "So you'd better answer it."

Cat picked up the phone slowly, never taking her eyes off his face. He did not seem to be angry.

"Sorry to call at this ungodly hour," Mark Goodwin said urgently, "but I've just called an ambulance for your mother. I think you'd better meet me at Downstate Hospital in Brooklyn."

"What happened?" Cat was fully awake.

"A mild heart attack, but at her age I feel it's better she be in the hospital for a few days. And she's asking for you."

Cat looked over at the digital clock beside her bed. It was six o'clock in the morning. Her first booking was at ten. "I'll be there," she said in resignation and hung up.

"My mother is in the hospital, and she wants me," she whispered, "and I don't want to go."

"I think you should." David was standing at the foot of her bed. She reached over and took his hand. "Do you want me to?"

"No, but it's the right thing to do." He leaned over and kissed her on the forehead.

She called Bernie and to her relief he was home. While dressing, she thought of her night with David. They were both high and had acted impulsively. She hoped her behavior would not change their relationship. She had wanted him but she should not have gone to bed with him. The timing was all wrong.

20

Clara moved into Alexandra's room when she was released from the hospital. It had been a mild heart attack, as Mark had said, and it was clear she could not go back to Brooklyn and live alone.

For Cat, the following days, which started with Mark's predawn call, were a nightmare. In her determination to get her finances in order, she had taken every booking which came up and although she did few of the important shows, she worked five, sometimes six shows a day, running from one fashion house to the next, as well as trying to reestablish her past contacts for the next season. Attending to her mother's move only compounded the busy schedule. She did not see David, but they spoke on the phone constantly and to her relief the night they slept together was never mentioned. Instead, their conversations centered on the possibility of starting their own agency. She had also postponed her date with Clay to the following Friday, but the days rushed by and suddenly it was Friday again and she realized she was looking forward to seeing him.

She finished work early and instead of going home, she decided to stop by the office. In spite of her talks with David and seeing all the advantages of going out on her own, she was still not sure as to what she should do. Assuming the responsibility for other models was not a simple matter. Staying with Pamela was far more practical. They had been together for a long time and although never worded, Cat was convinced that at one point Pamela would ask her to come into the agency on the managerial side. She did not feel she was misleading David. Once she joined the Fitzpatrick office, she would persuade Pamela to give him a staff position. He was bound to be an asset.

With Megan's pictures firmly tucked under her arm, Cat ran up the stoop of the building. Mel had been hounding her to talk to Pamela and she decided it would be a good way to start the conversation about her future.

The reception room was filled with young women, which surprised Cat. Cattle calls had long since been canceled. Pamela only saw girls by appointment and recommendations. The anxiety and tension could be felt the minute Cat entered. All eyes turned toward her, obviously wondering if she were the Great Pamela Fitzpatrick. Some of the girls tried to appear nonchalant, some smiled shy little smiles, some pretended to ignore her sudden appearance. But they were all posing in one form or another. When they realized she was not Pamela, they seemed to heave a silent sigh of relief. The tension reminded her of the one and only time she had exposed herself to a cattle call and she felt genuinely sorry for them.

"Hi, Mack." Cat walked over to the woman's desk.

"Oh, Cat, have you any idea where Pamela is?" Miss Mack whispered. "She said she'd be here at three and it's now three-thirty."

Cat raised her brows. It was unlike Pamela to be late for anything. Punctuality was a law with her. "Is it possible she forgot she had this call?" It was a superfluous question. Pamela never forgot anything.

"No. I personally think she blocked it out," Miss Mack said seriously. "Because frankly, why she suddenly decided to go through this charade again, I'll never know." She threw a disdainful look around the room. "Garbage, all of them, just garbage and you've got to believe these are the plums of what Lucille and I siphoned off as possibilities."

Cat glanced around, hoping the girls did not hear the comment. Turning away from the desk, she started toward Lucille's office.

"You're Cat Willingham, aren't you?" She was stopped by a very pretty young girl and she was flattered at being recognized. Unobtrusively she took in the girl's figure. She was quite short and thin, but not thin enough, and her shoulders were narrow. Too small even for junior shows, Cat thought automatically. She did have good hands and her feet were small. Sample shoes and gloves, possibly.

"My name is Dottie Gable," the girl said.

"How did you recognize me?" Cat smiled brightly.

"I've been living on fashion magazines ever since I can remember and I know your face as though it were my own."

The voice was pleasant. Maybe commercials, Cat thought. She stopped herself. This was ridiculous. She was thinking like a woman who was running an agency and she had not yet decided on it.

"That's very flattering," she said coldly as she headed toward Lucille's office.

Lucille was on the phone and seemed agitated.

"Where is Pamela?" Cat asked unceremoniously, when Lucille finished talking.

"She'll be here." Lucille hung up the phone, picked it up again and dialed another number.

Cat listened to her booker's pitch. Lucille was a master, and Cat wondered if she would have the guts to take Lucille away if Pamela did not want her to come in with her. Pamela had done it to Regency. It was an indecent thought and she was surprised at herself. She could never do anything as underhanded as that. Besides, Lucille and David did not get along and that would eliminate her immediately.

"What's this with the cattle call?" Cat asked when Lucille finally hung up.

"I think Pamela feels a need to replenish her ego, show her power. She certainly doesn't need more bodies, although I suppose seeing enough new faces can produce something worthwhile," Lucille answered noncommittally.

"It doesn't sound like her." Cat was disturbed by what Lucille was saying. "Pamela is more creative than that."

"Creative or not, she's doing it and she's the boss. Although I wish she'd get here. It's not fair to those girls out there." She paused. "What's bothering me is that I get the feeling she's doing it on purpose."

"Why would she do that?"

"Maybe she's really busy, but I have a hunch that keeping those girls waiting gives her a feeling of omnipotence. You know, like on the eighth day she created a model, or not, whichever way the mood hits her."

Cat was surprised at what Lucille was saying. She was one of Pamela's staunchest and most loyal supporters. Something was eluding her and it bothered her. "Come on, Lucille, what's going on?"

"Did you hear about Zoe?" Lucille asked suddenly.

"What about her?"

"She's opening an agency in Atlanta."

"When?" Cat asked cautiously.

"Never, if it's going to be up to Pamela. She's going to take out an injunction against her and then if that doesn't work, she'll sue her for every cent she's worth."

"That's unconscionable," Cat protested. "Pamela can't have the only agency in the country."

"What's that got to do with the price of beans?" Lucille laughed mirthlessly.

"Wait a minute," Cat continued, now angry. "Gillis McGill opened Mannequin, Ellen Harth has an agency, why not Zoe Smith?"

"Gillis and Ellen were top models before Pamela came on the scene. Pamela didn't create them, mold them. They owed her nothing. She needed them at one point probably more than they needed her. Zoe, on the other hand, was formed, created and exposed to the fashion world by Pamela."

"You make Pamela sound like God," Cat snapped. "Did she create me, too?" she asked as an afterthought.

"I would say she had a lot to do with your career, yes," Lucille said seriously.

"Which means that I'm beholden to her until I drop dead or decide to leave the modeling world?"

"Let me say that if you suddenly decided to open an agency, she would see it as a stab in the back."

Cat felt the color drain from her face. "I'll be eternally grateful to her for what she's done for me, but, Lucille, you were as responsible for me getting started as she was. It was you who encouraged, pushed, set up the appointments when I was too terrified to go anywhere." She stopped in frustration. "Why, you were the one who insisted I go up to Penn's studio that day . . ."

"Granted," Lucille interrupted, "but it was Pamela who took you from that point on. She was your staunchest supporter and still is."

Cat did not answer.

"But the truth is that in your case it's academic," Lucille's voice softened. "Pamela always looks to you when she's away, as she did over the summer. As a matter of fact, I think she's going to ask you to sit in for her when she goes to Europe this winter."

"But over the summer I was recuperating," Cat said slowly. "Now I'm working." She lowered her eyes, feeling uncomfortable.

Suddenly they heard Pamela's voice coming from the reception room.

"I can tell you right off the bat that none of you, and I mean none of you, stands a Chinaman's chance in hell of becoming models." She was obviously speaking to the waiting girls and her tone was insulting.

Both Lucille and Cat were startled as they stared at each other for a long moment.

"That's hardly the way I would do it," Cat said under her breath.

"Nor I, but it works for her."

Cat walked over to the door leading to the reception room and saw Pamela standing in the center of it, her face blazing with fury. She had a batch of pictures in her hand and kept looking at a photo and then scanning the room to identify the girl it belonged to. The silent hysterical vibrations emanating from the dozen or so girls was terrifying. Abruptly, Pamela turned and walked toward the stairway. Just before she started down, she turned around and with a well-manicured forefinger pointing like a dagger, she picked five girls and told them to come down when she was ready. "As for the rest of you, get out." It was then she spotted Cat and her expression changed. "Hey there, haven't seen you in a dog's age. Come on down."

Cat wanted to run out of the building, escape the cruelty she had just witnessed. She quelled the impulse and watched the humiliated, dejected girls file out, some quietly, some angry, others crying. She wished she could say something. In truth most of the girls were not likely to make it, but she knew there was no way to persuade them of it. Theirs was a dream which no one could take away. Just as it had been impossible to take it away from her once it took form.

"That was unnecessarily vicious," Cat said when she reached Pamela's office.

"I can't stand people who won't face reality," Pamela said, lighting a Turkish cigarette and inhaling deeply. "A pug nose and blond hair don't make a fashion model. And someone has to tell it to them right out."

"What's with the cattle call, anyway?" Cat asked.

"Just a whim," Pamela said evasively, as she buzzed Miss Mack, indicating she was ready to see the remaining candidates.

It was a torturous scene for Cat. Each girl who came down the circular stairway was verbally pummeled by Pamela. The nose was too long, the hair was too curly, the teeth needed capping, the posture was bad, the legs were heavy, the shoulders were narrow, the breasts were too full. What amazed Cat was that each girl took the abuse and seemed almost to be asking for more. Several asked if Pamela would reconsider them after they followed her advice. Her answer was noncommittal. Still they hesitated before leaving. Cat noted that Dottie Gable was not included among the girls who were asked to come down.

"Well, now that we've done that scene, how about a drink?" Pamela asked, opening a drawer and taking out a flask and a delicate Limoges demitasse cup and saucer.

Cat smiled to herself. She had given them as a gift to Pamela years back and Pamela seemed to cherish them.

"Not for me, thanks."

She watched Pamela pour herself a drink and gulp it down quickly. "Pamela, don't you feel badly for those girls?"

"Badly?" Pamela refilled her cup and looked directly at Cat. "Nonsense. This is not a charity organization and don't you forget it."

Cat's self-assurance began to falter. She did not want a confrontation.

"But they've been preparing themselves for this meeting for God-knows-how-long, looking forward to it, wanting to hear something encouraging. A kind word, a ray of hope, something!" she said in spite of herself.

"There were two that I'm going to have come in again," Pamela said, sifting through the pictures that the girls had left behind.

"Then why didn't you at least tell those two there was a chance?"

"I will in a day or so."

"How do you know they'll be around?"

"They'll be around. To get signed up by me is the prize. Even if they sign up with someone else within the next couple of days, which they won't, they'd break their backs to come here." Her self-assurance was infuriating.

"How can you be so sure about who can make it and who can't?" Cat said slowly.

"Gut feeling." Pamela lit another cigarette. "Educated guess."

"I must have been lucky, then. You were nice to me from the start."

Pamela smiled. "You had it! Insecure, frightened and all the rest, you walked into Penn's studio and I could tell you had it." Pamela threw her head back and laughed. "You were actually a mess. Your makeup was all wrong. You were dressed atrociously, as usual, but I could see you were a thoroughbred. And you had guts. Even Penn couldn't break you and he was a tiger." A faraway look came into her eyes. "And don't think I didn't try. They neglected to tell me I wasn't doing a single and it was the first time I ever did a shot with another model."

Cat ignored the insult concerning her wardrobe. Instead, her eyes wandered over to the far wall of the room. Framed in a simple lucite frame was the picture Pamela was talking about. Cat was not yet eighteen and Pamela was over thirty and they were both wearing evening dresses by Balenciaga. It was a picture of contrasts, Pamela with very blond hair wearing a black taffeta gown and Cat, with her dark looks, dressed in an identical white one. The dreamlike quality of the photo epitomized glamour, fashion and mystery. Although Pamela was a well-known model, photographed constantly by photographers all over the world and it was Cat's first job, it did not matter. The gowns they wore were of prime importance and the model's identity was immaterial. The regal quality, the serenity, the luxury the designer was looking to achieve, was the only concern of the editors. Cat suppressed a sigh. The years had flown by so quickly and the times had changed so drastically.

"Well, I still think you're being overly harsh and rash." Cat looked back at Pamela. "As a matter of fact, there was one little blond upstairs that I think had a quality."

"She's under sixteen," Pamela said coldly.

"How can you tell?"

"I can spot them a mile away and I refuse to get involved with kids. Eighteen is my bottom line. On a rare occasion I'll go as low as seventeen, but under that, never." Her voice became edged with anger.

Cat had heard this speech before but never questioned it. Today she suddenly wanted to understand the reason.

"What's the magic about being eighteen?" she asked haltingly. "I'm sure there are kids who are fourteen who are more mature than their parents."

"How mature are the parents?" Pamela laughed. "But the truth is that no matter how grown-up and sophisticated a girl is, a thirteen-year-old kid is emotionally thirteen. She may be bright, she may even be mature for her years, she's still thirteen, or fourteen, or whatever. And I don't want to be responsible for them." The anger returned briefly. "Eighteen is the age that the powers that be have deemed the age of consent and although God knows some of them will never grow up emotionally or in any other way, at least my sense of responsibility toward them is salved."

Cat looked down at the manila envelope containing Megan's pictures, which was on the floor beside her bag. She wondered if she should show them to Pamela. Mel had said Megan was nineteen and although she behaved as though she were twelve, Cat had no reason to doubt his word.

"What do you think of this girl?" She handed the envelope to Pamela and watched her closely as she took the pictures out and scrutinized them.

"Beautiful, exceptional, strange and scared and I wouldn't touch her with a ten-foot pole."

"But why?" Cat was taken aback.

"I don't know. I just don't want her."

"She's over eighteen," Cat said with exaggerated assurance.

"That's not my only criteria in judging who becomes a model with this agency. There are other factors."

"But," Cat started.

Pamela threw the pictures on the desk. "Forget it and stop being a talent scout."

The phrase offended Cat.

"Let's drop it," Pamela's voice softened, "and let's talk about more important things. How are things going for you?"

"Hopefully when word gets around that I'm back and still look the same, things will look up."

"And if they don't?"

"I'll cross that bridge when I come to it."

"By the way, I'm going over to cover the European collections for King publications toward the end of the year." Pamela refilled her demitasse. "I'm also going to take the time to look around for some new faces. Then Peter and I are going to the Greek Islands. Onassis invited us to a Mediterranean cruise on his yacht." She said the last with relish.

Cat looked at Pamela expectantly.

"Hi, everybody." David came down the stairs at that moment.

"Well, it's about time," Pamela exploded. "Where the hell have you been?"

"Around." He looked pleasantly at Pamela, then at Cat.

"You were supposed to be here at three."

"You can't win 'em all, can you?"

"Well, I'll be a son of a gun. You've learned to talk back." Pamela's voice grew syrupy.

"I think I'd better run along." Cat stood up. Pamela was being impossible and she couldn't stand it. Not for herself nor for David. She also did not trust herself to look at David. It was the first time she'd seen him since the night they went to bed together and the incident came alive all too vividly. Her heart began to pound when he appeared and she was not sure she could hide her feelings.

"You're forgetting your pictures." Pamela picked up Megan's photographs and handed them to David to pass on to Cat.

"Beautiful girl," David said pleasantly, but Pamela could see he was furious. His reaction puzzled her. She looked over at Cat. She appeared confused. Something was going on between Cat and David and it bothered her. She hated being left out of anything that was happening around her.

"You were saying something about a trip to Europe." Cat's voice broke into her thoughts and at that moment Pamela decided against asking Cat to sit in for her while she was gone.

"Oh yes," Pamela said pleasantly. "I won't be gone long and while I'm away Lucille and Mack will cover for me. So if you have any problems, just check with them."

Cat tried to smile but her heart sank with disappointment and she wondered what had made Pamela change her mind. Within seconds her disappointment turned to anger and she suddenly wanted no part of Pamela's agency.

"I'll be talking to you," Cat said, gathering her things and walking toward the stairway.

"Hey, I've been meaning to ask you, did you ever go out with Clay Whitfield?" Pamela's question stopped her.

"I'm seeing him this evening," Cat answered through clenched teeth, not wanting the conversation to take place in David's presence.

"I wouldn't be so nonchalant about it." Pamela ignored Cat's obvious irritation. "This could be the break you've been waiting for."

"Hardly."

"Well, he's the catch of the year, you know."

"I'll keep that in mind."

"Don't be sarcastic," Pamela shot back. "If you play your cards right you could end up on top of the heap, after all."

Cat started up the stairs.

"And above all, don't bore him with your troubles. Dating is an art which you're not too familiar with."

Cat felt her face grow red with rage.

"And don't sign any agreements before showing them to me," Pamela continued.

Cat turned around slowly. "Planning on taking a commission?" she asked coldly.

"No, this one will be on the house."

Pamela was being unusually nasty and Cat could not understand where the rage was coming from. She looked over at David. His face was expressionless.

"I'll be sure to check with you if I feel I need advice," Cat said icily as she turned and ran up the stairs.

Walking toward Park Avenue, Cat was overcome by feelings which had long been held in check. She was fed up with kowtowing to Pamela, trying to please her and pacify her. She owed Pamela a great deal, but Pamela owed her things, too. Insults that she had glossed over came back. Her anger grew. She could run an agency as well as Pamela and do it with greater dignity and more consideration. She would prove Pamela wrong on many levels.

By the time she reached her house, Cat was determined to start her move toward independence from Pamela and she would begin by making Megan a household name in the fashion world.

21

"Is that you, Catherine?" Clara called out when Cat entered the apartment. The television was blaring out the news and she could hear Emma clattering around in the kitchen. The apartment was alive with activity and Cat bristled. The scene was identical to the one she grew up with. Never once could she remember coming home without her mother being there, demanding to know where she'd been and ordering Emma to hurry dinner. This evening it was even more irritating, since she had a couple of hours before meeting Clay and needed time alone.

Entering Alexandra's room and seeing its total transformation was the last straw and Cat put her hand to her mouth, trying to stifle a cry. It had become Clara's room. The bed was covered with an old-fashioned quilt and huge European feathered pillows. An ancient chest, which Cat vaguely remembered from her childhood, had replaced Alexandra's simple desk and was laden with jars of cream and other toiletries. A small antique side table stood next to the bed and the large jewelry box overpowered its delicate form. It was as though Alexandra never existed. The idea was devastating and she wished with all her heart that Alexandra were in the room instead of her mother.

"Is everything all right?" Cat stiffly asked.

"Just a minute," Clara answered, her eyes glued to the television set.

Cat sat down on the edge of the bed and focused her attention on the tail end of a report about the war in the Middle East.

"It's not good, is it?" Cat said when the broadcast was over.

"I don't understand much, but somebody better help or there will be another Holocaust," Clara said with emotion.

The helpless feeling that Cat had when she first heard of the outbreak of the war came back. She wished Jeff were in New York so he could explain the situation to her. There were so few people she could talk to about it. Most did not care and the ones that did were not really knowledgeable about that part of the world.

"How did your day go?" Clara asked, settling back on her pillows.

"Nothing special," Cat answered, getting up. "How are you feeling and are you comfortable?"

"I'm all right, except that I was wondering where Alexandra will sleep when she comes home."

Cat could not help but smile. The question was typical for the self-centered, pampered old woman.

"Well, the fact is that Alexandra will not be coming home before June," Cat said slowly. She had avoided discussing her separation from Jeff or Alexandra's whereabouts and had been trying to decide how to break the news to her mother. The moment seemed as good as any. "She's gone to California with her father," she said, and waited for the reaction.

"You mean Jeff left you?" The wording struck Cat as an accusation.

"We decided on a trial separation."

"Why, what have you done?" It *was* an accusation.

"Mother, I haven't done anything. Besides, I thought you didn't like Jeff."

"That's not the point," Clara said indignantly. "After so many years of marriage, when there is a child to consider, you don't get divorced."

"No one is talking about divorce," Cat said defensively.

"And why is Alexandra with him? A daughter belongs with her mother."

"That's a long story but in a way it's just as well that she is. You need to be cared for and Alexandra is perfectly safe with her father."

"I miss her," Clara said suddenly.

"So do I."

"Why did you stop bringing her to visit me?" Clara asked, and Cat could hear the hurt.

"Mother, you know how teenagers are now." Cat tried to laugh it off.

"Not Alexandra. She's different and we had something special between us."

"When she comes back we'll get together more often." Cat wanted to end the conversation. "Now, I've got to run." She started to leave.

"Oh, Catherine, I've made arrangements for our dining room to be delivered next week." Clara's statement stopped her and she turned around in amazement.

"What do you mean?" she asked slowly. "I can understand you wanting your things in this room but where am I going to put a dining room set?"

"You've got a lovely dining area, which is totally bare," Clara said innocently. "And it's a beautiful Biedemeyer table and the chairs are magnificent. It will fit in perfectly."

"I don't want any furniture in that part of the room."

"But where do we eat?" Clara's face grew red. "Like this evening. It's Friday night and you don't have a decent table in the apartment."

"Mother, I'm not having dinner home tonight. I rarely eat dinner home and when I do, I'm really too exhausted to sit down and make a production of it."

"Not even on Friday night?"

Cat bit her lip in exasperation. "I don't mean to upset you, but I have a different lifestyle than the one you and Papa had. This evening, I'm being picked up at seven-thirty and that's that."

"Who are you going out with?"

Cat began to laugh. "I don't believe this," she said, and walked back to the bed. "Mother, please understand. I'm very glad that I have a place for you and I'll do everything to make you comfortable, but you cannot come into my life at this late stage and start dictating to me what to do."

"I'm very tired," the older woman said, sliding down on her pillow. "Just tell Emma to bring in a tray when she's ready."

Cat went into her bedroom and closed the door firmly. Mark had said that her mother was not to be upset but there were limits to her patience, too. She looked at her watch. It was nearly six o'clock. Throwing her bag on the bed she picked up the phone and called Bo.

Greg answered and was about to call out to Bo, but Cat stopped him.

"I want to talk to you, Greg," she said firmly.

"Oh, beg pardon."

"Have you found a model for the *Harper's* pages?"

He hesitated.

"I'm not suggesting myself," she said angrily. "I think I've got the girl for you."

"Who is she?"

"No one you've ever heard of, but believe me, she's the one."

"Let me get Bo," he said haltingly.

"Is he really a good photographer?" Cat asked when Bo came on the line. "He's so indecisive."

"He's tops, but you frighten him," Bo answered with annoyance. "You're far more formidable than you think. But that's beside the point. What's this about a model?"

"I've got just the one to do the *Harper's* pictures for you. She's gorgeous, unknown and I know you'll flip for her."

"When can I meet her?"

"I'll bring her over to your place tomorrow and if you agree with me, I'd like you to test her when I'm around. She's not that experienced, but has all the makings of the best of them."

"Is she signed up with Pamela?"

Cat laughed. She knew Bo disliked Pamela and Bo avoided using any of her models whenever possible.

"No, she's not."

"You've got a deal. Can you be at the showroom at ten tomorrow and if she's as good as you say she is, we can test her on Sunday at Greg's studio."

Hanging up, Cat picked up the receiver again and dialed Kevin. His Soho story would be ideal for Megan. "I'm just calling to confirm our date," she said flirtatiously.

"Cat, my darling, I've known you too long not to know that you've got something up your sleeve other than a desire to confirm a set date."

"Well, I have an idea for your Soho story."

"You don't even know what it is."

"It's not that hard to figure out what *Elle* would want from our version of the Paris Left Bank."

"That's what I love about you." He laughed in appreciation. "Tell me more."

"Well, I've got the model for you. She's gorgeous. She's from the South and as American as apple pie. She also plays the guitar. She's "today" as we would like to appear to the world."

"Sounds right on." He sounded pleased. "I can't wait to meet her."

Finished with Kevin, she called Mel Black.

"Will Pamela sign her up?" he asked the minute he heard her voice.

"Never mind that. I'd like to pick her up tomorrow around nine-thirty and take her down to Bo Shephard's."

"No problem, but what's it all about?"

"You and I will meet sometime next week and I'll bring you up to date. Just have her dressed and ready when I get there."

She felt exhilarated while talking on the phone and making the various arrangements. It was all going to work out, she thought with satisfaction. She started dressing and realized she still did not know how tall Clay was. She decided on high heels, anyway. The outfit called for heels and the look was all important.

She was ready by seven-fifteen and she settled herself in the small armchair, lit a cigarette and called Alexandra. She tried not to call too often, since Jeff had indicated that her calls upset the child. But she was feeling good and hoped her mood would transmit itself.

Alexandra came on the wire, sounding subdued.

"Are you enjoying your stay in Los Angeles?" Cat asked, ignoring the tone.

"It's okay."

"How's school?"

"Fine."

"Dad around?"

"No."

"Do you need anything?"

"No."

"Why don't you ever call me?"

"Would you like me to?"

"I would." The conversation was dreadful and Cat felt her feelings of well-being of minutes before draining away. "Incidentally, Grandma is staying here. Would you like to talk to her?" she said impulsively.

"Oh yes." There was now a hint of excitement in the voice.

Cat could hear the downstairs buzzer sound.

"I'll put her on." She rushed out and called to her mother to pick up the phone.

As Cat walked out the front door she could hear Clara talking excitedly to Alexandra. She wondered what they had to say to each other.

22

"Miss Willingham." The suave, impeccably dressed maître d' greeted Cat as she entered the fashionable Caravelle restaurant on Fifty-fifth Street. She was surprised that she was recognized, since she had never been to the place before.

"Mr. Whitfield told me that when the most beautiful woman entered this evening I would recognize her as Miss Willingham and he was right." He smiled graciously. "If you'll follow me, Mr. Whitfield is waiting."

Walking past the banquettes in the narrow corridor leading to the dining room, Cat felt people looking up discreetly. She sensed the luxury and special atmosphere that the place exuded and her excitement mounted. She was pleased she had made that special effort to look particularly glamorous. She had debated whether to wear a black Norell dress or the Bill Blass suit she had bought when she did his winter collection before she fell ill. She had chosen the latter—a lavender silk print in muted colors, with a georgette blouse. The lynx fur collar and cuffs added a touch of elegance and made her feel quite beautiful.

Clay stood up when she arrived at his table and by the look of pleasure that appeared on his face she knew she had chosen wisely. She was also pleased to see that having worn high heels, he was only slightly shorter than she. But it made no difference. She had forgotten how attractive he was and she was delighted to see him.

"You were right, Mr. Whitfield," the maître d' was saying. "I doubt that there will be any competition tonight for this lovely young woman." Clay smiled in agreement.

As soon as Cat was seated, the man disappeared and Clay turned to Cat. "You are more beautiful than I remembered."

"Thank you, Clay," she said sincerely.

"What will you drink?"

She was about to tell him that a drink after the exhausting day she'd had was hardly what she wanted but decided against it. She smiled inwardly remembering Pamela's warning about boring a date with her problems. "A glass of wine would be lovely."

A waiter appeared although Cat had not seen Clay call for him. It amused her and she found herself relaxing.

"What a lovely restaurant," she said, leaning back and taking out a cigarette. A waiter materialized out of nowhere and lit it for her.

"I rarely eat out, but I'm having my apartment painted and this restaurant is one of the few where I feel comfortable."

"Is it a new apartment?" Cat asked, wondering what the evening would be like. As pleasant as the surroundings were and as nice as Clay was, she had no idea what to say to him.

"No, but since the death of my wife, I felt I should make some changes."

"Are the changes such that you can't live in the apartment?" she asked politely.

"Drastic enough so that I'm staying at my club at River House."

"That's a lovely place."

"It's like my second home."

Oh, God, Cat thought. The evening was going to be a disaster.

"How about some food?" Clay asked after a short silence.

"I'd love it."

The dishes arrived without clatter, and the wineglasses were refilled automatically. The atmosphere was lovely, but sterile.

"Tell me about yourself, Catherine," Clay said when she finished her appetizer.

"Oh dear," she laughed self-consciously. "It's not very interesting. My life has been devoted to modeling. I've been doing it since I was seventeen and in a way it appears more glamorous than it really is." It was not what she had meant to say. She wanted to impress him. Instead she was running herself down.

"What does it involve?"

She thought for a long moment before she answered. "It's far more complex than one would think," she said finally. "Models, like me, who really work at it, must be conscious of the changing trends, different lifestyles, women's needs both at home and at work. I don't just put on a dress. I present it. I try to judge my audience. There's a way of showing a dress to a wealthy group of women who do nothing but spend their time at fashion shows. But it's a different scene when you're doing a line for working women. The designers are aware of it and quite a few of them take what we say and follow our advice. I'm quite friendly with several of them and we work very closely together."

"How fascinating." Clay was obviously impressed.

"And it's hard work." She laughed, aware that she had gotten

quite carried away. "Mind you, runway is quite different from print
. . ."

"Print?"

"Photography. You know, being photographed for magazines
and newspaper ads." She took a deep breath. "And now that I'm no
longer doing print, since age has a way of creeping up on models, I
find it just as exciting."

"But you're a child!" Clay exclaimed.

"Not to the camera."

He studied her carefully for a minute. "I don't see it. But if I
accept what you're saying, the life span of a model is rather short. So
what does she do when her career is over?"

The question made her squirm. She'd been living with the
thought almost constantly, but no one had ever asked it outright. The
answer still eluded her. For most of her adult life she had been a
successful model. Print, runway or whatever, she was a model. But
who was she when it ended?

"Well," she said slowly, "many girls are married and retire to
take care of their homes. Others go into fashion-related fields, such as
being stylists for designers, buyers for stores, some even begin to
design." Her mouth felt dry.

"And what will you do?" Clay asked with interest.

"I'm opening a modeling agency," she said, and was pleased she
could say it with assurance although she had not yet really decided to
do it.

"Fascinating," Clay murmured.

Cat watched him carefully. Although he was listening to her, she
knew her world was completely foreign to him. She had spoken with
great authority but he probably did not understand a word she said.
She remembered Pamela's words again and wondered if she had
bored him.

"Yes, it's a fascinating world," Cat said slowly. "But I'm sure it's
nowhere near as interesting as the work you do." She smiled warmly
at him. "You're in banking, am I right?"

Her statement sparked something in him and for the rest of the
evening Clay talked about his work. To her surprise she found it
engrossing and was completely absorbed in what he was saying.

"And now that we're into the Middle East, with gas and oil and
pipelines, it's opened up a whole new ball park," Clay said at one
point, and her interest was piqued even further.

"In what way?" Cat asked.

"Well, it's a world which we Americans don't really understand. I
have a slight edge since I was educated in Germany and England, so
the Middle East is not as foreign to me as it is to others."

"How does this present war affect the situation?" Cat asked slowly.

"It's hard to predict, since the fighting is still going on."

"The Israelis are taking an awful beating." She tried to keep the concern out of her voice.

"Yes, they are," Clay said thoughtfully, "but it will turn around. They'll get the upper hand and win the military victory. It's the political one they might lose."

"How come?"

"That's a long story and a complex situation." Clay smiled sadly.

"Have you ever been to Israel?" Cat asked.

"Several times and I must tell you it's the most fascinating country in the world." He looked at her. "Have you?"

"No," she said with embarrassment.

"You should go. Unfortunately, I shall not be able to do so for a long time to come."

"Why?"

"We work with the Arab world and as you may know, they really don't care to deal with people who travel to Israel."

"Do you travel much?"

"Constantly. We have offices in London, Paris and Zurich." He smiled wryly. "I was hoping my son-in-law would take over the London office, but I'm afraid, Brit, my daughter, is pulling strings which do not quite coincide with my plans."

"How old is she?"

"Twenty-six and a very aggressive young lady."

"Is she your only child?" Cat asked, remembering that Pamela said he had two children.

"Dee is twenty-four and she's much more amenable."

"Is she married?"

"Yes." His expression changed and Cat could tell that the younger girl was his favorite.

"What's her husband like?"

"A nice young man. He's going to the London School of Economics and I believe he'll be of much more value to me than Brit's husband."

"Well, obviously, Brit takes after you and Dee takes after her mother."

Clay's brows shot up in surprise. "What makes you say that?"

"It's not very difficult to figure out," Cat laughed pleasantly. "You're a man who runs the show and Brit wants to do the same."

"She's been a problem ever since she was very small." Clay's tone changed. "I simply can't reason with her. Never could. Take that man she married. He seems spineless, does everything she tells him, has no opinions of his own and now that Margaret is gone, we're at each other's throats at all times."

"Why is he working for you, anyway? Is he an expert of some sort?" Cat asked, marveling at the fact that bright and successful as he was in his field of business, he, too, was troubled by problems with his children.

He smiled sheepishly, and instead of answering he looked at his watch, and commented on how quickly the time had passed. "How about some coffee?" he asked, almost brusquely, and she understood he was embarrassed.

"I'd love some," she answered, and regretted that the evening was coming to an end. It had been truly exhilarating.

"I've had a most wonderful time," Clay said, and took her hands. "And you've been bored out of your head, haven't you?"

She looked at him and blushed. "Clay, I've had a lovely, interesting evening and I just hope I haven't bored you. The truth is, dating is not my forte."

"You're the first woman I've had dinner with who does not come from my circle of friends and I think we're both practicing. Do you mind being a guinea pig?"

She laughed. "Do you?"

He lifted her hand to his lips and kissed it. She noticed his hands for the first time. They were extraordinarily delicate yet there was a strength in them which fascinated her.

"Will you have a brandy with your coffee?" he asked, and suddenly he was no longer a stranger.

"Clay, if I had a brandy I'd fall flat on my face," she said, and the words came easily. She was talking to a friend. "I'm utterly exhausted."

"You really do work hard, don't you?"

"I don't think anyone knows how hard models work."

"But why?" he asked.

"Why do you work as hard as you do?"

"I've got obligations, I guess."

"So do I." She became defensive.

"I also love it," he said with sincerity.

"So do I," Cat answered without thinking and for the first time she understood Jeff's statement about her need where modeling was involved. It frightened her.

"How does your husband feel about it?" Clay asked haltingly.

"We're separated at the moment, but looking back, I don't think he minded." She thought for a long moment. "It was a pattern which started when we first married. He wanted to be a writer, is a writer, and he is totally absorbed in what he does." She shrugged her shoulders helplessly. "Frankly, I don't know any other way to live."

"I wouldn't allow my wife to be that tired from working."

Cat bristled. "Allow?"

"Miss Willingham, you're not going to drag me into a conversation about women's liberation. I appreciate women who work, but I'm a man who wants to take care of my woman. Is there something wrong with that?"

"Of course not." She lowered her eyes in confusion.

"Will I see you again?" Clay asked after they finished their coffee.

"I would really love it." It had been a lovely evening and she meant it.

Settled in the chauffeur-driven Rolls-Royce, Clay took her hand in his. "Would you like a nightcap?" he asked while the driver waited for instructions.

Here it comes, Cat thought with annoyance. "I don't think so," she said quietly.

"Fine. I've actually had a long grueling week and I'd just as soon turn in." He turned to the driver. "Jackson, take us to Miss Willingham's house."

Cat tried to quell her irritation. It had been a pleasant evening and she found Clay interesting and quite attractive, but she was not about to go to bed with him. Besides, her mother was in the apartment.

"Clay, I've really had a wonderful time . . ." she started.

"We must do this again, soon." He did not let her continue. "Maybe we could drive out to my house in Oyster Bay some Sunday."

"That sounds lovely and I'll look forward to hearing from you."

When the car stopped in front of her building, Jackson got out and opened the door for her.

She hesitated for a fraction of a second. Then extending her hand she smiled. "Good night, Clay," she said.

He pressed her hand. "Good night, Catherine, and thank you."

She was very aware that he did not make a specific date to see her again.

23

The last flickering of the Sabbath candles was the only illumination in the living room when Cat walked in and the sight startled her. Emma was dozing in the armchair. Cat woke her gently, fearful of frightening her. Then, giving her taxi fare, she made her promise to be back by nine o'clock the next day. During the evening she had forgotten all about Megan.

The evening had turned out well, but it was only ten-thirty and she felt restless. The fact that Clay had not made a date to see her again upset her. She had enjoyed his company, was interested in what he had to say and she wanted to see him again. She was not sure he felt the same way about her.

Turning on the track lights, she walked over to the dining area and tried to decide how her mother's table and chairs would fit in. She remembered them well. The table was an exceptionally pretty one and the chairs were covered in a magnificent red brocade. In the past, the candlesticks, which were now standing on the desk in her living room, had been placed on that table and she could almost feel the somber mood of yesteryear envelop her.

Somehow she was being dragged back into the past at a time when she was trying to carve out a future and she resented it terribly. She stormed out of the living room.

Her restlessness mounted. She wanted to be with someone who cared about her, who understood who she was and what she wanted. She reconstructed her conversation with Clay about retired models. To give herself an identity she had spoken about opening a modeling agency. It sounded important, made her appear like a person who knew what lay in store for her.

David came to mind. He understood her. He knew who she was, what she did, appreciated her needs. Clara was fast asleep and Cat decided she could meet David for a drink. It would just be for a short time, long enough to bring her back to herself. She would tell him about her plans for Megan and they would discuss their future. Impulsively she picked up the phone and dialed his number.

David sounded as though he had been awakened.

"Would you meet me for a drink at Moriarty's?" she asked, trying to keep the urgency out of her voice.

"Anything wrong?"

"No. I just want to see you."

While waiting for David, Cat reconsidered her decision about discussing her plans for Megan. It was all premature and she was not yet sure about opening her own business. Besides, Pamela was still getting assignments for her and handling her finances and there was just a possibility that her modeling days were not yet over.

"Cat?" David slipped in beside her.

She leaned over and kissed him affectionately on the lips. "God, it's good to see you," she whispered, and found herself wondering if she wanted to go to bed with him. Their first attempt at love-making had been unsatisfactory, but things had changed since then. They had grown closer. Now it would be different.

"Cat, you're trembling." David moved away and looked at her.

"Would you make love to me, David?" she whispered hoarsely.

"I don't think Mr. Moriarty would approve," David laughed, and put his arm around her shoulder affectionately.

She nestled in the crook of his arm and started caressing his upper thigh. David squirmed with embarrassment. She removed her hand and looked up at him.

"Couldn't we go up to your apartment?" she asked, and was surprised at herself.

"It's a rathole and I wouldn't dream of having you come up there." He sounded sincere.

"How about a hotel?"

"I couldn't do that to you. People know you around this town. We might meet someone you know and it'll embarrass you to death."

"Let's rent a car and go to a motel in New Jersey." She wanted to be made love to, wanted David to make love to her. David was young and she had an overwhelming need to touch that youth.

"Where could we rent one?"

"There's a place a couple of blocks up." Her voice became more urgent. "They know me there."

David paid for the coffee and Cat felt unsteady as they walked out of the restaurant. Putting her arm through his, she pressed herself close to him.

The rental office was closed.

"What happens now?" David asked, looking down at her.

She stared at him helplessly. Suddenly she started laughing. "God, I feel like a nymphomaniac."

"Don't say that." David put his arms around her and she leaned her head against his shoulder. If only her mother were not at the apartment, she thought, it would all be so simple. She felt David kiss her hair and she lifted her head and kissed him, trying to obliterate thoughts of Clara from her mind.

"I think I better take you home," David said after a moment.

Cat moved away slowly and they started down the darkened street. Was it possible that David was not attracted to her, she wondered. Was she making a fool of herself? She threw a sidelong glance at him. He did not seem upset or displeased. She felt his arm around her shoulder and the pressure of his fingers was reassuring. She had to get control of herself. Whether David wanted her or not, he was an integral part of her future and she could not risk losing him.

"How was your date with Clay Whitfield?" David asked, lighting cigarettes for them and handing one to her.

Her date with Clay, the luxury of the restaurant, the genteel atmosphere which had been so soothing, seemed remote, as though it never happened.

"It was fine. Just fine." She did not want to think of Clay.

"Pamela says he's richer than God."

"He also happens to be a very nice man," Cat answered quickly, feeling protective.

"I think I should tell you that Pamela offered me a job as her assistant," David said after a while. "And at the enormous salary of one hundred fifty dollars a week." The last was said with bitterness.

Cat swallowed hard. Lucille had said that David was heading for that position. Was he a homosexual after all? she wondered. But if he were a homosexual, she was making a fool of herself. Worse though was that David was working hard at denying it. Or was he possibly having an affair with Pamela? The thought infuriated her. Pamela was old enough to be his mother!

"Are you going to take it?" she asked when she felt she could speak normally.

He looked away. "I'd rather not, but what else can I do at this point?"

"What does the job involve?"

"Well, I have to be at her disposal almost day and night. Since she discovered I can type and take shorthand, I have to be up at her house three evenings a week to work on her column." He sounded defeated.

"What is this with her column, anyway?" Cat asked impatiently.

"I'm damned if I know. As far as I'm concerned, she doesn't give a damn about it and I get the feeling she doesn't really understand the politics she's writing about."

"That's surprising," Cat said thoughtfully. "When you consider that she's married to Peter, who's supposed to be a political genius."

"Be that as it may, the fact is that you're now talking to Pamela's new assistant and the only positive thing that comes of it is that I will probably be able to help you," David said, trying to bring enthusiasm to his statement.

"Me?"

"I'll be right there and I'll know exactly what's going on. I've told you before, I think you're being shafted."

Cat felt a surge of gratitude go through her. David was her friend. Unhappy as he was at how things had worked out for him, he was thinking of her and her well-being.

Within seconds all resolutions were forgotten and she found herself telling him about what she was planning for Megan. "And if it works, we could open our own agency," she finished breathlessly.

"Just let me know and I'll be right there when you need me," he said with sincere enthusiasm.

They were standing in front of her building and Cat was aware that the doorman was just inside the door so she restrained the impulse to throw her arms around David.

"Will I see you tomorrow?" he asked.

"I don't think so," she said slowly. "My mother still needs rest and quiet and the doctor feels we should not have any visitors." She was lying but could not help herself. She could not stand the idea of David having to confront Clara again.

"Will you call me?" he asked, looking forlorn.

Cat wished her mother would leave her house. "You know I will." She kissed him quickly on the lips and ran into the lobby.

The elevator man's eyes on her as she rode up and Cat could not help but smile. Just a couple of hours ago she had returned from her elegant evening with Clay, dressed in designer's clothes. She glanced at herself in the elevator mirror. Her hair was in disarray, her makeup slightly smeared and the top buttons of the bulky sweater were undone.

As she entered the apartment, Cat felt as she did when she was sixteen and had to tiptoe into her room after sitting on the stoop of her house waiting to see Jeff come home.

24

To Cat's relief and delight, Clay called her several days after their dinner date and she found herself blushing like a schoolgirl when she heard his voice. She had been thinking about him constantly and for the first time in her life her daydreams revolved around him rather than Jeff. She was still not sure she wanted to have an affair with him. But the invitation to have dinner at his club settled the problem. Clay could hardly invite her up to his rooms in that staid bastion of respectability.

Their second date was not much different from their first and was followed by dinners whenever he was in town and Cat was free. They all ended by his taking her home, kissing her affectionately on the cheek and saying good night. It appeared as though she did not appeal to him physically, and it offended her.

Although in a way it was for the best. Things began to look up for her workwise. She was called in as a replacement for ailing models, or she was asked to do last minute fittings, even if she did not do the actual fashion show. Hard as designers worked to meet their fashion week deadline, there was always the last minute alteration or some other disaster, and if their original fitting-model was busy, Cat was the ideal substitute. Her body measurements were perfect.

If these jobs offended her, she could not complain since she was paid her regular fee and dared not turn them down.

Also, Megan was proving to be a full-time preoccupation and an unexpected revelation.

As certain as Cat had been about Megan's abilities as a photographer's model, she did not expect the shy, frightened girl she met at the Osborne to come to life with the grace, elegance and flair which she exhibited in front of the camera the day Greg took the test shots of her. The editors of *Harper's Bazaar*, when they saw the pictures, were impressed and announced that they would be using Megan on their January cover. Cat felt a twinge of jealousy when she saw Megan in the wedding dress she had modeled for Bo's fashion show, but she put these feelings aside. Megan wore the clothes with the youthful air they deserved and Cat knew it.

She was convinced that once Megan appeared on the cover of *Harper's Bazaar* she would be on her way and what had started out as a form of revenge against Pamela's attitude was heading for great success. Mel Black was delighted and was already at work in building Megan up.

Cat had met with him shortly after Megan was photographed by Greg and told him what was happening. He picked it up like a quarterback with the ball on the twenty-yard line. Within days, stories about Megan began to appear in various newspapers and some feature articles for magazines were in the works for months to come. What bothered Cat was that they all focused on Megan's religious ardor. She was photographed in front of her church with her priest; she was shot playing her guitar to Sunday school children; her shabby apartment was described in exaggerated and glamorized detail, emphasizing the religious articles strewn around. But Megan seemed oblivious to the exploitive aspects of what was happening and appeared to be enjoying the attention. Cat could not shake the feeling that it was wrong and could lead to disaster.

With it all, Cat felt more relaxed about her own life. Opening an agency was almost a foregone conclusion and she was quite excited about it. Her friendship with David was solid and her mother's health was improving. Except for missing Alexandra, which was compounded by her growing relationship with Megan, Cat was mapping out a future in which her daughter played an important part. She still did not understand what had gone wrong with their relationship, but it was clear to her that she had to spend more time with Alexandra.

When Bo and Greg started scouting around for a location in which to photograph Megan for Greg's magazine assignment, Cat asked Clay if they could use his Oyster Bay home. He had spoken of it often and it sounded ideal. Clay was delighted with the idea and asked if he could come along.

The shooting fell on the Sunday before Thanksgiving and the weather was perfect for a drive to the country.

Cat was excited about the trip and was determined to show off to Clay the other side of her personality—Cat Willingham, the working woman. She chose her clothes with great care. On all their previous dates, she was dressed in glamorous designs, looking like the successful model. Today was going to be different. She wore a long, loose, tweedy jacket cut like a fisherman's overshirt, matching pants and a black turtleneck sweater, with a long white woolen scarf tied loosely around her neck. The effect was perfect. It was elegant and appropriate for the working woman executive.

Sitting beside Clay, listening to the exquisite tone of the stereo

which filled the car, Cat could not help but wonder what life would
be like with someone like Clay. She felt his hand clasping hers and
the touch was unnerving. A sigh escaped her and suddenly she
wished they were not going to meet Bo and Greg. A day alone with
Clay in his country home could have been far more exciting.

"Anything wrong?" Clay asked with concern, pulling her toward
him.

"No, I'm fine," she answered as she nestled against him. His
fingers began to caress her arm. "I was just thinking how lovely it is
being here."

He pressed her to his side and she closed her eyes wishing he
would stop the car and make love to her. That's what Jeff would have
done under the circumstances. The thought made her uncomfortable. Jeff and Alexandra did not fit into the present scene, especially
since it occurred to her that in all their years of marriage, she, Jeff and
Alexandra rarely drove out to the country, as she was now doing with
Clay. They were usually too busy, or she was too tired.

"I feel as though I've been transported back in time," Clay broke
into her thoughts, "when I used to drive my daughter to the country."

Cat moved away and tried to smile.

"Don't smile. You could be my daughter," he said looking over at
her.

"Nonsense," Cat said, taking a cigarette out and lighting it. "I
don't see you as my father."

"You certainly look young enough to be my daughter." He
pulled her back toward him. "And you smoke too much."

She ignored his remark about her smoking and leaned back to
look at him. He was no older than Jeff but they were as different as
could be in every way. Jeff was much taller and more gaunt-looking
with his sunken cheeks, Roman nose, his face etched with deep lines.
His hair was still too long and the overall impression was shaggy.
Whereas Clay was impeccable. He was far more handsome than Jeff.
His features were clean-cut and refined. His facial muscles were taut
and the strong jawline was not affected by drooping jowls. As always,
he was dressed to perfection for the occasion. His cashmere jacket
was faultlessly tailored, the white sports shirt was right for the silk
ascot tied around his neck. He carried his aristocratic ancestry with
dignity, and she realized she wanted to have an affair with him.

"I'm glad you're not my father," she said, and laughed self-
consciously.

Clay looked over at her briefly and laughed too.

They drove in silence for a while. Finally Clay turned off the
main highway and after what seemed like an interminably long,
twisted drive, they arrived at a three-story mansion.

"Good God, it looks like an English castle," Cat exclaimed.

The car came to a stop in front of an immense oak door. Within seconds it opened and a man dressed in a typical French houseman's apron over a white shirt with sleeves held up by black garters rushed toward them.

"Monsieur, you will forgive me for not being here when you arrived." He spoke with a thick French accent.

"But he was," Cat whispered to Clay in amusement.

"André thinks he should have anticipated our arrival by several seconds," Clay whispered back.

"Are Miss Willingham's friends here?" He turned back to the butler.

"They've gone down to the stream," the man said, as they followed him into the house.

Walking through a large gallery, Cat got a glimpse of a huge living room in which a fire was burning in the fireplace. She wanted to stay in the house with Clay.

"The gardens are much more beautiful in the summer when all the flowers are blooming," Clay said, guiding her out to the patio.

Cat was stunned by the sight which greeted her. Standing on the flagstone terrace, she could see wide shallow grass steps which led down in a pencil-straight line from the terrace to what appeared to be an Olympic-sized swimming pool. Flanking the steps were endless plantings and several redwood trees. Beyond the pool, a large grassy area stretched toward a wooded hillside. Even though it was fall, there were colorful flowers intermingled with small trees bearing ultramarine blueberries. In the far distance Cat could see a small stream gleaming under the pleasant fall sunlight. Immense as the garden was, every inch was cared for and it was clear that great skill and constant, loving attention went into making the place so awesomely beautiful.

"I don't think I've ever seen anything like this before," Cat said after a minute.

"Margaret loved gardening and spent a great deal of time here."

"Do you come here often?" Cat asked, feeling uncomfortable at the mention of Clay's wife.

"Not since Margaret died. I don't think you know it, but she was ill for a long time and this was the house where she spent the last year of her life." His voice was low and filled with emotion.

"I feel like an intruder."

"Nonsense. Your beauty does this place justice."

"Cat," Bo's voice reached her from afar. "Could you get your ass down here?"

She looked over at Clay with embarrassment. He seemed nonplused.

Greg had his camera equipment set up next to a small fish pond and Bo was accessorizing the outfit Megan was wearing. The design was totally outrageous, but Megan was completely captivating in it.

"What do you think?" Bo asked Cat.

With authority she walked over to Megan and adjusted the sleeve. Taking some pins out of a box, she pinned up the hem. She and Bo then moved back to get the effect.

"And I don't think she should be standing next to that barren tree," Cat said, looking around. Spotting a small patch of flowers clustered nearby, she took Megan's hand and led her toward it.

They were completely absorbed in what they were doing. Greg made suggestions from time to time, Bo objected, and Cat kept finding the compromise. She was in complete control and she loved it.

Cat was so absorbed in what she was doing that she almost forgot Clay was watching from the sideline.

At one point, when Megan had gone to change, Cat walked over to Clay and smiled apologetically. "It won't be long now," she assured him. "I hope you're not too bored."

"I don't remember being so interested in anything in a long time," he said sincerely. "But I can see where this sort of work can take a great deal out of you."

"I told you that when we first met." She put down a light meter she was holding and took a cigarette, but seeing Clay's displeasure she threw it away. Her action surprised and amused her.

"Does she get well paid for all this work?" Clay asked, looking over at Megan, who was just coming back dressed in a magnificent red and white, little-girl outfit.

"Not very much for what she's doing today. This comes under the heading of editorial, and magazines don't pay much for that."

"To work that hard and not get adequately paid makes no sense." Clay shook his head in disapproval.

"Editorial photography is one of the best ways of building a model's reputation. Once you appear in *Harper's Bazaar* or *Vogue*, every advertiser wants you. And when that happens, the money rolls in. Lots of it, if you click."

"And will she?"

"I'm not sure," Cat said thoughtfully. "At the moment I get the feeling she does not have the patience and drive for modeling. She wants movie star recognition." She smiled ruefully. "I can't seem to explain to her that more and more models today are known by name. It's going to become a trend, and if she makes it, she could be one of the new breed."

"And she doesn't believe you?"

"No." Cat answered too abruptly. Megan's greed when it came

to money was a constant source of amazement to Cat. Why she needed it, Cat could not tell. Megan rarely bought any clothes or food. Mel took care of all her expenses and except for going to church, Megan rarely went out. But what was even more disturbing was the change that would take place in her when money was discussed. Her face would take on a look of a woman haggling in an open marketplace. It was in total contrast to the sweet, submissive girl that Cat knew.

"And what's in it for you?" Clay broke into her thoughts.

"At this point, nothing, but if I can work with someone like Megan, build her up, I may take her on as a client when I open my agency." She said the last words with relish. She was beginning to feel good about the prospect.

"Well, she's very beautiful and I'm sure she'll make it," Clay said with confidence.

"Unfortunately, being beautiful is not enough," Cat said thoughtfully. "But if she doesn't make it, it won't be because I'm not trying." She rushed on, "The truth is I love that child."

"You keep calling her a child," Clay said. "How old is she?"

"Nineteen."

"She looks older." Clay scrutinized Megan for a long moment. "She appears young. She acts like a kid, but there's something almost worn out about her, as if she's had a hard life."

"I don't see it and thank God the camera doesn't, either. Although I figure her to be in her twenties. But nineteen seems to be the acceptable age for beginners. You're still a teenager." She laughed. "That's what I said when I first started, and mind you I was just sixteen. But that is changing. We'll be seeing kids of twelve and thirteen in high-fashion magazines soon." A bitterness she could not hide crept into her voice.

Clay put his arm over her shoulders. "My poor, aging friend." There was merriment in his voice. "How old are you?"

"Clay, no one ever asks a lady such a question." She tried to make a joke of it.

"I'm serious. How old are you?"

"Almost thirty-seven," she answered and was shocked at her truthfulness.

"Thank God," Clay said with relief, "although that's still too young for me. I thought you were in your late twenties and I refuse to get involved with anyone that young."

"Young or old, I've got to get back to work."

"Why?" His voice was low and there was a definite seductive quality to it.

She looked at him for a long moment and ran off.

The whole conversation about age bothered her. The talk about

Megan upset her. But what disturbed her most was the phrase "I love that child." It was said automatically and she tried to remember when she last applied it to Alexandra.

"How about all of you joining me for a late lunch?" Clay asked when the shooting session was over. It was nearly four o'clock in the afternoon.

"Won't that be an imposition?" Cat asked.

"André and Suzanne prepared it all before they left and I'm sure it'll be delicious."

Cat was pleased with the invitation. She wanted Bo to get to know Clay and like him.

Lunch turned out to be a disaster.

It was served in an exquisite, small, round-shaped dining room, which was furnished in authentic French provincial furniture. A large basket filled with fresh vegetables served as a centerpiece and the dishes were magnificent pewter. The setting was enchanting and Cat, knowing Bo's love of beautiful things, was convinced he would react. But he seemed impervious to it all. Instead, he and Greg behaved outrageously, flaunting their relationship in an almost vulgar manner. Cat was shocked at Bo's indiscriminate behavior. Her upset grew when the conversation turned to fashion, Bo's career and Greg's photography. It was as though Cat, Clay and Megan did not exist. Megan was no help. She was withdrawn and seemed completely out of place. She was worried about missing evening Mass and kept looking at her watch. Clay tried to discuss religion with her and Cat was again struck by how devout she was. But Clay talking about religion with Megan was hardly what Cat had hoped for.

For the first time since they arrived at the house, Cat wished David had come along. It would have been easier. He had wanted to come but Bo disliked him and she thought it would strain the atmosphere. Of course if Jeff were around, he would have been the ideal person to have along. Cat was sure that Clay and Jeff would have had a great deal in common. Thoughts of Jeff talking to Clay startled her.

Jeff, Clay, David. Given the choice, she wondered which one she really wanted. She smiled inwardly. She was not being given a choice.

"How about some dessert, Catherine?" Clay asked, and her speculations came to an abrupt end.

"I'd rather not. I'm gaining weight."

"You're as thin as a rail." He sounded paternal.

She handed her plate to him obediently, feeling Bo's eyes on her. He obviously disapproved of the whole scene.

She was relieved when the meal was over and Bo, Greg and Megan finally left.

Clay had his arm around her when Bo's station wagon drove away and they started back into the house.

Once indoors, Clay pulled her toward him and kissed her on the mouth. All the events leading up to that moment were forgotten. She was alone with Clay and that was what she wanted.

Being made love to by Clay made Cat aware that she had forgotten the meaning of physical passion. To her surprise and delight, she discovered that the elegant, restrained man she had been seeing in solemn, stuffy surroundings, was someone who obviously loved women and a lover who wanted to please her while fully enjoying himself. He was both gentle and forceful and she felt wanted and accepted. His fingers caressed her body masterfully. She found herself crying out, oblivious to her surroundings. Thoughts disappeared and dormant feelings came alive. When she felt him come, her joy for him was boundless. Finally the frantic passion turned to passive lovemaking, which she found equally thrilling.

When she woke she could see him standing at the bar pouring them drinks. She ran to him and sank to her knees and made love to him again. He placed his hands over her head and pressed her close. Then lowering himself to her, they lay in each other's arms and she felt him enter her again. The fervor of their passion was as great as it had been when they first started making love.

The embers in the fireplace turned gray and lying beside Clay, with his spent erection touching her body, she still trembled with excitement.

"I knew it would be like this," Clay whispered.

"I wish I knew you even thought about it," she answered. "I honestly wondered whether you were attracted to me."

"My darling, Catherine, I would have happily raped you at the Caravelle."

"Then why didn't you?"

"They're very stuffy about that sort of thing," he laughed, and within seconds she felt him harden and she accepted him with great ardor.

It was past midnight when they drove back to the city. She was sitting close to Clay, her hand pressed between his thighs while his fingers caressed her breasts. She could feel he still desired her, but his manner had changed. They were coming back to his staid world and abandoned, mindless love-making was not part of it.

"I'm leaving for Palm Beach tomorrow," Clay said after a while.

Cat moved away, feeling hurt and rejected.

"My daughters are meeting me there. It's a family Thanksgiving ritual which has been going on for years."

"When are you coming back?"

"I'll be back for a couple of days in December, then I'm flying off to South America."

Cat held her breath, wondering if he would invite her to join him. She couldn't go even if he did, but she wished he would ask.

"But I'll be back for New Year's Eve and I'm giving a party which I want you to come to. It would mean a great deal to me."

"That's a long way off," she said coolly.

He looked over at her and smiled. "Will you come?"

"You know I will."

He did not kiss her when they arrived at her house. Instead, he took her hand just as he did the first night they met. She shook it solemnly.

25

Cat tiptoed into her bedroom and switched on a dim light. The room was in a shambles and the sight made her blush. She had been so determined to appear elegant yet professional that she had tried on every outfit she had in her closet. Now, looking at herself in the full-length mirror, she felt like a fool. The way she was dressed did not make the difference. Bo had probably been annoyed that she did not wear one of his designs. Greg was too absorbed in his work to notice. Megan certainly couldn't have cared less and Clay would probably be hard-pressed to remember what she wore. How do I look. The question was part of her existence ever since she could remember. Would it never end?

She lay down on her bed, lit a cigarette and tried to recount the events after Bo left Clay's house and suddenly she felt embarrassed. Although she had behaved much as she had with Jeff during their married life, there was a difference. Jeff and she had made love. With Clay it was simply sexual gratification. But then, she was in love with Jeff and she was not in love with Clay.

She dismissed the thought quickly. Comparisons were not in order. She had so much to offer Jeff and he had needed her on so many levels. She had nothing to offer Clay.

Feeling tired and defeated, she started toward her bathroom, switching on her phone machine as she passed it. She stopped in her tracks when she heard Alexandra's voice.

"Mom?" Alexandra sounded conspiratorial. "It's Alexandra." Cat smiled in spite of herself. "Mom, if you come in before midnight our time, which is three in the morning in New York, call me. But please, please don't call if it's after that. I must talk to you."

Cat looked at the clock. It was 1 A.M. She dialed the Coast.

"What's the problem, honey?" she asked when Alexandra answered.

"Oh, thank God you called," the child squealed with delight.

"You sounded so mysterious." Cat felt happy talking to her. "Anything wrong?"

"Well, yes and no," Alexandra began to hedge. "You see, Mom, I need my allowance."

"Doesn't your father give you one?"

"Sure, but with Neva's miserly ways, she's convinced him that ten dollars a week is all I need."

"I thought you liked Neva."

"She's all right," Alexandra said impatiently. "But her idea of what people need is very different from yours."

"What's the ten dollars supposed to cover?" Cat knew she was being set up but this was the first time since Alexandra left that she had called and asked for anything and she did not want to turn her down. Cat was sure Jeff would be furious at her reasoning.

"Oh, everything. Lunch, movies, sodas, you know."

"How much do you want?"

"Well, you used to give me twenty-five a week and we've been here since October." She paused. "Mom, could you send me one hundred dollars?" Alexandra began to sound frantic.

"One hundred?"

"Please, Mom." Now the child was pleading.

"What's it for?" Cat asked quietly.

"I borrowed it from a friend and I've got to give it back."

"One friend had that much money to lend you?"

"It's been over a long period." Alexandra became indignant. "This is almost December."

"Your father obviously doesn't know you're calling me."

"And you won't tell him. You mustn't."

Cat did not answer.

"Oh, Mom, promise you won't. He'll be furious and Neva will split a gut. God, she's a bitch. And so tasteless. She's as fat as a pig and I really hate her."

"That's ridiculous, Alexandra." Cat grew angry. "You don't mean that. Neva is a good lady and I'm sure she's being very kind and understanding." She paused for a minute. "Alexandra, would you like to come home?"

"We'll be home in June." The girl became evasive.

"I mean, would you like to come home now?"

"Oh, Mom, you know as well as I do that in January you start the fittings, in February you do catalogues, in March you'll probably go to Europe and April and May are collection time."

Cat was staggered. She never knew Alexandra was that aware of her schedule.

"Will you send me the money?"

"I'll think about it," Cat said, but knew she was being unfair, since she had already made up her mind to do so. "I'll send it but that'll be your Christmas present."

"But I'll get it before Christmas, won't I?"

"Yes, honey, you will."

"Oh, Mom, I love you."

"I love you too, baby."

She hung up. She knew she ought to call Jeff and talk to him but that would be disloyal to Alexandra. The child was in trouble and had come to her for help. That's what mothers were for. And ten dollars a week was hardly an allowance for a girl who was going on sixteen.

She undressed quickly and got into bed. She wished there were someone other than Jeff that she could talk to about Alexandra's request. Clay would have been ideal. He had discussed his daughters with her at great length during their evenings together. His formal behavior when they parted made her dismiss the idea.

For the first time she wondered what she would do for Thanksgiving. Her mother's dietary laws made eating out impossible. Those damned rules and regulations which had been a nuisance ever since she was a child! She tried to recall what it was like when Jeff and Alexandra were with her in the past. Nothing special came to mind. Too often she had accepted doing some collection in Europe at the end of November when other American models wanted to stay in New York.

Turning out the light, Cat was trying to wipe all thoughts from her mind when the phone rang.

"Did I wake you?" It was David.

"No," she answered, allowing a deep sigh to escape her.

"Was it that bad?" he asked.

"No. As a matter of fact it went very well, except that Bo and Greg made a spectacle of themselves over lunch."

"In what way?"

"Oh, you know. Horsing around like little boys."

"I know they're friends of yours, Cat," David said seriously, "but fags who have a need to make an exhibition of themselves are really quite revolting." His voice rose in righteous indignation.

She was sorry she had mentioned Bo's behavior and decided to ignore David's remark, although she could not help but feel that he was overreacting and it annoyed her.

"And how was Megan?" David asked, ignoring her silence.

"I don't really know," she said seriously. "She was magnificent and followed instructions to a T, but there's something about her which bothers me and I can't put my finger on it."

"Oh, come on, Cat. She's young and needs guidance." He paused for a long moment. "You will go on working with her, won't you?"

"I guess so, but it's hard work."

"I'll help, you know that. And now that Pamela is off to Europe, I'll have all the time in the world."

She did not reply.

"Cat, you're not backing out of the agency idea, are you?" He sounded concerned.

"Heavens, no," she answered with exaggerated assurance. Opening an agency was probably the only avenue open to her if she were to maintain any semblance of her being. Her mind wandered briefly to her day with Clay. She was a plaything to him, in spite of his having seen her working. "No, of course not," she said more forcefully.

"Incidentally, I've got several bookings for you the weeks before Christmas," David said slowly.

"Really? Isn't Lucille around?"

"She's around all right, but as I told you, there are quite a few jobs that she somehow gives to others rather than to you."

"Thanks for trying, David," Cat said, genuinely grateful.

When she hung up, a jab of disloyalty toward Lucille sprang up. Or was it possible that David was misrepresenting what was actually happening at the office? She wiped both thoughts from her mind before they took root. All she knew was that somehow she had to get the money and move out on her own. It was not only for herself but for David, as well. He was doing so much for her and she did too little for him. But most important, Pamela's office was no longer interested in her. Pamela with her grand airs, living in her fool's paradise, lording it over her, feeling superior. Pamela who took credit for her career and always talked down to her. Well, she was in for a surprise. She would open an agency and would give Pamela a run for her money. She would take David as a partner and they would make it.

The need to defeat Pamela was overwhelming.

26

While waiting for Dan Grayson to come on the wire, Cat stared at the December snow coming down and blanketing her terrace. It was a week before Christmas and she hoped it would mean a white Christmas.

"Miss Willingham," the secretary's voice came on the wire, "Mr. Grayson will be with you in just a few minutes. Do you mind holding on?"

"Not at all," Cat answered, and wondered what it was he wanted of her so urgently. She had been quite definite about not being interested in his offer to go on the road and was almost annoyed that he was still hounding her. It would have been difficult to meet her commitments on thirty-five thousand dollars a year when he made the offer. Now with her mother living with her, and medical bills piling up, having to pay almost a full salary to Emma, added to her other expenses, that salary was out of the question. Besides, she was modeling all the time. Granted, she was doing jobs she would not have accepted in the past, but it meant earning money and she had put her pride aside. Lucille was annoyed but David was encouraging. And in truth, she was being seen and there was always a chance that the next season would be different. No one had yet said she was too old to model. She was also deeply involved in Kevin's Soho story. It was being shot at night and both Kevin and Megan wanted her around. It was exhausting but it did prove David's point. She could do both—work as a model and start her own agency.

Absently, she scanned the photographs of potential models that David had been sending her. None were Pamela's clients and, although she suspected she was looking at girls who were going to the Fitzpatrick Agency on cattle calls, Cat did not think it unfair to be considering Pamela's prospective clients.

She picked up the guest list that she and David had drawn up for the Christmas party they were planning. It was to be a testing ground for their agency. For the first time, Cat wondered when Pamela was due back. Although she and David had intended to send telegrams in lieu of written invitations, even an open house affair required some advance preparation.

Thoughts of her future plans with David and their modeling agency gave Cat a sense of well-being. In a way David had given her a new lease on life just when she thought everything was over, and there was nothing that could make her leave New York now. But even more important, Clay Whitfield had begun to play an important role in her life and, although she did not know where the relationship was heading, she looked forward to spending time with him when he returned to New York.

"Is that my gorgeous Cat Willingham?" Dan's voice boomed through the wire. "How's it going?"

"I was just thinking about it and it's going pretty well," Cat laughed happily.

"Let me get right to the point. Those pictures of the Baynes girl you sent me, well, she's a real knockout."

Cat was stunned. She had not sent him Megan's pictures. Then she remembered that David had asked to see Greg's pictures of Megan and she had given him a set, never dreaming there was a special reason for his request.

"You know, she reminds me of you when you did the Helena Rubinstein ads, years back," Dan laughed, unaware that he was being insensitive. "She's almost too perfect for words and you were right on as far as Chameleon is concerned."

"Yes, she is magnificent, isn't she?" Cat found her voice. Chameleon. The name was almost symbolic.

"Well, we'll be making our decision within the next couple of weeks and to date we haven't really found anyone who is being seriously considered except for Jeannie Lester. You know, Pamela's latest sensation from England, but frankly, between her and Baynes, I'll up for Baynes."

"That's wonderful." She was still too numb to react.

"What agency is she with?"

Cat felt her throat go dry. "She isn't with anyone, actually."

"Don't tell me you're going into the flesh-peddling business?" he laughed good-naturedly.

The phrase stung.

"No, she has a manager. I'll have him call you."

"No rush, the first week in January would be fine. And I appreciate your thinking of me."

"Well, you're my friend, aren't you?" She tried to sound pleasant.

"Haven't changed your mind about my offer, have you?"

"You'll be the first to know if I do."

She hung up and stared at the phone. David should not have done it. They were going to open an agency and talked about it constantly, but it was still a ways off. But what made it worse was that if Megan got the job, Jeannie Lester would be out. As estranged as she felt from Pamela, Cat did not want to hurt her or do anything underhanded where she was concerned. Besides, Cat herself was still signed up with the Fitzpatrick Agency.

She picked up the phone and dialed David's number.

"Hi, beautiful." David sounded happy.

"Who the hell gave you permission to send Grayson Megan's pictures?" she said unceremoniously.

"Hold it, Cat." His tone changed. "What happened?"

"Dan Grayson just called and thanked me for sending him her pictures and you know I did no such thing."

"What else did he say?"

"What difference does it make? We're not in business yet. Besides you know the front runner for the Chameleon campaign is Jeannie Lester and she's with Pamela and I told you I won't do anything like that to Pamela."

"She'd do it to you," he said jeeringly. "But that's not the point. What's important is that Grayson obviously liked Megan's pictures and that means he's considering her for the ad campaign, right?"

"David, I'm not ready to quit Pamela," she hissed through clenched teeth. "Opening an agency is all very well and fine. I want it and you know I'm keeping my eyes open to what's around, but what I'm earning as a model at the moment barely pays the bills around this house. It certainly leaves nothing over with which to go to the expense of opening offices and all the rest."

"Afford it or not, it didn't stop you from getting Megan to do the Bo layout for *Harper's Bazaar*. Just as you went right ahead and got her the fur ad for Maximilian. Not to mention the cover for the French magazine. And the grapevine has it that several Italian editors are panting to have her. That little press agent of hers is a genius with all that religious garbage and she's fast becoming the hottest item around."

"It's not garbage. She is religious," Cat said indignantly.

"Who cares?" David laughed her statement off. "It works and she's going to be a big moneymaker. Every one of the jobs you've gotten her is commissionable, you know, and I wanted to talk to you about it, but it was all chicken feed and I figured it wasn't serious. But the Grayson deal can mean big money, for her and for the agency she's tied up with."

Cat listened carefully. She had done every one of the things David mentioned, but she had done it out of pique, trying to show Pamela up. She was certainly not in a position to take a commission from Megan or from Mel Black.

"You mean, you want me to sign her up now?" The idea was distasteful.

"Yes, that's exactly what I mean. Sign her up; make it official that you represent her." He stopped abruptly. "But if you're not interested, forget it." He caught his breath. "Oh, shit, Cat. I was just thinking of you and our future."

"I am interested." Her anger was dissipated. "It's just that you're rushing me."

"No. Let's drop the whole thing." He sounded indifferent. "Now, I've got to run. Pamela's back and she wants me to come over. So, as they say, I'll be talking to you."

"Pamela is back?" Cat gasped.

"Yes, she came back last night."

"Is she giving a Christmas party?"

"I think so," he said matter-of-factly. "Cat, I'm really rushed."

"Don't hang up," she pleaded.

"What else is there to say?"

"Look, why don't you come by on Sunday. I'll have Megan over and we'll talk." The words tumbled out before she could stop herself.

"You mean your mother is no longer living with you?" he asked sarcastically.

"It'll be all right." She became flustered.

"What time?" His voice softened.

"Make it around four for drinks."

She regretted her impulsive outburst but could not retract it. Although her mother had never mentioned David after that first meeting, Cat did not want another encounter. But that was not the only reason for keeping David away. Since leaving Brooklyn, she had kept her two worlds separate. She worked hard at creating an image which she presented to the world, and Clara Wallenstein was not the mother of that image.

She looked down at her hand still resting on the phone, and the reason for her call to David came back to her. He was wrong to send the pictures to Dan without consulting with her, but then again, if Megan got the account it would mean that they would have the money to start their agency. He was her friend and he had done it for them both. She could not afford to lose his friendship now.

"Who was that?" Cat's head jerked up in surprise when she heard her mother's voice. She turned quickly and saw Clara walking laboriously toward her armchair, which had been brought from Brooklyn.

Finally settled, Clara leaned forward and took her needlepoint from the massive wooden sewing box which stood at the foot of the chair. The sight of the aging woman sitting in her chair, working on the canvas, angered Cat. Neither her mother nor her mother's furniture belonged in her living room. They were out of place in her home and in her life. Everything she had worked for was somehow wiped away, almost within days of Clara's arrival.

"Who was that on the phone?" Clara repeated her question.

"Just a friend," Cat answered noncommittally, wondering how much of the conversation her mother had overheard.

"Hardly a friendly conversation, though." Clara did not look up.

"A slight misunderstanding." Cat kept her voice light.

"It sounded to me as though you're being pushed to do something you don't want to do."

"Mother, it's really nothing," she said pleasantly. "Incidentally, I'm having a couple of friends over for drinks on Sunday."

"How nice. Anybody I know?"

"As a matter of fact, you know the man. You met him the first time you came up here."

Clara stopped working and looked up. "Oh, the young man with the pretty face?"

"Mother, stop it." Cat tried to laugh it off. "He's a very good friend and he's much more than a young man with a pretty face. I work with him and he's been of great help to me." She hesitated for a minute before continuing. "As a matter of fact, we're working on a project which can lead to a big business."

"Well, I certainly hope he's not the only one you're going to depend on."

"It's really a very big project and I'm quite excited about it." Cat decided to ignore the remark.

Clara did not take her eyes off her daughter.

"Which reminds me, I might be giving a Christmas party. I think everything will be ready by then." Cat spoke quickly, almost slurring her words.

"A Christmas party?" Clara tried to keep the shock out of her voice.

"Well, you know what I mean. Christmas, Hanukkah, house-warming."

"You wouldn't actually have a Christmas tree?"

"I might." She was being childish but she could not stop herself.

"Have you ever had one?" Clara's voice was barely audible.

"No, but most of the people who'll be invited would probably expect it."

"I doubt it." Clara picked up her needlepoint work again. "Although that young man probably would." She paused briefly. "Yes, I can see where you would do something that would actually be out of character to impress him." She spoke with unusual calm but the viciousness with which she pierced the canvas gave away her full anger.

"That's absurd," Cat stammered. "David would be the last one to care."

"Yes, that's his name, David. David Thomas, if I'm not mistaken."

"Let's drop this idiotic conversation," Cat suggested, feeling that what had started as an unimportant exchange was turning into a confrontation.

"Not idiotic at all. You're feeling lonely and afraid of growing old and you're reaching out for companionship. It's understandable but your choice is what's so sad."

"For God's sake, Mother, what could you possibly have against a young man you don't even know?" She tried to sound reasonable. "I'm a grown woman and I know what I'm doing."

"Yes, you're a grown woman but I should have thought that by now you would have learned to choose your friends more carefully."

"What's wrong with David Thomas?"

"What's right about him?"

"I told you. He's part of my work. He's bright, charming, knows lots of people and he's trying to help me with my career."

"I doubt it," Clara said evenly. "Your Mr. Thomas is a nobody. At best he's a lap dog, at worst he's a paid gigolo."

Cat clenched her fists, trying to control herself.

"What brought this whole thing on?" she asked, when she felt she could speak naturally.

"I just think Mr. Thomas is all wrong for you," Clara said slowly. "What I see is that you're reaching out for a relationship which must in the end hurt you. He's from a different world and has different values."

"He's from a world I work in, and live in, a world I understand and which he does, too."

"That's not what I'm talking about." Clara paused briefly. "Who is he? Where is he from?"

"Frankly, I don't know, but what difference does it make?" She stopped abruptly. "Wait a minute, are you talking about his not being Jewish?" She began to laugh. "I'm not planning on marrying him, you know. But even if I were, it would make no difference."

"Wouldn't it?"

"Mother, this is the second half of the twentieth century. I'm past thirty. Have you any idea how ridiculous you sound?"

"You are who you are no matter how old you are."

"I didn't ask to be born Jewish, you know."

"Neither did I," Clara snapped back, "but we were and to try to ignore it by reaching out to a Mr. Thomas can hurt you deeply."

"Stop it!" Cat screamed. "Did it ever occur to you that I hate being Jewish and I always did?"

"That's not true." The older woman was trying to hide her hurt by lowering her eyes and concentrating on her needlepoint.

"Of course it's true. I didn't just move out of Brooklyn. I moved out of everything it represented. I didn't just change my name, I changed inside. Why do you think I kept Alexandra away from there?" She had lost control, but could not stop. "Sure, I made all those stupid excuses as to why we stopped visiting you, but the truth is that I wanted to spare her the misery that you and everyone around that neighborhood lives in. Rules and regulations dragged out of some ancient past which have nothing to do with today's world. Being different, different, different, at all cost, no matter how difficult. I am Cat Willingham and I make my rules and they don't hurt anyone."

"That's a fine speech, Catherine Wallenstein, but in the final analysis, it won't be you who decides who you are. There's a world out there that makes that decision."

"And damn it, that's the world I want to belong to."

The words were out and she knew she had gone too far. She stopped and waited.

Clara raised her eyes slowly and stared silently at her.

For a brief moment Cat felt elated. She felt liberated. She had worded all that the child in Brooklyn had never dared say. But within seconds the familiar sense of guilt returned and shattered her. Frantically, she ran from the room.

Once in her bedroom, she felt a deep sense of loss and could not understand where the feeling came from. Slowly she crawled into bed and pulled the cover over her, wanting to wipe away the dreadful scene which had just taken place.

27

Cat rolled over on her back and realized she had dozed off since it was now quite dark. Slowly, as consciousness returned, a feeling of emptiness rose in her accompanied again by the dreadful feeling of loss, although she still could not pinpoint what it was she had lost. Was it her youth? Her innocence? Her looks? Her mother's love? She had never had that love. Yet, in the last few weeks, a warmth and acceptance had developed between them and it had given her a feeling of well-being. Now suddenly, out of nowhere, the pent-up rage, which she had hoped had been put to rest, rose and splattered the house with a venom she could not explain.

The scene with Clara returned to pound in her ears. Her words were harsh, harsher than she had meant them to be and she could not understand what had triggered them. What had caused her to lash out so viciously at being Jewish, when she knew how much it meant to her mother?

It had nothing to do with David per se. Or even the talk about the Christmas tree. It was the combination of both which represented a foreign world to Clara.

Turning on the light Cat walked over to her dresser and opened a drawer. From under several layers of sheer undergarments she brought out her safe deposit box and opened it. It contained some documents and a framed picture of her father as a young man, a prayer shawl draped around his shoulders, and he was standing next to his regal-looking mother. Beneath it all lay a small brown sack. Removing it from the box, she reached into it and took out a tiny dusty Santa Claus.

She had bought it when she was six years old. She remembered being in an enormous department store filled with radiant decorations. The place was crowded and everyone seemed to be full of electricity like the flashing colorful lights on the tinseled tree. Trailing behind her mother she watched a group of babbling, happy children who were standing in line waiting to talk to a man with long white whiskers, dressed in a red fur-trimmed suit. Their excitement was contagious.

"May I stay here and watch?" she asked.

Her mother hesitated. "All right, but don't move away from this spot until I come back."

The warning made her recall her mother's other warning—forbidding her to talk about something called Christmas. "That's a foreign holiday which we do not celebrate."

The decorated trees, trimmed with gold and silver tinsel, filled her with joy, and the incandescent lights seemed to be winking at her. She wanted it all, but mostly she wanted the round beautiful balls of dazzling colors which glittered and reflected magic and dreams. Putting her hand in her coat pocket she took out the money she had received for Hanukkah and looked around furtively. Then, as though in a trance, she walked toward the counter where the enchanted ornaments waited. She picked one up and was amazed and delighted at how light it was—light and delicate and yet so brilliant.

"It is for my tree," she said, watching the salesman place it in a small brown sack.

"And here is a little present for you," he said, throwing in a miniature figure of Santa Claus.

She looked back at the squealing, joyful children. Now she belonged.

Her mother was laden with packages and Cat was forced to sit next to the taxi driver. Tenderly she put her hand on her bag.

As soon as they arrived in front of their house, she jumped out and ran up the stoop. She missed a step and fell to the ground. She felt no pain. She only heard the faint, sickening crunching sound inside the bag.

It had happened thirty years ago and Cat, looking down at the miniature doll, wondered if the powder clinging to it was dust or the remains of the Christmas ornament which had broken so easily.

"That's a foreign holiday which we do not celebrate."

That was what the fight had been about. Her mother was trying to pull her back from her new world. David and the talk of the Christmas tree were part of a world Cat had been living with for a long time. She did not want to go back.

Still holding the doll, Cat looked down at the framed picture of her father and grandmother. Her father was staring directly into the camera and her grandmother was looking up at her son with love and pride. They were both dead, yet even in the ancient yellowing picture Cat could feel their dignity and their love for each other. It survived.

She pressed her memory back. There was a time when her father looked at her with pride and love. Even when it turned to pity, she still hoped for that love. But then he died and the world she lived in turned sad and full of tears and she wanted to escape. He had abandoned her and she could not bear the pain.

She fondled the small doll in her hand. It represented that different world which she wanted to belong to. It had accepted her, she was part of it. Or was it possible that her standing with it would prove to be as fragile as the delicate Christmas ball?

Cat turned her face away and caught sight of herself in the large mirror. She almost did not recognize herself.

The dreadful sense of loss returned. A tear rolled down the side of her face, then another. She did not wipe them away. She was alone, absolutely alone and one of the few privileges it offered was that she could permit the pent-up feelings to be released. She did not know why she was crying.

A gentle knock on her door made Cat wipe her eyes before opening it.

"Miss Catherine," Emma was standing at the door, "there is a Mr. Black on the phone."

Picking up the phone, it occurred to her that she had not spoken to him in quite a long time.

"How are you?" she asked pleasantly.

"How can a press agent be when he has nuts for clients?" he answered and laughed. "Not that I'm complaining. The nuts bring in more money than the normal ones. But that's not what I'm calling about. It's Megan."

"What about her?" Cat asked suspiciously. She did not like his tone.

"She's going to perform in some variety show off-off-Broadway. You know, in one of those crazy places and I'm against it."

"Megan is going to act in a play?" Cat gasped.

"My attitude precisely, but I can't talk her out of it. And frankly, if I didn't have a movie deal in the works for her, I'd drop her like a hot potato."

"Oh, Mel, come on. Who's going to see her in it?" Cat protested.

"I don't really give a shit. No one is going to hire her for her talent, I know that. The truth is," he paused with embarrassment, "the money is drying up and she's beginning to cost me a bundle."

"What are you talking about?" Cat tried to sound composed. She needed Mel at this point. He was her front where Megan was concerned. Although she was responsible for most of Megan's assignments, it was Mel who was considered her representative and Cat was looked on as a concerned friend.

"I'll level with you," Mel said. "I had a deal with a friend of hers back in her hometown who was paying the bills. I don't know the man, but he sent in a monthly check for her support. I didn't figure it to be a bad deal for him, since I still think she's gonna make it. But now he's upset about all that religious publicity and he's cutting out."

"Who's the man?" Cat asked.

"I'm a press agent but I'm also a gentleman." Mel assumed a virtuous manner. "So you see, kid, if I don't get that movie deal, which I'll know about this weekend, and if there's no more money from home, plus the fact that she's too dumb to listen to my advice, who needs it?"

"What can I do?" Cat asked haltingly.

"Try to talk her out of doing that show, for starters. And pray that she gets the movie contract."

"When is the show taking place?"

"This Sunday, at five in the afternoon."

"Are you going?"

"Ya got to be kidding."

"I'll talk to her," Cat said quietly. "And let me know what happens with the movie deal."

When she hung up she wondered if she should call David but decided against it. If she could not talk Megan out of doing the show, she and David would go down together and see her at the theater. She was pleased she had not mentioned the Dan Grayson possibility to Mel. He was obviously not concerned about Megan and she would simply have to figure out another way of handling Megan until she opened her agency.

28

David awoke with a start. He sat up in bed and felt the perspiration running down his back. It was still dark and he looked over at the clock on the bedside table. It was 5:30 A.M. Automatically he reached over for a cigarette, lit it and lay back on the pillow. He felt apprehensive and could not understand why. He looked around. He was in his own room, in his own bed, yet something had shaken him out of his sleep. It was a dream, one of several recurrent dreams which haunted him. As always, he was alone, isolated and terrified. This time, however, there was something else. He pressed his memory. . . . He was in a casket. No, it was a vase . . . an urn. That was it! He was trapped in an urn. The urn lent a new twist to the nightmare and he felt stifled.

Dawn was beginning to come through the window and David realized it was raining. It would be a grim, cloudy day. Somehow he had expected it to be sunny. His eyes wandered over to Megan's picture, which he had hung over his bed. He'd been living with her image since the day he first saw her picture on Cat's terrace and had been trying to understand what it was about her that caused him to react so violently. She was beautiful, but there were other beautiful girls around. He certainly did not desire her physically. If anything, the mere thought of going to bed with her made him tremble with horror. Yet he felt a need for her, a need to be around her, to be with her. Her success would ensure her presence in his life. But he could not make it happen alone. For that he needed Cat. And this was going to be the day when he would force Cat to make the commitment which would bind his future to Megan.

Thoughts of Cat angered him. She was so indecisive, so frightened, so insecure. He had such high hopes when they first discussed their plans. They had to move cautiously, which was right. But that was before Megan came on the scene. Setting up the agency, now, was a matter which had to be attended to without delay.

The room was suddenly hot and David climbed out of bed. His head began to spin and he rushed over to the window and opened it wide, hoping the fresh air would cleanse away some of his unhappiness. The instant of daybreak passed and he stood staring at the vacant street below. The muted gray buildings became clearer as the fog rose from their rooftops, exposing them in their full ugliness. Even the rain did not seem to clean away the deep-rooted dirt which the years had etched into the very marrow of the brick. They would stand as they were for many more years until they caved in and the people within them would be squashed under the rubble. The misery which he felt minutes before grew worse. He refused to be buried with them.

He crawled back into bed.

When he next woke it was past three in the afternoon. He dressed quickly and ran out of his apartment.

The rain was coming down furiously as he hurried down First Avenue. The shops he passed were locked and barred against the unprecedented and outrageous thievery which was growing commonplace in this section of the city. Except for a few people walking by quickly, the neighborhood was deserted.

When he had moved here after arriving in the city he was only concerned with the idea that it was more fashionable to live on the East Side. It did not take him long to discover he lived too far uptown and too far east. Anyone in the know understood that. He lived on the fringe. The thought infuriated him. He lived on the fringe of everything. He hastened his step. He was fed up with living on the sideline. It had to come to an end. He had to see Cat alone before Megan arrived. She was the one who could help him enter a world he longed for.

A clock was striking four as Cat's house came into view.

"Good morning, Mr. Thomas." The doorman tipped his hat. The greeting of the building staff always pleased him. The doormen, the elevator operators, the other attendants had accepted him as part of Cat's household. He had not been around for a while, but they had not forgotten him. Being whisked up to Cat's apartment he felt calmer.

Ringing the doorbell, David tapped his foot impatiently. Somehow he had to force Cat into making a decision.

The door was opened by a wizened old lady whom David assumed was Emma. She looked at him suspiciously.

"I'm David Thomas and Miss Willingham is expecting me."

She moved aside slowly, never taking her eyes off him. It made him uncomfortable. Briskly he walked into the living room and for a minute he thought he was in the wrong apartment. The added pieces of furniture had distorted the decor, but that was not the only difference. The atmosphere had undergone a complete transformation. It was no longer Cat's living room.

"Miss Catherine is going to be with you in a minute. She's with the doctor in her mother's room." Emma seemed to be standing guard in the doorway.

David ignored her and wandered aimlessly around, looking at the aged wooden sewing box and examining the various bric-a-brac which had been placed around. A small framed picture caught his eye and he picked it up. It looked like a photograph taken on Coney Island where people were placed behind a cardboard on which turn-of-the-century figures were painted dressed in the fashion of the day. He thought he recognized Cat. He had no idea who the young man was.

"Hello, David." Cat's voice was soft and filled with warmth.

"That's a great picture of you. Who's the boy?"

"That's my grandmother and my father," Cat laughed. "But how flattering of you to say so. I think she's gorgeous. I always did."

"The resemblance is uncanny."

"I wish it were." She came over to him and kissed him lightly on the cheek. He could feel her tension the minute he touched her.

"You okay?" he asked, and before she could answer he saw Clara walk into the room on the arm of an elderly, bearded man.

"Mother, you remember David Thomas, don't you?" The strain in Cat's voice was obvious.

"Mr. Thomas." Clara came closer and stretched out her hand graciously. "Of course I remember him. How could anyone forget such a handsome face."

David bowed his head slightly and shook the extended hand. "Thank you for having me." He raised his head and looked directly at her. For a moment their eyes held. The hate which he saw staring at him shook him.

"And this," Cat said, quickly turning to the man who was standing next to Clara, "is Dr. Mark Goodwin."

David shook the doctor's hand and scrutinized him carefully. Cat had told him about Mark but he'd never really listened, assuming the man was an old portly doctor who was simply a friend of the family. He was in fact old, but there was a vibrancy and sensuality about him which made David uncomfortable. He disliked him immediately and was surprised that he reacted so violently to someone he had just met.

"Delighted to meet you," Mark said agreeably.

"Let me get you a drink, David," Cat said. It seemed as though she had held her breath throughout the introduction. "How about you, Mark? A drink or some tea?"

"Tea would be nice." Mark smiled warmly at Cat.

There was a feeling of family about these people, David thought, and he resented them. He had never looked on Cat as a stranger, but standing in the company of her mother and the doctor, she appeared different.

"I'll help you." David rushed after Cat, who was heading for the kitchen. He wanted to get away from Mrs. Wallenstein and the doctor.

"When's Megan coming?" he asked when Cat handed him his drink.

"She's not, but it's okay," she continued hurriedly. "We'll be seeing her later." She started busying herself with preparing the tea. "The truth is, I've got a surprise for you," she said with her back to David. "Megan is appearing in a play this afternoon and I promised Mel we'd go."

"A play? A stage play?" David started to laugh but caught himself.

"I tried to talk her out of it but there was no way. She wants to be a big star." Cat tried to smile. "You will come, won't you? And I figured we'd talk to her afterward."

"What time is this thing going on?" he asked, knowing he had to meet Pamela at her office at six. "And where is it?"

"It starts at five and I've got the address written down. It's somewhere near the Bowery."

"Will it be a disaster?" he asked after a moment. Megan had to be established as a model first, not an actress. By the time he and Cat were ready to go public, Megan had to be the hottest model around.

"With friends like you and Mel, she doesn't need enemies," Cat said bitingly.

"What's that supposed to mean?"

"He's hoping for a Hollywood contract and he didn't want her to do this thing."

Megan going off to California! David felt sick.

Clara's voice could be heard calling for Cat and he felt Cat's eyes staring at him intently. He tried to relax.

"We'd better get out there," Cat said, and started out of the kitchen.

David caught her arm. "Don't you and I have to talk seriously before we meet with Megan?"

"We will," she said pleasantly. "As a matter of fact, I've thought about it and I've got a plan of action all worked out." She continued with assurance, "I even figured out where to get the money. So just give me a little more time and trust me, David. I know what I'm doing." She smiled encouragingly. "Now, come along and be sociable for a few minutes. We don't have much time."

Preceding him into the living room, Cat was amazed at how easily she had lied to David. She had no idea where to get the money for the agency but she knew she had to hold on to David's interest.

29

The theater turned out to be a converted Chinese movie house and the neighborhood was teeming with people. A huge picture of Megan, dressed in nun's garb, was displayed out front and was totally incongruous with the surroundings.

"Oh my God," Cat whispered.

"What is she playing, the Virgin?" David asked sarcastically, but his voice betrayed his unhappiness.

"I don't know anything about it. As far as I knew this was some sort of a variety show."

The curtain had just gone up when David and Cat sat down in the back row of the shabby theater and found themselves watching a juggler doing his routine. The juggling act was followed by a skit dealing with pornography. The audience was loud and vulgar and David looked over at Cat in disbelief. She seemed equally uncomfortable. He wanted to leave but knew he had to stay until Megan appeared. He hoped it would be soon since he could not be too late getting to Pamela's office. Suddenly a hush fell over the audience and the stage darkened. He turned his attention back to the stage. Megan, dressed in a simple black dress, was kneeling center stage, talking to an unseen vision in what appeared to be a cave or grotto. She was alone and was completely immersed in the role of a young St. Bernadette. Her exquisite face glowed under the spotlight, which enhanced her saintly appearance. As her monologue began to unfold, so did the soul and spiritual beauty of the character she was portraying. The audience, which had been silenced by Megan's appearance, grew restless and then began to laugh, drowning out Megan's voice. When she finished the scene and left the stage, no one applauded.

David was stunned. He grabbed Cat's hand and they ran out of the theater just as a comedian began his routine.

"What the hell was that all about?" David asked when they were out on the street.

"I don't know," Cat whispered. Her thoughts came and went before any of them could take form. "It was brilliant, but it didn't seem real," she said finally. She had accepted Megan's beauty and eventual success as a model. She was unable to deal with her talent.

"It was the most impressive performance I've seen in quite a while," David said.

"That was the real Megan," Cat said without thinking, and realized instantly that it explained the phenomenon they had just witnessed. "Of course, that's it. We saw Megan tonight. All of her. She wasn't acting at all. She was playing herself." Cat did not bother to hide her relief.

"Is she an actress?" David asked slowly.

"That would depend on how many Bernadettes you can find in plays." After a pause, she added, "No, the truth is she's not. What we saw just now was it. I don't think she could even repeat what she did this afternoon. She simply does not have the inner resources nor the taste of selection."

"What the hell does that mean?" David asked with annoyance.

"Extracting, removing what is superfluous and adding what is important." She spoke slowly, trying to explain something which Bo and Pamela had taught her many years back and which she had not been applying to herself in recent months. The realization bothered her and she forced her mind to return to the conversation at hand. "Anyway, I'm really glad we came," she said finally. "It explains so much about her."

"Good or bad?"

"For whom?"

"Does it help her or doesn't it?"

"In her career or in her personal life?"

"You know what I'm talking about," David said impatiently.

"Let me put it this way. It would be absurd if someone saw her in this performance and thought she could do any other role," Cat answered soberly. "If she were given a role she could not handle, it would be a disaster." She paused briefly. "It could destroy her."

David remained silent. Megan was crucial to him and he refused to accept what Cat was saying. Megan was not going to be destroyed. He would make her a famous model and then he, David, would get her a movie contract. She would become famous and rich and he would be at her side.

"A penny for your thoughts." Cat touched his arm.

"They're not worth even that," he said flippantly. Then realizing his rudeness, he smiled. "I agree that we did the right thing by coming. Now what say we go back and congratulate the star?"

"No," Cat replied quickly. "No, David, I think we should leave her alone this evening."

For no apparent reason, she recalled David's expression the first time he saw Megan's pictures and she felt a need to protect Megan. She felt responsible for her in the same way she did for Alexandra.

"David, I don't know why, but I'm frightened," Cat whispered.

"I'll tell you what you're frightened of," David said angrily. "You're frightened of making a commitment. To Megan, to me, to yourself. Remember, we were going to talk to Megan about signing up with us?"

Cat was silent.

"Well, I'm not frightened and I intend to go backstage and tell her we saw her and enjoyed her performance. Then I'm going to discuss her future with her, just as we planned. She may not be much of an actress, but she sure as hell is going to be the hottest model in this city and I intend to be around when that happens."

"Please, David, not right now," Cat pleaded.

"You're behaving like a child and I'm damned if I know what's gotten into you."

"I'm not going in," Cat said stubbornly.

"As you wish." He turned quickly and ran into the theater.

Cat hesitated for a moment and then, as though compelled by some unknown force, ran in after him.

As unsavory as the front of the theater was, backstage was worse. Performers were standing around drinking and laughing loudly, throwing empty cans on the floor, oblivious to the fact that the show was still in progress. The scent of pot was overwhelming.

They found Megan sitting on a bench in a large empty dressing room, looking forlorn. She looked up when they came in. She had obviously been crying.

"You were wonderful, Megan," Cat said, sitting down beside her and taking her hand.

"You're not angry?"

"Why on earth would we be?" Cat asked.

"They shouldn't have used that picture of me out there," Megan said, and tears started streaming down her cheeks. "I thought they were going to use one of the pictures Greg took."

Cat felt uneasy as she looked over at David, who appeared equally puzzled. The picture out front seemed like the least of what had gone wrong for Megan.

"My mom is angry that I don't seem to be taking my religion seriously enough."

"Oh, you spoke to your mother?" Cat asked with interest. Megan was very secretive about her background, except for talking about how much Cora Baynes meant to her.

"No, but Jeb Kimbrough called to tell me she's upset."

"Would you like me to call your mother or Mr. Kimbrough?" Cat asked haltingly. Megan was more of an enigma than ever. A conversation with people who knew her might clear up some of the mystery.

"Oh no!" It was a vulgar shriek and Cat was taken aback. "Please, please don't!" The little girl quality returned. "Cat, swear to me that you'll never call my mother. She'd worry herself sick if you did. And Jeb would be so upset."

Cat nodded.

"Megan, who got you into this thing here, anyway?" David asked suddenly.

"Well, you know, with the publicity which Mel got me, all sorts of people have been calling, and Mel was handling everything. But this man, he's from the South, and he came to my house, said he was a producer and told me I could do any part I wanted."

"And?" David said impatiently.

"Well, I've always wanted to be St. Bernadette," she said breathlessly. "And he paid me two hundred dollars to do two performances."

"You're not planning on doing another," David said cautiously.

"Didn't you like it?" Megan looked hurt.

"You were very, very good, honey, but I think your mother is right. And that picture out there could harm your career," Cat said patiently. She was upset at Megan's lack of understanding of what had actually taken place while she was on stage. It was Megan's hysterical, vulgar outburst, however, which rattled Cat most. Clay's comment about Megan looking as though she'd had a hard life came back to her.

"If you think so, then I won't do it," Megan acquiesced immediately. "But won't the producer be angry? And will I have to give back the money?"

"I'll get you out of it if I can find him," David said with assurance. Cat was convinced he was right. Whoever the man was, he had probably gotten paid for getting Megan to appear and was no longer around.

Megan smiled for the first time. "You know that you two are my dearest and most trusted friends. Except for Mel, of course."

"That's sweet," Cat said nervously, "but you must know that no one is completely dependable." She was thinking of Mel deserting Megan and wondering how the girl would react when she found out. "We're all only human."

"Did I say something wrong?" Megan asked, sensing Cat's restless mood.

"No, of course not," David intervened. "You can depend on Cat and you can certainly depend on me." He took hold of Megan's free hand and held it firmly in his.

Guiltily, Cat placed her arm around Megan's shoulder. "Actually, David is right. You can depend on us. We are your friends."

Megan looked from Cat to David and back to Cat. "If you can really get me out of doing tomorrow's performance and I don't have to give back the money, then I can go to Queens tonight."

"What's in Queens?" David demanded.

"I'm going to spend the holidays with the sisters in their convent. Someday I hope I can become a nun." She stood up and she was beaming. "I was going to go tomorrow, but now I can go today."

"What's this about becoming a nun?" David choked the words out with difficulty. "What about your career?"

"It won't happen for a while. But I wish I could get a movie contract soon. It's taking forever."

"Megan, let's not go through that again. Your modeling career is moving well and I know that in the end it's your best way of getting into the movies," Cat said firmly.

Megan smiled at Cat. "It's because I believe you that I'm working so hard at modeling." Then, with practiced ease, she removed the nun's headdress and slipped into a long, simple black coat. "I'm going now, and won't the sisters be surprised that I came early?" She sounded like a little girl.

"Would you like me to take you there?" David asked.

"Oh no," Megan said firmly, "I must go alone."

"David," Cat spoke up, "this is obviously a personal matter between Megan and her faith."

Megan looked at Cat gratefully and threw her arms around Cat and hugged her, much as she had the first time they met. "I love you almost as much as I love my mom," she whispered emotionally.

The awkward silence which followed Megan's departure infuriated Cat. She watched David begin to pace and suddenly she wondered if David was in love with Megan. The idea shook her. It was not that she was in love with him, but somehow she had never thought of the relationship between David and Megan as anything other than a business affair. It also dawned on Cat that his great concern for her future had nothing to do with her and was motivated by his interest in Megan. The idea was humiliating.

"I just don't understand what's going on," David broke into her thoughts. "Weird is weird, but this is complete nuttiness," he hissed. "The sisters will probably persuade her to join the convent now just so they can exploit her."

"She's being exploited anyway, so why not for something she believes in," Cat said quietly. "Weren't we going to exploit her?" She bit her lip as the truth of what she said struck her.

"That's nonsense. She stood to make a great deal of money with us," David shot back. "Which brings me full circle. Where the hell does that leave us?"

"You mean where the agency is concerned?" she asked with interest.

"Of course."

"Nowhere different than where we were a few hours ago."

"What's that supposed to mean? Megan is our drawing card, Cat, and don't you forget it."

"Megan will never be a nun," Cat said slowly. "The church was not created to take in people who want to run away from life."

"Is that what she's doing?"

"I think so," Cat said and somehow she knew she was right.

They walked out of the theater, each absorbed in their own thoughts. Once outside, Cat looked over at David. She could barely see his face in the dim light, but his pain was evident. She wanted to ask him how he felt about Megan but was too frightened of the answer.

"David, I think we should rethink about working with Megan," she said instead. "There are many girls we can find who could be as sensational as she is. I'm sure of it."

"If you say so," he answered, and without another word he turned and walked rapidly down the street. He seemed to have forgotten she was there.

Cat stood for a long time looking after the disappearing figure. She was upset about Megan, but David's reaction was far more devastating.

It was now quite dark and the streetlights came on. Cat looked around and realized she was in a bad part of town. She started walking. The pain, frustration and feelings of dejection were unbearable and she barely noticed that people were jostling her.

She was unaware of time passing when suddenly she found herself on a deserted street, in an unfamiliar shabby neighborhood. She wondered why she was not afraid. She looked up at the sky. It was black with heavy clouds almost touching the rooftops of the dilapidated houses. The silence around was ominous and she felt as though she were the last survivor on earth. She felt completely abandoned. Everybody she cared for had deserted her: Jeff, Alexandra, David, her father. Even Clay did not really want her.

Suddenly she heard someone cry out, "Somebody please love me." She looked around but saw no one. Her throat was aching and she wondered if it was she who had spoken. Then an echo came rushing back at her. "Somebody please love me." She recognized her voice.

30

David hailed a cab and settled back after giving the driver Pamela's office address. He was aware that he had run out on Cat, left her alone on a deserted street, but he had to get away from her, from the theater, from the whole scene which he found himself embroiled in. Seeing Megan on stage, followed by her strange behavior in the dressing room after the performance, discombobulated him. Cat was of no help, with her exaggerated motherly concern and thumbnail analysis. He needed time to think, be brought back to reality. Pamela was real, the only realistic player in the game. He stared out the cab window, wondering if she would still be there when he arrived. It was important for him to see her, talk to her, be with her. The loathing he felt for her only hours before was forgotten.

It was nearly seven o'clock when he walked into the office.

"Hi, Pamela," he said pleasantly. The room was thick with smoke and the pungent odor of her Turkish tobacco filled the air.

She was sitting at her desk, systematically sorting through a pile of paper. When she heard him, she glanced up briefly, nodded her head and continued with her work.

David felt better the minute he saw her in spite of her obvious displeasure. Throwing himself into an armchair, he spread his legs wide before him and stared at her. She could still be a good-looking woman, he thought, if she'd drop that bitchy, petulant look. He watched the overshot chin, fascinated by the movement of her strong jawbones as if she were grinding on a piece of hard candy.

"That's an elegant Givenchy you've got on today," he said finally, referring to the faultlessly tailored suit she was wearing. He knew she would be pleased he had recognized the designer. Pamela was impressed with famous labels.

Again she looked up and smiled, then returned to what she was doing. She was obviously furious and he wondered what he could do to pacify her. He could think of nothing and his mind drifted back to Cat and Megan. Between Pamela and Cat, Pamela was the lesser of two evils. At least Pamela was paying him a weekly salary, whereas

Cat was making demands and giving little in return. Megan was a different matter. She had a great deal to offer. The Chameleon account could mean a lot of money. It could set him up on his own and he would be free of Pamela and of Cat. Then he remembered Cat saying something about Mel Black working on a movie contract for Megan. It would mean Megan would be going to California. He could not allow that to happen. He wanted Megan in New York.

"I'd like a light." Pamela's voice cut through his thoughts and David looked up startled. She was leaning back in her chair, a cigarette held between her thumb and forefinger.

He jumped up and lit it. She smiled her thanks and, opening up her desk drawer, she took out her flask and Limoges cup.

David returned the matches to his pocket and walked back to his seat as thoughts of Megan returned. Somehow he had to keep her in the city.

"Pamela," he started slowly, "I want to help someone but I can't do it alone. I need your help."

"You mean, darling, God helps those who help themselves to others' help." She sipped her drink slowly, observing him carefully.

"Something like that."

"Who is she?"

"A beautiful girl who I believe is going to make it," he said cautiously.

"Do I know her?"

"No."

"All right." Pamela's face was a mask of innocence. "Let's play three questions, shall we?" She finished her drink and poured herself another. "One, she's a model, and not with my agency, obviously. Two, she wants a job in the theater. Three, you want me to use my contacts to get it for her."

"One, she's a model and is doing extremely well. Two, it is I who want to get her a job in the theater. Three, right on." His mouth felt dry as he waited for Pamela to speak. He was acting impulsively and had not thought out the consequences of his request.

"Tell me more, Davie," Pamela said, knowing he hated to be called by the diminutive form of his name. "Why do you want to help her?" She paused briefly. "She's not one of those poor little things from an orphanage whom you're trying to save." She was mocking him. "This is most unlike you."

"I don't know." His confusion mounted.

"Speak up, boy." Pamela's voice was biting and she hit the last word to emphasize her contempt.

"I said I don't really know why I want to help her." His mind was racing for a plausible answer but none came to mind. "But what difference does it make? Why does there have to be a special reason?"

"There's always a reason." She was enjoying his discomfort. "It'll come to you."

"What reason did you have for taking me on?" He was suddenly angry. "We both knew I wouldn't make it as a model."

"True."

"Then, why?"

"Because, my dear David, I know who you are. I knew who you were the minute I saw you." She spoke slowly, emphasizing every word. "You're a pale imitation of me and, at the risk of sounding immodest, even my watered-down counterparts don't grow on trees." She never took her eyes off him. "We're both insatiably hungry. Hungry for different reasons, mind you, but hungry, nevertheless."

"Hungry?"

"Ravenous." She grew serious. "We feed on other people's guts, on how they look, what they say, what they know and what they do. We're voyeurs and it pays off both financially and emotionally."

David did not want to listen but dared not interrupt.

"We live vicariously," Pamela continued. "Sort of like Dracula, only we're not as messy. No one sees the blood." She poured herself another drink, swung her chair around, so he could not see her face.

"That's because we dilute it with alcohol," he said furiously.

"Touché." Pamela turned back, pleased that he was angry. "Incidentally, what's her name?"

"Megan Baynes."

"Megan Baynes," Pamela repeated the name as though she were tasting a hot red pepper. "That's Cat's friend, the religious one who's getting all the publicity." She broke out into a loud, ugly laugh. "Oh no. That's too delicious, simply too delicious and very interesting." Then her face went blank, except for her eyes, which began moving around rapidly.

David realized that in his hysterical need to keep Megan in New York he had forgotten that Cat had shown Megan's pictures to Pamela. Would she now guess what he and Cat were up to?

"You didn't want her, remember?" David found his voice.

"I still don't."

"So I'm not really cutting into your domain and you're not interested in your models beyond their modeling careers anyway."

"True, true." She nodded. "Still, I hate competition." An uncomfortable silence followed. "Who's her agent, anyway?" Pamela asked as an afterthought.

"Mel Black." He shot the name out almost too quickly.

"Oh, Sammy Glick is expanding into another media," she sneered.

"Well, anything you can do would be nice." David got up and started pacing. It was a close call and he wanted to get on to a safer topic.

He lit a cigarette. "And how was your day? Do anything special?" Feeling more in control, he looked at her with pretended interest.

"Peter and I went to Vera Maxwell's house for cocktails."

"I thought Peter didn't care for the world of fashion and its people."

"Vera Maxwell is a brilliant designer and she also happens to be one of the most imaginative hostesses in the country."

"Who was there?" David asked, wondering if she would have taken him had he been at the office on time.

"Everybody from the publishing world and the entertainment world. Paley from CBS, Bill Buckley, Walter Cronkite, some big shots from California and several theatrical personalities," she answered with relish. "And Peter just adores Buckley. I couldn't get him to leave, he was having such a good time."

David bit his lip. That was the world he wanted to be close to. Peter talking to Bill Buckley. David wondered what they talked about. He tried to conjure up Peter's face but could not. In all the time he worked for Pamela, he only saw him occasionally when he brought Pamela home. Peter would greet them from the library door, as Pamela whisked David up to her study where he helped her with her column. It was almost as though she were embarrassed to have them spend time together. It had not bothered him before. Now it did.

"Did you get some great scoop for your column?" David asked in disdain.

"You don't really like my column, do you, David?" she asked, refilling her cup.

"Frankly, no," David answered without thinking.

"But why?" she asked mockingly.

He regretted his candid outburst but knew he had to answer. "For starters, I don't believe you have your heart in it. I've never been able to figure out why you write it."

"Oh, there are several good reasons." Her face took on a serious expression. "I am where I am because my name is known. As a woman who runs a modeling agency, I could just go so far, but when your name is in print, every day, you begin to have some clout. Not to mention the fact that prowling around the city I do get a pretty good idea of what's happening in our world and it's a way of keeping an eye on the models who are signed with me. At least the ones who earn the money. And believe it or not, it also gives me untold satisfaction."

"But your column is so unfocused. You write about everything and therefore nothing. It's not a gossip column. Your political comments are accurate but never complete. As for your fashion bits, what's fashion?"

"I'm delighted that you don't think it's a gossip column. I'm overjoyed at your statement about the political stuff, but don't sell the fashion world short."

"But, Pamela, the fashion world is such a small, insignificant one," David protested.

"Larger than you think and it's an indicative world. A very significant one. It's connected to how we live, think and behave. Fashion is not a frivolous theme. It's part of a wider culture which has an enormous impact on our lives and influences our whole way of living. It may appear small, but the way that little world goes, so will other little worlds go." Her smile widened, stretching her thin lips so that the redness disappeared almost completely. She looked like a snake ready to spit poison. "The people who make up fashion, going back to whoever designed the fig leaf through to what the executive lady of today wears, wield an enormous power. They have their finger on the pulse of what's going on. Even the crazies who contort their bodies to show off the latest fads are significant."

David did not believe a word she said. He was the one who typed up the items she dictated, and he could have sworn it meant nothing to her.

"As a matter of fact, I see myself as a social historian. Someone who is writing notes for future historians who will read what I wrote and get a picture of what this generation was all about. Why, I might even write a book someday."

David tried not to laugh. The idea of Pamela writing a book was completely ridiculous.

"Then I am the assistant social historian," he said seriously.

"No, my dear David. As of now you still only see yourself and are trying to fulfill your very petty little needs. You have no perspective." She squashed out her cigarette. "You may never get it."

"Hey, what brought on this lecture, anyway?" David asked, aware they had wandered away from the subject of the party.

"You asked me if I got a scoop for my column. And the fact is that I did get something quite marvelous out of it. I believe I've wrapped up the Chameleon account."

"Really? Who's the lucky girl?" David asked, trying to sound indifferent.

"Jeannie Lester. That's why I brought her over from London and kept her here all this time. I knew she'd be ideal."

"Have you signed on the dotted line?" Despite his shock, he succeeded in sounding indifferent.

"No, but I got word from the horse's mouth, so to speak, that it's all set."

"From Dan Grayson?"

"Oh, you are a quick learner, aren't you?" Pamela laughed almost gaily. "No, that would be getting it from the horse directly. I spoke to one of his top aides, which is just as good."

"I wouldn't bank on it," David said casually.

"What are you talking about?" Pamela got up angrily.

"Well, you've always said that until it's signed on the dotted line, it isn't final," he said innocently.

She eyed him suspiciously. "Do you know something I don't know?"

"No, Pamela, not really."

"Just remember, David. You work for me and don't you forget it." She turned quickly and started pushing papers into her ostrich leather attaché case.

David stood up. "Need me for anything else this evening?"

"Get the car and drive me home," she ordered. "That silly column has to be worked on tonight."

It was Sunday and he wanted to protest, but did not dare. He had succeeded in offending her and she was very angry. He also knew that he had talked too much.

With measured steps, he walked over to the phone and dialed the garage.

31

Peter Hazeltine came out of the library to greet Pamela and David as they entered the imposing townhouse in the East Eighties.

"What a lovely surprise!" he said graciously, putting his arm around Pamela's shoulder and pecking her on the cheek. "But, God, you look tired." There was real concern in his voice. Then looking over at David, he continued, "She's working much too hard. You really should try to slow her down."

"Not very likely." David smiled politely.

"New book?" Pamela asked, indicating to a book Peter was holding in his free hand.

"Yes, first edition," he said enthusiastically. "It's a gem. A real gem."

"Peter collects antique books," Pamela explained to no one in particular. She started removing her gloves and placed them along with her attaché case on the round Empire table which stood in the center of the oval-shaped foyer. Then she turned back to Peter. "When are you leaving for Washington?"

"I'm taking the ten o'clock shuttle. But I do have time for a drink. How about it?"

"Wonderful idea," she answered. "Let me just go up and get into something comfortable."

"Shall I bring them up to your study or will you come down?" Peter asked.

"I'll be down in a few minutes." She started up the cantilevered stairway and stopped midway. "Incidentally, Peter," she said without turning around, "David doesn't like my columns." Then she turned around slowly, "Especially the political items. He thinks they're incomplete. You did say that, didn't you?" She directed the question to David.

David felt himself blush.

"Do you agree, Peter?" she asked sweetly.

"As a matter of fact, I would say he's right on."

David, watching Pamela, could not figure out what game was being played but he knew it was a game, a vicious game. Pamela was now staring at Peter. David tried to decide what was going through her mind. She was no longer angry, nor was she amused. Husband and wife continued to stare at each other for a long moment. Peter had a friendly smile on his lips.

"Well, isn't that too bad," she said in a saccharine voice and rushed up the stairs.

At that moment it came to him. Peter wrote the column, Pamela rewrote it, and for some unknown reason she got the credit.

"Come along," Peter turned to David. "Let me fix those drinks."

David followed him into the walnut-paneled library but his thoughts were wrapped up in his new discovery. He knew nothing about their personal life and until this evening he did not care. He had assumed, as everyone did, that theirs was a marriage of convenience which had spanned many years and was too entangled to dissolve. What made no sense was why Peter was allowing Pamela to distort and misrepresent his ideas.

"What will it be?" Peter asked, opening the old wooden cabinet.

"Scotch straight, please," David said, looking around. He had been in the library before but never spent any time in it. He took the room in carefully. It was the kind of room he would want. The dark wood paneling, the massive desk, the big leather armchairs and bookcases lining most of the walls from floor to ceiling, all exuded an air of masculinity. It had no superfluous accessories except for a Limoges urn sitting on the wooden fireplace hearth. The sight of the urn made him gasp. That was the urn in his dream.

"Pamela does look tired," Peter repeated his concern as he poured the drinks.

"Yes, I guess she does," David murmured, trying to get a hold of himself. "But a good night's rest and she'll be refreshed in the morning."

Peter nodded his head in agreement. "Of course, you're right." He smiled warmly as he handed David his drink.

David took a sip and observed his host. His clothing was meticulous, his manner perfect, his posture correct and when he smiled, David noted that his teeth were white and flawless. Everything about him was right, which made him more of an enigma, and made everything that was happening more sinister. It was even difficult to guess his age. He was not old nor was he young, not ugly nor handsome, neither short nor tall. David tried to pinpoint his impressions. The man was simply vague, yet it all went together, and David found him enormously attractive, and appealing. The realization made him uncomfortable.

"I'm really pleased about the book," Peter said, breaking the silence, and David watched him as he patted the protective leather covering affectionately.

"May I see it?"

"Of course," Peter handed the book over eagerly.

David opened it and studied a few of the pages. "Fascinating, but not quite a first, you know."

"Oh?"

"Anna Karenina first appeared in installments in a magazine."

"I know that," Peter said with relief. "You frightened me. I meant publication of the novel, the actual publication of the whole book."

"Well, it certainly is a valuable find." David handed the book back.

"That was very interesting, your being aware of the history of the book."

"I'm interested in a lot of things," David answered, aware that he wanted to impress Peter.

"Well, in that case, come let me show you something," Peter said enthusiastically. He waved him to the farthest wall of the library, which was lined from ceiling to floor with books.

As David walked over and stood beside him, he was surprised to see that Peter was almost as tall as he was.

"Turgenev, Tolstoy, Dostoyevsky. They're all here." Peter's eyes were glistening with pride. "That's only part of my Russian collection. English, French, German are over there." He pointed to other shelves. "And I've done it all alone. So few people are interested or have the time."

"May I offer my help?" David said with sincerity. "I browse a great deal whenever I can in the old bookshops just off the beaten path. And if I come across something interesting, I could possibly get it for you." He was determined to ingratiate himself.

"Do you collect books, too?" Peter looked like a suspicious child. "I hate competition."

David smiled inwardly. Pamela had said the same thing earlier that evening.

"No, I'd just like to do it. Books and I have always been good companions."

"That's damned decent of you. I'll pay you back immediately."

"I'm afraid that would have to be part of the bargain. I certainly couldn't afford it." He looked back at the book shelves. "To think you keep them all hidden away where nobody can see them."

"I know they're here," Peter said. "And anyone who is interested knows they're here." His comment made David uneasy. "How about another drink?" Peter asked as he walked over and poured himself one.

"Not for me," David answered, turning his back on Peter, fearful his expression would give away his feelings of discomfort.

"I love beautiful things," Peter said, and something in the man's voice made David turn around. It sounded like a declaration of love. Peter was looking directly at him. David felt himself blush and was surprised that Peter's words did not upset him. He had heard rumors that Peter was one. Looking at Peter, David wondered if it were true.

"It's a fascinating library," David said, not knowing what else to say, and turned his attention to the wall nearest him. "If I'm not mistaken, this entire wall contains nothing but books about American history."

"I've always been interested in history," Peter said, walking over to David. "As a matter of fact, I've recently begun writing a book and I believe that future historians will be able to study my writings and learn what this generation was all about."

David was stunned. It was like a recording of his conversation with Pamela. Peter was writing the book and Pamela would get the by-line. The question again was why Peter was permitting Pamela to get away with all the credit.

"I didn't know you wrote," David said finally, aware that his silence was weighing heavily in the room.

"He writes lovely letters to his friends." Pamela was standing in the doorway, one arm lifted upward, her hand pressed against the framework. It was a model's pose, and she did it well.

"Your drink, darling." Peter walked over and handed her the glass.

With a slight nod of her head, Pamela entered the room and sat down gracefully, arranging her long powder-blue robe into proper folds.

"David, have you noticed my prize Impressionist painting?" she asked, smiling pleasantly. "That's the one hanging over the fireplace, dear." Her manner became insulting. "Peter gave it to me as an anniversary present."

The abrupt change in conversation did not escape his attention and David became wary.

"You mean Matisse's 'Still Life of Apples'?" he said without turning to look at the painting. He had spotted it the minute he walked into the room. "It was painted at the tail end of his decorative period, if I'm not mistaken, and although decorative, it lacks profundity." He said it pleasantly but knew that Pamela got the message. If she was going to play him for a fool, he was going to dispel the notion. Somehow he felt the time had come for her to realize he was a worthy opponent, if not partner.

"I'm not interested in when an artist painted his pictures." Pamela paled visibly.

David walked over to the fireplace and looked up at the painting as though studying it carefully.

"It's worth a great deal of money, that's for sure. But the period of his work which this represents has never been my favorite." He turned and spoke directly to Pamela. "I prefer his later works, the flat, formal, simplified compositions which are more realistic and detailed. But that's my personal taste." He spoke hesitantly and although looking at Pamela was fully aware that Peter was listening. "And that, ladies and gentlemen, is the end of Art Appreciation I." He grinned self-consciously, thanking heaven for his photographic memory.

"All that in just Art Appreciation I?" Peter laughed good-naturedly.

"One, two or three," Pamela broke in, unable to control her fury, "you certainly are full of little surprises this evening, David, aren't you?"

"Is that good or bad?" he asked, trying to sound light.

"I'm not sure which it is. You know I hate surprises." She sounded like a spoiled little girl who had not gotten her way.

"Well, I love them," Peter said, "and I must admit I enjoyed every minute of my visit with David. We really must do it again, soon." He stood up. "But now I must run out and catch a plane." He walked over to David and extended his hand. "And I do want to thank you for helping Pamela. She may not like my saying it, but I do believe she depends on you, and now I know why." He held David's hand a fraction too long, and it caused a strange sensation to go through him. "You are truly a delightful young man."

"I'd be flattered to think that I even help." He wanted Peter to stay.

"I'm sure you do," Peter said, seemingly oblivious to what had transpired around him. Leaning down, he kissed Pamela on the cheek, "Good night, my love. I'll see you tomorrow."

"Tomorrow?" she echoed in a hollow voice. She sounded defeated and David could not understand her mood. It would have made sense if she were angry. He had made her angry in the past, and he knew her rage. Tonight there was something deeper. He was sure it had to do with Peter.

"I think I'll have another drink." Pamela broke the silence when they heard the front door close. Her tone was suddenly pleasant and David was caught off guard. He looked at her and she was smiling. "Would you pour it for me?" She sounded almost coquettish.

As he poured the drink, his feelings of discomfort grew. Her behavior was strange. She was totally undiscriminating in her sexual preferences, except, as he discovered soon after joining her agency, she never had affairs with anyone connected with her office.

It bothered him only to the extent that she titillated him and on occasion he actually desired her. With time, he accepted his position, although anyone seeing them together assumed they were having an affair. Her behavior certainly encouraged these assumptions. There was an element of sadism in it, and a definite put-down of his manhood.

Being alone in her house, he wondered if she were jabbing at his masculinity again. As long as Peter was there, he felt confident. With Peter gone, all his insecurities returned.

"I've been giving thought to your little friend," Pamela was saying. "You know, Megan Baynes. Well, Sidney Karsten is doing a play and I believe I could talk to him."

"Karsten is doing a musical," David said quickly. "Megan is not a dancer."

"Oh, if she's talented it won't matter. Besides, she would be hired for her looks, not her talent."

David bit his lip. Cat had said Megan's talent was very limited. A part in a musical would be out of Megan's range. What Pamela was suggesting could destroy her.

"You're really very beautiful, David," Pamela said softly, walking over to him. She touched his face with her fingertips seductively. "But you know that, don't you?" Moving away, she turned on the radio and began to sway to the rhythm of the music while sipping her drink. A small smile hovered over her lips.

"Would you like to dance with me?" She came over to him again and pressed her body against his. Automatically David put his arms around her waist. Pamela was real. She was flesh and blood. Megan was elusive.

"Let's go upstairs," Pamela whispered.

They started out of the library and David knew that he could not make love to her. He was embarrassed, aware that Pamela would never forgive him, but he had to get away from her, get out of the house, escape. He felt the pressure of her hand as she pulled him toward the stairs. He closed his eyes, trying to stifle a cry.

"David!" He heard her calling him. He looked up. Pamela was halfway up the stairs and her smile was mocking.

"Pamela, I have to go," he whispered hoarsely, and without another word he turned and ran out of the house.

Walking along the darkened street, David felt empty, like the ornately wrapped Christmas box which he had once received at a foundling home. It had nothing inside. A cruel prank at a joyless Christmas party. The memory made him feel weak and he leaned against a lamppost. If only there were someone he could turn to. Cat's face flashed through his mind. She wanted things from him which he was unable and unwilling to give. Megan's face replaced

Cat's. He could do things for her. He would make her a superstar and she would be his creation, his property. Then he could hold his head up with pride. Still, the pungent feeling remained. Suddenly Peter's face appeared and lingered. It startled him, but it also soothed him. He felt better.

As he looked around for a taxi, he remembered leaving Cat alone outside the theater and he wondered if she were angry with him. Well, even if she were, he was sure he could pacify her. He had always succeeded in doing it in the past.

32

Cat followed the butler into the large circular gallery of Clay's Beekman Place apartment. Her eyes wandered around the room as she removed her coat and handed it to the waiting butler.

"Gwenny will take you to the terrace," the butler said, nodding toward the maid who was waiting nearby.

As Gwenny led her through the paneled library, Cat paused to compose herself. The room was imposing, immense by any standard. She expected it to be luxurious, but there was more than just money involved in what she was seeing. The Oyster Bay house was lovely and was obviously the house of rich people, but this house had an aura money could not buy. It had a feeling of tranquillity, an atmosphere of permanence. She looked at the lighted paintings and recognized a Gainsborough. Several sculptures were placed casually around, as well as a collection of primitive African art which was magnificently displayed behind a glass enclosure. All the priceless things, collected over the years by Clay's ancestors, those indomitable kinsmen whom Clay had told her about and in whom he took extravagant pride. Permanence. The word struck and lingered. A gnawing feeling that she wanted to be part of this world prickled her spine.

If she could marry Clay, she would automatically enter this world. That was what Pamela had meant. Coming out on top! Marriage to Clay. In all the times she had seen him, she had given it only a passing thought. Now that she was in his home, she wondered if she could turn their relationship into a more serious affair. She liked him, on occasion she even thought she was in love with him. Getting to know him was proving difficult because he traveled so much. Still, he was a mature, attractive, tasteful man who knew what he wanted.

Gwenny coughed politely and Cat became aware that she was waiting for her. Quickly she glanced at herself in the bronzed mirror which hung over the fireplace and followed the maid to the open

French doors. Just before she stepped out, she wondered if Clay's daughters would be here. The idea made her nervous.

Standing on the threshold of an enormous glass-enclosed terrace, she looked out on what appeared to be a small private park. Tiny lights flickered through the mass of planted shrubbery. Several tall trees were standing in large stone basins. Potted flowers were everywhere and at the far end she could see a small water fountain sending a colorful spray of water into the air. People were milling around, talking in muted voices. Cat knew no one and a flash of insecurity shot through her. She wondered if she were overdressed. She had chosen a Mary McFadden design, a simple pleated column in black, feeling that the classic cut accentuated her special look. She was going to meet Clay's friends for the first time and she wanted to impress them. Instinctively she knew the evening would be important and she wanted to come off in the right light. Now she noticed that most of the women were dressed in colorful dresses and she felt out of place.

Composing herself, Cat was trying to find Clay when she spotted Nancy Stuart. She wanted to rush over to her but realized it was not the thing to do in front of these strangers. She would be making a spectacle of herself and it would embarrass Clay.

Taking a cigarette from her evening purse, she nearly jumped as a waiter lit it for her. It was then she saw Clay.

He was talking animatedly with some of his guests and he had his back to her. The sight of him excited her. He had been gone since Thanksgiving but he called her almost daily from various parts of the world, and she realized she had missed him. The impulse to rush over to him was great, but again she held back. At that moment he turned and looked at her as if conscious of her stare.

"Catherine," he called out, and her name sounded pleasant coming to her from a distance. As he approached her, she could see excitement clearly written on his face.

"I'm so happy you finally got here." He reached out and took both her hands in his, pressing them eagerly. "And you look ravishing. But I knew you would." Then he turned to his guests. "I want you all to meet Catherine Willingham."

With his arm around her shoulder he guided her around, introducing her to the various men and women. Everyone shook her hand formally. She was too nervous to catch any of the names. She noticed the men looking at her appreciatively. The younger women, obviously new to the social hierarchy, smiled pleasantly; the older, dowager-like ladies exuded displeasure.

Finally they reached Nancy and her husband.

"Cat, how wonderful to see you." Nancy's pleasure was only evident in her eyes, as she leaned over and kissed Cat on the cheek.

"Oh, you know each other," Clay said happily. "So I know I'm leaving you in good hands." He rushed off to greet some newly arrived guests.

Cat turned to look at Jack Hastings. He was a big, muscular man with a shock of white hair. He was ruggedly handsome and must have been an athlete in his youth. Now, because of his age, too much rich food and an overindulgence in liquor, he looked like a retired elder statesman. His blue eyes were examining her as though she were a prize poodle in a dog show.

"So you're Clay's new little woman." His face finally broke into a smile.

Cat sucked in her breath at the condescending remark.

"Cat and I worked together for years, Jack." Nancy broke the tension.

"Did you now?" He did not seem pleased. "Pleasure to meet you, anyway. And now I think I'll have another drink." He turned to Cat. "May I bring you one?"

"A glass of white wine would be nice."

"How about you, Nancy?"

A look of panic crossed Nancy's face, but it passed too quickly and Cat decided she imagined it.

"No thanks, Jack." Nancy shook her head. "A soda is all I want."

"Sure?" he asked.

"Positive," she said, too forcefully.

"Who are all these mummies?" Cat whispered to Nancy when Jack was gone.

"Now, now, Cat, behave." Nancy seemed to relax. "And as soon as Jack brings your drink I'll take you over to the ladies and if you just take them all with a grain of salt, you'll find they're really quite nice, especially if you don't rock their little boats."

"Nancy, are Clay's daughters here?"

"No, they took Papa's yacht and went sailing."

"I'm starved." Cat realized she had not eaten all day. "Do we get dinner, too?"

"That's rocking the boat," Nancy laughed. "Of course you get food and it's going to be delicious. Clay has one of the best chefs in the United States. But you never, never rush a good chef."

"Haven't we met somewhere?" An impeccably dressed, petite woman came over to them.

"Serena Graville, Cat Willingham," Nancy said. Then without a pause, "What a perfectly glorious Galanos you've got on."

"Would you believe the dear man had it finished for me between Christmas and today?"

Cat was about to say she had modeled it, but Nancy interrupted, as if on purpose. "Incidentally, Serena, Grace's tea for the retarded children was really done beautifully, don't you think?"

"We have met, haven't we?" Serena would not be put off.

"I don't think so," Cat said politely, and threw a bewildered look at Nancy, wondering if Nancy were embarrassed about having been a model. It amused Cat. She herself had always been very proud of being one.

"I never forget a face," Serena persisted.

"Why don't we go and sit with Lady Joynsen-hicks?" Nancy suggested, and they walked over to an aging woman who was sitting in a huge armchair which she filled completely with her mass. Whereas everyone else in the room was festively dressed, the heavy-set lady was wearing an ill-fitting man-tailored suit and she seemed to carry it with defiance.

"Lady Joynsen-hicks has come over from London for the holidays," Nancy explained, while the older woman examined Cat.

"Delighted," Cat said, feeling like a fool. The pretentiousness of the situation was irritating.

"I'd like you to meet Lady Beatrice," Lady Joynsen-hicks clucked, and Cat found herself shaking hands again with an attractive woman of undetermined age, with blond hair and the peaches and cream complexion which British women are noted for. "Lady Beatrice went to school with Clay's daughter Brit," she continued, scrutinizing Cat.

"Lady Joynsen-hicks runs the most prestigious finishing school in London," Nancy helped Cat out.

"I've got it," Serena said suddenly. "You were the model who showed at the Plaza several months back. You were wearing Shephard's see-through wedding dress, weren't you?"

Cat summoned her most imperious look and smiled down at the woman. "Bo Shephard is a fabulous designer, isn't he?" She smiled carefully. "You know, he's being considered for an award this year because of his originality."

"No one would ever wear that dress," Serena said indignantly.

"Probably not, but you did remember it, didn't you?"

"You're a Mannequin?" Lady Joynsen-hicks asked.

"Yes, I am."

"Some of my girls have been approached by our designers asking them to be photographed, but I really don't think it's the right thing for them to do."

"Why not?" Cat was having a hard time hiding her annoyance.

"Well, there's something exploitive about it. Just because they are beautiful, one should not assume they are for sale." Her accent had become even more pronounced.

"Lady Joynsen-hicks, being a model is work." Cat spoke deliberately. "Hard, honest work. The ones who do it as a lark do not make good models. Having one picture taken isn't modeling. Doing it year in and year out, applying yourself to it totally, as any working person in any field would, permits someone to call herself a model."

"I wouldn't let my daughter do it," Serena said testily.

"Dinner is served," the butler announced, and Cat heard Nancy heave a sigh of relief.

The food, as Nancy had predicted, was superb. The waiters, all wearing tuxedos and white gloves, worked smoothly, making the meal even more of a feast. The conversation centered around business and world affairs. The gentlemen seated to each side of Cat were pleasant, but were far more anxious to participate in what was being said around the table than talk to her. She found it a novelty.

"Do you go to these things often?" Cat asked Nancy when they finally escaped to an upstairs sitting room off the guest bathroom.

"Too often," Nancy answered wearily, walking into the lavatory.

Not wanting to go downstairs alone, Cat walked out to the hallway and peeked into the various rooms whose doors were open. Each room was more beautifully furnished than the other. They were done in various periods, and to the best of Cat's understanding of antiques, each appeared authentic to the last detail. She wondered if she would want to live in another woman's house. The idea was distasteful.

She was about to re-enter the guest sitting room when she overheard Serena talking, and she stopped in her track, since she was obviously the subject of the conversation.

"If at least she were really young, I'd understand. But, God, she's pushing forty if she's a day. And a model! You'd think Clay, after nearly thirty years with Margaret, would find someone who could remotely give him what Margaret did. At this point I'd even accept Eve Simpson."

"It's a shame," the other woman answered. "But that's what happens. These women who've struggled all their lives have that ability to sell someone like Clay a song and dance, and being as vulnerable as he is, she just might make it."

"Heaven forbid." Serena's voice rose in indignation.

Cat walked in, determined to stop the exchange. Nancy was just coming out of the lavatory. She, too, had heard the conversation.

The women looked confused, uncertain as to how much had been overheard.

"Betty," Nancy emphasized the other woman's name. "That green dress you're wearing matches your complexion and reflects your personality to a T."

Betty blushed and within seconds both women left the room.

"And who the hell is Eve Simpson?" Cat asked Nancy the minute the women were gone.

"She's someone who works with Clay and they've been together for the past few years," Nancy said, and looked uncomfortable. "You do know that Margaret was ill for nearly five years."

Cat took out her compact and stared at herself, hoping Nancy would not see her confusion.

"She couldn't hold a candle to you," Nancy said, trying to be helpful.

"Oh well." Cat put her compact away. "I don't think I could take all this, anyway." She laughed bitterly. "Frankly, I feel like Joan Fontaine in the movie *Rebecca*. The only thing missing is a portrait of Margaret Whitfield hanging at the head of the stairs."

"It was there, but Clay had it removed when he did some redecorating recently," Nancy laughed good-naturedly.

"What do these women actually have against me?" Cat asked after a moment. "Or against that Eve Simpson?"

"Honey, each of these witches has a dozen available lady friends whom they were going to introduce to Clay as soon as he gave them the go-ahead. It would have been a feather in their cap to make the match, not to mention a good excuse for lavish entertaining."

"And neither Eve nor I fit the bill."

"In a way she would be easier for them to take. She's an office executive and as far as they're concerned she knows her place. You're gorgeous and seem independent. That's why I tried to stop you from mentioning you're a model."

"But they accepted you."

"It was a tough battle, believe me."

"How do you take it?" Cat asked in exasperation.

"Badly, if you must know. If I could at least have a drink I'd probably do better, but Jack would pull the rug out from under me if I did."

"Pull the rug out?"

"He'd divorce me like a shot."

"What are you talking about?"

"Cat, my love. I don't just take a drink. I usually finish the bottle. And it is understood that if I pull another binge, like the ones I've been known to do, the marriage would be over and that prenuptial agreement I signed would leave me high and dry."

"You mean you actually signed one of those things?" Cat grimaced. "How humiliating."

"Oh, I don't know. Do you think being married to someone like Jack Hastings is not work?" She leaned against the wall and lit a cigarette. "Let me tell you, I'm working harder now than I did when we used to have to get up at four in the morning to do a sunrise shot and work through the day and then some."

"Then why the hell is everyone breaking their backs to marry money?" Cat knew she sounded naïve, but it was as though she were trying to understand something in herself for herself.

"It sounds great for starters and there are compensations. The fringe benefits are the best. You know, not having to worry if your bank account is overdrawn, because there's a secretary who puts money in the account automatically. Being able to buy anything you want without having to look at the price tag. Reading a menu from left to right rather than the other way around." She stopped and took a long drag on her cigarette. "And there is another thing. There is something very seductive about being close to power." She smiled bitterly. "Unfortunately, what most don't realize is that the ego of powerful men is insatiable and their need to break everyone around, make them knuckle down to them, is never-ending, especially if they know you have a will and a personality of your own."

"Power?" Cat mulled the word over. "You're equating money with power?"

"It's as close as you come to it in our democracy. You see, in England it's people like that dikey Joynsen-hicks, who's a hundred times removed from inheriting the throne, who still wield power because of their titles. But here? Money! M-O-N-E-Y!" She spelled out the last word for emphasis.

"But there's always someone around who has more money than the next guy," Cat protested.

"True, and that's the contest. As a matter of fact, I love watching Jack grovel when he's in the company of the ones who do."

"To each his own pleasure," Cat said. "To me it sounds revolting."

"Not if you found yourself with four kids and an ex-husband who's an honest cop and who was fool enough to fall in love with a drunk."

Cat regretted her statement and reached out and pressed Nancy's hand.

"Let's go down or they'll wonder what happened to us," Nancy said, covering her emotions.

"No, wait," Cat stopped her. "I have to ask you a question which you must take in the spirit in which it's being asked." She searched for the right words before she continued. "I know why you married Jack, but why did he marry you?"

"You mean, why didn't he marry a young, beautiful, sexy, fluffy doll who would drool all over him?" Nancy asked seriously. "Well, I'll tell you why. Firstly, you're confusing rich playboys and retired, older men who inherited their money and have an ego problem about who they are, with men who worked for what they have. They may have even been born rich, like Clay Whitfield, but they doubled and quadrupled their inheritances and they're still at it. Jack was poor but he made it. And men like Jack are terrified of young people in general and young women in particular. Men like Jack and Clay don't marry for sex. They can have as much or as little of it as they want, whenever and with whomever they want. They're also not interested in having any more children. Jack has two sons and a daughter. A young, wide-eyed little bride would deliver him a bundle of joy and suddenly he'd find himself embroiled in a family situation which would tear him apart. He may get away with a premarital contract with the bride, but the ransom note is attached to the delivery of that offspring."

"So why does he get married?" Cat asked.

"He's old-fashioned. Plus the fact that people like Serena or Betty and even Clay expect it."

"And what does he expect from you?"

"To run his six homes and his yacht. See to it that the servants are honest and do their work. Entertain as befits his standing."

"A secretary and a good housekeeper could do that."

"But could they step into a Bill Blass or a Chanel or a Dior and look right on his arm?"

"Nancy, there's something missing in what you're saying," Cat said thoughtfully. "I love you, I think you're the greatest, but I still don't get it. Why you and not some attractive, bright, single lady who would probably like him more than you do."

"Because I was married. I ran a home. I've had kids. I knocked around and know the price of eggs and milk." She stopped. "Do you?"

"Do I what?"

"Do you know how much a container of milk costs?"

Cat blushed. "Skimmed or pasteurized?" She tried to laugh off the question.

"Don't laugh. Do you?" Nancy persisted. "You don't, honey, because you and many career ladies have arranged it so that someone else does it all for them."

"Does Serena know? Did Margaret Whitfield know?" Cat got defensive.

"They could tell you exactly what the price of pork was last week compared to the price today."

"Oh, come on, Nancy. I don't for one minute believe that Serena or Margaret Whitfield did their own grocery shopping," Cat remarked.

"No, but they sure looked over the bill when it arrived," Nancy said coolly.

"I think I'll go back to eating kosher food," Cat laughed, and Nancy joined her.

33

The ringing in of the New Year was accompanied by waiters pouring vintage champagne, the lights being dimmed and everyone greeting each other in the spirit dictated by the occasion.

Clay, the gracious host, kissed the women, shook hands with the men and came over and put his arm around Cat's shoulder, kissing her gently on the lips.

"You will stay after everyone leaves, won't you?" he whispered.

She smiled and nodded. Then she caught sight of Serena's eyes staring at her. Do I appear to be just another model who is having an affair with a wealthy man? Cat wondered. It was an unappealing idea.

"Now for some decent holiday cheer," Jack said when the lights came up and the butler wheeled in the liqueurs.

The room cleared out shortly thereafter with only three couples remaining. Jack and Nancy, the Fieldstons and another couple whose name Cat could not remember. She was relieved that Serena and her husband were gone as well as Joynsen-hicks and her companion. Vaguely, Cat wondered if the women were lovers, or if the younger one was brought as a prospective bride for Clay. She did, after all, have a title, and horse-trading went on everywhere, why not here? She glanced over at Nancy, who was holding a glass of Perrier. She looked sad and Cat felt sorry for her. The other women were chatting with each other and the men were having a serious discussion. Nancy seemed out of place in spite of her beauty and magnificent grooming.

Cat tried to follow what the men were saying and gathered they were talking about oil prices and the effects of the Middle East War on the world situation. As Clay had predicted, the Israelis won the battle on the military front but were being pushed on the political front. She found it difficult to follow their thinking. Finally giving up, she relaxed into a feeling of contentment. The luxury of the surroundings, coupled with the superb brandy she was drinking, lulled her again into thoughts of what life could be like if she were married to Clay.

She would stop working. She would have all the time in the
world to spend with Alexandra. Clara would have the best of care. As
for David . . . She realized she had not thought of him all evening.
It left her feeling strangely empty. Although he had not called her
since the evening they saw Megan's performance, he was usually on
her mind. For the first few days after the incident, she was too hurt
and angry to care. She almost hoped the strange attachment to him
was over and that she would somehow open an agency on her own
when the time was right. But as the days went by and he still did not
call, she got worried. She could in no way run the agency alone and
she knew she needed David. She wanted to call him but had little to
say and even less to offer.

"It's those fucking kikes." Jack's voice boomed through the room
and Cat was jolted back to the present. "That goddamned war,
whether they instigated it or not, is going to kill the whole deal with
the Saudis. They've started the embargo, which I couldn't care less
about, but that pipeline deal is in jeopardy and those Israeli bastards,
with their hysteria about being wiped out, have got this country by
the balls."

Cat felt her throat go dry and a rage she never knew she pos-
sessed was hurting her gut.

Clay, sitting next to her, seemingly impervious to her reaction,
placed his hand on her arm. It was done unobtrusively and appeared
to be a simple affectionate gesture. She felt the pressure, however,
and glanced over at him. His expression was impenetrable.

"Such talk with ladies around isn't quite the thing, Jack." His
voice was pleasant.

Nancy got up quickly. "This has been a long and wonderful
evening and I think I'm going to take my little boy home to bed." She
reached out and took Jack's hand and pulled him out of his seat. Cat
knew Nancy was furious and she could not help but marvel at the
masterful exhibit of her self-control.

Cat did not join them as they walked toward the front door, but
could see and hear them clearly. The customary salutations were
exchanged and Jack, who was quite drunk, put his arm around Clay.

"I'll have the contracts ready for signing right after this fucking
holiday is over and I'll send them over to your office."

Clay disengaged himself from the embrace and a formidable
look came over his face. He was white with rage, his nostrils taut, his
lips colorless.

"I wouldn't bother, Jack," his voice was even, the tone cutting.
"We're going with another bid."

The statement sobered Jack somewhat. He grew red and he
tried to focus his eyes on Clay.

"Buddy, you don't mean it. Mine was the lowest bid around."

"Good night." Clay leaned over and kissed Nancy on the cheek and nodded to the other departing guests.

Cat stood up and walked around the room, waiting for Clay to come back. She had never actually been exposed to anti-Semitism. She obviously knew of its existence, had even participated in social situations where the unflattering references to Jews were bandied about, but it was always in good humor. On the rare occasions when the remarks got out of hand, someone in the crowd would stand up and fight with conviction against bigotry. What she had witnessed this evening was shocking, almost obscene, and, except for Clay's comment, no one in the room seemed to care.

"Thank you for not saying anything." Clay came back into the room. "I don't know if I could have restrained myself if I were in your position."

"I was just wondering if I really would have had the guts to say anything," she said slowly. "I don't know that I would have found the right words."

"Once you started, you would have, I assure you."

"You canceled a deal with him, didn't you?"

"Irrevocably canceled."

"But he's supposed to be some sort of a powerhouse in his field."

Clay smiled and seemed embarrassed. "Yes, he is. But in this particular context, I'm more powerful."

This is what Nancy was talking about, Cat thought, and for the first time she wondered if it was Clay's power and money which made him so attractive to her. She had witnessed the battle of lions and she was on the winning side. She loved it.

"Forgive my immodesty, but did you do it on my account?"

"No. I happen to hate people who hide from what they are."

"Meaning?"

"Jack Hastings is a man who takes no pride in who he is or what he comes from. I don't trust people like that."

"You mean he's Jewish?"

"Yes, he is."

Cat was quiet for a moment, then said impulsively, "I changed my name."

"Yes, I know."

She raised her brows.

"Catherine, I know a great deal about you, if only from the purchase application you made when buying the apartment. It was an estate sale, remember? And our offices handled it. The woman who lived there was an old friend of my mother's and I handled her portfolio personally."

"How does Nancy take it?" Cat asked after a minute. "He's vulgar, he drinks too much and tries to ply her with liquor when he knows she can't take it. I can't begin to imagine what it must be like living with him."

"I doubt that you ever could. But at the rate he's going, his drinking, his whole lifestyle, will leave her a very rich widow, I assure you."

"If she outlives him."

"For some it's a worthwhile gamble, when the stakes are that high."

He came over to her and brushed her face with the back of his hand. "Don't look so pensive," he said gently.

She pressed his hand to her cheek. It was cool and comforting.

He leaned over and brushed her lips with his. She responded immediately. When he kissed her more passionately, she reacted, throwing her arms around him. He lifted her to her feet and with his arm holding her waist they walked up the stairs.

Entering his bedroom, Cat was struck by the complete austerity of it. It was a room which could have been hosed down without damaging anything. The highly polished floors were bare. The bed was large, it's wood uncarved. She wondered if Margaret had slept in this room.

She looked over at Clay. He had removed his jacket and was placing it carefully on the wooden valet. She averted her eyes as he started to unbutton his shirt. It was very different from their affair in the country. It bothered her and she thought of leaving but when she felt his arms around her, felt his naked body close to her, she started to unzip her dress. He moved back as her dress fell to the floor, and she could see the look of desire cross his face. He was rich and powerful. He ruled over his empire, but at that moment she was the object of his desire. Her excitement rose.

The passion, the need to please, the nuances which their love-making had had in Oyster Bay were all there as they made love, but as the hours passed, Cat felt a difference. She did not belong; she was a guest in a house which belonged to another woman.

Later, lying next to Clay, Cat stared ahead, listening to his steady breathing. Finally, she turned her head and looked at the sleeping man. She wished he would wake up and take her in his arms and help dispel her feelings of displacement.

As quietly as she could, she crawled out of bed, not wanting to disturb him. Somewhere in the house she heard a clock strike 3 A.M. Her mother was home alone and she needed to get back to the apartment. The thought almost made her laugh. She was a woman who had lived away from her mother for nearly twenty years and now she was rushing home to Mama.

She was almost dressed when Clay woke up. Within seconds he was out of bed and pulling on his robe.

"I'm sorry I woke you," she smiled, and walked over to him. He put his arms around her and kissed her affectionately.

"Must you go?"

"It's been a wonderful evening, Clay, but the party is over and the real world out there is waiting for me."

"Real world?" He seemed amused.

"And how," she answered seriously. "Within the next week I've got to figure out how to handle my career as well as Megan's."

"What do you mean?"

"Well, Megan is back. She stayed with the sisters over the holidays and she's got quite a few assignments. Her career is mushrooming and now that I don't have Mel, I've got to figure out how to work it so that I can represent her without coming out with it."

"But isn't that what you wanted, setting up a modeling agency of your own?"

"I'll be able to do it sometime toward the end of May, beginning of June, but until then I've got to figure out how to work it." She was too tired to explain the situation. "There are certain commitments which I must fulfill before then. Plus the fact that I haven't really chosen the other models I want to sign up." She picked up her evening purse. "But all of that is really my problem." She headed for the door.

"Wait a minute." Clay stopped her. "I've got to leave the city for several days, but if you need anything at all, just call my lawyer, Martin Drew. I'll leave word that he is to do anything and everything to help." Quickly he scribbled the name down and handed her the paper.

She smiled her gratitude.

"Now let me get Jackson to drive you home."

"You mean to tell me you'd wake your driver at this hour?" The idea was absurd. "I won't dream of it and besides, I know this may come as a shock, but I'd be embarrassed on several levels."

"Of course you would. I'm sorry." He started looking around for his clothes. "I'll dress and take you home."

"No need. I live ten blocks away. I'll walk it in five minutes."

"You're not walking home alone at this hour," he said firmly. "I won't hear of it."

"You'll have to. I could use the walk and frankly, I want to think. Believe me, nothing is going to happen to me."

"How about my giving you cab fare or something?" Clay said helplessly.

She kissed him quickly on the lips and left.

As Cat headed up First Avenue, she suddenly remembered herself at seventeen with a hundred dollars for cab fare, given to her by some man whose name she could not recall. She had thought at the time that she could use the money to help her with her modeling career. Clay had just offered her cab fare . . . She threw her head back and laughed out loud. Nothing ever changes, she thought, and continued up the street.

34

The February snow stung Cat's face as she looked up at the clock outside the Sherry-Netherland Hotel. It was twelve noon and she was meeting David at their office. She was running late and was worried that she could not attend to all her appointments before her date with Clay at eight that evening. She felt extremely pressured.

Her modeling career was limping along, but she had not given up. It meant pounding the pavements of Seventh Avenue, where she had once been queen. She knew everyone around and they all greeted her as though nothing had changed, although, in fact, everything had. There was a form of masochism in what she was doing, but she could not help herself. And she did succeed in getting jobs, especially with the young fledgling designers, who were pleased to have her to work with them. Also some of the old-time manufacturers, whom she had not worked for in years, were delighted to have her. It was humiliating for the most part, but she pressed on.

It was Megan's career, however, which was keeping her truly busy. Since word got around that Megan had gotten the Chameleon account, she was in great demand.

Cat's first impulse, the day right after the New Year, when she got the call from Grayson, asking who represented Megan, was to call Pamela and ask her to handle the deal. She felt totally ill-prepared to undertake the negotiations, which could run into six figures. Much as she wanted to be on her own, she panicked when the opportunity presented itself.

She called David instead. He was surprised to hear from her and his efforts at sounding hurt and aloof irritated her. She was tempted simply to wish him a Happy New Year and hang up. But she needed advice from someone she could trust. His manner changed when she told him about Megan and mentioned that she was thinking of handing the package over to Pamela.

"Don't you dare give it to that woman. It's ours." The pretense was gone and he sounded like his old self. She also noted his use of the plural pronoun, which gave her confidence.

"But, David. I don't intend to stop modeling. I've got to go to Paris at the end of March to do a show for Bo and as you know I'm still signed with Pamela." She waited for his reply. It was a perfect opening for him to say that her modeling career was over.

"We'll work it out," he answered, his voice filled with confidence.

Her next call was to Martin Drew, Clay's lawyer, and as Clay had promised, Martin took charge. When Cat explained that she was still not able to open an agency in her own right, he set up the Megan Baynes Corporation, gave Cat space in his enormous offices in the General Motors building and put a secretary at her disposal. He handled the terms of Megan's contracts with Grayson, personally. His patience with Megan was incredible, especially since Megan seemed to misunderstand the enormity of the deal she was getting. Instead, she haggled over the size of the commission which Cat and David were to get. Cat was both upset and embarrassed. Again she noticed that strange vulgar streak in Megan and wondered where it came from. Certainly the devout and loving Cora Baynes could not be held responsible. It bothered Cat, but Martin succeeded in glossing it over and the deal was finally set.

The only time Martin proved difficult was when Cat insisted David be made an equal partner in the corporation. He seemed to feel that David had nothing to contribute. Cat ignored his reaction. She needed a partner and she felt David deserved it.

If David proved to be less than helpful in running things, Cat refused to admit it. She was, however, aware that the flamboyant, self-assured young man who had stood on her terrace months earlier, outlining how they would run their agency, was nowhere to be seen. She succeeded in rationalizing it away. There was little David could actually do for the agency at that point without jeopardizing his position with Pamela. Megan was their only client and there was nothing for him to do. It was Cat who found herself sitting in on photography sessions, holding Megan's hand. If people wondered why she was there, she explained that Megan was her friend and she was simply helping out. David would not have been in a position to do that.

More and more, Cat wondered if she should quit modeling and announce openly that she was running a bona fide agency instead of skulking around. But she was set to do Bo's show in Paris in mid-March and was secretly hoping it might turn the tide for her. That was how she had rejuvenated her career after Alexandra was born. The fact that fifteen years had gone by since then did not escape her. Still, she wanted to give it a try.

Entering the office, Cat found David sitting at her desk, sifting through a pile of photographs. For a brief second she resented his sitting in her place. She dismissed it quickly.

"Hi," he said when he saw her, although he did not get up. "What do you think of these girls?" He held up some pictures.

Cat scanned them quickly and shook her head.

"You're worse than Pamela." David got up and walked to the window. He sounded upset.

"David, we've got some twenty girls that I think are sensational and we can't even talk to them, much less sign them up at this point." She threw her bag on the desk, staring at David's back. Their relationship had changed. It was now quite formal and Cat missed the light banter and camaraderie that had existed between them in the past.

As though feeling her eyes on him, David turned around and looked at her intently. "You sure look beat," he said finally.

"I think I could sleep for a week," she answered, kicking off her shoes, and settled herself on the sofa which stood against the wall of the small office. "Unprofessional designers are far more exhausting to work for." She continued wearily as she lay down and tried to relax.

"Why don't you lie on your tummy and I'll massage your neck?" David walked over to the sofa.

She did as he suggested. She felt him unzip her dress and his hands began to move soothingly down her back.

"Miss Willingham." Cat heard the secretary come in. "Oh, I'm sorry." She sounded embarrassed at the sight of David and Cat on the sofa.

"No, come in." Cat sat up, pulling her dress over her shoulder. "What's the problem?"

"Well, these are the calls I got for Miss Baynes today." She handed Cat a sheet with the names of various photographers, designers and ad agencies who wanted to book Megan.

Cat glanced through them quickly and, picking up a pencil, she started checking the list. Absently she told the girl she could leave as she continued making her notations.

"Well, I can tell you one thing. There is no way I'll let Megan be interviewed by *New York Magazine.*" Cat looked up at David, who was watching her closely.

"Why not?"

"They'll cut her to ribbons."

"Oh, come on, Cat. It's a wonderful magazine. The publicity would be great. Besides, why would they want to hurt her?"

"Not intentionally. But when Megan starts talking about her religion, interviewers think she's putting them on and they report it that way."

"It's what's got her this far so quickly," David said casually.

"I don't care. The answer is no," Cat said with finality.

"I think you're hampering her progress with your caution." David said slowly.

"I resent that." Cat was outraged.

"You can resent it all you want but the fact remains that when Mel Black was in charge she was forging ahead and was someone people took note of. Now, with your pussyfooting around, I think she'll be forgotten as soon as her ads stop appearing."

"I believe in building a career slowly and solidly," Cat said, trying to control her temper. "Working her to the bone, overexposing her, is not really the best way to keep her on top, you know."

"Says who?"

"David, the girl is working night and day. Have you seen her recently? She's down to ninety-eight pounds and for her height that's a disaster."

David did not answer.

"Have you seen her?" Cat demanded, and she realized that she wanted to know if David was seeing Megan behind her back. She did not care personally, because of her involvement with Clay, but there was something about David's reaction to Megan that troubled her.

"You're running this show, so far be it from me to interfere." He ignored her question and started toward the door. "I've got to run," he said over his shoulder

"Pamela waiting for you?" The question slipped out.

He turned around slowly. "Cat, for whatever reason, you won't go public about your involvement with Megan. And I can't spit into my bowl of grub either."

"Oh, so that's it." Cat put her pencil down. "That one hundred fifty dollars is what's keeping you so loyal to Pamela," she said bitingly.

"Until we get some of the commission from Megan's work, that's what I'm subsisting on." His face had grown white with rage.

"I'll match that one hundred fifty dollars anytime," Cat said impulsively.

"Don't be an ass." He spat the words out and slammed out of the office.

The intercom on her desk sounded and Cat flicked the button. "There's a call for you," the secretary said apologetically.

Cat was about to lash out since no one was supposed to know that Cat Willingham was in any way connected with the Martin Drew office.

"It's a Mr. Phillips and he says he's your husband."

Cat felt the blood drain from her face as she picked up the

phone. If her mother had given the number to Jeff something terrible must have happened to Alexandra.

"Is Alexandra all right?" Cat asked the minute she heard Jeff's voice.

"She's fine," Jeff said quietly, "but no thanks to you."

"What's that supposed to mean?"

"You're a goddamned fool, Cat," he continued, and the calm manner frightened her. "If I didn't know better, I'd say you were purposely trying to destroy the child."

"You must be drunk," Cat said, knowing full well that Jeff never drank.

"You really believe that money is what Alexandra needs or wants?"

"What are you talking about?" she asked, although she knew immediately what he was referring to.

"Money! Your money is not what she needs," he said, and he sounded tired and hurt.

"Jeff, one of the reasons I work is so that my child can have the things she wants," Cat said evenly.

"Drugs are what she wants. Drugs so that she can forget what her real needs are."

"Jeff, I've got an appointment for a fitting. Why don't we talk this evening when you're all calmed down?"

"Oh my God. You poor woman."

"How did you find out about it anyway?"

"Alexandra obviously wanted me to." A strange laugh escaped him. "Don't you understand that she, too, wants to survive?"

The phrase shook her.

"Jeff, I want her back. I want to help her. I want to do things for her." She felt desperate. "If you could just tell me what it is she needs, what I can do for her, I'll do anything."

"That's something you'll have to figure out for yourself."

"I've been trying to but I can't come up with the answer."

"That's a shame, but for now, Cat, please don't send her money without telling me about it first."

She wanted to ask him how he was and how Neva was, but she thought she would sound insincere.

"Are you still planning on coming back in June?" she asked instead.

"Yes, and as a matter of fact Alexandra was accepted at the Art Institute in New York."

"Is she still painting those awful . . ."

"I'll be speaking to you, Cat," Jeff said and hung up.

She was tempted to call him back but remembered she had a one o'clock fitting and had to be at Bo's at three. She got up and automatically walked over to the mirror and started repairing her makeup. Alexandra, Jeff, David, Megan, her mother—they were all nibbling away at her. Clay was the only one who seemed willing to give her things. Their relationship had settled into a routine which was quite pleasant and even though it, too, was lacking, at least she could relax with him.

Why had things worked out so badly for her, she thought angrily. What had she done that had brought her to this state? She had jumped into the stream of life without knowing how to swim and she was one of the few who made it. In a way, she had it all, but it was not enough. She wanted more. What was it she really wanted? Recognition? Success? To be adulated for her beauty? Love! That was the underlying drive. She wanted to be loved and somehow it was eluding her.

Her face came into focus and she looked old.

In confusion she picked up her bag and stormed out of the office.

35

"You're terribly jumpy today," Bo said, taking the pins out of his mouth and stepping back to scrutinize the muslin draped loosely on Cat.

"I've been standing in this position for the last hour and it's getting pretty difficult," she answered, trying not to show her fatigue.

"It won't be much longer." He knelt down and pinned up the hem. "Now turn slowly and try not to move your arms."

She did as he asked and her eyes took in the various sketches tacked on the cork board. Each was outrageously different from the designs forecasted by the various fashion experts but Bo did not care. He had found the formula. Shock value, high prices and becoming the darling of the editors and the wealthy jet set—that was all that mattered.

"How does the thing feel?" Bo asked when Cat turned full circle.

"A dozen twelve-year-old girls will be able to put it on and still breathe," she laughed.

"You know what I mean." He laughed, too.

"Well, it's a little too short and I think you should let the sleeves out around the elbows. Maybe make them bouffant."

Quickly, he did what she suggested and stood back again. "You're right." He grinned at her with pleasure. "But then you usually are."

"Can I get out of this now?"

She stepped out of the fabric carefully.

"Good God, Cat, you're thinner than I've ever seen you," Bo exclaimed in shock.

She stared down at herself wearing nothing but the flimsy bikini panties and knew he was right. She reached for a robe, put it on quickly, and looked at him. Was this the moment to ask him if she were through?

"Are you sure you're all right?" he asked with concern.

"I'm fine, really," she said out loud, silently pleading with him to say it.

"Just don't go getting sick on me before that Paris show. I'm depending on you," Bo said sternly.

"Wild horses couldn't keep me away." She hurried toward the dressing room, feeling better. Bo needed her. Depended on her. She was not through.

"Incidentally, that Megan is sure going places," she heard him say as she slipped into a pair of slacks. "And whoever is masterminding her career is doing some hell of a job."

Cat was tempted to tell him that it was she who was in charge of Megan's career. He could probably help her, advise her, make some constructive suggestions. But she dared not take the risk.

"Look at that," Bo said as Cat emerged from the dressing room. *"Vogue, Sports Illustrated.* Seven pages in the New York *Times* fashion magazine. And I hear there are two more covers in European magazines and, now that she's signed that unbelievable contract for the cosmetic ads, she's set for life." He handed her a copy of *Vogue* and Cat smiled wanly.

"I hear Pamela Fitzpatrick had a hemorrhage when she heard about Megan getting the job," Bo continued, oblivious to Cat's silence. "Have you spoken to her lately? What did she say?"

"I've been too busy," Cat said evenly. "I haven't been near the office in weeks and weeks."

"I think she'd kill whoever got that contract for Megan."

"What the hell can she do?" Cat's nerves got the better of her.

"I don't know that she can do anything, except I'd hate to be on that barracuda's hit list."

"Bo, I'm exhausted and I've got a date this evening."

"Who with?"

"Clay Whitfield."

"Oh, my dear, you're really going at this one, aren't you?" he said in that affected feminine manner that Cat hated and which she knew indicated his displeasure.

"Bo, I think you should know that I'm very much in love with Clay." It felt good to say the words out loud.

"Well, to each his own."

"Oh, come on, Bo. I know you don't like him, but why?"

"What are you in love with, him or his money?"

Cat thought for a long moment before answering. "I can't really divide Clay from his money," she said slowly. "Would I love him if he didn't have any?" Again she stopped. "I don't know. But believe me, Bo, I don't believe I'd fall in love with money if it wasn't attached to someone named Clay." She smiled feebly. "Not very much of an answer, I know. But why don't you like him? I'm curious."

"He doesn't fit into my scheme of things, just as I don't fit into his." He walked over to her and hugged her. "But if you're happy, who am I to argue?" Then pushing her away he said seriously, "Try to get some rest."

"I'll try."

"See you tomorrow?" he asked, walking her to the elevator.

"You know you will."

The minute Cat settled in the cab heading home, she felt better. She was meeting Clay at eight and the thought of spending the evening with him made all the day's rejections and hardships evaporate. He'd been gone for several days and she had missed him desperately.

Clara greeted Cat at the door when she walked into the apartment. She seemed flustered.

"You all right?" Cat asked.

"Fine. Fine." Clara repeated the word, obviously upset.

"I've got to shower and dress." Cat decided to accept the statement and rushed toward her bedroom. "I've got to meet someone at eight o'clock and I don't want to be late."

"Mr. Whitfield?" Clara asked haltingly.

Cat stopped and turned around. "Why, yes," she said slowly.

"He called about an hour ago and said he would pick you up here."

Cat felt the blood rush to her head. "Really?"

"Well, I suggested it." Clara's agitation grew.

The feelings about having her friends meet her mother came back as though she were still a little girl in Brooklyn who was embarrassed about her immigrant family.

"I'll go dress," she said, and slammed into her room.

As she dressed, her rage grew. What the hell would Clara and Clay Whitfield have to say to each other? she thought in frustration.

Clay arrived just as the clock announced the hour. Much as she wanted to see him, her nervousness about how her mother would behave, how she would appear to Clay, dampened her enthusiasm.

Clay was alone in the living room when Cat emerged. He clasped her to him with great warmth.

"Drink?" she asked moving away.

"Love one."

The minutes ticked by and although Clay seemed perfectly happy to be in her home, admiring the furniture that Clara had brought from Brooklyn, enjoying the various changes that Cat had executed since she took over the apartment, Cat was aware that her mother was not coming out of her room.

"I'm starved," she said finally.

"No problem. I promised to feed you and I will." Clay finished his drink.

"Let me go in and see how my mother is doing before we leave," Cat said, wondering if she would be spared the painful encounter.

Clara was sitting in a chair staring out the window. She was elegantly dressed. Her hair was neatly combed and, as always, she looked extremely dignified. Her discomfort, however, was evident.

"Aren't you coming out to meet my friend?" Cat found herself saying and, for the first time, she realized her mother was as nervous about being introduced to Clay as Cat was about introducing her. The brusque manner, the arrogance, the indelicate way in which Clara had always behaved, was due to her own insecurities. She was not a worldly person, her education was limited and she was self-conscious about her accent when she spoke English. The revelation shocked Cat.

"I'm a little tired," Clara started.

"Don't be silly. Come out and just say hello."

Clay stood up when they walked in.

"Clay Whitfield, my mother, Mrs. Wallenstein," she said, and held her breath.

"Ich freue mich Sie kennen zu lernen," Clay said in fluent German.

The look of relief on Clara's face made Cat want to cry.

"Herr Whitfield." Clara stretched out her hand graciously.

Standing outside her building, Cat could not hide her gratitude. "That had to be the sweetest thing you could have done."

"What have I done?"

"Talking German to my mother. You made her day. Her year. Her decade."

"Nonsense. The truth is my mother was Dutch and no one butchered the English language as she did. So I know the feeling from way back." He pressed her arm to his and they started walking. "Where shall we eat?" he asked when they reached the corner of First Avenue.

"What are my choices?"

"Caravelle? Côte Basque? Twenty-One? You name it."

"I'm not really dressed for any of those places."

"Well, there is always Chez Whitfield," he said cautiously.

"I've eaten dinner there once. On New Year's Eve," she said seriously. "It wasn't bad."

The apartment was dimly lit when they walked in and Clay took her in his arms the minute he closed the door.

"I've missed you terribly," he whispered. Then pulling away he turned on the lights. "I'm afraid I brought you here under false pretenses," he said in mock seriousness as he started to lead her into the living room. "The chef is off tonight. Jackson and Gwenny are out and all we've really got to eat is what they've left in the chafing dishes."

"That's the problem with small, unknown restaurants." Cat picked up his mood. "No consistency."

He turned and looked at her.

"And since the place is so crowded, why don't we go upstairs?" she continued, starting toward the stairway.

36

Flipping through an advance copy of April's *Vogue* magazine, Cat caught sight of several photographs of Megan dressed in various designers' clothes. One photograph was more beautiful than the other and Cat tried to evaluate her feelings. She would be lying if she did not admit that the coverage caused her a twinge of envy, but since she was responsible for Megan's success, she felt a sense of satisfaction which balanced out her jealousy.

On the whole she felt good. Things were working out and except for a few loose ends, she was almost ready to face the future. Her fight with Jeff on the phone had cleared the air, somewhat, and they talked often and were able to discuss Alexandra more rationally. The old camaraderie was almost back. Her mother's health was improving and she would be able to move back to Brooklyn when Cat went to Paris at the end of the week. Even her earnings had picked up. But it was Megan's commissionable income that made it possible for her to catch up financially. Even before the contract was signed, Megan had started working on the cosmetic ads. It was six weeks of grueling work, in which all the still shots were taken as well as most of the television commercials filmed. She was going on location sometime in April, to finish off the rest of the TV spots, but the payments had already started coming in. David was around and although she felt a lessened enthusiasm on his part where their agency was concerned, she was sure that it would change when they announced its existence publicly.

She stopped turning the pages of the magazine and looked over at Clay and Clara, who were sitting on the sofa chatting in German.

Watching them, Cat wondered how her mother would react if she knew that she was Clay's mistress. Mistress! She hated the label but how else could she be described? She, who had prided herself on being a loyal wife, a mother, a working independent woman, had succumbed and was now the rich man's ladyfriend. There was a difference, however. She was madly in love with Clay. He had become a serious part of her life. She missed him terribly when he was away, loved going to bed with him, enjoyed listening to him, wanted to spend every minute with him. And although she sensed he was not in love with her, he made her feel wanted, exciting and beautiful.

At that moment Clay looked up and Cat had to check the impulse to walk over to him. She wondered if he felt the same and knew that even if he wanted to, he would never do it. Certainly not in front of her mother. He was far too disciplined. She could not wait to meet him in Paris. Maybe things would be different if they were with each other for more than just a few hours. They had never slept together through the night or gotten up in the morning, as lovers do.

Putting aside the magazine, Cat picked up *Women's Wear Daily* and tried to absorb herself in what she was reading. A picture of Megan hiding her face with her hand caught her eye. The caption underneath read: "The secret is out! The popular religious model, Megan Baynes, attends early Mass every morning at . . ."

"Oh, Christ!" Cat exploded, crushing the newspaper angrily.

Clay and Clara looked up at her.

"I promised Megan there would be no more publicity about her involvement with the church," she said in frustration. Megan had finally understood she was being exploited, and was deeply upset by it.

She stood up and started pacing. "I wonder who could have done it?" she raged. "Mel hasn't been around her in months." But even as she spoke she knew the answer. It was David and the question was why?

"That's what happens when you become a public figure." Clay's voice distracted her. "As a matter of fact, I've seen her pictures several times in magazines and they always mention her religious devotion."

Clara stood up and Clay did too.

"That young lady should go back to her mother," Clara said.

Cat bristled. Clara had met Megan several times and reacted to her much as she did to David.

"That's ridiculous," Cat said evenly. "She's got a brilliant career ahead of her and I see no reason for her to give it up."

"I'm going to take a nap." Clara ignored Cat's remark and turned to Clay. "You are leaving for Europe, I understand. When will you be back?"

"I should be in New York sometime in the middle of April." He leaned over and kissed the older woman on the cheek. "Now, you take care of yourself."

With Clara gone, Clay came over to Cat and put his arm around her shoulder. "My dear, you take it too much to heart."

"I can't help it. Megan depends on me."

"What will it be like when you have many models to take care of?"

Cat leaned against him. "It would be different."

"In what way would it be different? Every model would have the right to make demands on you."

"But if I have a running agency, I'd have a staff who would help," Cat protested.

"Catherine, are you sure you want this agency?"

The question startled her. "How can you ask such a question? I've been planning it for so long."

"Somehow I get the feeling it's not really important to you. If it were, you wouldn't be going off to Paris at this time . . ."

"David is here and he can take care of everything while I'm gone. We worked that out long ago," she interrupted quickly.

"Martin wasn't very impressed with him," Clay said, moving away from her.

Cat bit her lip. "What does Martin know about running an agency?"

"Well, I know you have a passion for modeling, but you don't have that same passion for managing. As I see it, the only way for you to do it is as a hobby. Take on two or three girls and do whatever it is one does in a modeling agency without consideration for the money. Then you could call the shots and relax and enjoy it."

"I don't believe I could be a dilettante at anything even if I could afford to be one." She stopped in confusion. "Clay, I'm a working woman. I don't know how to be anything else. I don't want to be anything else."

"I keep forgetting that," he smiled indulgently. "Okay," he said after a moment, "I won't be in Paris when you arrive but the suite at the Crillon will be ready for you. Jackson, of course, is at your disposal here whenever you want him and if you have any problems, Martin will be around."

He sounded patronizing and Cat resented it.

At the door, Clay lifted her face to his and kissed her tenderly.

"You're sure you want to do this Paris show?" he asked haltingly.

"I wouldn't dream of not doing it." She was outraged. "I've made the commitment and nothing in the world would make me back out. I think the only excuse for not showing up would be if I dropped dead. But more than that, these ten days will bring me a lot of money." She saw him try to hide his smile and her voice rose. "Don't belittle it!"

"I'm not, except that I would have liked you to come to Munich with me."

"Germany has never been of particular interest to me," she said dryly, and was surprised at the statement. It was not something she had thought about before.

"Okay, my pet. On this note I leave you." He kissed her on the forehead and left.

Closing the front door after Clay's departure, Cat stood for a long time staring into space. Was she being a fool at not taking him up on his offer? In a way he was the embodiment of her dream and he did desire her, wanted to be with her, had even offered to take care of her. Yet she was still trying to reestablish her modeling career. She could not help it, since she did not really trust Clay. She had dreamed of becoming a top fashion model and the dream had come true. What she had not realized then was that it was a dream which by its very nature had to be short-lived, had to end in spite of her. A life with Clay could be another short-lived dream. He had left Eve Simpson. She had replaced Eve Simpson. It could happen to her too. The thought of Clay leaving her was unbearably painful.

Walking into the living room, Cat wondered if she would feel differently if Clay asked her to marry him. She dismissed the thought. Clay would expect her to be an appendage to him. She would cease to be a person in her own right. His remark about the modeling agency was proof of it. David would never say a thing like that. She shrugged her shoulders and decided that in a way having Clay as a lover and David as a friend gave her the better part of two worlds.

For no apparent reason, Jeff came to mind. She knew what Clay expected of her; understood what David wanted. What was it Jeff had wanted?

"You're looking very thoughtful," Clara said, coming back into the room and settling herself in her chair.

"Not really, Mother. I was just thinking about how life plays itself out." She looked closely at Clara, who was quite pale. "Are you all right?" she asked with concern.

"I'm fine. Really fine. I think I'm just lonely and miss my home."

In the past, Clara's statement would have upset her, but now Cat realized there was no malice in it. "Why don't you invite some of your friends over here?" she suggested.

"Catherine, we're all old and we don't travel well."

"Don't say that." She walked over and sat on the floor next to the wing chair. "Mother, you're looking forward to going to Brooklyn when I leave for Paris, aren't you?"

Clara hesitated. "Well, yes. I miss my things."

"I can understand that."

"Each one had deep meaning to me and your papa."

"You loved each other very much, didn't you?"

"He was my whole life," she said slowly. "You and I were all he had."

"I didn't count. He didn't love me," Cat said sadly.

"In a way he loved you more than he loved me."

"Oh, nonsense. He felt sorry for me," Cat said quickly. "And after all these years, I can finally face it." She spoke with assurance but there was little conviction in her statement. The pain was still there.

"He never felt sorry for you." Clara became indignant. "Why, every time he looked at you his heart broke because you reminded him of his Chatsie who was killed in Auschwitz. You replaced her in his life and he was scared that something would happen to you." Her voice had risen with emotion.

Cat could not decide if she wanted to laugh or cry.

"I couldn't have reminded him of her. She was so beautiful."

Clara did not reply and Cat felt the childish resentment of years ago. She was considered beautiful by so many, except her mother.

"But he never stood up for me when you attacked me and hurt me with the way you felt about me."

"Attacked you?" Clara was flabbergasted. "I was worried sick about you. You were so thin, so sickly-looking. You were a strange child, doing everything differently from all the other children. I was afraid you were going to get into trouble and we would not be able to help you. You were all we had and I didn't know what would become of you."

Cat looked at her mother and was amazed at the simplistic thinking. And what was even more amazing was that she probably believed every word she was saying.

"Why don't we spend the evening together, Mother?" she said finally. "We'll get dressed and I'll get a car to come and drive us to some good fish restaurant. You haven't really been out since you got here and I'm sure Mark wouldn't mind, especially if we bundle you up properly."

"I'd like that." Clara's face lit up with excitement.

"It's all settled then."

The phone rang at that moment. Cat glanced at her mother before picking up the receiver.

It was Megan and she sounded upset.

"I know why you're calling, honey. It's that awful picture in the newspaper," Cat started out immediately, although surprised, since she was sure Megan never read the papers.

"I've got a script." Megan had not heard a word Cat said. "Someone sent me a script which they want me to do."

"What kind of script?"

"It's a musical and I don't know if I can do it." She seemed to be on the verge of tears. "Would you read it?"

"Of course I will," Cat assured her, but her mind was racing. "I'll send a messenger over and read it right away." She listened to Megan's sobs subside. "But tell me more about it. Who gave it to you?"

"A Mr. Karsten. David told him about me."

Cat stiffened. "Okay, I'll read it this evening and call you as soon as I finish it." She lit a cigarette. "Incidentally, what does David say?"

"He thinks this is a big break for me and I do trust him."

There was something in Megan's manner which bothered her. "You've decided to do it, haven't you?" Cat said slowly.

"You will help me?" she pleaded, ignoring Cat's question.

"I'll speak to you later," Cat said, and slammed the phone down. "God damn it all," she screamed. "Of all the destructive things that one can do to a human being." She squashed out her cigarette and threw herself on the couch in frustration. She was sure David had given the item about Megan to the newspaper and she was going to talk to him about it. Getting Megan a part in a musical, however, was sheer lunacy.

Clara stood up.

"Oh, Mother." She had forgotten she was there. "I'm sorry, but this is important."

The older woman walked over to Cat. Gently she put her arms around her and pressed Cat's head to her breast. The gesture was strange and caught Cat off guard.

"Don't let anyone push you around, Catherine. Don't get involved in anything that you don't feel is right. Do whatever it is you really want to do. Remember that."

Cat pressed herself closer to her mother's bosom. It was the only time she remembered physical contact between them. She did not shrink away. Did not want to. Instead, she put her arms around Clara's waist and hugged her. She wanted to cry, yet she felt strangely at peace.

37

Pamela felt her eyes sting with pain, warning that tears might come. Quickly she removed her false lashes and rubbed her fingers over her eyes to prevent the pent-up anguish from coming through. She would not allow an overt display of weakness even within the confines of her office. Opening the bottom drawer of her desk, she extracted a bottle of scotch and took out her cup. Balancing it on its matching saucer she filled it deftly, then slowly she raised the drink to her lips and sipped it. She allowed the liquid to stay in her mouth for a moment until she felt the tense muscles of her jaw relax, then she swallowed it with relish. The familiar taste sliding down her throat was soothing. Quickly she drank the remaining whiskey and poured herself another, this time popping a small gray-green pellet into her mouth. She placed the Limoges cup carefully on the desk and stared at it intently. It was so very delicate, so very beautiful and so breakable.

The drinks helped and the pill would soon work its lovely magic. Within minutes she felt better and started shuffling through the photographs lying on her desk. None were of interest, and, in an effort to stave off another bout of misery, she poured herself another drink, then stood up and walked over to the window, which faced the street.

Although it was mid-March, the days were still short and at seven o'clock dusk barely lingered. It was Friday and the movement of the people walking along the street seemed leisurely and serene as though readying themselves for the weekend. It made little difference to her. Every day was the same in her life. She tried to absorb herself in one particular couple, wondering what it was like to walk along with someone whose arm hugged your waist, trying to imagine what they were saying to each other. She had never done it. She closed her eyes and reached out to her youth and sadly realized that there never was a time when she was truly young. She had gone from childhood to womanhood without a pause. For the first time in her life, she missed those years and it startled her.

Turning away from the window she looked around the room and took in the pictures of herself spanning the years from the time she started modeling over thirty years ago. She had that inborn elegance from the start and it had served her well. Her eyes came to rest on the picture of Cat and herself taken by Penn. She was in her thirties then and it struck her that she was almost as old then as Cat was now. It seemed unreal. Somehow she still saw Cat as a young girl who needed to be cared for and protected. She remembered their first encounter. She identified with the excruciatingly thin, tall, almost gawky kid from the start and threw herself into creating Cat and her instincts had proven correct. Cat had all the ingredients of a top model. Aside from her height, the bone structure and her thin figure she had ambition, was inventive and single-minded. She was competitive but fair, never devious or underhanded.

In a way, it was Cat who made her decide that the time had come to tone down her own modeling career and start an agency. She had always known she would. It was simply a matter of timing and persuading Peter to come back to live in the States.

Pamela returned to her desk and poured herself another drink, gulping it down with a pill. She did not want to think of those years, but she could not put Cat out of her mind.

Cat had never been devious, at least not until now. Many people had betrayed her over the years, but she had never thought Cat would. The idea that she had been wrong about Cat after all this time hurt her deeply. Had anyone else tried to cross her, she would have known it immediately; but her deep affection for her protegée blinded her.

First she was sidetracked by Cat's pathetic dependence on David. She saw it first when Cat came in with Megan's pictures. Cat's interest in Megan seemed to be just a friendly gesture by an experienced model toward a beginner. What disturbed Pamela that day was the look that appeared on Cat's face when David walked in. Although she had never approved of Cat's marriage to Jeff, David was hardly a substitute and she became engrossed in the need to break up the relationship.

It was David bringing up Megan's name several weeks later that made her wonder if he was planning on starting his own agency. It amused her. David could never run an agency on his own. He was too unscrupulous and greedy. Besides, she was in full control of David and knew he would never leave her. Her amusement turned to fury when she discovered Megan was up for the Grayson account. It was then that it began to fall into place. Someone who understood the modeling world had to be behind David and as hard as it was to admit, Pamela knew it was Cat. From that moment on she was no longer fighting to protect Cat. She was fighting for her agency. It was

not even Megan getting the job that troubled her. In spite of Megan's
meteoric success, Pamela knew instinctively that there was an insta-
bility in the girl and it would eventually be exposed. It was how to
deal with Cat and David in the interim which preoccupied her.
Although convinced she was right, she had no actual proof. They had
done it very skillfully. Megan was originally represented by Mel
Black, just as David had said. But her contract with Grayson was
handled by some powerful attorney who had incorporated Megan.
There was an office in Megan's name in the attorney's office. No one
there had ever heard of Cat Willingham, or David Thomas.

Thoughts of firing David were with her at all times, but somehow she could not bring herself to do it.

Pamela poured herself another drink. Why had she not fired
him? He was no different from any other assistant she'd ever had.
They all served their purpose and she would send them on their way
when they had begun to bore her. None had achieved a position she
did not wish them to have.

She started pacing again. She did the hiring and she did the
firing, she thought desperately. Yet, when it came to David something happened to her that had made her lose control.

Quickly she picked up the phone, dialed David's office and ordered him to come down.

David waited for Pamela to hang up before slamming down the
receiver.

"You fucking bitch," he whispered furiously as he settled back,
determined to let her wait. She was ruining everything he had
worked for. He knew it the day she announced that she had gotten
Megan the job with Karsten to do the musical. He had forgotten his
impulsive request of months back and was shocked when she
brought it up. She announced it innocently, and although he could
not imagine why she was doing it, he was sure she had a purpose and
that purpose was not in Megan's interest. He remembered all too
clearly Cat's warning about placing Megan in a situation she could
not cope with. More than ever he knew Cat was right. What bothered him was that he could have prevented it and could not explain
why he did not. What was even worse, he knew he would convince
Megan to do it. It made no sense, but his whole relationship with her
was warped. There were times he hated her but the thought that she
would leave him made him break out into a deep sweat. With time he
had accepted her strange hold over him, and though it caused him
unbearable pain, she settled into his subconscious, as though she
belonged.

He put thoughts of Megan aside. What troubled him now was
Cat. He could not convince her that Megan had to do the role. He

had met with her earlier in the day and their meeting ended with her storming out of her office. His greatest concern was that she would cut him out of the agency and deprive him of his commission from Megan's earnings.

Somehow, Cat no longer cared about him. Like everyone else, she too was abandoning him. Frankie had abandoned him. His father had abandoned him, and his mother. He remembered her standing with him in front of the orphanage. He was five years old. It was dusk and he could not quite recall her features. She smiled and waved.

"I will be back," she called to him as she was led away to a large black car.

She never came back.

The phone on David's desk rang out shrilly.

"I thought I told you to get down here." Pamela's voice sounded like a metallic hammer hitting a nail.

"I'll be right there," he said quietly. How he hated to be ordered about.

He glanced at the pile of composites on his desk that he had accumulated. In a way, Cat's leaving for Europe the next day could be a blessing in disguise. With her gone he would approach Megan on his own. He would sign her up and then he would never be ordered around again

Quickly he locked up all but two photographs in a drawer and rushed down to Pamela's office.

"What's up?" he asked as he walked in. The tension in the room was obvious and the mess on her desk unusual. He caught sight of the demitasse cup and the vial of pills.

"Isn't it early for that?" he asked, pointing to the cup. "The evening is still young."

"When I want advice, I'll see an analyst," Pamela said, and deliberately poured herself another drink. "And instead of all this sincere, touching concern for my well-being, suppose you tell me about all these idiotic pictures you've been feeding me these last few months." Her voice rose. "Why, there isn't one interesting girl here. Not even one remote possibility." And picking up a large gold-sprayed wire basket which was brimming over with photographs she began waving it in the air. Photographs flew up and landed around the room. "How do you think I've stayed on top all these years. Certainly not with what you've been bringing in." Her hands began to move around frantically, scanning the faces in the pictures that still remained on her desk. "This cannot happen. I've come into my office for years, long before you came on the scene, and I've always found something I could use." She bit her lip and tried to regain her composure. "Finding new faces is the only real pleasure I have." She

stopped briefly to catch her breath. "This garbage, it's nothing but
. . ."

"Shit," David finished the sentence for her.

"Don't use obscenities in my presence. You know I loathe them."

"Think obscene but talk clean." He smiled. "That's our motto,
right?"

Pamela glared at him for a moment. Suddenly her expression
changed. "David, you've been holding out on me, haven't you?" The
thought seemed to amuse her. He was the one who convinced her to
start cattle calls again, and in the hope of keeping him busy, she had
agreed. Now she understood why. "You have, haven't you?" she said
almost appreciatively.

"What do you mean?" David asked innocently.

"You know all too well what I mean, you dirty little thief. You've
been taking the cream off the top of mother's milk, haven't you?"

"I wouldn't do a thing like that." His voice was calm. He knew
his expression betrayed nothing. She was bound to figure it out
sooner or later but he knew she could not prove it. What was even
better, he knew that she knew she could not prove it. He had done it
skillfully. Sitting in on the cattle calls, he would take note of the girls
Pamela rejected, knew her well enough to know whom she considered a possibility and who was of real interest to her. Getting dupli-
cates from the various models was no problem and those were the
ones that he sent over to Cat for her consideration. Since Pamela
never rushed to sign anyone, he had ample time in which to make up
his mind and even wait for Cat to make up hers. He had rehearsed
the scene which would be played out when Pamela discovered what
he was up to and now that it was being played, he felt very secure.

"As a matter of fact, Pamela, the reason I took so long in coming
when you called was that I was looking for two pictures in particular
that I thought you would be interested in." He stopped and watched
her face take on an eager look. Slowly he walked over to her desk and
put the photographs in front of her.

"These girls are probably twelve or thirteen years old," Pamela
said furiously.

"Maybe fourteen," David nodded his head. "But they are gorgeous, you must admit."

"Forget it," Pamela snapped.

"Pamela, you've run a modeling agency all these years with the
motto that the public's insatiable need for the new must always be
satisfied. Well, this is what they're looking for now. And as a social
historian, you should know that better than most." He tried to sound
serious, although by now he was convinced that her interest in her
column was a farce. The column was Peter's and for some unknown
reason Peter allowed her to publish it under her by-line. "Obviously

the trend today is toward very young girls, and I'm sure that serious sociologists are taking note of it and if you're writing a book . . ."

"Shut up, David," Pamela hissed. "I'll sign any girl that I think is a worthwhile model, but I will not abuse innocent kids."

"Innocent kids?" David started to laugh. "Why, these girls could teach you and me a thing or two or three."

"David, if you don't shut up, I swear I'll do something violent." She swiveled her chair around so he could not see her face.

The silence in the room was ominous. Suddenly she began to speak and she sounded different from any other time that he remembered.

"You didn't know I had a child once, did you?" she asked, turning around to face him. "Yes, I had a beautiful little girl named Missy."

Although she was looking directly at him, David was convinced she was not seeing him.

"She was ours, completely ours, conceived by us, given birth to by me. She was Peter's claim to manhood and mine to womanhood and I loved her with every breath I took. I loved her with every bit of feeling given to a woman and she loved me." She stopped for a long moment and her face clouded over. "She was twelve years old when she died." She seemed to be transported back in time. "I was doing a job for *Vogue* in Monte Carlo. I remember it clearly. It was summertime and it was evening when I got the call. She shot herself with her father's gun."

A small shudder went through her. "I rushed back to our house outside Paris and Peter was too broken up even to lie. It seemed the child had walked in on her father making love to a young man." Her voice grew hoarse with emotion. "I've hated Peter ever since and my only salvation is to make him suffer every single day. I think I've succeeded." She looked at David for a long moment. "So you see, David, no young girls in my agency."

"Well, what do you know. You've got a soft spot after all. You're human, deep down inside." It was not what he meant to say, except that he felt stifled by what he had just heard.

"Yes," Pamela answered. "Yes, David. I'm human and I do have a soft spot, which is why I am where I am and you won't ever make it. You have no soft spots anywhere. You think you're compassionate. You think you feel. You think you care. But the truth is you're hollow. You don't love and no one really loves you and no one ever did and no one ever will. And if ever you brush past anything resembling love, give or take, you'll destroy it. You'll use anything and anyone, anytime, for whatever suits you. For you there are no rules. You'll break anything and anyone around if it suits your immediate need and you'll pick on the small and defenseless if necessary." She stopped talking and with a deft hand swept up the papers and photographs from her desk and turned toward her typewriter.

"How do you know?" David found his voice.

"Instinct—and I'm usually right."

He watched her face. It was set in the usual hard lines, with her brow furrowed. Suddenly he understood why Peter's column carried Pamela's by-line. It was part of her revenge for the tragic loss of her child. He felt sorry for Peter but he felt worse for himself. Pamela was wrong about him. He had loved. He had loved his brother, but he died. He was almost sure that at one point Cat loved him and he was able to accept her love. He even thought that someday he might be able to reciprocate that love. Megan came to mind. His feelings for Megan were deep and true. Yes, Megan, she was the proof that Pamela was wrong. He wanted to tell Pamela about Megan but knew she would not understand.

Pamela took a cigarette from the gold case on the table and from habit David jumped to his feet, lighting a match as he approached her. She had her lighter out and the cigarette lit by the time he reached her side.

"You'd better blow it out," she said condescendingly, indicating the lit match in his hand.

David looked down at the burning match, which was precariously close to burning his fingers. He blew it out and walked back to his seat. It was a minuscule incident but within seconds he was again the flunky, the legman, the "assistant" to the top modeling agent in the business.

"You're tired, Pamela," he said when he felt his voice would not betray his hurt. "You look really beat."

"Thanks a lot." She did not turn around.

"I didn't mean it that way," he protested feebly. "I just think you need some rest. Let me sort this stuff out and you go home and turn in early."

"Not a bad idea." She smiled and looked like her old self. "Let's just close shop and turn in for the night." The smile turned malicious. "As a matter of fact, Peter has been asking about you. He will be pleased to see you."

David caught his breath. That, too, was part of Pamela's game. Titillating Peter with her young assistants. The idea was revolting, but the thought that Peter wanted to see him was far more important. If he could win Peter over, he could take a stand with Pamela. He remembered how self-assured he felt in Peter's presence. Somehow he was convinced that Peter would help him.

"Sure you're not too tired?" he asked, trying to check his excitement. "I'll be only too happy to finish things up here." He started piling up the photographs on the desk when the intercom buzzer sounded. Pamela turned and flicked the button and as she did the demitasse glass crashed to the floor.

"Cat's here and wants to come down," Lucille's voice came through the box.

David gritted his teeth. They had had a fight that morning and since she was leaving the next day, he hoped he would not have to see her again before her departure. He was wondering how he could avoid her when he caught sight of Pamela's expression and he froze. She was staring at the broken china as though hypnotized.

38

"What happened?" Lucille asked, hearing the crash over the phone and looking over at Cat, who was sitting opposite her.

Pamela did not reply and Lucille stood up quickly and headed toward the door. Realizing that Cat was not following, she stopped and said impatiently, "Come on, Cat."

Cat got up reluctantly. She did not want to see Pamela or David. She had come by to talk to Lucille and had made the date for this late hour convinced that neither Pamela nor David would be in. When she was ready to leave, Lucille insisted that Cat had to say good-bye to Pamela. Finally Cat relented and Lucille called down.

"What broke?" Lucille asked the minute they reached the bottom rung of the stairs.

Cat took the scene in with distaste. David was deathly pale and Pamela did not look like herself. Cat felt no sympathy for either of them.

Walking over to the desk, Cat looked down at the broken porcelain. "It's only broken in two parts, Pamela. It can easily be fixed," she said calmly.

"Don't bother. I loathe patched-up things." Pamela looked up at Cat as though she were recovering from a deep shock. Then she turned to Lucille, "Have the maid clean it up when she comes in."

Lucille hesitated for a minute. "Okay, I'll see you on Monday." She turned to Cat. "You behave yourself, hear?" Then softening her voice she continued, "And have a good trip and call me when you get back." Without acknowledging David's presence, she walked up the stairs.

"I should have thought you'd be busy packing," David said to Cat. He was worried that her sudden appearance would prevent him from going with Pamela to see Peter.

"I couldn't leave without saying good-bye." Her voice was saccharine and she wished it had not been. But her anger at his getting Megan the part in the musical would not leave her.

"How sweet," Pamela interjected, sounding like her old self. "That calls for a farewell drink."

"I'd love one," Cat said, and was amused to see Pamela's expression. "Don't look so surprised. I've developed a taste for the stuff recently."

"Will a scotch do?"

Cat nodded and Pamela poured the drinks. Her need to know if she had been right about Cat's betrayal was overwhelming.

"It's been so long since I've seen you," she started slowly. "Have you acquired any other new and interesting habits that I should know about?"

"I'm off to Paris to do Bo's show and that's new. I haven't done a European show in years," Cat said pointedly.

"I noticed you've been working all the wrong shows around town." Pamela lit her Turkish cigarette and for a moment disappeared behind a veil of smoke.

"They pay my price and that's all that counts," Cat snapped.

"That's wrong thinking," Pamela said. "My advice . . ."

Cat stopped listening. Pamela loved giving advice about everything to everybody. Being listened to gave her a feeling of superiority. How shocked she would be, Cat thought, if she knew how utterly uninterested she was in listening to her at this moment. The droning voice stopped and Cat realized Pamela had stopped talking.

"Well, thanks for the drink and thanks loads for your words of wisdom. I'll keep them in mind."

"Incidentally, Cat," Pamela's voice stopped her, "I was wondering how that friend of yours is doing—you know, the one whose pictures you showed me back then. I could have sworn she was a loser."

"I'm sure you know she's doing very well," Cat said with annoyance. "Although she's about to do a musical which I think is all wrong for her." She looked toward David to see if he were paying attention.

"Do you really?" Pamela said innocently. "That's a shame. I was instrumental in getting it for her. Karsten, as you know, is a friend of mine and I thought she would be perfect."

Cat's expression did not change, although her stomach turned over in disgust. David had told her he had gotten the part for Megan. Her anger toward him turned to uncontrollable loathing.

"She is going to do it, isn't she?" Pamela asked.

Cat dared not speak, afraid her voice would betray her feelings.

"She *is* going to do it, isn't she, David?" Pamela's voice was demanding.

"How the hell would I know? The last I heard, she was planning on it."

"Temper, temper," Pamela said soothingly. "That's no way to

talk about a friend." Then she turned back to Cat. "And then what are her plans?"

"I'm going to try to persuade her to go back South for a while." Cat found her voice. "I had a long talk with her a few hours ago and that's the way I feel. She's so distraught about this musical, I couldn't really get a clear answer from her."

"What the hell is this whole thing about her being that upset?" David burst into the conversation, unable to control himself.

"I don't really know how to explain it," Cat said innocently. She had tried to convince Megan not to do the show but Megan was adamant.

"I think her leaving New York is absurd, idiotic," David said heatedly. "She's got a great career ahead of her."

"Why, Davie, what's it to you?" Pamela asked.

"You're right." He regained his equilibrium. "Actually it's none of my business."

There was a venomous undertone hovering around both David and Pamela which could be cut with a knife, and for the first time Cat wondered what this brilliant, successful woman saw in David. She knew what her need was for him. And now, even she had seen through him and was trying to disengage herself from him. But Pamela . . .

Suddenly Cat felt very tired. "I really must run," she said again.

"No, wait," Pamela said quickly, and turning to David, she ordered him to get her car.

"I'll call the garage and have them deliver it," David said.

"That's not what I said," Pamela said coldly. "You go get it."

"Pamela, I'll see you when I come back. I still have so much packing to do," Cat said when David left. She did not want to be alone with Pamela.

"How long will you be gone?"

"Three or four weeks." Cat picked up her bag. "I'm meeting Clay Whitfield after the Paris show and we're going to the South of France."

"Is it serious?"

"Who knows?" Cat shrugged. "He's a wonderful man." She tried to sound indifferent. Clay was too important to her to discuss with Pamela.

"Could you marry him?"

"He hasn't asked me."

"Yes, you probably could," Pamela said thoughtfully. "I wouldn't have thought so six months ago, but today I think you could swing it." The insult was blatant.

"And what's that supposed to mean?" Cat regretted the question the minute it was out of her mouth. How could she explain to Pamela that she was hopelessly in love with Clay.

"The Cat I knew could never have compromised herself, could never have accepted what goes along with being married to someone like Clay Whitfield. But you're no longer the same lady."

Cat did not want to listen, but she felt as though she were glued to the spot.

"Why did you do it, Cat?" Pamela asked simply.

"Do what?"

"Betray me," her voice was strangely soft. "You of all people betrayed me and I don't understand why." Her sincerity upset Cat and involuntarily her eyes swept up the stairs.

"It was David, wasn't it?" Pamela laughed softly. "You really got involved with him, didn't you?"

Cat felt like a child being lectured to by a schoolteacher, and it annoyed her.

"It's really none of your business," she said firmly.

"You couldn't begin to cope with someone like him."

"I noticed you're working at it rather diligently."

"You fool. I can afford it. I'm a grown woman, whereas you're still an overprotected child."

"I resent that," Cat said indignantly. "I've been on my own since I was seventeen, working my ass off, mostly for you, and doing a pretty good job of it."

"Working doesn't necessarily make you grow up."

The silence grew heavy.

"You were one of the few people who really meant anything to me," Pamela said finally.

"You had a hell of a way of showing it the last few months."

"Maybe you're right, but in the final analysis, I would never have let you down and you know it. Or you should have known it."

Cat felt torn. Since walking out of the office that day with Megan's pictures, she had not called Pamela, had not talked to her and had allowed a rage to grow. A rage which, she now realized, was nurtured by David.

"I think you're overdramatizing the whole thing. I did not betray you. You started this agency around me and I'm going to build one around Megan. I came to you first, remember, and you turned her down. As for the Grayson deal, that was a lucky break."

It was out in the open and Cat watched Pamela closely. Her expression did not change, but Cat knew that Pamela would never forgive her.

"She won't make it, you know," Pamela said evenly.

"I don't know about that."

"I'll see to it that she doesn't."

"How?"

"Why don't you wait and see?"

Cat walked over and poured herself another drink. She did not really want one but was feeling shaky and needed fortification for what she was about to say. Then turning to Pamela she cleared her throat.

"Pamela, you play with people and for the first time since I've known you I can tell you, I don't like it. Worse, I don't like you." She took a deep breath before continuing. "Out of habit or whatever, I've taken the shit you handed out but it's over, finished, done with."

A look of pain shot across Pamela's face and Cat wished she could retract her words. It was not that she did not mean most of what she said, but she should have couched it with a little more kindness.

Turning around quickly she started up the stairs.

39

David was relieved to find Pamela alone when he returned.

She stood up shakily when he walked in and he realized she was drunker than he had ever seen her. He watched her look around in a dazed manner; then she picked up her phone and dialed a number.

"Peter?" she said after a moment. "I'm leaving the office now. No, I'm not quite sure when I'm coming home." She listened for a moment. "Well, I hope you have a nice time and I'll see you in the morning." She stopped. "Yes, David will see me home." There was malice in the last phrase.

David, watching her, felt revulsion at the look of satisfaction that gleamed in her eyes. He had listened to similar conversations between husband and wife on other occasions when Pamela and he left the office together. Tonight, the sickness of the relationship took form. He was aware that he was a peon in the overall scheme of their game, but it did not bother him. He wanted to see Peter and that was all that mattered.

He tried not to rush as he helped Pamela into the car and got behind the wheel.

"Home?" he asked, wanting to get there before Peter left.

"I don't want to go home." She sounded like a spoiled child.

"Come on, Pamela. It's been a hectic day."

"No. We're not going home. I want to go to the Factory." She was a little more alert, although the expression of something akin to despair began to appear on her tired face.

He dared not disobey.

To the casual observer, seeing her in the various spots they visited that night, nothing in Pamela's behavior indicated she was in any way different from her usual self. But David knew she was really unaware of much of what was happening around her. He watched her drink her scotch, smoke her Turkish cigarettes, pop pills and pretend to observe the crowds. He kept wondering when he could take her home.

By eleven o'clock, he was drained. Pamela was nearly incoherent, having switched from cigarettes to pot. "Pamela, I don't know about you, but I'm going to turn in."

"You're going to turn in?" she sneered. "Do that and you'll see how fast you're turned out." Her eyes blazed briefly under the highly arched brows. "You will go when I am good and ready for you to. Is that clear?"

David's fingers dug deeply into the cheap velour seat of the seedy East Village discotheque. She was insufferable, gloating over the power she wielded even in her incoherent state.

"I often wondered if Missy's hair would change color as she grew older." Pamela's voice softened abruptly. "I'm so glad it stayed penny red. Penny red. Penny red." She repeated the phrase as she reached over and touched David's hair affectionately.

David had never seen her so out of control. He almost felt sorry for her as he saw her trying to put a reefer to her lips. She was physically helpless and he wondered if her mind were equally dulled. He had to chance it. Getting up, he signed for the drinks and taking her by the arm led her out of the bar. She did not resist. Her subservience made him uncomfortable.

The house was quiet as they entered the front hall. Peter was obviously out and David was relieved. As much as he had wanted to see him, this was not the time.

Leading Pamela past the study, he guided her toward the stairs. Once in her room, he sat her down on the bed. She opened her mouth as if to form a word but it was too garbled. It sounded as though she said "drink." He assumed she wanted her usual nightcap and barbiturates. He watched her fumbling on the enormous bed, still trying to formulate intelligible words, as she reached clumsily for the small vial of sleeping pills standing on the night table next to her bed.

His feelings of compassion for her evaporated. She had so much. She had position, power, admiration. She was wealthy and accepted, and she was abusing it all. And why? Because of a tragedy that occurred years ago? He did not belittle her pain, but his hurt was as great as hers. The tragedies in his life had stunted him, whereas Pamela's misfortunes had made her mean and cruel. If he were in her position, he would reach out to people. He would try to do good. He would share what he had.

Thoughts began to pound at him, thoughts of what he might have if Pamela were gone. If Pamela were no longer around, he would be number one. "If Pamela were dead." The idea was fantastic, but it also frightened him. Out of the corner of his eye he saw her struggling with the vial of pills, mumbling incoherently. If Pamela were dead, he could have the power he craved so desperately and it was now within his reach.

Slowly he walked over to the bar and poured a full glass of whiskey into a cut-crystal tumbler. Then, taking the vial of pills from Pamela, he poured all of them into his palm. A cold sweat broke out on his forehead and he felt hot flashes run up each side of his neck. His hands began to shake as he extended the pills and glass toward her. She looked at them and then stared into his face. For a minute she seemed to smile. He returned the look and wondered if she knew what he was doing. If she did, she gave no indication. Instead, she reached out her hands and held them in space, waiting to receive the liquor and the pills. There was a look of gratitude on her face.

Suddenly he panicked. *She knew what he was doing.* She would take the pills and throw them in his face. She would expose him. She would laugh and then she would throw him out, and he would be abandoned forever.

Frantically, he replaced all but one capsule into the vial. He poured the liquor down the bathroom sink and refilled the glass with water. Back in the bedroom, he handed Pamela one pill along with the water. She put the glass to her mouth and drank thirstily. Some of the water dribbled down her chin. Then, like a marionette whose strings were cut from above, she dropped her head on the pillow. Within seconds he saw her body relax, and the smile, that amused knowing smile, appeared around her lips.

David did not move. The one and only Pamela Fitzpatrick was high on a trip, he thought derisively. She was totally defenseless, completely at his mercy. He could have killed her and no one would have known.

Before leaving the room, he turned to look at her once more. She was fast asleep. Her mouth was partially open and her hand hung limply over the edge of the bed.

His step was light as he bounced down the spacious stairway.

"Why, David, how nice to see you," Peter said, coming in the front door just as David reached the bottom rung. Then Peter's expression changed. "Is Pamela all right?"

David froze. Although it was not unusual for him to be in their house at that hour, he took a minute before answering.

"Of course she is. She did get slightly high tonight, but she'll be fine in the morning." He sounded natural and he was relieved. "Just let her sleep it off."

"She was deeply unhappy this evening when she phoned," Peter said with concern.

"Pamela is never happy."

"Tonight was different."

"I was in the room when she called and I didn't notice anything different. She sounded the same to me."

"Not to me. I know her too well."

"Maybe you're right," David said evenly. He felt calmer. Talking to Peter made everything seem simple and pleasant.

"How about a nightcap?"

He hesitated briefly. Pamela was out for the night. It would be nice to have a drink with someone who made him feel the way Peter did.

"I'd love one."

While waiting for Peter to pour their drinks, David's eyes came to rest on the urn and he remembered his nightmare. But what made him shudder was that he now knew what the urn contained. Missy's ashes were in it. Pamela was cruel enough and vengeful enough to make Peter live with them in his study.

"David?" Peter said, and his name sounded foreign in the way Peter pronounced it. "David?" Peter called his name again in a soft whisper.

He turned slowly. Peter was standing close to him. He felt Peter's hand slide down his arm, then onto his hand. Clearly he knew he had anticipated this very moment when he accepted Peter's invitation to have a drink with him. He thought of moving away. Instead, he closed his hand over Peter's and held it tightly in his own.

The bargain was sealed. It did not seem wrong to hold Peter's hand. It seemed natural and reassuring. Neither of them spoke.

I need him, David thought, and the idea startled him. Incredible soft lips covered his. Infinitely gentle lips. All the scorn, the abuse, the ridicule he was ready to hurl upon himself did not materialize.

So this was the way it was. It was not like the stories he had heard countless people joke about. He himself had joined others in deriding such a relationship. Why was it so unforgivable? Why did he not feel like sneering now? At this moment, such a kiss reassured him. It told him he was accepted, wanted. People had wanted him before, but not quite this way. Tonight, for the first time in his life, there was no pretense. Tomorrow, perhaps, he would feel shame. Tomorrow he would feel disgust, ignore the episode, wipe it out of his mind, pretend it never happened. But not now. Now it was real. All the emptiness, the gnawing, endless emptiness was gone. It was as though some magical god had made it go away.

With a clarity that amazed him, he knew that never again would he be pushed around.

As David climbed into his bed later that night, he looked around his shabby room and relived the moments with Peter. Of course, he knew why he had done it. It was not because he really wanted to. It was one of those things that had to be done. Peter was important to his future.

David closed his eyes, content with his explanation, oblivious to the pleasure, the tenderness that Peter afforded him only a short while ago.

40

Traffic to Kennedy Airport was almost at a standstill and Cat hoped she would not miss her plane. She was late, since she had started packing only that morning. Normally, she would have packed the night before, but the scene with Pamela had upset her and she had spent most of the night mulling it over. She had been too cruel. After all, Pamela was convinced that whatever she did was for Cat's own good, just as Cat felt that what she was doing for Megan was for Megan's good. Both she and Pamela had presumed to take control of people's lives without realizing they were projecting their own needs and ambitions. Coming to that conclusion was difficult, but when she finally recognized it, Cat knew that she had moved to another plateau. It was not a higher or lower one. It was just a different one. It was followed by the acceptance that she was not going to model again.

To her surprise, the decision was not accompanied by pain or despair. She was relieved. Never again would she be placed in the position of being inspected by prospective designers, producers, manufacturers or buyers. She could stop looking expectantly at faceless receptionists, wondering if they knew who she was, or having to be charming and pleasant when she did not feel like it. But most important, she had come to the decision on her own. She was quitting because she wanted to.

The revelation and relief were so great that she wanted to share it with someone and she called Jeff. She was bubbling with excitement when she heard his voice.

"I'm quitting the modeling field," she said without preliminary salutations. "And I'll have all the time in the world to spend with Alexandra. I've worked it all out. I'm going to run a small modeling agency and that will give me enough money to support us and it won't take up too much of my time."

He did not react immediately, and then he said quietly, "If that's what you really want to do, Cat, that's great."

She felt deflated by his reaction. She had been sure he would be pleased.

"What time does your plane take off?" the driver asked.

"It's a 10 A.M. flight."

"I hope we make it," he said. "This traffic is terrible."

"We will," she said with confidence, and leaning back, she closed her eyes. Her thoughts returned to her conversation with Jeff.

"If that's what you want to do . . ." The phrase was the crux of what was wrong with their marriage. It also pointed out the difference between Clay and Jeff. Clay told her what to do. It was he who suggested the small agency. She had dismissed it at the time, but he was right. She would have no more than six models and although not all would be big money-makers like Megan, somehow she would manage.

It did not matter what Jeff thought. She was happy with her decision.

The airport, when they arrived, was crowded and there were long lines at the ticket counter. It was nearly nine-thirty when Cat boarded the plane.

Buckling herself into her seat, Cat felt good. She had attended to most things, not the least of which was her call to Jeb Kimbrough to ask him to go to Megan's opening. He became very emotional when he heard who she was and what she was calling about. He had a thick Southern accent and she had a hard time understanding what he was saying. His genuine concern, however, was clear and Cat was glad she had called. When she hung up she wondered if he were Megan's lover. The thought surprised her. Megan was terrified of men and, to the best of Cat's knowledge, had never dated anyone since she came to New York. She put the thought aside. She was pleased Jeb was coming up. She wanted someone who cared to be with Megan on that night.

She had even spoken to Grayson just before she boarded the plane and told him she was Megan's agent. In a way, that call established her in her new career. Except for feeling uncomfortable about the state of her friendship with Pamela and her uncontrollable loathing of and disappointment in David, she felt free. She was embarking on a new life and although tired, the excitement seeped through.

The plane started its take-off. Cat stretched her head to see the New York coastline grow smaller as the plane rose into the air. She loved the city but was grateful that Bo had asked her to do his collection in Paris. It was right that this should be her last modeling job. Clay would be arriving the morning after the final showing. Her thoughts lingered on him. They would have ten days together. Three in Paris and the rest in Monte Carlo. She wondered what the suite at the Crillon was like. She had never stayed there and was looking forward to it.

"Would you like a newspaper?" the hostess asked.

Cat took a New York *Times*, placed it on her lap and looked to see if the No Smoking sign was finally off. It was. She took out her cigarettes, lit one and inhaled deeply.

She wondered how Clay would react if he knew she was in love with him? Would it change their relationship? Could she maintain it if Alexandra came to live with her? Would she interfere with what she and Clay had between them? Of course, if she married Clay, it would be so much simpler. She mulled over the last thought. She would not push it, but she really was someone who liked being married. But if she married Clay, could she go on working? Even a small agency would require work. He probably would not allow it. But that was what she loved about him. He made decisions. She smiled to herself. She was daydreaming again.

"Coffee or tea?" The hostess brought her out of her reverie.

Cat took the small tray and placed it on the drop table in front of her and looked down at the newspaper. The front page dealt with world affairs. She turned the pages slowly, skimming the headlines absently. She froze as the words PAMELA FITZPATRICK FOUND DEAD jumped out at her.

She looked over at the man sitting beside her. He was sipping his juice calmly. She peered at the people across the aisle. They were talking to each other quietly. The hostess was chatting amicably with someone in the seat ahead. Cat looked back at the headline and her eyes took in the short bulletin beneath the headline.

. . . her husband, Peter Hazeltine, who discovered the body of his fifty-two-year-old wife in the couple's bedroom when he returned home late last night, said he believed his wife's death was accidental.

"Pamela had just begun a new medication and she had had a couple of drinks and I think she did not know that the two did not mix," Mr. Hazeltine said. "It's a tragedy, because she was in the prime of her life."

Police today questioned David Thomas, an assistant to Ms. Fitzpatrick, who is believed to be the last person who saw her alive . . .

Cat raised her eyes and stared out the window at the vast white clouds which seemed to stretch to eternity. The plane appeared not to be moving at all. Everything looked so peaceful and serene. She felt suspended in space both physically and emotionally suddenly. Pamela's face was superimposed on the bleak emptiness outside the window and Cat wanted to get back to New York. Somehow she had to stop the plane and get back to the city. She had to be there before her friend was buried. She had to see Pamela and tell her she cared for her. Maybe her words would breathe life back into her. Pamela could not be dead.

"You may now unfasten your seat belts. Breakfast will be served in a few minutes." The announcement came over the loudspeaker and Cat could not adjust to the idea that no one around cared about her great loss.

"Would you like scrambled eggs or fried . . ." The hostess was smiling pleasantly at her.

"I'd like a double scotch," Cat said, and noticed that the man next to her stared at her in amusement.

Cat did not remember the rest of the flight.

"Miss Willingham?" A chauffeur came toward her. "Mr. Whitfield asked me to pick you up and take you to the hotel."

Cat tried to focus her eyes on him. Clay was taking care of her. Where was Clay? She wanted to get back to New York. Pamela was dead and she had to see her just once more. If Clay were here he would tell her what to do.

The car stopped in front of the Crillon and Cat stumbled out. She did not want to stay there alone. She and Pamela always stayed at the Élysée Hotel and she wanted to be with Pamela.

"Miss Willingham, how delighted we are to have you. Mr. Whitfield has made all arrangements. If you would follow me." The elegant young manager was smiling graciously at her.

"I must call New York." She slurred her words. She did not care. She had to talk to Lucille.

"I'm catching the next plane back to New York," she said, and she did not recognize her own voice. It was the first time she had spoken to anyone who understood her pain.

"You'll do no such thing," Lucille said wearily. "You're committed to do Bo's show and that's just what you're going to do."

"He'll understand," Cat wailed. "I've got to be at Pamela's funeral. I've got to!" The hysteria poured forth. "I, more than anyone, have a right to mourn her at her graveside."

"What graveside?" Lucille said harshly. "Pamela will be cremated in the morning. There will be a short service and that's it."

Cat hung up the phone slowly. Pamela would be cremated and she would never be able to tell her how sorry she was for the harsh words spoken at their last meeting. Angry as they were with each other, one did not wipe out twenty years of friendship because of a misunderstanding. There would not even be a grave where she could go and place a flower, a token of her love and gratitude.

For the first time she recalled the days of mourning following her father's death. It was a nightmare which she avoided thinking about, but now she remembered the painful period. The funeral procession was vague, but the seven days of shared sadness following the burial were vivid. Although her father was dead, he continued to live in the thoughts and minds of everyone who came and sat with her mother and her. He was not passed into oblivion so abruptly as Pamela was through the act of cremation.

"May I take your bags up, madame?" the manager asked, and Cat knew she would not stay at the Crillon. It would not be the place to mourn Pamela.

"No," she said quietly, "I won't be staying here." She wanted to be at the Élysée, where she felt she belonged.

The concierge at the Élysée did not recognize her and Cat realized that it had been several years since she had been to Paris. She asked for the rooms she and Pamela had shared years back but they were occupied. The feeling of displacement mounted. Pamela was dead and Cat was clinging to an existence that was alive only in her mind.

Once in her room she wondered why she had bothered. Did it matter if she were at the Crillon or anywhere else? She tried reaching Bo but he was not in. Coming to Paris had meant so much to her. She could not remember why.

Cat sat in a chair staring into space, and found herself reliving her early years with Pamela. They had been exciting and carefree. Everything seemed to come so easily. Yes, there had been rejections, but they were so quickly forgotten when acceptance came. And Pamela had been there to smooth the way. Who would ever be able to cushion her pain again?

The knock on the door startled her. She looked at her watch. It was almost midnight and she realized she was cold. Wearily she got up and went to the door. Clay was looking at her with deep concern.

She threw herself into his arms.

"I just heard the news about Pamela Fitzpatrick's death," he whispered, holding her close. The tears which had been held back since she read the news item gushed forth uncontrollably. Clay cradled her in his arms and let her cry. Then maneuvering her gently toward the bed, he let her rest her head on his shoulder. She snuggled up to him for safety and comfort.

"Cat, I think you've struggled alone for too long," he said when her sobs subsided. He lifted her face to his. "I want to marry you. I'd like to take care of you and make you happy. I've given it a great deal of thought. We'll have a good life together. I have a great deal to offer you and I know you've got a great deal to offer me."

She kissed him on the lips and the pain, the sadness, the world around her faded. She was lying in the arms of the man she loved and she wished the moment would last forever.

"I love you, Clay," she whispered.

"You're like a little girl." He smiled ruefully. "You don't have to say you're in love with me. I want to marry you because you are you."

She sat up. "You don't understand. It has nothing to do with whether you want to get married or not. I've been in love with you from that first night we had dinner, but it was a while before I realized it."

He patted her shoulder warmly.

"You've got to believe me," Cat persisted. It was crucially important for him to know how she felt. "I was going to tell you that just being with you was all that mattered."

He kissed her and, pushing her away gently, he stood up. "I've got to leave in an hour. My plane is waiting for me at the airport. But I'll be back in ten days and you'll give me your answer then."

She looked up at him. She did not want him to go.

"The suite at the Crillon is waiting for you," he said quietly.

"I think I'd better stay here while I'm doing the shows. It's part of a life which I'll miss and I want to be close to it for just a while longer."

He kissed her warmly and he was gone. She was painfully aware that he did not say he loved her.

41

The cacophony of the music which filled the grand ballroom of the George V Hotel was, in fact, brilliantly orchestrated to match the variation of designs Bo had created for his Paris showings.

On this last evening of presentations, Cat, who had been Bo's fitting model in New York for the entire collection and had worked in Paris both as model and Bo's watchful helper, was nervous as she watched the young girls burst through the curtains to the raucous rock music. She knew the clothes, and worried that the models, in their exuberance, would forget that designs were being presented, not their own personalities.

It had been a grueling ten days and Cat was grateful for the hard work. She was the only American model and Bo involved her in every aspect of the shows. At first, the European models were wary and suspicious of her, but when they saw her on the runway, they began to look to her for approval as much as they did to Bo. It was gratifying, it kept her busy and gave her little time to think.

Standing in the small dressing room, Cat slipped into the final design, which was Bo's *pièce de résistance* and which had all of the Parisian fashion world agog. She allowed her dresser to zip up the back. She barely had time to glance in the mirror when the music suddenly stopped and she walked quickly toward the curtained entrance to the ballroom. The sudden hushed silence from the audience in the ballroom was almost eerie.

"Now," Bo whispered, and on his command the curtains parted. Cat stood immobile as a floodlight, dim at first, grew brighter, and the notes from a single guitar began to filter through the room.

Maintaining the proper somber air, Cat was the perfect model for the gown, which was made of thousands of brilliant red bugle beads touched off with glints of black. The halter top in hand-beaded Kabat silk chiffon mushroomed out into a balloon shape and came down to just below her hipbones. From there, the pencil-thin skirt of the same fabric, hugged her thighs and fell loosely to the floor. Slowly she lifted her bare arms and touched the tight-fitting black cap which covered her head and was swathed in sheer black lace, which was gathered toward the center of her forehead and held by an enormous red satin rose.

Cat heard the gasp of appreciation rise from the crowded room, followed by thunderous applause. She started to walk slowly, allowing a small smile to appear on her lips. The solo guitar was then joined by the rest of the band as she began to move down the runway. Gliding toward the turn, she lingered, turned sideways long enough to give a new line to her body and outfit. Then, as though growing bored with the pose, she turned her back to the audience briefly, stopped and, placing a blood-colored manicured hand across her hipbone, she looked back longingly over a curled shoulder. Her body began to sway to the sound of the music, which had now grown to full pitch, and the audience stood up, pushing back the elegant gilded chairs in their enthusiasm, their voices rising in appreciation.

The sound of clicking cameras, the flashing of bulbs and the warmth emanating from the crowded room reached Cat through a haze and for a brief moment a flicker of excitement ignited in her and she allowed herself to feel the old joy of being accepted and loved. It disappeared as quickly as it had come. It was as though a mist surrounded her and she could not push it away.

The cheers followed her back to where Bo was standing. He was beaming.

"They loved you," he whispered, and kissed her on the cheek. Then he clapped his hands like a schoolmaster and the dozen models who had participated in the show walked out to the runway to take their final bows.

Bo took Cat's hand and together they followed the last model out to the ballroom, where colorful strobe lights were now circling the audience. The room took on the gaiety of a discotheque.

The models began to mingle with the audience, everyone kissing and hugging each other as though they were long lost friends. It was an unusual sight for a Paris fashion show, but Bo Shephard had presented them with a magnificent collection and the normally staid audience was swept away with enthusiasm.

Several people came up to Cat and greeted her by name and although she recognized the faces, she could not quite remember when or where she had met them.

As discreetly as she could, she edged her way to the dressing rooms. She was far more tired than she realized and she wanted to get to the Crillon. Although it was not yet midnight and Clay was not due in until three that morning, she wanted to have a rest and be awake when he arrived. It was to be their first night in Paris together.

"Coming to our little soiree at the Lancaster?" Bo came toward her, his face flushed with excitement.

"Not tonight. I'm exhausted and I'd like to get some shut-eye." She purposely did not mention Clay.

"Then I'll take you home."

"Don't be silly. Besides, I'm going to walk and that will take quite a while."

"Greg will hold down the fort," Bo said firmly. "And I'll be delighted to walk down the Champs-Élysée with the toast of Paris."

"Hardly that." She smiled, looking down at the dungarees, sweater and sneakers she was wearing. "And you'd look awfully suspect walking with me dressed as you are in that magnificent tux."

"Fear not, lady," he grinned. "These are, after all, my working clothes."

Walking along the wide boulevard arm in arm, Bo Shephard and Cat Willingham did not look like the elegant designer and famous model they had been just a brief while back. Bo, like Cat, had changed into dungarees and sneakers.

The street began to grow emptier as they passed the Rond Point and the Élysée Palace's lights could be seen through the trees. It was a perfect April night, with a pleasant breeze moving gently through the freshly planted spring flowers. The dim streetlights accentuated the beauty of the surroundings, and the atmosphere was romantic and filled with nostalgia. Cat felt Bo's arm pressing hers protectively. They had walked in a similar fashion many years back and both were absorbed in thoughts of the past.

"You're not going to model anymore, are you?" Bo broke the silence.

She threw him a sidelong glance. "How did you know?"

"You were superb tonight. Magnificent, stupendous, but there were two things which gave you away. You never once looked into the mirrors surrounding the ballroom to see yourself and you never really saw the audience."

He is right, she thought sadly. She had been unable to make eye contact with anyone, not even herself.

"Was it that obvious?"

"Only to someone who knows you and loves you as much as I do," Bo answered. Then after a brief silence he asked, "Why?"

"Don't you think it's time?" she said slowly, and found herself holding her breath, waiting for his answer.

"Yes," he finally said.

She had girded herself for the answer and yet when it was worded she felt a stab of pain shoot through her.

"Now mind you," Bo continued thoughtfully, "you can go on modeling. Most models who look like you, and model as well as you do, could squeeze in another few seasons, but not you. You're smarter than that."

"How I wish I weren't so smart," she said sadly. "It's hard to give up that applause, the feeling that everyone is looking up at me, smiling at me, appreciating me. Even tonight, I felt it for a couple of seconds and how I wished I could have held on to it . . . forever."

"What will you do?" Bo asked and he, too, sounded sad at what she was saying.

"I was thinking of opening a modeling agency. As a matter of fact, I should tell you that I was handling Megan Baynes and as you yourself said, whoever was mapping out her career was doing a damned good job."

"You're saying it in the past tense," Bo said suspiciously.

"Clay asked me to marry him."

Bo stopped walking and looked around. "Where are we walking to, anyway? I thought you lived at the Élysée."

"I moved into the Crillon today. Clay has a suite of rooms there which he uses whenever he's in Paris."

Bo sucked in his breath as if trying to control his emotions. Then he put his arms around her and held her close. She folded him in her arms adoringly.

Then pushing her away, he looked directly into her eyes. "My precious funny face, are you sure you'll be happy?" he whispered.

She felt the tears well up in her eyes. "The way I feel these days, I wonder if I'll ever be happy again."

He touched her face, wiping away the tears. "Who would believe that you are the woman who has dazzled Paris for the last week, captured the imagination of hundreds of thousands through the years, and is now standing on a street corner longing for . . ." He stopped and searched for the word. "For what?" he asked finally.

"I don't know." She lowered her eyes. "To be wanted? To be needed? To be loved?"

"Just like everybody else," Bo said quietly. "Except that in your case, you know you can come into my showroom anytime and get it all. Remember that, always."

With that he turned away quickly and she watched him rush back toward the Champs-Élysée, waving frantically for a passing taxi.

Slowly Cat started toward the Place de la Concorde.

42

Cat heard the muffled sound of the phone ringing, but she refused to wake up. Bad as the nights were, when sleep finally came, thoughts would disappear, and with them the confusion which she had been living with for the last few days.

The ringing continued and she finally reached over and picked up the old-fashioned antique receiver.

"New York calling for Miss Willingham," the international operator announced.

It was another call from Lucille and Cat wondered why she had not taken Clay's advice to leave word with the hotel operator that no one should be put through unless announced beforehand. She had been tempted but could not bring herself to do it. There was something pretentious about it.

"Cat, for crying out loud, when are you coming back to the States?" Lucille asked unceremoniously when she heard Cat's voice. "I'll be charged with murder if you don't come back soon."

"What's the matter?" Cat asked cautiously. Sitting up, she glanced at the small clock. It was twelve noon and she was shocked. She had never slept that late in her whole life.

"David Thomas is a monster. No, he's the devil incarnate. I believe he's going to destroy everything Pamela built over the years in a couple of months, unless someone stops him. And you're the only one I can think of."

"What's he done?" Cat asked, trying to keep calm. She was not ready to take on the agency. She had not really accepted the fact that Pamela was gone. She reached for a cigarette on the nightstand. There were none there. She gritted her teeth. Clay was trying to get her to cut down on her smoking and at that moment she was ready to scream.

"I think the oldest model he's taken on in the last few days is about ten years old. The third floor has been turned into a nursery with dolls and balloons."

"You're exaggerating," Cat said impatiently.

"Of course I am, but not by much, and I'm telling you I won't stay on. I swear it's only my feeling of obligation to Pamela's memory and my loyalty to the models whom I've known for so long that makes me come in every day."

"Is the agency making money?" Cat asked coldly.

There was a long silence.

"Well?" Cat demanded. "Are the girls he's signing up money-makers?"

"In the short run," Lucille snapped.

"That's your opinion. It might not be so."

"Why are you defending him?" Lucille asked angrily.

"I'm not defending him. I'm simply stating a fact."

"You don't sound like yourself." Lucille's tone changed.

"I can't imagine what you're talking about," Cat said noncommittally, although she knew Lucille was right. In the time she had spent with Clay, especially the last ten days since moving into his suite at the Crillon Hotel, she had changed. Watching him deal with people, listening to him cut through highly charged business meetings with the one criterion overriding all else, whether the project generated money, she had learned a great deal. She could not decide if she liked herself in this new light, but it was better than getting caught up in the hysterical tailspin in which Lucille was trapped.

"Okay," Lucille said. "I guess I'll have to play it by ear for now." There was a pause. "But when are you coming back?"

"In a day or so. I promised my mother I'd try to spend Passover with her," Cat answered, and was about to hang up when Lucille spoke again.

"Incidentally, there's a Mr. Kimbrough looking for you."

Cat pressed the phone closer to her ear and waited.

"It's something to do with the Baynes girl, who smashed her knee while performing in some out-of-town show."

"Smashed knee?" Cat echoed the words.

"Something like that," Lucille said, unaware of the impact the news was having on Cat.

"Is it serious?"

"This Kimbrough guy seems to think so."

"I'll call you when I get back to the city." Cat choked out the words and hung up quickly.

Everything was falling apart around her, she thought dully, and she had no way of controlling it. Pamela was dead and Lucille wanted her to come back and take her place. She had not been able to fathom the loss, much less think of replacing Pamela at the office. She had succeeded in skirting the full horror of it while doing Bo's shows, and being with Bo and Greg helped. She had hoped that spending time with Clay would relieve the pain. It did for a while but his work was so demanding that he could not fully devote himself to her state of mind. But Megan hurt was more than she could stand. Pamela's death caused in her a deep sense of mourning but there was nothing she could do about it. Megan in a hospital was a different matter. Cat felt totally responsible for it. She should have forbidden Megan to do the musical.

A feeling of futility gripped her as she climbed out of bed and slipped into a robe. The silk fabric next to her skin and the tickling of the feather trim as it brushed against her chin irritated her. She was living in a fairy tale setting and the time had come to wake up.

Angrily she took the robe off and picked up her old terry cloth one, which was lying on the chair.

Walking over to the ancient armoire, she opened it and stared at the numerous designer clothes, which Clay insisted on buying her. In all the years she had modeled, she had occasionally splurged on an outfit which she bought at a reduced price when the shows were over. Even then they were expensive and she considered them an extravagance. Her lifestyle while married to Jeff rarely, if ever, called for dressing up in haute couture clothes. Buying them at full price was outrageous. It struck her that they had cost more than she had earned over a period of several months and she felt foolish. Clay had asked her to forego the work and until this moment she had not realized that in his calculations, her earnings were negligible.

"Is madame ready for her coffee?" Marie, the maid appointed to take care of her, had come into the room and was holding a small tray.

Cat waved her hand indifferently, indicating the tray be placed on the table.

"May I open the blinds?" Marie asked.

Cat nodded and wondered at her manner. It was unlike her to treat a maid so indifferently.

"Thank you." She forced the words out and wished she were back at the Élysée Hotel. Staying at the luxurious Crillon as Mr. Whitfield's guest was like living in a gilded cage.

As soon as Marie was gone, Cat picked up the phone and made a reservation on the first flight to New York early the next day. Clay would simply have to understand that she had responsibilities and obligations which she could no longer ignore. She had already stayed longer than she had intended.

Sipping her coffee, Cat walked into the living room. The enormous, magnificently furnished room struck her with awe, much as it did when she first moved in. It was flooded with sunshine coming through the ceiling-to-floor windows and she could see the obelisk of the Place de la Concorde outside. Looking down at the grand plaza, decked with early spring flowers, she could not understand why they did not give her pleasure. Their beauty was breathtaking.

She wondered when Clay would be back. He made everything bearable, she thought, as she walked over to the far end of the living room and peered into the large bedroom which also served as his study. It was empty. She smiled sadly to herself. He had promised to spend every minute with her from the day she stopped working and moved in with him. It had not happened. His work consumed him totally and although they spent the evenings together, they, too, were, in a way, part of his work. Nothing had turned out as she had hoped. She could not get him to spend even one hour with Bo and Greg. She was going to marry Clay and it was important for her that Bo know Clay and like him. But the biggest shock since moving in was having Clay go to his bedroom after they made love. Clay was a man of set habits. Sleeping alone was one of them. The first night it happened, she lay awake long after he left and thought of Jeff. Whether they made love or not, she and Jeff slept together, held on to each other. No matter what, he was there. She could reach out and touch him and he would acknowledge her existence.

Turning from Clay's room, she felt awkward thinking about Jeff but could not put him out of her mind. She tried to imagine him in these luxurious surroundings. He would have appreciated the beauty but would have laughed at the waste. It would have infuriated her, but secretly she would have agreed with him. She wondered what he was doing at that precise moment and wished she had Alexandra with her. Would this beautiful room make her daughter happy? she wondered. The temptation to pick up the phone and call her was overwhelming, but she knew it would be pointless. The six months were nearly over and Cat was still at a loss as to what it was she had to offer Alexandra. Money was obviously not the solution. If anything, it emphasized their flimsy relationship.

The phone rang again and Cat picked it up automatically. Clay, she was told by his secretary, was on his way back to the hotel and wanted to have a drink with her before lunch. It would be the first time they lunched together since she came to Paris. It touched her. He did care, after all.

Quickly she rushed into the bedroom to dress.

Clay was on the phone when she walked back into the living room. She had chosen a glove-thin, navy leather slack suit with matching leather coat, an outfit she knew Clay liked. Kissing him on the cheek, she leaned her head against his shoulder and he held her while continuing to talk on the phone. Finally, hanging up, he looked at her and smiled.

"I don't think I'll ever get used to how beautiful you really are." His voice was filled with affection.

"Thank you, Clay."

"You always thank me when I compliment you. Why?"

"It's quite simple. I work hard at looking as I do."

"Well, you succeed." He walked over to the bar and poured them a drink. "Now, Catherine, I've made a reservation at a very fine restaurant on the Left Bank for you and Prudence Langley. She's the lady we met last night at the ambassador's dinner and you'll be joined by the wife of a Kuwaiti banker who's in town. You'll be hosting the lunch. The chauffeur will get you there and the maître d' is expecting you so there's nothing to worry about. You ladies can order whatever you want to eat. The bill will be attended to and I've ordered the wine."

"Aren't Kuwaiti women supposed to abstain?" Cat asked off-handedly.

"Christ, you're right." He walked over to the phone. She heard him cancel the wine order. "That was very clever, Catherine," he sounded like a proud father. "And I think you'd better wear a skirt rather than those pants. Kuwait is not quite into the twentieth century." He laughed pleasantly. "You don't mind, do you?"

Cat was about to say she minded dreadfully, but restrained herself. She had hoped to lunch with him and tell him that she was leaving the next day. She wanted to ask him what he thought she should do about Megan. She hated herself for her silence.

"Oh, I forgot." Clay stopped her as she was about to go into her room to change. "I bought you something." He took a small box out of his pocket and opened it. It was a magnificent diamond ring. "I thought you should have some sort of engagement present." He kissed her on the forehead. "I believe you've never been engaged before. Am I right?"

Cat stared at the ring. It was nothing she would ever wear, although it was quite beautiful and obviously expensive. She was also convinced it had been bought by Clay's efficient French secretary.

"Do you like it?"

"It's beautiful."

"Catherine, is anything wrong? Aren't you happy?"

Happy. The world sounded out of place, almost ridiculous.

"Clay, I have to talk to you. There are things which I must discuss with you."

"We'll do it tonight. I've arranged for tickets to the opera and then I've made a reservation at the Tour d'Argent and it's only you and I." He pressed her hand. "Now, let me put the ring on your finger and then you'd better hurry and change."

"I'm not yet divorced, remember? I'm not even legally separated."

"Martin Drew will attend to that when we get back to New York.

I shouldn't think there will be any problem," he said with authority. "But if it'll make you feel better, let's call it a friendship ring for now."

Cat changed into an Yves St. Laurent suit and remembered her conversation with Alexandra the day she left for boarding school. Cat had wanted her to wear a different outfit and they nearly had a fight. The child had more guts than she did.

Lunch was a dreadful bore. The women, although charming, were extremely conscious of their positions and unbearably stiff. Prudence played the role of the flighty lady, pretending to have no opinions or convictions about anything. The Kuwaiti woman was reserved and trying to be correct in the presence of the two American women. Except when they discussed the latest fashions, Cat had little to say and preoccupied herself with thoughts of Pamela, Megan, the agency and what Lucille had told her. There was a reality in her life in New York and Cat missed it. She worked hard, sometimes too hard, but that was who she was—a woman working to survive. Lunching with ladies would be what Clay would expect of her when they were married. Suddenly the idea was abhorrent. Nancy Stuart had said that being Jack Hastings' wife was harder work than modeling. If she married Clay, it would be worse, since he was far less volatile and much more domineering in his quiet, subtle way. Marriage to Clay would allow no overt emotions. There would be no fights as she had with Jeff, no raising of voices, probably not even disagreements. It would all be geared to surface elegance. Could she do it? Pamela had said she had changed, that she was ready to forfeit who she was for the sake of a marriage to power and money. She had meant to hurt her with that statement. But Pamela did not know that she had fallen in love with Clay. Still, her doubts were growing. She was not ready to be just Mrs. Clay Whitfield.

Arriving back at the hotel, Cat discovered that plans for the evening had changed. Martin Drew had flown in from New York and was joining them for a drink before dinner. The opera was out.

Cat chose her evening clothes carefully. She still wanted to please Clay. In spite of her trepidations, she had not abandoned the idea of marrying him. She settled on an extremely glamorous Marc Bohan black silk taffeta gown. She sifted through the jewelry which Clay had bought her and tried to understand what pleasure some women got from owning expensive gems. They gave her none. She recalled Pamela's ostentatious need to display her jewels. Cat was convinced that they had added little joy to Pamela's life. She finally settled on a string of pearls and shut the box firmly. It was the simplest ornament in the box.

Clay and Martin were still in the study when Cat walked into the living room. She poured herself a glass of wine. Her growing doubts

about marrying Clay disturbed her on another level. Even before
Clay's proposal, she had booked herself out from work until further
notice. She was depending on Megan's commissions to carry her
financially. Her decision not to go on with her modeling career was
also predicated on those commissions. Now Megan was ill and Cat
had no way of knowing if she could meet her contractual commitment to Grayson. There was every possibility that she would have no
income when she returned to New York. No income and no work to
go back to. Not going back to work had seemed so exciting. She was
going to sleep late, shop, go to matinees and lunch with friends.

She finished her drink and began to pour herself another. She
stopped midway. Having lunch with what friends? Everyone she
knew worked.

The door to the study opened and Clay and Martin came out,
putting an end to her speculations. She noted that Clay was flushed
and it surprised her.

"I'll get right to the point, Catherine," Martin said. "I've drawn
up a premarital contract for you to sign and I think you'll find it
eminently fair."

Cat was startled for a minute and then she started to laugh.

"Did you have a nice flight, Martin?" she asked pleasantly, and
was pleased to see him flush with embarrassment.

"I'm sorry, Catherine. How are you?" he said, and she could see
he was annoyed at having been put in his place.

"Catherine, it's just a contract which Martin feels, and I agree,
has to be signed." Clay intervened to ease the tension.

"Isn't it all a bit premature? I'm still married to someone else."
The whole idea of a contract was preposterous.

"I don't think you understand," Martin became aggressive again.
"This is something that cannot be left to the last minute. There are all
sorts of legal ramifications . . ."

"Martin, I'm not really interested in your legal interpretations of
why I'm being asked to sign this. Just leave that piece of paper on the
desk and I'll look it over when and if I have the time or inclination to
do so. I shall sign it or not, accordingly." She turned away and refilled
her wineglass.

"Clay can't go into an open-ended contract situation." Martin
would not be put off.

"My marriage to Clay, if it should come to be, will not be a
business transaction." She looked over at Clay. He was smiling.

"Okay, Martin." Clay hid his amusement. "You've earned your
salary for the year. Now, suppose you let me handle my future wife
my way."

From his flippant expression, Cat knew he was sure she would
sign the contract. Her resentment rose.

Sitting across from Clay at the Tour d'Argent, with Paris spread out beneath them, Cat watched Clay order their dinner and listened as he chose the wine. His elegance, his self-assurance, his commanding manner fascinated her, and she was shocked when her thoughts suddenly turned to Megan. Such thoughts seemed incongruous at that moment.

"You look pensive," Clay said when the waiter was gone.

"I was thinking of New York and wondering how to break the news to you." She stopped and saw his brow wrinkle. "I've got to go back first thing in the morning. I've already made the reservation."

"But why?"

"Well, for one thing, Megan Baynes has been hospitalized."

"What happened?"

"She's had an accident."

"Serious?"

"Broken knee."

"That doesn't sound too serious," Clay said. "And surely you're not responsible for her. You're her friend, not her mother."

Cat winced. "I feel like her mother."

"Catherine, you are Alexandra's mother. You can feel sympathy for Megan, but you can't rearrange your life for her. Besides, you can't help her now. It takes time for a knee to heal."

"I do have to speak to Grayson. Megan has commitments . . ."

"Martin Drew can attend to that," Clay said firmly. "Right now you've got to think of yourself. You have to establish who you are, what you are and where you're going."

Cat bit her lip. "Clay, that's all part of it. I'm trying to establish who I am and that's another reason I've got to get back to New York."

"I can tell you one thing. You're going to be my wife."

"What happens to Cat Willingham?"

"Cat Willingham is someone with a wonderful past, who can look back on having been one of the top models in New York. And as Mrs. Clay Whitfield, there's a wonderful future to look forward to."

"I'm leaving in the morning," she said, and lowered her eyes.

He reached over and took her hand. "I won't be able to leave until sometime next week, but if you feel you must go, I'll cable Jackson and tell him to meet you at the airport."

He had lost the round, Cat thought, but he was obviously not intending to lose the battle.

"Now, let's just enjoy the evening as planned," Clay said.

Leaning back, Cat heaved a sigh of relief. "You're really a very kind man, Clay," she said finally. "You do make me feel like a princess in a fairy tale."

"That's what I'm trying to do," he said seriously.

The waiter brought their wine and Clay lifted his glass in a silent toast.

"How far I've come from that little girl in Brooklyn." Cat sipped her wine slowly and pondered her last statement. "My mother would be so proud. She has such a love for elegance."

"Will she come to our wedding?" Clay asked.

"If I invite her, I'm sure she will."

"Will she mind if it's at the Episcopalian church in Palm Beach?"

"Of course she would. So would I."

"What do you mean?"

"Clay, you don't for one minute think I'd be married by a minister?"

"But, Catherine, I thought you understood that I would expect you to convert."

"Convert?" Cat gasped.

"You're not going to tell me that religion really matters to you. You're hardly observant. I belong to the Episcopal Church and it does mean a great deal to me."

Cat had never seen Clay as emotional as he was at that moment.

"But that's not who I am," she said defensively.

"There is no way I would offend anyone's religious beliefs. But forgive me when I say that your Jewishness has hardly been of great importance to you, and frankly I didn't think it would matter." He paused briefly. "Besides, on a practical level, I travel in areas where my wife's being Jewish might cause, shall we say, an embarrassment." The conversation was obviously difficult for him and he looked around impatiently before turning back to her. "I must confess your reaction seems to smack of stubbornness rather than conviction."

Cat tried to follow what he was saying and she could not disagree with him. But she also felt humiliated.

"Catherine," Clay's manner softened, "what makes you Jewish?"

She looked at him for a long moment. "What makes me Jewish is the fact that you are asking me to convert," she said slowly. Then feeling that she might have sounded flippant, she continued. "That may not sound like much of an answer, but it's part of it." She paused again, trying to gather her thoughts. "But what I do know is that the idea of converting, getting married in a church, confuses me and I don't think I can do it."

The silence which followed her last words made the mood grow somber. Cat felt completely lost.

What Clay was asking of her was to make a choice. To make a commitment to his world and abandon her own forever. That was what she had wanted for so long. Now she was not sure she could do it.

"I pray that we never have to make that choice." Mark had said months back when the Yom Kippur War started. She dismissed it then, since she felt it did not apply to her. Suddenly she understood the deeper meaning of the phrase, and her confusion mounted.

Disjointed memories raced through her mind. Her father sitting at the Sabbath table wrapped in his prayer shawl; the gleaming candles over which her mother had said her Friday night prayers. The peace and tranquillity which her childhood had forced on her at holiday time and which she resented then but which she suddenly realized she missed. The caring that existed among everyone who lived in her neighborhood, which she rebelled against then, but which she now knew meant a great deal. The total commitment to survival after the Holocaust; the togetherness which permeated everyone's existence because they all shared a common past. The battles with her father over not wanting to be different from her classmates, she now realized, had given her an identity that had sustained her.

"Clay, why do you want to marry me?" she asked after a long pause. "There are so many women who would suit you more than I would, who could give you what you really want."

"I was married to one of them for nearly thirty years," he answered soberly. "Margaret was a wonderful wife, but I don't want to repeat that life. You're different. Your whole approach to life is different and it excites me." He put his hands over hers.

She lowered her eyes. She was so close to her dream, so close to the life she had hoped to attain, and she could not understand her hesitancy about reaching out and grabbing it. She was also painfully conscious that Clay had still not mentioned that he loved her.

For no reason, she remembered the flowers Clay had sent her after their first meeting.

"This is reality, isn't it?" she said almost to herself.

Clay looked surprised.

"Remember the flowers and the note you sent me and the one real rose which pricked my finger?"

He smiled ruefully. "Yes, this is nitty-gritty reality."

"The pain lasted for days."

"It doesn't have to."

"I'm afraid it will."

"If it does, it will be your choice."

"My choice," she repeated the words. Something was eluding her and she could not figure out what it was.

"I need time to think," she said slowly.

"Of course. You've been hit with a lot today—the news about Megan; converting; that agreement . . ."

"That I could almost live with," she answered, and was surprised at what she was saying. She felt him press her hand. "Clay, would you take me home and make love to me?" she whispered. "I just don't want to think about anything else tonight."

43

While on the plane coming back to New York, Cat could think of nothing but her conversation with Clay. She could not understand why she could not do what he asked of her. Her ambivalence grew when she found Jackson waiting for her at the airport. The man's respectful manner, the ease with which she went through customs, the luxury of having everything taken care of, made her wonder if Clay were right about her simply being stubborn. Still, once back in her apartment, she knew that her decision could not be made because she was hungry.

Lucille came over a couple of hours after Cat arrived home and within minutes Cat found herself going through the pictures that she had brought over. Youngsters of thirteen and fourteen were staring up at her, all exquisitely made up, dressed in sumptuous gowns and looking extraordinarily grown-up. Yet the fact remained that they were all children.

"Being skinny is no longer the only criterion for being a photographer's fashion model," Lucille said harshly. "Prepuberty helps. And David Thomas is feeding the need. And as bad as the kids are, you should see their mothers."

Cat put the photographs down slowly. "For the first time I understand what Pamela was talking about when she said she didn't want kids as models." She shrugged her shoulders helplessly. "If that's the way the modeling world is going, I certainly don't want any part of it. There's no way I could take it."

"But you don't have to," Lucille said impatiently. "Sure, there are agencies who will sign up their children, but most people work with highly professional, serious young men and women, which is what I'd like us to do." She paused briefly. "Cat, believe me, I never thought I'd want to run an agency," Lucille pressed on. "I frankly didn't think you wanted to run one either but damn it, I like being a booker. I'm damned good at it and although you might have another couple of years as a model, you've got to think of the future. I think we'd make a great team."

Lucille's references to her remaining years as a model made Cat smile. "I wish I'd known I could go on working for a couple of more years several months back. I might not have been so frantic."

Cat got up and walked around the room. "Well, we could work out of the apartment," she said. "Alexandra won't be moving back to live here." She tried to say it lightly, although she had still not digested the fact completely.

She had called the Coast the minute she came in from the airport. There had been no way she could persuade Alexandra to come live with her. The rewarding part of the conversation was that Alexandra sounded bright, alert and filled with excitement. Surprisingly, she wanted to know if Cat would be moving in with them. Jeff, too, sounded cheerful when he came on the wire. Their conversation had overtones of the warmth which always existed between them in the past, with him asking her advice about how best to furnish the renovated five-story landmark building he had bought. It was clear, although not worded, that Neva was not coming back with them.

"Where's Alexandra going to live?" Lucille asked.

Cat looked around in surprise and realized that Lucille had no idea about her separation from Jeff. "With her father in a house he bought on Willow Street in Brooklyn Heights."

"Those are beautiful houses," Lucille said wistfully. "And that's a gorgeous block."

"Yes, I know."

"So you'll be living there and this place will be empty?" Lucille asked innocently.

"Not quite." She paused. "Lucille, Jeff and I have been separated for the last six months. It was sort of a sabbatical which we took from our marriage," Cat said more forcefully.

Lucille's brows shot up briefly. "Well, it certainly explains a hell of a lot which I did not understand," she said, watching Cat carefully.

"Meaning?" Cat asked cautiously.

"Your hysteria of the last six months." Lucille did not take her eyes off Cat. "Look, I don't know Jeff well, but he was the one who gave you a balance all these years. You gorgeous broads can lose sight of what it's all about, unless there is someone sitting on the other end of that seesaw of your lives. As a matter of fact, I've always marveled at how cleverly he held on to his end of that board, so that even when you were way up, he could bring you down gently without hurting you, and then making it possible for you to go up again, unbruised. That takes doing."

"Be that as it may," Cat said with finality, not wanting to go into the details of her personal life, "we could use this room as a reception area and I could work with the girls here in the evening."

Lucille picked up the hint. "I've spoken to Zoe Smith. She's willing to go into partnership with us so we'll have the benefit of her agency and girls in Atlanta."

Cat swung around in surprise. "Weren't you taking an awful lot for granted?"

"What can I say except that I was praying you'd agree and I wanted to be as helpful as possible."

It all sounded so reasonable, yet Cat felt she could not quite make her decision at that moment.

"Give me a few days," she said finally. "There are a couple of things I've got to figure out before I can make the commitment."

"Fine, but can you at least take some assignments while you're making up your mind?" Lucille asked, handing Cat the latest Fashion Calendar. "Look it over. I've marked the shows which are still booking."

"You really believe I can still work?"

"Of course. You're a phenomenon in the business," Lucille smiled. "Pamela was like that. She decided when she wanted to quit, and I believe you're going to be the same."

"So, what the hell happened last season?" Cat asked in exasperation. "I felt I couldn't get myself arrested."

"At the risk of repeating myself, you were hysterical and running all over the place. I figured you needed time to recover emotionally from the operation, so I left you alone. Obviously, it was more than just the operation . . ."

"It's sort of hazy, but I get your point," Cat smiled. Then lighting a cigarette she waited a minute before wording her next question. "Tell me about David," she said as casually as she could. Talking about opening an agency of her own was so emotionally tied with him.

"There's nothing to tell except that he's totally driven and is pretending he's Pamela, which is revolting." She shuddered. "And for a while he's going to succeed, except that he's too greedy and inexperienced and that's going to be his downfall."

Cat nodded thoughtfully, aware that she wanted to see him, had to see him just once more. Somehow she had to understand her feelings about him. Her rage, whenever she thought of him, was still too acute and debilitating.

"I'd like to get in touch with him but his number has been disconnected and the referral number is the office," Cat said casually. "And I'd rather not call him there."

"He's living with Peter Hazeltine," Lucille said with obvious malice.

Cat gulped. "What do you mean, living with Peter Hazeltine?"

"Cat, I do believe that you're the only person in New York who did not know that David was a closet homosexual." She saw Cat squirm and her voice softened. "Although, now, in a way, I can understand your attachment to him. He is terribly good-looking and with that sly and devious manner he has, he knew he could put something over on someone who's as vulnerable as you were. But what's really tragic about him is that he doesn't only lie to others. He lies to himself. That's why he won't give out his new telephone number. He's still pretending."

"But in this day and age!" Cat exploded indignantly. "Who cares if he's a homosexual—especially in our field?"

Lucille shrugged her shoulders. "Why do you think I loathed him so?" She stood up. "But David is really the least of my worries now that you're back."

The downstairs buzzer rang.

"There's a Mr. Kimbrough to see you, Miss Willingham," the doorman said. He sounded unhappy. "Do you know him?"

"Send him right up," she said quickly, wondering what kind of man she was going to meet. From the doorman's tone, he sounded unappetizing.

"Lucille, you've got to forgive me, but this is important," Cat said, coming back to the living room.

"No problem. Just call me as soon as you can."

The doorbell of the apartment sounded.

"I'll call you within a couple of days if not sooner," Cat said with assurance as she ushered Lucille toward the front door.

Lucille's expression, as she walked away after meeting Jeb, matched Cat's reaction.

She did not know what she expected but it certainly was not this large, heavy-set man whose huge frame filled the doorway.

"Miss Willingham?" he said in a soft southern drawl, walking into the apartment.

As she preceded him into the living room, Cat wondered if he, too, was trying to get in on Megan's success. He had not sounded like that when she spoke to him on the phone. Now she was not sure.

Waving him to a chair, she watched him as he looked around the room with obvious admiration. He was dressed in a gray-blue large check suit, blue shirt, the collar buttoned tightly around his fleshy neck, a colorful tie with a large tie clip in the form of a dog, all completely incongruous with the spurred boots. His hair was completely gray and she noted that his blue eyes were unusually gentle.

"Before you say a word," he said quickly, "I want to thank you for being so good to Megan."

"Please sit down," she said, feeling somewhat relieved. The man's appearance compared with his sincerity were a study in contrasts. She believed he was honestly interested in Megan's welfare.

"Would you like a drink?" she asked politely.

"Haven't touched the stuff in fourteen years."

"Cigarette?"

"Gave them up, too," he laughed. "My only remaining vice is cussing. Can't seem to shake that one."

Cat laughed politely, then, unable to keep herself back, she worded her main concern. "How is Megan?"

"Bad. Very bad." His expression of benign friendliness turned mournful.

"A smashed knee . . ." Cat started.

"Smashed soul. Smashed brain would be more like it."

Cat froze. "Surely she's going to be all right?"

"With God's help, maybe. But right now she's lost."

"Mr. Kimbrough."

"Jeb."

"Jeb, I understood she has a broken knee. Now that can't be too serious."

"It's much more than that. She's very sick."

"Where is she?" Cat decided to humor him.

"In the hospital where they took her after that awful show she was in." He stopped. "She should never have done it."

"Can you tell me what actually happened?" Cat asked patiently.

"I don't really know," Jeb said, scratching his head thoughtfully. "I arrived after their final rehearsal. She was very nervous, although the director seemed pleased. When she first saw me, I was sure she was happy I was there. But then she wanted to know why I didn't bring her mother along. I tried to explain that Cora was busy, but Megan didn't believe me. She didn't say so, but I could tell she didn't." He stood up and walked around the room. "Then on opening night, sometime during the second act, when she was dancing around, she seemed to catch sight of me and she lost her balance, hit her knee against something sharp and went down like a rag doll." He turned around, looking troubled. "It was that look before she fell which makes me sure she did not believe my story about Cora." He came back to himself. "She should never have done that show."

"Yes, I know that, but if it's only a broken knee . . ." Cat started.

"The knee will heal."

Cat was relieved. "Well, that's good news. And then, you can take her back to her mother." She lit a cigarette, aware that she was losing her, allowing her prize model to slip through her fingers. But it seemed like the right thing to do. "Cora Baynes must be a wonderful woman," Cat said absently. She had lost interest in the conversation. Megan was going to be all right and would be going home. That was it.

"Cora Baynes is nothing but a two-bit whore," Jeb replied almost matter-of-factly.

Cat gagged and her hand shook as she lifted her cigarette to her lips and waited for Jeb to continue.

"Not worth a pinch of salt," he went on, more animated. "And how Megan ever turned out the way she did, all things considered, beats the hell out of me. You gotta admit, Megan's a wonderful little girl."

"Yes, she's very sweet," Cat said slowly.

"That's what I mean. Hell, if you went by what these psychologists say, Megan would turn out to be a no-count tramp like her mother."

"But Mrs. Baynes must have cared for Megan deeply. Maybe circumstances forced her into doing things she did not want to do."

"Cora Baynes don't give one shit for Megan, excuse the language, and it makes me so mad."

"You mean Megan's mother isn't interested in Megan?" Cat asked, in spite of herself.

"Only in the money Megan sends her."

"When was Megan in the convent?" Cat asked.

"I got her in there when she was nine, to get her away from Cora, but Megan wanted to be with Cora and she ran away and stayed with her for another year or so. I was coming around to visit at that time and I could see that Cora was grooming Megan to follow in her footsteps." His face grew red. "I couldn't stand it and I offered to take Megan to live with me and my wife. But Cora had a nose for business. She wanted me to pay for Megan."

Cat, listening attentively, felt she was going to be sick.

"And then what happened?" She did not want to hear anymore but knew she must.

"Well, Megan was always well developed for her age, if you know what I mean, and she won some beauty contest and that's when Cora got the idea that Megan could make money by being photographed." His laughter sounded like a sob. "That poor kid, she was no more than eleven years old. When she saw how happy it made her mother that people were taking pictures of her, she couldn't be stopped." His face was contorted with pain. "I saw some of those pictures and most of them were disgusting. So I got the convent to take her again."

Cat stood up and walked over to the window. She wanted some fresh air. The effort exerted at opening it gave her time to collect herself.

"Why didn't Megan stay in the convent and become a nun?" Cat asked, turning her back to Jeb.

"Never could figure that one out," Jeb said thoughtfully. "Seems the nuns couldn't cope with her. The fact is that the day Mother Alba died, Megan ran back to Cora."

"How old is Megan?" Cat held her breath.

"Sixteen. But when you consider what she's been put through she could be one hundred and sixteen."

Oh my God, Cat thought. Megan was Alexandra's age. She stared up at the ceiling, trying to control her tears.

"How did she get to New York?" Cat whispered.

"Well, the minute she was back with Cora, the picture-taking started again. Some were pretty good, and someone suggested she could be a model or a movie star. Cora found a friend to take Megan to Shreveport." He sounded tired and defeated. "I tried to find her and get her back, but she heard about it and ran away." He became emotional and Cat could see he was suffering. "Then I got a call from a Mel Black. He found Megan somewhere in New York and gave me a long song and dance about how famous he could make her. I didn't trust him, but what could I do? I told him that I'd pay him to take care of Megan, figuring Cora would leave town at one point and then I'd come and bring Megan home." He stopped. "Damn him. Exploiting her religion, the only thing Megan ever had that meant anything to her."

He stood up in a rage and started walking around the room.

Cat wanted to cry. She and David had exploited her more than anyone else.

"Most people have lots of things which are important to them." Jeb swung around and his words seemed to bounce off the walls. "Megan only had her faith and no one had the right to take it away from her."

Alexandra had her paintings, which meant so much to her, and Cat had belittled them, not understanding their importance. But Megan was not Alexandra!

Cat looked away. Everything Jeb said was probably true but at that moment she could not cope with any of it. She needed time to understand what had caused her to ignore what was happening around her. She had sensed something was wrong with Megan, had even spoken about it to David, but somehow she had let it happen.

"Miss Willingham," Jeb said urgently, "will you help me get Megan back?"

"How?"

"Would you go and see her? She'll listen to you."

Cat hesitated for a long moment. "What's the name of the hospital?" she asked finally.

"Lakeland State Hospital."

"That's an asylum!"

"I know."

Cat wanted to say she was busy, that she would be of no use. She hated institutions. Clay had said she could feel sympathy for Megan, but was not responsible for her. She was responsible for Alexandra. "I

really don't know that I could be of any use . . ." she started haltingly.

"Megan told me you have a daughter," Jeb was pleading. "So
you've got to understand and try to help me."

Cat stared at him numbly.

"Cora always said Megan was mine but I didn't believe her. Now
I feel she is."

He turned around and walked out the door without another
word.

44

Cat stared at the door through which Jeb had left and wanted to call him back. She did not want to face the horror of what she had just heard, alone. But she knew she must.

Slowly she walked back into the living room. She could still feel Jeb's presence and heard his plea coming at her from the lacquered white walls, as though they had soaked up his voice and were forcing her to comprehend what he had said.

She sank down into her mother's large wing chair, which had been left behind, and closed her eyes. The picture of Megan's life began to fall into place slowly. Megan's description of her mother was nothing but a fantasy which she wanted desperately to be true. The love that Cora presumably had for her was nothing but an unfulfilled dream. It brought Megan into focus and she realized that there was no Megan. The beautiful, sweet, vague creature whom she had been nurturing as a substitute for Alexandra was nothing but a figment of her imagination. Cat had tried to create perfection out of a lovely but empty vessel who could not live up to her expectations, just as Alexandra did not live up to what she had hoped for her. But Alexandra was loved by people who existed and that was why she would be saved from escaping into a world of unreality. Suddenly, Cat knew that she had been jealous of Megan. But it was not of her youth or beauty. She was jealous of Megan's love for Cora and what she had assumed was Cora's love for Megan. She had wanted to be loved by her mother and love her daughter and was too blind to see that both were hers. Megan had come into her life when she was uncertain about many things, and one of them was her struggle with whether she was a mother or a daughter. She was both. She could be both.

Cat ran her fingers over Clara's velvet chair and snuggled deeper into it. She was Clara's daughter and she was Alexandra's mother. The lines were clearly defined. She did not have to choose.

Her thoughts returned to Megan. Could she have prevented her breakdown and was she responsible for what happened to her? That was what she had to deal with now. Sympathy alone was not enough.

She wondered what Jeff would say. "You must do what you think is right for you." She could practically hear him say the words.

At that moment she knew that she had to help Megan.

She and David would help her get back on her feet. They owed it to her.

For the first time since she heard about the tragedy, she thought of David and his strange relationship to Megan.

The confusion returned. For a few moments she thought she had begun to understand her feelings. But David had not been included in the overall picture.

More than ever she had to understand who David was and what part he played in her life. Whatever the involvement, it had to be brought into perspective. Somehow she had to put the anger she felt toward him to rest.

Quickly, she picked up the phone and dialed David's office. While waiting for him to come on the wire, she decided not to tell him about Megan until they met face to face. She suspected he would not meet her if he knew.

"Hey there." He sounded happy to hear from her. "I was going to call you but I wasn't sure when you were coming back. . . . When did you arrive and how was the trip and how are you?" he rushed on gaily.

"I'm fine and I arrived just a few hours ago," she said in a measured voice.

"You sound as lovely as ever and I'm dying to see you."

"That's what I'm calling about." She swallowed hard. "Why don't we have a drink this afternoon, for old time's sake?"

"Not for old time's sake," he laughed. "For new time's sake. Where would you like to meet and when?"

"Today and you name the place."

"Make it at five at the Stanhope Hotel on Fifth Avenue."

"Perfect." Cat hung up thinking that the Stanhope was just two blocks away from Pamela and Peter's house.

The jet lag was catching up with her, but Cat refused to give in to it. She had to see David.

Sitting in the bar of the Stanhope Hotel, Cat watched David order their drinks. She could not help but marvel at the fact that she had spent so much time with this man who now appeared like a stranger. He was wearing a dark green suede Eisenhower jacket over a thick, expensive white turtleneck sweater and his face was as handsome as ever. A little harder, perhaps, but the extraordinary features, the unusual coloring, were all there and she tried to understand what it was about this beautiful boy that could bring out such anger in her. Was it possible that she was actually angry at herself for placing such emphasis on external appearances and had projected the anger at him? Looking at him now, she felt no anger. Instead she remembered the fragile, colorful Christmas ornaments that she had coveted as a child. David was that exquisite and transparent ornament which had been crushed so easily, so many years back. She wished she did not have to tell him about Megan.

The waiter walked away and David turned to her and reached over to take her hand.

"Now, tell me everything," he said, and his exaggerated self-assurance was touching.

"There's really nothing to tell," she smiled feebly.

"But what are your plans?" He was taken aback.

"I don't have any," she answered. "How about you?"

"Oh, I've got my work cut out for me," he said cautiously. "It's not as easy as it looks, you know." He lit a cigarette and she could see that he was becoming edgy.

"How does it feel to be boss?"

"It feels good, damned good." The bravado barely hid the lack of enthusiasm.

"I suppose you miss Pamela, though."

"Yes, sure. She was a great lady. A great agent. A real pro." The answer sounded rehearsed.

"Was she in love with you?"

"Pamela loved nobody."

"Nobody?"

"Well, she loved children, I guess." And he broke into an unpleasant laughter.

"What's so funny?"

"The truth, I guess."

Cat smiled politely. "What did you learn from her, David?"

"That liquor and drugs don't mix."

Cat could see his façade cracking. She felt sorry for him.

"David, Megan had a nervous breakdown and she's at Lakeland State Hospital," she blurted the words out.

The waiter arrived with their drinks at that moment. David looked up at him and Cat realized the expression on his face was identical to the one she had seen when she first showed him Megan's pictures.

He looked back at her and she felt he was not really seeing her.

"David, I'm going up to see her and I was wondering if you'd come along."

"I couldn't possibly get away," he said, coming back to himself.

"Don't you feel any sense of responsibility toward her?" Cat asked wearily.

"No, I really don't, and I don't think you should," he said forcefully. "Frankly, I think you should try to reach her mother. She's the one who's responsible."

"Oh, dear God. That woman couldn't care less if Megan lives or dies. That's all part of it."

"Well, what do you know." A strange smile appeared on his face. It almost appeared to be a smile of satisfaction.

For the first time since meeting him, Cat wondered where his mother was. He never spoke about his family, never mentioned a past. He seemed to have sprung from nowhere. Her feeling of sadness for him grew.

"Will you ever see Megan again?" she asked instead.

"There would be no point. I'm perfectly satisfied with my behavior toward her. I've done all I can do for her."

"Maybe it's the other way around." A flicker of rage rose in her but was quickly extinguished when she realized he really believed what he was saying.

"Funny that you should say that. She's the only person I've ever wanted to help. Wanted to do things for."

"But you did use her. I used her. We all used her."

"I was going to help her make a career. Make her the star she wanted to be."

"It was all a fantasy."

"Megan was no fantasy," David said adamantly.

"Oh yes, she was."

"Megan was real and like you and me, she had dreams."

"Megan had fantasies, not dreams. Dreams have their place. We carve them out of our desires and frustrations and strive to achieve them. They are an extension of our reality. Whereas fantasies are built on quicksand and when confused with dreams they result in destruction."

"You're playing with words."

"Maybe you're right. But I can't ignore the fact that Megan was part of my life and I have to understand what happened to her so that I can live with myself."

"That's the real point." David hit the table with his fist. "It's not Megan you're talking about. You're talking about yourself and you're trying to project your feelings on to me."

"David, she walked into our lives asking for nothing except some warmth and kindness. She had nothing to offer except her transparent loveliness. She never pretended to be anything else. We created her to satisfy our own needs. We never thought about who she was or what she wanted. I know she wanted love. Everyone wants someone to love them."

"Love?" David smiled derisively. "Love, my dear Cat, is only a secretion of the glands."

Cat stared at him numbly.

"Let me tell you something," he continued after a moment. "Pamela once said I was hollow, that I could never really love or be loved. Well, maybe she was right. But in the long run that makes me the stronger one. Love makes people vulnerable, makes them dependent, causes them to live with the fear of losing it." He looked more alive and animated as his voice rose. "Think of it. You're vulnerable and open to hurt because you need to be loved. Megan was obviously destroyed by that need and Pamela rotted because she had lost it."

Cat listened attentively, never taking her eyes off him. What he was saying was the anguished cry of an orphan, a lonely, unwanted child who had never been loved, whom no one had ever cared about. He had to believe it because he had given up hope of ever loving or being loved.

"David," she said gently. "There's nothing wrong with wanting to be loved or in being dependent, if you know who you are."

Her words made her pause, as the full impact of their meaning struck her. Unlike Megan, who was struggling with her reality through madness, or David, who would always cling to his fantasies to avoid reality, she, Cat, existed. Jeff knew it and respected it. That was the reason he always deferred to her judgments and wishes for herself. She had a past, she came from somewhere, she belonged to something. She was not only Cat Willingham. She was also Catherine Wallenstein. She had an identity before she became a model because her father and mother had given it to her. She was part of their lives and they instilled in her thoughts and values and traditions. They made her aware of their past, which they took pride in, and they gave her a foundation so she could grow up with the ability to determine her fate. But most important they gave her memories. Megan broke down when Jeb arrived and her horrendous memories of the past had surfaced. David's memories were probably too unbearable and he therefore eliminated them completely from his mind. But Cat knew that her memories were tangible, and she was grateful for them. And if she had ignored them and seemed to have forgotten them, they all came back when Clay assumed she would convert.

She knew at that moment that she could not marry Clay. She also knew the answer to Clay's question as to what made her Jewish. It was all so simple and so clear. She was Joe and Clara Wallenstein's daughter. They were Jewish, her grandparents had been Jewish and she was the continuation and reaffirmation of their existence. By giving up that part of herself she would be denying what they were, what she was and what Alexandra could become.

Tears which had been held back started streaming down her cheeks. She was crying for David and Megan, who had touched her life in a moment when she was frightened and lonely and for whom she could do nothing. She was crying for what might have been her life with Clay. But she was crying most for Alexandra, who had so little to fall back on. She had been so busy trying to survive that, in the process, she had neglected to give her daughter concrete memories to sustain her when the pressures of life crowded in on her.

She stood up quickly. "I've got to run," she said, trying to compose herself and aware that David looked completely lost as he stared at her. "I'm taking a cab." She felt more in control. "May I drop you?"

"Sure thing." He looked at her almost tenderly. "I hate to see you in such a state."

"Where to?" the driver asked once they were seated in the taxi.

"Just up the street, driver," David said. "I'll tell you where to stop." Then realizing what he was doing, he looked confused for a moment. "I've got to pick something up from Peter."

Cat watched him walk up the stairs of Pamela's house. He hesitated but did not look around. Then he began pounding on the brass knocker and within seconds the door opened and Peter was standing there smiling. He extended his arms toward David and pulled him into the house.

It was all so pathetic, Cat thought. David with his grand speech about not needing to be loved. Megan, in the asylum, had more of a chance than David to survive.

Arriving at her apartment, Cat let herself in and took off her raincoat. Dropping it on the bench in the hallway, she kicked off her boots and pulled the rubber band out of her hair. She looked at her watch. It was seven o'clock.

Walking into her bedroom, she opened the dresser drawer and removed her safe deposit box. With great care she took out the little brown paper bag. Brushing the dust off the small doll, she placed it on the round table in front of the window. The childish fantasy had finally been put to rest. Now she could see the tiny figure for what it was: a small memento of childhood. It would make her smile whenever she looked at it.

Throwing herself on her bed, she turned on her recording machine and listened to her messages.

Bo's voice sounded frantic, as usual. Nancy Stuart called and said it was urgent. Clay called from Paris. Her mother called to say she was expected the next evening at Seder, that she must not be late and that she was not to drive up to the house in a car on a holiday.

Cat picked up the phone and called Lucille.

"Meet me here at 9 A.M. tomorrow," she said officiously.

"I've got several bookings for you for day after tomorrow," Lucille answered in an equally professional tone. "Do you want to write them down?"

"I'm booking out for good." She laughed. "And as for the day after tomorrow, it's a Jewish holiday so I'm not working. But sometime next week we've got to get that agency running."

"Which one?" Lucille asked cautiously. "Pamela's?"

"Not on your sweet life. It's the MB Agency."

"What's that mean?"

"Stands for Megan Baynes."

"Why?"

"She was our first client and it's her commissions that are getting us started."

"Can she work with a broken knee?"

"You ask too many questions."

Lucille laughed. "You know, you really do sound different."

"I am different," she answered, and hung up.

Then with an ease which amazed and pleased her, she picked up the phone and dialed the Coast.

PART THREE

EPILOGUE
1983

EPILOGUE

Dan Grayson leaned back in his chair and watched the test commercial of a beautiful young model dressed in Calvin Klein jeans and sweater, talking about the Van Cleef and Arpels diamond necklace, earrings and tiara. She smiled sweetly and spoke of the value of owning gems.

The screen went blank and the lights came on.

"What do you think?" a young executive asked.

Dan poured himself a drink, gulped it down and lit his cigar.

"I don't believe she could afford to buy the pants, much less the jewels," he said finally. "Do you? Would anybody?"

"But Mr. Grayson. She's one of the top models around. She was voted 1982 Model of the Year."

"I don't give a shit about that. I want someone who people will believe. I want a model who can convince the audience that she thinks the jewelry is worth it, because she looks like she knows fine jewelry and can afford to buy it." He stopped and looked around the room.

The ad agency people sat silently, waiting for him to continue.

"Anybody seen Cat Willingham recently?" Dan asked suddenly.

"I saw her the other day at McMullens with her husband. They were celebrating their daughter's art show opening," someone said. "She's running a modeling agency with Lucille . . ."

"I know that. But what does she look like? That's what I'm interested in," Dan barked.

"Better than ever. She's a classic."

"That's who I want," Dan shot out. "Get her."

Also available in Methuen Paperbacks

ROSALIND LAKER

Jewelled Path

It is the last decade of the nineteenth century, a time of opulence, decadence, and, above all, style. Art Nouveau is the latest fashion, free and sensual, arousing passionate responses in Irene Lindsay, daughter of a famous Bond Street jeweller. A trainee jeweller herself, and very much a 'modern' woman, she soon finds herself at odds with her father and must break away from him and his past, to explore a revealing, brilliant and loving life of her own . . .

Best-selling author Rosalind Laker's unforgettable romance moves from London to Paris and the splendours of Monte Carlo as we follow one woman's search for her true fulfilment.

JOHN BRAINE

The Two of Us

The uneasy calm which has settled on the strangely enduring marriage of Clive and Robin is disturbed by the reappearance of Stephen Belgard, Robin's former lover, and a new challenge to Clive's supremacy within the family firm of Lendrick Mills . . .

This powerful novel, which is also a sequel to *Stay With Me Till Morning*, sees John Braine's return to the Yorkshire landscape he evokes so well and the territory of passionate relationships he has made so very much his own.

'Mr Braine writes with an authority and confidence that are wholly beguiling . . . his ability to establish the details of how people live, to catch the tone and flavour of life as it is experienced, gives his fiction the quality of vitality, so hard to define.'

Allan Massie, *The Scotsman*

INGRID PITT and TONY RUDLIN

Eva's Spell

A novel of the Peróns

She was a legend in her own lifetime. Eva Duarte, the small-time actress and radio announcer who turned Juan Perón from an ambitious soldier into the most charismatic leader Argentina had ever known.

Perón was ambitious, and had used the ferment of World War Two to secure massive favour – and finance – with the Nazis. But it was Eva's magic, her flair for publicity and her instinct for the will of the people which brought his career to its pinnacle.

Together, Juan and Eva formed the most electric partnership in South America. Insatiably power-hungry and utterly ruthless, for a while the world was theirs, until the wheel of fortune began to turn again . . .

Ingrid Pitt and Tony Rudlin's sweeping novel of the Peróns' rise and fall vividly recreates the drama and tragedy of the nation who fell under Eva's spell.

JAMES FOLLETT

Dominator

A terrifying thriller for the 80s – and beyond –
by the author of *The Tiptoe Boys*.

High above the earth's surface orbits one of
NASA's latest space shuttles, *Dominator*. But
the crew and cargo on board are beyond the
control of the US space agency. *Dominator* has
been hijacked and a nightmare is about to be
unleashed.

How could it happen – and how will it end?
James Follett's heart-stopping novel spans
three continents as it follows the fearfully
possible outcome of a new deadlock between
the warring Middle East factions and the
United States. Standing innocently at the
centre is Neil O'Hara, ex-astronaut, ex-drunk,
whose rare skills and debatable loyalties may
ultimately be the only barrier between us and
the holocaust . . .

VLADIMIR VOLKOFF

The Set-up

Double cross, and then double cross again —
the art in which the KGB are supreme masters.

Psar wanted to go home. A White Russian,
living in Paris, he is not the most obvious
immigrant to the Mother Country. But there is
a way — if Psar will only collude with the KGB
in a dazzling plot to confound both the
dissident movement and Western liberals
alike. Psar must agree, and so begins a
nightmare of manipulation and obscure but
increasing danger, as the steely web of the
KGB's all-pervasive disinformation network is
revealed in its ruthless complexity.

Seldom has the seamy and dangerous world of
espionage been so relentlessly explored as in
this brilliant and disturbing award-winning
novel.

'This book may be pure entertainment, but it
gradually builds up a picture of world politics
as a great amoral game of chess in which
Russians are supreme masters.'
                    John Weightman, *The Observer*

SOL YURICK

Richard A

Set against the building tension of the Cuban
missile crisis, Sol Yurick's mesmerizing
thriller exposes a secret internationalist
agency that uses ultra-sophisticated mind-
control technology to penetrate both the CIA
and the KGB. Richard A, a hapless radio-ham,
stumbles accidentally upon them and their
terrifying technology of phone-tapping,
bugging and 'brain-washing' techniques – and
soon finds himself caught up in one of the
most terrifying threats of infiltration of both
sides of the Cold War.

'A wonderfully wicked view of life in the spy
chambers and boudoirs of international
travellers'

Gay Talese

'Sol Yurick is a gifted, experienced writer . . .
Scenes dovetail, merge, intersect; the book is a
literary switchboard, a console of a novel'
The New York Times Book Review

'One of the cleverest and most chilling
espionage thrillers yet . . . The whole narrative
hums with tension'

Publishers Weekly

DAVID BUTLER

Lord Mountbatten: The Last Victory

At midnight on 14 August 1947, an event took place that would change the world. That moment marked the dawn of Independence for India, the birth of Pakistan and the end of the British Raj — the last days of the greatest empire in history.

The seemingly impossible task of bringing about Independence fell on the shoulders of a remarkable man, Lord Louis Mountbatten. Faced with a group of hugely influential and charismatic men — Pandit Nehru, Mohammed Ali Jinnah and Mahatma Gandhi — he had to find a way to resolve irreconcilable differences and formulate a plan for Partition agreeable to all parties.

David Butler's novel brilliantly evokes the scope and magnitude of that momentous time, the terrible bloodshed and the immense, enduring affection felt for Lord Mountbatten and his wife Edwina.

12.25 2.95 F. S.

These and other Methuen Paperbacks are available at your bookshop or newsagent. In case of difficulties orders may be sent to:

Methuen Paperbacks
Cash Sales Department
PO Box 11
Falmouth
Cornwall TR10 109EN

Please send cheque or postal order, no currency, for purchase price quoted and allow the following for postage and packing:

UK   55p for the first book, 22p for the second book and 14p for each additional book ordered to a maximum of £1.75.

BFPO   55p for the first book, 22p for the second
& Eire   book plus 14p for the next seven books, thereafter 8p per book.

Overseas   £1.00 for the first book plus 25p per copy for
Customers   each additional book.

While every effort is made to keep prices low, it is sometimes necessary to increase prices at short notice. Methuen Paperbacks reserves the right to show new retail prices on covers which may differ from those previously advertised in the text or elsewhere.